# ASH & AMBITION

### BOOK ONE OF NOR FANG, NOR FIRE

# ARI MARMELL

# Ash & Ambition

## Book One of Nor Fang, Nor Fire

# Ari Marmell

ISBN 978-1-77400-012-0

# DEDICATION

Too many names to list, and too many names that can't afford to be listed. This is for everyone who's been forced by society to hide who they are. You are magnificent and powerful, every one.

# CHAPTER ONE

Everything ached.

Even the parts he wasn't yet accustomed to having.

The world swayed and juddered to a song of ear-rending shrieks and moans. The sun, though modestly veiled behind a translucent and wind-kissed overcast, was blinding through the shadows of the bars. On those winds wafted the sour stench of sweat and offal. Directly overhead, the sky was wooden, the patterns in the grain suggesting—

*Wooden? Bars?*

"Smim?" His voice was ragged and parched.

The one that replied was no less a croak, though something about its nasally, savage timbre suggested it wouldn't have sounded pleasant even under more comfortable circumstances.

"I'm here, Master."

"Where are we?"

"The wagon, Master. Remember?"

*The wagon? The* cage!

Oh, but he remembered now. Furious, he sat upright, and nearly collapsed all over again as the world, already swaying, began to spin. The creaking of the wheels, jolting over every imperfection, separated themselves from the pounding deep in his skull—just as the warmth of midday now paled against the feverish heat from within.

And above all that, the agony, the infection, the *intrusion*, in his chest.

Clinging with desperate intensity to a lucidity that threatened to dissipate with every breath, the injured man forced himself to look around.

He was, indeed, within a heavy cage on wheels, lying beside a flattened board intended as a bench. There were others, many others, crowded in with him, but first and foremost, there was Smim.

The goblin leaned over him, concern evident in the rheumy eyes that peered from a rounded, swamp-skinned face half-hidden by strands of coal-black but moss-textured hair. Whether that concern contained an iota of true affection or merely represented Smim's fear of being left to fend for himself, he neither knew nor cared.

"Your nose is crooked."

Smim's grin, revealing jagged gray teeth, was feeble. "As it ever has been, Master."

"No." The protuberant, almost root vegetable-like snout was definitely even less centered than usual.

"I may have had something of a misunderstanding with several of our fellow internees," the creature admitted.

At that, squinting through the pain, the wounded man examined the others. All human, save Smim, or so at least they appeared. Many glared sullenly his way, though whether in general resentment over their situation or particular animosity due to the goblin's presence, he couldn't say. Most were men, a few women. None of obvious nationality; hair color varied, and skin tones ranged from nearly snow-pale to the brown-black of lush soil, and every hue between—though even the darkest of them showed a certain greyed pallor from hunger and fear.

*Elgarrad*, he thought, drawing the two primary human ethnicities of Galadras from deep memory, *and Cennuen. Mostly a mix of both.*

Which thought, in turn, caused him to raise a hand and examine his own skin, his own flesh, alien as it was. A rich, chestnut hue: abnormally dark if his blood were substantially Elgarrad, about average if Cennuen. He wondered, idly, if that implied any cultural connotations with which he might need concern himself in the future.

Then again, given his current circumstances, he wondered if he'd have any sort of future in which it mattered.

*No! None of that! I've survived too much already to—*

A particularly sharp bounce of the wagon, followed by an equally stabbing jolt of torment through his skull, obliterated the rest of his internal rant. He clutched his forehead, groaning.

"People travel in these contraptions regularly?" he demanded.

"Most of them keep to the roads, Master," Smim pointed out helpfully. "I would imagine that makes their journeys somewhat less arduous."

Indeed, the view between the bars showed no trace of a roadway, or any sign of civilization at all. Open fields of poor grasslands and the sporadic copses stretched far to the east, first rolling gently before rising to veritable waves of hills at the edges of vision. Between the wagon and those hills, invisible due to the land's contours but just audible above the protests of vehicle and passengers, ran—he scoffed inwardly at the name—the Dragon's Tail, tributary of the Dragon River.

He focused as best he could on the rushing waters, trying to block out the more immediate noises and the constant agony. Eventually he fell back into a feverish half-doze, in which he dreamed, or perhaps hallucinated, of a sword the size of a mountain, one that cruelly sliced bits of him off and added weaker, incongruous parts back in their place, all while he whimpered in fear or prayed for succor to gods he scarcely recognized.

When he awoke once more, when those whimpers and prayers penetrated deeply enough for him to recognize them as genuine sounds rather than products of his near-delirium, the wagon had halted. Beyond the bars, unshaven men of a particularly rough mien, clad in leathers and armed with cudgels, passed bowls of a pasty gruel to prisoners' grasping hands.

He didn't recognize his captors. He *did* recognize their cudgels.

*He remembered staggering from the foothills and out onto the plains, every step a fresh hell, his heart the center of a web of agony so intense as to make madness a welcome respite. Step by step, each an impossible act of will, leaning heavily on Smim's wiry frame lest the next stumble be the last. They made for a border that might as well be worlds away—the untamed region known by most as the Outermark was broad indeed—beyond which lay at best a feeble hope.*

*Then shouting, shapes rising from behind this boulder, that knoll, swinging those massive, knotty clubs... Sharp pain, in arm and leg and skull, and that pain was welcome for its distraction from a torment far greater, a relieved smile around a mouthful of blood...*

The memory faded, the here-and-now returned. The wagon was already moving once more, the prisoners greedily clutching their pathetic fare, eyeing their neighbors like sworn enemies. Smim, a cracked and battered bowl in each hand, knelt beside him, one arm extended. "Here, Master. You should—"

"You won't be needing that." The fellow who spoke was a hairy, unwashed tree-trunk of a man. Clad in tattered rags like the rest of the wagon's occupants—including Smim and his master—he nonetheless stood out. Not merely his size marked him as different, but the healthier flush to his tanned skin, a lesser cracking of his lips. This one wasn't near so hungry as the others, and it took no contemplation at all to understand why.

A quick whisper. "The one you 'disagreed' with earlier?"

Smim nodded, flinching. Then, to the larger prisoner, "My mas—my friend is sick. He requires food and—" The goblin yelped, only partially able to dodge the kick aimed his way.

"If he's sick, there's no cause to waste good food on him. And as for you, you damn garbage-eater—"

The ache in his head, in his limbs, seemed to fade; even his wounded chest subsided just a bit. "The goblin is with me."

"Yeah? So?"

Fury blazed, burning away what remained of the pain. "Have you any idea who you'd defy, you stupid man?! I am—"

"Master!" Smim hissed, alarmed.

*Damn it!* He wanted to scream his frustration, but the goblin was right.

It took him an instant to remember, though. "Anvarri," he said, somewhat anticlimactically. *My name, for now. I can't afford to let myself forget.* "Nycolos Anvarri."

The other prisoner appeared not merely unimpressed, but irritated, even disgusted. "Never bloody heard of you," he grunted, reaching again for the goblin. The other miserable souls, who had paused their meals to watch the altercation, looked equally ignorant.

All save one or two. These, if Nycolos read their expressions accurately, indeed recognized the name—they just didn't *believe* it.

Interesting, and worth further study. Later.

For now, even as Smim fell back to the floor of the wagon, trying to avoid his tormentor, Nycolos grabbed the larger man's arm in an impossible grip. He allowed the other a moment to stare, locking his eyes with Nycolos's own, jaw gaping in the beginning of a shocked, suffering gasp...

And then he twisted, snapping bone midway between elbow and wrist.

The agonized scream, accompanied by a chorus of softer, startled sounds from around the cage, was the first noise Nycolos had heard since he'd awakened in this damned rolling prison that didn't cause him pain.

Still, he was weak, injured, distracted, far from his best. He failed to notice one of the other prisoners rise, fists raised, moving to help the first.

He failed to notice, but Smim did not.

Another horrid shriek joined the first as the second man also collapsed, clutching the back of his mangled, crippled ankle. Smim rose from a crawl behind him, teeth and lips smeared with blood where he'd bitten clear through tendon and flesh.

"Would anyone else," Nycolos demanded, rising to his full height, head brushing the wooden ceiling above, "take what is mine?" The sobbing bully still dangled from his fist, arm flexing horribly in his grip.

Nobody so much as met his gaze.

It was not only a small victory, but a short-lived one. The wagon halted, and the cruel men with their cudgels seemed uninterested in Nycolos and Smim's protestations of self-defense. Even as his many pains returned twice-over, however, as he felt consciousness slipping away again beneath the pounding of the heavy clubs, Nycolos was satisfied that he had made an important point.

Not only to the other prisoners, but to himself.

*For all that has changed, I am still me. And I will fight to keep—and to reclaim—what is mine!*

———

When he awakened again, the aches were worse than before, but his mind was clearer. When he ground a hoarse "Where are we?" through ragged throat, it wasn't that he had once again forgotten the wagon. He meant, and Smim properly interpreted, his question in a much broader sense.

The goblin pressed his face to the bars, peering out into the long shadows and pooled murk of twilight. For the nonce, Smim's night vision was far better than Nycolos's own. He could remedy that, but the requisite change in his eyes would almost assuredly be noticed.

"We've been traveling west," Smim announced after a pause. "I can see the ridges winding southward, far ahead. I'm afraid, Master, that we must be nearing the mountains."

Nycolos choked softly on a self-mocking laugh. The Outermark Mountains—or simply "home," as he'd called them—was where they'd *started* this hellish, fruitless trek! That they approached the mighty range far north of where they'd begun was hardly consolation. It still meant that the bulk of their efforts had been neatly undone.

Before Nycolos could come up with profanity sufficient for the situation, the wagon slowed, accompanied by a brief symphony of human grunts, equine snorts, and wooden creaking.

"Apparently we're to be examined before 'delivery,'" Smim informed him in response to a curious glance. "Or so I believe I overheard. I cannot be certain I heard properly, of course. The others seem disinclined to allow me near them."

After what had happened earlier—and Nycolos couldn't help but notice that the two men he and the goblin had mauled were nowhere to be seen—that was hardly surprising.

"Master..." the goblin continued, his ugly voice dropping. Had Nycolos possessed only a human's hearing, he'd never have caught the word at all.

"What is it?"

"You're too strong, Master. You need to fix that."

Nycolos repressed the urge to hiss. "I will do no such thing! I'm feeble enough as it is!"

"I understand, but..." Smim scooted closer, fingers twitching anxiously as the vehicle came to a full stop and their captors approached. "You should not have been able to do what you did earlier, to that lout's arm. It was noticed."

"I'll be more careful."

"Master, you know I would never show you disrespect, but—"

"Out with it!"

Smim sighed. "You lack your usual patience. Perhaps it is your injuries, or our present circumstances. Perhaps your blood simply burns hotter now than you are accustomed to. And you've rarely before had need to restrain yourself when your anger burnt brightest. You're not used to it. Master, you *can't* simply 'be careful.' Not at this time."

"Smim…"

"I'm sorry. But you know I'm right. And you *will* be noticed. You cannot afford that; *we* cannot."

Nycolos felt his shoulders slump, an odd feeling in and of itself. Everything inside him screamed defiance, railed against the notion of making himself weaker still, of giving anything to these… these *animals* who dared cage him! He had little left to him, but that short list included his pride.

But Smim *was* right. Nycolos had precious little experience with these feelings, with enemies he could not overpower or at least meet on equal terms. The goblin did.

"You can always regain your might," Smim reminded him, doubtless sensing his hesitation, "should you require it."

Another sigh, a nod, and Nycolos closed his eyes in brief concentration. Beneath his skin, muscle and bone rippled, shifting, softening. In instants, he possessed a strength impressive, perhaps even remarkable for a man of his height and build, but no longer unnatural.

After that, there was nothing for it but to rise, the ragged tatters of his shirt and trousers tugging loose from his flesh where the congealing blood of his injuries tried to paste them, and present himself, like freshly slaughtered game, for inspection.

The sting to his pride burned hotter than any fire.

The men came, hauling open the door of the cage. They poked, they prodded. They checked teeth, as though purchasing a herd of old nags. They stripped rags away, studying physique. They squeezed muscles. They pushed. Occasionally they slapped. Nycolos nearly bruised the bone of his jaw, so tightly did he clench, biting back an angry protest or worse.

"This?" A heavily mustached man with old cheese on his breath, jabbed a finger at the red and angry wound in Nycolos's chest, exposed when his shredded tunic was tugged aside. "You'd best not let this cost us." He conveniently ignored the other injuries, the ones he and his fellows had themselves inflicted. And just as well, really; had he scrubbed away the caked blood and the dust, he might have been startled at just how swiftly those wounds, unlike the one beneath Nycolos's heart, were healing.

"Perhaps you ought have considered that," the seething captive spat, "when you crept up behind me and clubbed me over the head, you cowardly—!"

The slap, made dismissively with an open hand rather than fist or cudgel, startled several birds from a nearby branch, where they had warily studied the wagon and the gathered people. A furious heat washed through Nycolos, from his cheek outward; a tide of rage, not pain.

He heard screaming, and couldn't be certain at first whence it came. He felt leathers and fabrics bunched in his grip, flesh flattening against bone beneath his other fist. His vision cleared, the crimson veil boiling away, to reveal his captor's bruised face and bloodied nose hanging inches from his own.

"Master! No! Stop!"

It wasn't Smim's beseeching cry that brought him up short, however, but the overheard muttering of the other captives.

"Idiot."

"Fool."

"Madman."

"Get himself killed."

The goblin had said it, mere minutes ago. His temper was no longer as it had been. His judgment, his patience…

*Who am I allowing myself to become?*

And, of perhaps more immediate import, *How quickly will this new "me" get me killed?*

Nycolos released his tormentor-turned-victim and stepped back, hands raised, well before the man's compatriots reached him. He expected, at best, another severe beating. With luck, he might survive it.

But while many of his captors clearly intended precisely that, cudgels and even a few small blades raised, one man reined them in with a gesture and a sharp bark. His bald head bore signs of peeling, having seen far too much of the midday sun. The ends of his dark mustache dangled low to vanish into the equally dark fur mantle he wore over a battered breastplate of old steel. It was, to Nycolos's memory, the only armor he'd yet seen among his jailers that wasn't of leather and hide.

"You're fast," the bald one said in a voice more befitting a boy than a man of his size and age. "Not many can get the drop on Inju way you just did."

"He startled me." Nycolos wanted to vomit, to throttle himself before he let the words escape, but he would not allow his pride to be the end of him. Not today, not this way. "It won't happen again."

"We should kill you," the other continued. "Attacking one of us. And you already cost us two perfectly good slaves."

*Slaves.* Nycolos was no fool, regardless of what his fellow captives thought. He'd known these vermin for slavers, known since he'd been taken that he had value only to those who traded in muscle and flesh. Nonetheless, hearing the word nearly set him off once more. It was only an iron-willed effort, one that nearly had him breaking out in a new sweat, that kept him still.

"If I'd let them harm us, or starve us, you'd have lost just as much," was all he said.

"You wouldn't have starved." The bald head shook. "You're strong, stronger than you look."

Nycolos ignored the almost accusing sideways glare from Smim.

"Assuming that doesn't pus up and kill you with infection," the slaver continued, pointing at Nycolos's chest, "you're worth any two or three of these sorry creatures. So you got one more chance. *One.* Step out of line, though, and you die ugly. Understood?"

*Patience. Let them have their meaningless victory. Patience...*

"I understand."

"Good."

Nycolos saw the blow coming, squeezed his fists tight against every instinct he had, and allowed it to land. Pain burst through his jaw—though less than the bald slaver might have expected—and he crashed back against the wagon before slumping to the earth.

By the time he'd hauled himself to his feet, the examination was concluded and the other slaves were being marched back into the cage. Biting his tongue and refusing to acknowledge Smim at all, Nycolos followed.

The wagon did not, however, lurch back into motion, not immediately. After a brief argument up near the horses, several slavers returned to the rear and entered the cage. Eyes darting nervously about them, they moved to stand over Nycolos. While one kept careful watch on the other prisoners, the second knelt and produced a few lengths of ratty bandage and a small handful of crushed leaves. These he mixed with a splash of water from a skin at his belt, then slathered it roughly across Nycolos's chest without so much as a word.

Nycolos wondered if he was supposed to feel something beyond the caustic pain of contact with the infection.

No act of kindness, this. They'd just told him he was their most valuable piece of cargo; surely this was nothing more than protecting an investment. Still, if the salve did any good at all, Nycolos didn't care why they'd provided it.

Was it stinging, burning, a bit less? Or was that merely hopeful imagination? He sat still and focused on nothing else as the wagon once more wobbled and shook across the Outermark.

It kept him from dwelling on the other wounds, the wounds to his pride—those he'd already suffered, and the many more he knew must lay ahead.

———

Her name was Justina Norbenus, his was Rasmus. Nycolos knew that much from eavesdropping on the conversation between slavers and, presumably, their clients.

He knew, too, that he hated them, and not merely because they prepared to purchase him like some low beast of burden.

While the slavers had been of mixed ethnicities, boasting every tone of skin and hair, these customers were all of a single type. Even had their pallid, patrician features not been sufficient to announce their nationality far and wide, the cream-hued drapes with colorful trim they wore pinned over one shoulder— hers burgundy, his robin's egg blue—and certainly their names, were a dead giveaway.

Ythani.

In his disdain for that nation's aristocracy, Nycolos stood in accord with the majority of southern Galadras. Opportunistic, sycophantic, and bullying, Ythane remained the only human state to retain its fealty, into the modern age, to the fey of Tir Nallon, and their so-called Bronze Emperor.

The thought brought Nycolos up short, as he stood waiting for his own examination. Could a true denizen of that declining inhuman empire see through him? His transformation was absolute, but unnatural; would it deceive equally unnatural sight? The mountain fey, with whom he'd had occasional dealings, would be unlikely to penetrate it, but the elves of Tir Nallon were a more uncanny, more uncertain thing.

It probably wouldn't matter. The rulers of Tir Nallon rarely appeared in the company of their human vassals. As elven focus and appetites turned ever inward, they left Ythane largely to its own devices.

Nonetheless, the possibility, however slim, made Nycolos nervous.

"Start with that one."

Several slavers marched toward Nycolos from the opposite side of the wagon, Justina and Rasmus in their midst. Their bald leader gesticulated wildly, doubtless boasting of the slave's strength and value. Inspection of the "livestock," to ensure the buyers received their coins' worth, was about to begin. Nycolos, for all that the notion of being bought and sold was abhorrent to him, found himself grateful to be getting it over with.

"He's injured." Justina Norbenus's voice was taut, upper crust with a bit of an accent Nycolos could only assume was Ythani.

"As I warned you, Lady Norbenus," the slaver reminded her. "But with a bit of treatment—"

"It's far worse than you led me to believe, Sanish. You cannot possibly expect me to pay full price for damaged merchandise."

*Deep breaths. Don't react.*

"He's quite strong. He'll make a good worker."

"Are you?" It took Nycolos a moment to realize she addressed him directly, now, since she couldn't be bothered to look him in the eye. "Are you as strong as Sanish claims you are?"

"I don't know. How strong does Sanish claim I am?"

Now the aristocrat *did* glare directly at him, with something less than amusement in her expression. The bald man—Sanish, apparently—flickered swiftly from murderous glower to sickly smile. "As I said, he can be a bit mouthy. But he's learned his lesson about disobedience or causing trouble."

*Oh, have I?*

Justina snapped her fingers, then pointed imperiously at a pile of stones that must have been placed here, at the edge of their camp, specifically for this purpose. "I want those in the wheelbarrow. Given that you seem incapable of keeping either your mouth or your injury shut, you had better be *quite* strong indeed."

Swallowing his disgust, Nycolos swiftly and efficiently loaded the rocks. It took some doing—the task didn't come nearly as easily as it might have, had he been willing to resume his earlier strength—but he was winded only a little by the time he finished. "I could do even better," he noted, returning to his spot by the wagon, "if I could get this wound properly treated."

The woman nodded, more to Sanish than to him, and moved on to the next slave. Rasmus—seemingly some sort of bodyguard or lieutenant to Justina—snarled something unintelligible at him before following.

Nycolos ignored him, instead examining the mining camp that would apparently be his home for a while. Built up against one of the peaks of the northern Outermark Mountains, the structures were surprisingly roomy and well constructed. Logs were carefully slotted together to avoid shifting or drafts, and the roofs were evenly shaked. Smoke curled languidly from several chimneys: Cooking fires, to judge by the aroma of meat lurking within. Some sort of stable or corral stood nearby, its presence betrayed by the smell of horse and horse-leavings, but from this angle it must have been concealed behind one of the other buildings.

Of the few people moving to and fro between those buildings, most were clad either as Justina and Rasmus were, or wore sculpted breastplates and greaves, and carried spears. The bulk of the slaves were doubtless asleep, and probably confined to the mines themselves, rather than the more comfortable quarters enjoyed by camp personnel.

The observant prisoner couldn't help but note that the guards made a regular practice of looking up, into the darkening night sky, as well as around. Clearly these Ythani weren't careless, whatever else might be said of them. They'd heard and taken seriously the rumors that a colony of wyverns hunted the peaks of the Outermark.

Nycolos knew well it was more than mere rumor—though the wyverns spent most of their time further south. *If they were here now,* he wondered idly, *could I convince them of who I am? Or would I die as just another few mouthfuls of prey?*

*Hardly the most pleasant way I could possibly go, but surely among the most ironic.*

"...for the whole lot of healthy ones," Justina was saying as she and the slavers wormed their way back into Nycolos's attentions.

Sanish, despite his nod, was frowning. "In what coinage?"

The woman looked at him as if he'd just asked the color of her unmentionables. "Ythani dinar, of course."

"It's just, not everyone is entirely happy about taking—"

"Silver is silver."

"This is a mine! Couldn't we—?"

"It's not a *silver* mine," she reminded him with a sneer.

"Well, what are you—?"

"Ythani dinar, Sanish. Take it or leave it. You've been good to work with, but you're hardly the only slaver."

"Fine." He chomped each word from the others like jerked meats. "You have a bargain."

"I'm so glad. Rasmus, please take our new workers to their pallets. Oh, Sanish?"

The bald slaver grunted.

"If you're going to kill the rejects, please take them further from camp. We had real problems with carrion eaters and vermin last time."

Nycolos scarcely turned his head at the gasps and cries as a handful of prisoners were separated from the rest. Of course some would be deemed inappropriate for mining work, and it couldn't possibly be worth the slavers' time to transport them all the way back across the Outermark in hope of another buyer. Poor fortune for them, but not anything he—

"Master?"

A whisper, scarcely audible even to him, but enough. Now he *did* turn, tensing as Smim was shoved into the smaller group. Standing upright beside the others, it was clear why he'd been rejected. Although tall for one of his people, Smim only came up to about the ribs of the man beside him.

"The goblin is far stronger than his size suggests," Nycolos called out.

Rasmus spun, a short bullwhip seeming to unfold from nowhere in his fist. "Nobody told you to speak, slave!"

Justina, at the same moment, snapped, "I'm not paying good silver for a *goblin*." Revulsion dripped from her voice, so thick Nycolos was surprised it didn't form into a puddle large enough to slip in.

What now? Nycolos couldn't fight the lot of them, wasn't willing to risk his life for his servant—not without *some* reasonable chance of victory. Yet standing helpless while his only companion was wrested from him was intolerable. What should he—?

It was Smim himself who saved him the trouble. "If I might be permitted to offer up an argument on my own behalf?"

The humans stared. "And now he's mocking us with his speech!" Rasmus accused.

"I assure you," the goblin protested, "it is most certainly not with my speech." Then, before the taskmaster could work through that one, "If my elocution seems formal to you, it is only because I learned the human languages with which I'm familiar from..." A quick, subtle glance at Nycolos. "...a teacher and master who insisted on being addressed thus."

Nycolos had always felt the precise decorum was his due, but now he felt a touch of embarrassment over it.

"I don't care how you talk—" Rasmus began, but a gentle cough silenced him.

"Very well, goblin," Justina challenged. "Convince me."

"For one, my frame allows me to work in spaces that might be excessively confining for a human of comparable strength. Of greater import, however, is my sight. You require workers for a mine? I can see far beyond any of your human laborers, and in greater detail, with only the faintest torch- or candlelight."

The noblewoman leaned in, whispering to her lieutenant. "Yes, that might prove useful," she acknowledged after a brief exchange. "Rasmus, have two of the men take him into the mountain to prove his claim. If he's telling the truth, we'll buy him. If not, Sanish won't *have* to kill him."

Nycolos watched Smim marched away, relieved not to lose his only ally.

Then Justina's guards gathered around, leading the slaves at an awkward shuffle into the mines, and relief faded to the last thing on Nycolos's mind.

# CHAPTER TWO

*"Cart!"*

Nycolos muttered something vile under his breath and wrestled with the wooden frame, forcing the conveyance to rotate on protesting, grinding wheels. Had the tunnel been wider, he might have had an easier time with the various maneuvers his new duties required of him, but their Ythani masters saw no need to "waste" the labor required to enlarge the mine. After all, the narrow confines weren't inconveniencing *them* overmuch.

*I'd have been wiser to make a poorer showing of my damn test.*

In order to best make use of Nycolos's obvious strengths, without putting a pickaxe or other potential weapons in his hands, they'd expanded the loading and hauling of rocks from test to task. It was his responsibility to clear away the rubble his fellow slaves left behind in their search for more valuable ores. Hour after hour, for days now, his life had consisted of pushing the damn cart up and down uneven tunnels of sagging and poorly buttressed roofs, pausing only long enough to load up here or empty out there before making another pass. The almost ebony hues of his skin were concealed beneath a patina of sweat-matted dust, and he had discovered the delightful twin experiences of blisters and calluses for the first time in his life.

His chest wound, at least, had been treated—adequately, if not well—and might have begun to show some signs of healing had his labors not constantly aggravated it. The lessening of the pain was more than countered by the frustration caused by his knowledge that, if they'd just give him some time, it might be far better still.

Between that, the exhaustion, the constant hunger, and the overall humiliation, Nycolos's mood could best be described as "borderline murderous." He'd found swiftly that he was best served keeping his mouth shut and speaking as little as necessary, lest he come out and accidentally say something he'd soon regret.

It was an attitude the guards appreciated just fine, and if it didn't earn him any friendships among the other slaves, at least it didn't earn their enmity either. Most of them had, early in their captivity, felt similarly. Nycolos, in turn, felt no particular animosity, and even a faint sense of camaraderie and shared purpose, with his fellow captives.

"You! Rock boy! Hurry it up!"

Well, with most of them.

Nycolos stabbed a rancorous glower at the speaker—a grizzled "veteran" of the mines, one slave among a handful who were given small clubs and no observable duties Nycolos had yet seen, who snickered with one of his companions—and made a small show of stacking more broken stone into the already overloaded cart.

"Sorry about that." Keva, a wiry worker of mixed but light-skinned heritage and no obvious nation, shrugged an apology, then waved his heavily scarred pick over the heap of rubble his efforts had left scattered about. "I told them I didn't need this cleared away yet, but…" A second shrug.

Nycolos grunted noncommittally. Then, more because his fellow slave seemed to expect it than because he had any desire for conversation, "I'd have had to get around to it eventually, one way or the other."

It was Keva's turn to grunt, and then the smaller slave went back to pounding at the wall, half-stumbling a step with a chorus of small clatters. He wore a pair of rusty manacles around his ankles, long enough to let him work but restrictive enough to occasionally get in his way—and definitely enough to keep him from running. Perhaps one in three or four slaves were similarly restrained. Nycolos guessed they all had escape attempts or some other disobedience in their past.

He started to turn away, grappling again with the cart whose high-pitched screeches of protest echoed in the cramped mine in way that the flatter impact of steel on rock did not. Those efforts were interrupted, however, by the appearance of Rasmus himself, followed by a pair of bucket-toting slaves. "Water break! Ten minutes!"

Nobody actually dropped their tools—that could only bring trouble—but they laid them down swiftly and sat or leaned against the rocky walls, catching their breath, wiping feebly at perspiration and dirt, waiting for the buckets to reach them.

Perhaps spurred on by the low hum of other conversations, Nycolos decided now was as propitious a time as any to learn more of his new—however temporary, he swore—home.

"Collaborators?" he whispered to Keva, aiming his chin at the older slave who'd summoned him earlier.

"More or less, yeah. Prove yourself trustworthy, and just maybe you get guard or oversight duty instead of rock pounding. Or hauling," he added.

"Hmm."

"The old man you talked to is Veddai. The, uh, 'collaborators' don't have a rank structure, but if they did, he'd be near the top. Been watching over us for a while, now."

Nycolos felt his brow furrowing. "There are an awful lot of guards here," he noted. "Surely more than necessary just to keep us from being troublesome."

It was the taskmaster, Rasmus, who answered as he approached, whip dangling with a deceptively gentle sway from his belt. "Rival miners in the area. And they wouldn't treat you near as nice as we do."

"That... seems odd," Nycolos objected, trying to couch his doubt in more delicate terms than he felt. "Surely this mine isn't producing so much ore as to make a raid worthwhile. Besides, shouldn't the guards be *outside* the mine, then? An attack's not going to come from—"

"Shut your mouth and mind your own duties, slave! Unless you want to go without your water ration this afternoon."

Nycolos clapped his lips together, but his mind was racing. Not only was the lie obvious to anyone with a brain in his head, but he couldn't shake the suspicion that Rasmus had no good reason for the deceit. He just enjoyed even so petty a display of power over his captives.

"Gnomes," Keva breathed, leaning in. "I know it sounds insane, but—"

His whisper was not, apparently, silent enough. Rasmus spun, his whole face taut with fury, and snapped his fingers. Two of the slaves Nycolos had dubbed collaborators descended on Keva, fists flying. Several others, along with Rasmus himself, watched Nycolos carefully, just waiting for him to interfere.

He was tempted, not from any affection or loyalty to Keva but out of shared hatred of their oppressors—and, even more so, out of curiosity regarding what the man had been about to say. It was a temptation he resisted, however, patiently waiting for his water and closing his ears to the meaty thumps and cries of pain.

---

"I don't believe I'm familiar with the term, Master."

The overseers had assigned Smim to scout the new exploratory tunnels, counting on his gaunt build and sharp vision to help them locate traces of ore. Night, in the slave barracks, was the only time Nycolos had to speak with his goblin ally. They sat slumped, side by side, awaiting the evening meal (if one could dignify it with such a term).

The barracks were not within the mine proper, as Nycolos had initially assumed, but rather in the least comfortable and most poorly built of the camp structures. Breezes and sounds wormed their way through chinks in the logs, then back out again when they decided the place wasn't worth staying in. It was all one great room, without the slightest gesture toward privacy, and it reeked of unwashed bodies and leaky, crusted chamber pots.

The pair kept their voices low, each relying on the other's inhumanly sharp hearing, to ensure that the cramped confines and gap-ridden walls didn't carry their words to an unwanted audience.

"Gnome?" Nycolos asked. "A term in multiple human tongues. Something they came up with long ago to refer to the mountain fey."

"Ah." The goblin nodded. "Like 'elf' for the fey of the wilds or the Bronze Empire?"

"Precisely. A tiny, insufficient word for a notion far too large and too alien for them to comprehend."

"So also like 'dragon'?" Smim prodded with a faint smirk.

Nycolos ignored that. "It might just be a precaution, inspired by superstition and rumor, same as their fear of wyvern attack. Or they might have actually encountered the mountain fey. I'd very much like to know which…"

A short procession marched in through the barracks' door, a cluster of slaves carrying large bowls of a thick, unappetizing gruel. Or stew. It varied day by day and was often difficult to tell. Overseen by those same collaborators, including Veddai, they began scooping the slop into smaller bowls, cracked and clumsy little things, before handing them out.

"Why not ask?" Smim suggested, pointing at one slave in particular. "You might have a receptive audience."

Safia, on meal duty tonight, hadn't made any particular effort to engage with Nycolos, and he had no reason to count her as an ally. She was, however, a friend of Keva's—a fact that would have been made obvious, even if Nycolos had not already known, by her expression during Keva's punishment. Given Keva's efforts, slight as they'd been, to make Nycolos feel welcome, that might inspire her toward sympathy.

Unless she blamed him for getting her friend beaten.

Once Nycolos had his own bowl, he moved to her side and walked with her, so they could speak without forcing her to pause in her task. She appeared puzzled by his approach, but he took her lack of obvious hostility as a positive sign.

This close, he observed she had similar features to their captors, suggesting Ythani descent, but her mixed heritage was clear in her duskier eyes and skin. Otherwise, nothing much differentiated her from any of the other slaves. If her friendship with Keva was based on a common home or any ties of blood, neither of them showed it.

"How is he?" That, Nycolos decided, would prove the most effective opening.

Safia frowned. "I'm not sure." She pointed with one of the bowls she carried, nearly spilling it. Across the crowded room, Keva sat huddled in the corner, bruise-pocked arms wrapped around his doubtless aching gut. "Someone else is serving that half of the room tonight. Deliberately, I'm sure." Her bitter tang might have spoiled the food she was delivering.

"So… What, do those vermin hate the rest of us so much? They enjoy the opportunity to beat us?"

"Some. Others work to earn the overseers' trust because standing watch is easier than the rest of our duties." She paused, handed a bowl off into grasping hands. "They aren't really even assigned to watch *us*, you know. They're meant to be extra eyes to assist the guards. But some of them feel they can prove their loyalty by reporting the 'infractions' of fellow slaves. And even the ones who don't? They're not going to disobey, if they're ordered to…" Again she gestured Keva's way. "Well, do that."

It was as smooth an opportunity as Nycolos could have hoped for. "What is it exactly they're supposed to be watching for, if not—?"

"Oh, no. Vizret take them!"

Across the chamber, another slave—acting, most assuredly, on Veddai's orders—had delivered Keva his own "supper": a tiny dollop of gruel, scarcely more than a mouthful, and not even in its own bowl. The battered young man was forced to catch what he could in cupped, unsteady hands, then lick and slurp at them like an animal.

Veddai and his fellow collaborator cackled, each holding a bowl notably fuller than anyone else's. Clearly the gruel that should have been Keva's wasn't going to waste.

"Bastards!" Safia's whole body was tense, her expression livid—and utterly helpless.

Damn them, indeed, for their timing if nothing else. Was Nycolos never to learn even the simplest of the answers he sought? Frustrated and again swallowing a rising fury, he began to turn away.

And yet...

How long would he be trapped here, in this hellish subservience? Either a great while, in which case he might require allies beyond Smim, to help keep him alive; or he would find, or *make*, an opportunity to escape, which also might require assistance. Blood of his ancestors, apparently he needed allies just to learn what was going on in this wretched mine!

He could already hear Smim's arguments, that it was best, safest, to keep his head down, to avoid trouble; that he was ignoring the third option, which was that he offended the overseers enough that they chose simply to kill him. And yes, such arguments contained more than a kernel of wisdom, but Nycolos chose to rely on the fact that Justina Norbenus had, mere days ago, paid good silver for him. She wasn't about to have him slain for a single infraction.

It was sheer justification, hiding his true motives, he knew, but he quashed that knowledge deep inside.

"What are you doing?" Safia demanded, alarmed by whatever tensing or shift in his posture she'd sensed.

"Just going to reason with them."

She hissed something he didn't bother to hear, but when he took his first steps toward Veddai, she followed a few paces behind.

Veddai's companion tapped the grizzled older man on the shoulder and pointed, so he might turn to meet Nycolos's approach.

"You want something, slave?"

"A moment of your time." Nycolos chose not to comment on the fact that, his favored position notwithstanding, Veddai was no less a slave than he. "Surely Keva's been punished enough?"

"What business of yours is that? Unless you're looking for some of the same?"

The sounds of conversation, muted as it already was, faded throughout the chamber, leaving only soft slurps. The prisoners might not want to miss whatever was about to occur, but they weren't about to stop eating for it.

"I only wanted to point out, if Keva's too weak to work, it's going to hurt productivity. Justina and Rasmus can't possibly want that."

Safia's soft sigh of resignation from behind was clear indication of how well she expected *that* argument to work. Come to think of it, Nycolos was probably far from the first slave to voice it.

Veddai laughed. "Guess the rest of you will just have to work hard to make up for it. And maybe help remind Keva of how unhappy you are about it the next time he looks like he's about to yap out of turn."

"I see."

"Or the next time *you* are," the collaborator added, poking him in the shoulder, hard with a wooden serving spoon.

There it was. The real motivation, the one Nycolos had tried to bury beneath a topsoil of reasoning and justification along with his ever-simmering resentment and blazing pride: the hope that one or the other of these two brutes would do something very much like this.

Because now, for whatever miniscule difference it made, this was self-defense.

His grin grew wide enough nearly to split his face. From the rear of the room, somehow sensing what was about to occur, Smim muttered a fervent, "Oh, shi—"

To a chorus of shocked cries, Nycolos lunged.

No. He *leapt*.

Mere feet from his victim the slave hurled himself through the air, propelled by an enraged strength. Hands and knees slammed into Veddai, carrying him back as though struck by a ballista before taking him to the floor. His jaw twisted in an inhuman snarl, Nycolos struck, over and over, tearing flesh and cracking bone.

But he didn't strike with fists.

Shocks of pain shuddered through his fingers, but it wasn't enough to stop him. Hands held spread and bent, talon-like, he practically *dug* at the collaborator, slashing and ripping. Deep gashes gaped wide, oozing thick rivulets of blood, very much as if Nycolos struck not with fingertips and nails but with genuine claws.

Shocked by the speed and savagery of the assault, Veddai's companion hesitated a long moment, but his friend's screams ultimately spurred him into action. Rather than take the extra seconds to draw a weapon, he raised a fist high and brought it down, aiming the blow at Nycolos's collarbone.

Nycolos saw the strike coming, but instead of raising an arm to block it or dodge aside, he twisted so the fist landed instead on the outside of his shoulder. It ached, yes, but it was the attacker who caught the worst of it. Expecting a more fragile target, the man recoiled, howling at what had to be at least a fracture in his fingers.

Nycolos rose, turning to face him, sparing only a quick glance downward to be sure Veddai wouldn't be rejoining the struggle any time soon.

The older man looked as though he'd been savaged by an animal. Narrow crevices of blood crossed his cheeks, his chest, his throat—which had not been torn wide open through sheer luck alone. Nycolos's hands were drenched in crimson past the wrist, and slender, crinkled ribbons of skin dangled from his nails.

It was neither the blood nor the brutality that brought Nycolos up short, however, froze him in his tracks. Those he had expected, welcomed, reveled in. No, it was the sudden confusion that his actions weren't suited to his form, that he had fallen back on instinct and possibly given away far too much.

*This is not how humans fight!*

He was still overwhelmed with conflicting urges and a bewildered fear when the first of the guards, drawn from outside the barracks by the sounds of mayhem, tackled him to the earthen floor.

———

"Nycolos Anvarri. What in the name of Straigon's missing jawbone am I to do with you?"

He stood before Justina Norbenus in what could only be described as some peculiar merging of an office and a sitting room. An ornate—to say nothing of heavy—sequence of manacles and chains linked his ankles, wrists, and throat. Three guards, fully armed and clad in cuirass and greaves, surrounded him, just beyond arm's reach, but well within range of their narrow-tipped spears.

The mine-owner herself reclined on a sofa of scarlet velvet cushions, transported here across the Outermark at who-knew-what difficulty and expense. At its head stood a rounded table with an ingenious rotating top, allowing her to keep all necessary ledgers and papers within reach. At the moment, however, it was turned to allow her access to a plate of berries that had, quite possibly, been even more difficult and costly to acquire than the furniture. In all four corners, small shelves held bowls of posies, their aroma cutting, if not concealing, the harsh odors of the nearby mine and its many workers.

"In the days you've been here," she continued, when it became clear Nycolos wasn't prepared to answer her question, "you've proven yourself a good worker. Strong. In that regard, worth every mark I paid for you.

"But it's equally clear that you've not learned your lessons regarding troublemaking as well as Sanish claimed."

"Veddai struck me first," Nycolos offered with, thanks to the manacles, an absurdly loud and metallic shrug.

Justina's wave of dismissal spattered a single drop of berry juice across an open ledger. "He is one of the First among you," she said, referring not to his length of service but his position as what Nycolos called collaborator. "He's *allowed* to strike you, with sufficient reason. Hitting back is not a right you have earned."

"So make me one of the First."

A moment of stunned silence, and then Justina burst into a disbelieving guffaw. "You want me to *reward* you for crippling one of my best men?"

"Hardly crippled. With a chirurgeon's attentions and sufficient time to recover, he should be…" The slow twisting of his owner's expression warned Nycolos that this was probably not the right approach. "I'd be good for it," he said, changing tack. "You said yourself I'm strong. I'm fast. And I know something of the mountain fey—the gnomes. That *is* who the guards and the First are really watching against, isn't it?"

"And what would you know of gnomes?"

"That if there *are* any in this stretch of the mountain range, for one, they're going to consider a mine such as yours to be an intrusion on their domain. And they're not likely to notice, or care, for the difference between willing intruders and slaves. We'd *all* be in danger.

"Sanish's men *did* waylay me near the Outermark Mountains," he added at her questioning glance, "albeit farther south. I've had plenty of time to learn much of the region's threats." *You have no idea how much time, you stupid little creature...*

"I see." Justina tapped a finger on her lower lip. "You very well *might* make a solid First, at that.

"But no. Even if I were to ignore the incident with Veddai—and make no mistake, I'll do no such thing—you've not been here remotely long enough. I don't trust you enough, and the precedent... No." She snapped her fingers, and the trio of guards straightened. "Take Nycolos back to the barracks. Remove the manacles from his neck and arms, but he's to work hobbled until I order otherwise. Nycolos, you will receive four lashes a day, and short rations, for a week. I think you're tough enough to weather that without too great an impact on your work. When that's done, if you've endured well enough and your behavior's improved, that'll be the end of it. If not... Well, we'll see."

Another snap, and the guards began marching the chain-swaddled slave toward the door. As the first of them reached for the latch, however, Justina spoke up again.

"Nycolos?"

He tilted his head but said nothing.

"You *are* strong, and I suspect you may not fear pain the way many do. I also don't know how close you are to the goblin, or why you spoke up on Keva's behalf. But if we have another incident, if I have to discipline you again, they will share in your punishment."

There seemed little enough to be said to that, and the guards hustled him from the room before he might foolishly decide otherwise.

———

Justina might have been correct, that Nycolos didn't fear pain as much as most, but that didn't mean he felt it any less.

His back *hurt*.

The overseers weren't foolish. They whipped him at the end of the day, not the start, so as to affect his work as lightly as possible. Further, they allowed the other slaves—mostly Smim, with assistance from Keva and Safia—to treat his lashes with a salve meant to protect against infection or putrefaction.

It *still* bloody damn well hurt!

He sat now on his pallet, hunched over to gaze absently at the short length of chain linking his ankles. The posture was painful, tugging at the wounds, but less so than lying on them or leaning back against the wall. From all about him came the rough snores, sighs, occasional sobs, and other sounds of despair that even slumber could not fully erase.

Nycolos burned not with despair, but frustration.

He could be free. In a mere instant, he could shatter these chains, shatter these *walls*, slaughter everyone here who had harmed or offended him—and anyone else he chose. Freedom or death, all at his whim. He would be, for all practical purposes, a god unto them.

For a few minutes. And then he would die, his heart punctured by a triple-damned sliver of eldritch steel so small it should be less than an irritant! Just as that bloody knight should have been, the knight who wore an ever-more familiar face and bore an ever-more familiar name...

Nycolos clenched both fists in his hair, tugging almost hard enough to rip tufts out by the roots, to keep himself from screaming aloud.

And just as swiftly he stopped. *His fists...*

He remembered the assault on Veddai, fingertips stabbing, and he wondered.

In the desperation of the moment, weeks ago, it had taken all he had, every iota of effort and will, to change his shape to one that the intruding magical shard might not instantly slay. In the intervening days, he had adapted his ears, regaining a touch of the hearing he'd possessed before becoming a man. He knew he could permit his eyes to resume their prior form, ever so slightly, allowing him to see in the dark, and to gaze farther and more sharply than normal—but also that the effect was visible, marked him as something other than human. And he could control the strength inherent in his alien form, of course, as Smim had encouraged him to do; that he could, if he wished it, grow mightier than his human body should allow, albeit still far weaker than he once had been.

What else, then, could he do? He had never truly experimented with a *partial* shapeshift, had performed the aforementioned feats as much by feel and instinct as by intent. He dare not reshape his body as a whole, or any of the organs deep within, for that most certainly would reawaken the sorcery that sought his heart.

He started with his hands. He held them before him, after ensuring that everyone near enough to see him was, indeed, asleep, and concentrated. He remembered the feel of tearing flesh, the hunt, the many lives his "hands" had taken in their prior form.

His nails began to harden, to blacken. They grew curved, melding with his fingertips, lengthening...

Earlier he had struck as though his fingers were talons, the claws he remembered of old. Now they truly *were*.

As he had forced himself to swallow his earlier scream, so now did he fight back an almost hysterical laughter. More intense concentration and they had reverted. His hands were, again, entirely human.

What else?

If he could strengthen his muscles, what of his skin? Could he armor himself against the blows of his enemies, turn aside blades—or at least cudgels, and the lash—as once he had?

Again he concentrated, focusing on only the surface of his body, his outer flesh, far from the organs that pumped air and blood.

Yes! He felt a change, though he at first saw no alteration to the deep brown skin of his arm. He tapped it with a finger, and then—after regrowing it yet again—a claw. Tougher than human, but still normal mammalian hide. It would still bruise, still cut, but not readily. Would turn aside at least a glancing blow.

Useful, certainly, but could he go further?

The skin grew obviously thick, leathery; impossible to pass for human except in deep shadow. And then…

Nycolos's arm took on a pattern of tight, overlapping scales, iridescent as a jungle snake. In the dim confines of the slave barracks they appeared a reflective black, but he knew, in better lighting, they would boast a deep, magnificent purple. Deeper than wine, deeper than twilight, yet shimmering as he moved, as the sun or the moons shone down upon them, reflected from them, dark yet radiant…

With a sharp gasp, he forced himself to revert, until his skin was, once more, just that. Tougher than it had been, enough to take the edge off the sting of the lash, but not enough to draw attention. Subtlety, for the time being. Secrecy.

But he knew, now, that he was capable—even in this miserable body—of so very much more. And one day soon, he would reveal it. Revel in it.

In the gloom and grim misery of the slave barracks, Nycolos could not suppress a widening grin.

# CHAPTER THREE

How long he labored in those mines, making his so-called "owners" wealthy, Nycolos was never certain. In the monotony of those efforts, a seemingly changeless purgatory, he lost count of the days. Measuring the passage of time in such tiny increments had never much concerned him, and it was a knack he would have had to learn even under circumstances far less mind-numbing than these.

Weeks, at least; of that much, he was positive. The sentence Justina had degreed had come and gone long since.

Which was not to say that things had gone back to the way they were during his first days here. Branded a troublemaker, he still—like Keva and some others—wore manacles around his ankles. The chain was long enough that his walking steps were unimpeded, but try to climb one of the sloping passages, or to run for any reason, and he found himself hobbled and off-balance. It made his task of pushing the rock cart that much more frustrating, which in turn provided no end of amusement for the Firsts and the guards.

Oh, but they held a grudge over what he had done to Veddai, one that would not be satisfied by a week of the lash and short rations. The end of his formal chastisement was not, by far, his last taste of the lash. The collaborators—particularly Veddai's friend, whose name Nycolos never bothered to remember—took every opportunity to direct the guards' whips against him. The slightest delay in responding to a call for the cart, a word that could be twisted and massaged until it became an insult or other mark of disrespect, anything was justification if his tormentors were in the mood to make it so. Their penalties were never severe; a single stroke, maybe two; a half-empty bowl at the next meal, or short sleep the next night. Never enough to significantly impact his work, or to attract the attention of Justina or Rasmus.

Well, Justina. Nycolos had his private suspicions that Rasmus was fully aware, and approved. Although the taskmaster himself treated him no differently than any other slave, the man couldn't quite repress the occasional smirk or knowing gaze.

Nycolos bore it, as he'd borne everything else—a trial made rather easier since he'd toughened his skin, so that the kiss of the whip was markedly less agonizing than it had been.

Thus did time, however much of it, pass. The mine slowly grew, creeping deeper into the mountain like a curious, questing tendril. The corridor of rock and wooden beams became familiar as any home; the slaves, particularly Keva and Safia, as recognizable as the many servant creatures Smim had once managed for him.

Not comfortable, never comfortable. And never acceptable. But, until he came up with a way to either escape his circumstances or turn them to his advantage, unavoidable and, in the day-to-day, unremarkable.

So he never knew how long he'd waited for something to change before it finally did.

Nycolos had dragged his cart over to a trio of slaves working one particular vein, chipping and picking at the walls to reveal more valuable ore, and had just begun loading their latest detritus into the cart when he heard it. He froze, a hefty chunk of rock in his hands, head tilted, trying to listen and wishing the grunts and the panting and the tools would go silent for just a moment.

"You! Nycolos!" Veddai's friend; of course it was. "Get the hell back to work!"

*Couldn't they all just* shut up *a minute a let him listen?*

"You just go deaf? I told you—!"

"*Quiet!*"

It wasn't just the bellow, thundering as it was, but the fact that a slave had dared to make such a demand of a First—and in front of other workers, no less—that grabbed everyone's attention. Whether in shock or in fury, the entire tunnel indeed went silent.

For a few breaths only, of course, but that was long enough for Nycolos's more than human hearing to confirm what he'd thought he'd sensed, that nobody else present could possibly yet have noticed.

The stone surrounding them had begun, ever so faintly and oh so deeply, to hum.

*They've come.*

"Oh, that's it, you stupid bastard!" The First was near apoplectic with fury, but a note of gloating had wound itself into his snarled and spit-drenched words. "I'm going to enjoy having you flayed and roasted for—"

Nycolos had absolutely no time for that idiot right now. "Everybody step back!" he cried out, shuffling toward the center of the tunnel as fast as his manacles would allow. "*Back away from the walls!*"

Not that they couldn't come from the floor or ceiling just as readily, but at least there would be a chance…

The captives had little reason to trust Nycolos's judgment, nor had they any notion of what had triggered his sudden alarm, but these were men and women accustomed to following commands. Most did as he'd ordered, stepping away from their work and from the walls of stone. Even several of the Firsts and guards had done the same, only slowly realizing that they'd just accepted the command of a mere slave.

Others, however, including the enraged First, only grew angrier and more resentful that Nycolos dared think to order them about. Their shouts and threats and curses filled the mine, echoing from the rock as they advanced, fists and cudgels and whips raised high.

Yet even they could no longer drown out the alien song of the stone that had finally risen high enough for human ears. Slaves gawped in growing panic, and many clutched pickaxes and shovels to their chests, feeble weapons indeed but all that stood between them and a threat they sensed but could not begin to comprehend. The air in the passage grew heavy with a peculiar earthy scent.

The mountain fey had finally come to Justina's mines.

The rock disgorged them like jellyfish on the tide. They varied widely in size, some taller than Nycolos, some little larger than a child's marionette. A few boasted wings, though to what purpose Nycolos couldn't have said; others extra legs or arms, which they used to scrabble across wall and ceiling as readily as floor. Beyond such details, however, they all looked very much alike.

It appeared some sculptor or toymaker had abandoned his work halfway through. Their faces were greatly detailed, though lacking in any human expression. Eyes and mouths were rounded hollows in the stone, twisting and writhing as they shrieked their rock-grinding cries. Those faces were misshapen, often bulging and stretching around cheeks and chin, doubtless the source of the "beards" such creatures wore in bedtime tales told to children. Their bodies, however, were far less intricate, consisting only of vague shapes that approximated gaunt torsos and spindly limbs, far too long and possessing far too many joints. All were simple stone, though several possessed striae or embedded crystals granting them additional color and even a touch of beauty.

They clawed at the air even as they emerged, spindly fingers of rock swiping through empty space where the workers had stood only moments ago. Nycolos's warning had spared a dozen from injury or death, though whether that respite was to last more than a few seconds remained to be seen.

The first of the mountain fey to completely leave the wall appeared near the man who had been so eager to see Nycolos beaten, and Nycolos gave half an instant's thought to letting him suffer whatever fate had in store. But no, if he was to fight, he would fight.

Strength rippled through his body, the culmination of an internal effort he had begun the instant he sensed the coming fey. He sprang forward, leaping hard and twisting in the air, then kicked out with both feet.

The cart, only partly full of rocks, cracked along one side as its wheels left the earth, hurtling back to slam against the wall—and the fey creature that stood in its path. Nycolos didn't know if such an impact would be enough to kill the thing, but surely it would at least be injured, slowed.

His jaw hanging in a stunned and vaguely sickly gape, the First retreated back into the midst of his fellows.

Still, that man was not the only one to have ignored Nycolos's warning, and not all the rest were so fortunate as he. Even as one of the armored guards dropped her whip and fumbled for the short sword at her waist, another of the fey slid from the wall and raked its fingers across the exposed flesh of her bicep.

The woman's scream choked off halfway through as she collapsed, her body going into shock at the unnatural injury. The triple gashes through muscle and flesh calcified instantly into solid stone, severing arteries, destroying tissue, and further tearing the skin around them. Even if she survived the shock, Nycolos knew, the best she could possibly hope for was to lose the arm.

Others were unluckier still, the blows delivered by the mountain fey piercing and petrifying organs or closing off throats, leaving a small but growing heap of cadavers part statue and part flesh.

Hysteria and dread spread before the fey, and the screams of the living swiftly overwhelmed the cries of the dying.

Until another shout came, louder still. "Panic and die!" Nycolos roared. "Fight back! You *can* hurt them!"

Not *well*, they couldn't. The steel of the picks and spades would require a great deal of strength to damage the rocky bodies of the mountain fey. Accustomed to hard labor, the slaves were assuredly strong enough—but whether they could deliver such blows swiftly, consistently, or for long was doubtful.

But picks and spades were not the only available weapons. For all their connection with the mountain, he knew, still these were fey, with everything—and every vulnerability—that entailed.

Hoping that what he was about to do would, like his kick to the wagon, be attributed to desperate strength bestowed by the heat of battle, Nycolos reached down and snapped the chain free of the manacles. Hefting the short length in one fist, he swung it in quick circles, links whistling as they cut the air.

Not the most accurate weapon, nor simple to wield. More than once, he came nearer to striking himself than any legitimate target. Still, as the wall disgorged another of the fey, Nycolos swung, catching the creature across the head with the chain.

The chain, made not from steel but from plainer, purer iron.

Wailing piteously, broad flakes of stone "bleeding" from the side of its head in a bizarre, sifting torrent, the fey creature retreated into the wall as rapidly as it had emerged.

"Unlock the chains!" Nycolos shouted. "We need iron, not steel!"

No longer hesitant to follow his orders, guards leapt to obey, fumbling at heavy keys. Several of the slaves equipped with older or simpler tools of iron—a prybar here, a hammer there—moved to protect their friends, or else passed the weapons to men and women in better shape and of braver mien. Nycolos was unsurprised, and yet strangely gratified for reasons he could not define, to see both Safia and Keva among those who had taken up iron.

The next wave of fey threw themselves at the assembled workers. Nycolos's chain lashed out, not unlike the whips he'd so recently endured, smashing a small depression into a skull of stone. Keva had wrapped his own chain around and through his fist to make an awkward cestus and punched like a taproom brawler, while Safia thrust the long end of her prybar like an clumsy spear. Others along the line struck with varying effect, but Nycolos hadn't the attention to spare them.

Faced with unexpectedly effective resistance, the mountain fey paused to reassess, but not for long. They advanced again, slower, more cautiously, even as a second wave clambered from the floor, reaching up and out as though from some premature grave. Workers and guards alike screamed and toppled as fingertips raked their feet, transforming tendon, flesh, and bone to lifeless rock.

A hand appeared inches from Nycolos, and he whipped his chain down and around him, kicking up a cloud of rock dust. Another rose and snatched at Keva; Nycolos yanked his fellow slave from its path and literally off the floor by his ragged tunic, then kicked to the side so the manacle around his ankle impacted and shattered the flexing stone digits.

Yet another fell to the spinning chain, but Nycolos's good fortune with the awkward weapon had finally run its course. In its fervor to escape the burning and cracking touch of iron, the fey spun away as it crumbled, winding the links around its body. The unexpected weight yanked the chain from the slave's hand, carrying it several yards down the passage before it finally landed in a heap of broken rock-flesh.

He'd taken one long stride toward the fallen weapon when he heard the cries and grunts from behind. Safia and several others were pinned in a tight cluster with their backs to the half-broken cart. Nobody else seemed able to reach them (assuming any would even have made the effort), and the few iron weapons they wielded only barely kept the grasping, swarming creatures at bay.

Cursing under his breath, a string of profanities that nobody present would have recognized had they heard them, Nycolos bolted across the passage. Certain that the others had more to occupy their attention right now, he focused on his left hand, fingertips warping into blackened talons. He grabbed the first of the fey from behind and tossed it away. Those he rescued could never have seen that his grip punched *into* the creature's back, severing whatever it might have in place of a spine. With his other hand he scooped up a short sword from where it lay beside a fallen guard. A second fey fell before him—not dead, for the blade he wielded was of steel, but temporarily pinned through the chest to the body of the sword's former owner.

Even now, as they turned to face this new assault, he grabbed a third from where it clung to the wall—both his hands were, again, entirely normal, merely human—and hurled it with bone-crushing force to the floor. There, before it could recover, he stepped beside its head, closed his iron-clad ankles around its neck, and twisted.

It wasn't much, but it opened a small gap through the converging fey. Still laying about them with what weapons they had, Safia and the other slaves broke through, racing to join with the larger band further down the passage. They, in turn, swarmed over the nearest of the creatures, making for the mine entrance. Thanks once more to his enhanced senses, Nycolos heard not only the panicked retreat, but the pounding footsteps of more guards charging this way, having finally overheard and reacted to the mayhem from within the mountain.

He had no idea, of course, if these new combatants carried weapons that could significantly harm the fey—but then, neither did the fey themselves. Having anticipated a slaughter, not a battle, and uncertain what they might soon be facing, they began to slide back into the walls and the floor whence they'd come.

Not that their efforts at slaughter had been wasted. The corridor lay strewn with bodies of the dead and dying, people with injuries of solid stone that no mortal being could heal. Doubtless Justina and Rasmus would order the survivors put out of their misery; not out of kindness, though it was the most compassionate option, but because it was cheaper and easier than trying to keep them alive.

Before the overseers arrived, however, Nycolos had something of his own to accomplish. Swiftly he returned to the side of the fey whom he had impaled, and who still struggled to free itself from the corpse to which he'd effectively staked it.

The harsh sounds contorting his jaw so that it instantly began to ache, tearing at his throat until he felt it might bleed, he spoke to it in its own inhuman tongue.

*"You do not drive the invaders from your kingdom of stone, not this way. Not without great loss. Hold off your attacks until I call to speak with you once more, and we can both have what we desire."*

He yanked the sword free with a piercing screech and a fainter *squelch* of steel through flesh. *"Go."*

It made no response, this creature of the mountain, but it peered at him long enough that he knew it understood—though whether it would heed his words, or bother to relay them, he couldn't guess. Then it was gone, as a fish vanishing into the deep waters of a pool of earth, an instant before the first of the guards appeared.

Mind racing and hope for freedom burning bright for the first time in weeks, Nycolos allowed his shoulders to sag in only partly feigned exhaustion and moved to meet them.

———

It was remarkably average, as cudgels go. Not quite thirty inches of hardwood, narrowed at one end, a heavy knot at the other, very similar to those carried by many of the guards and several of the First among slaves. And like those others, it had recently been altered to better serve against the mountain fey. Nails had been hammered into the knot and along much of the length, creating makeshift but brutally effective iron studs.

The only thing that made this particular club at all significant, as compared to the others like it, was that Nycolos wielded it.

Justina Norbenus was no fool. Although she was, indeed, concerned with precedent, with ensuring the complete dependability of any slave to whom she granted the tiniest sliver of authority, she recognized the severity of the immediate threat. Clearly not all the tales she'd heard of Nycolos's performance against the fey were accurate; some were contradictory, and many described feats of strength or prowess that were blatantly impossible. In the terror and chaos of the battle, the workers' eyes must have deceived them. That he had proven effective, however, and that his initial warning had saved the lives of many, was in no doubt.

Thus, though she had laughed off the suggestion as ridiculous only weeks earlier, she had indeed promoted Nycolos to the ranks of the Firsts.

Rasmus hadn't been thrilled with the notion, the slowly recovering Veddai even less so, but the others were grateful to have him at their side, watching their backs. The other slaves, too, seemed happy with the situation. Nycolos was still one of them, having achieved his position without playing sycophant to the overseers, and he seemed to take his duties seriously. He proved immediately that he had no interest in spying on his fellow captives for infractions, but was focused solely on standing sentinel against the return of the fey.

Or so he made himself appear, while he worked out how to go about the next steps of what he generously and jokingly called his "plan."

"So what *are* we waiting for, Master?" Smim asked one night as they huddled against the wall, side by side in the barracks. As a First, Nycolos could have claimed a larger space for himself, but he preferred to leave his living conditions as they were. If nothing else, it allowed him to keep having these conversations with his goblin companion.

"Them." Nycolos tilted his head, then emitted something equal parts growl and sigh.

Smim followed the gesture across multiple pallets to Keva and Safia, who were engaged in a similar conversation of their own. "I see. Is there something in particular that they ought to be engaged in?"

"Something in particular I'll need them for."

"And you don't believe they'll be amenable?"

"That's just it. I don't know. They very well might, but I don't *know*. If I ask this of them and they refuse, if they report me, the entire plan falls apart."

"A conundrum indeed," the goblin said. And then, "Now that you are a First, perhaps you might explain something to me."

The subject change was obvious and, Nycolos knew, quite deliberate. It was something Smim often did when playing the part of adviser, to let a topic sit for a few moments, let the mind work on it while the mouth was occupied elsewhere.

Though Nycolos never had entirely figured out if the goblin did it so he could ruminate on the subject, or so his master could.

"Yes?"

"If the overseers knew they were watching for an attack from the fey, why were they not already equipped with weapons of iron? Why were you required to improvise?"

Nycolos snorted. "That was the first question I asked. Apparently they just *assumed* that fey of mountains and stone wouldn't have the vulnerability to an ore that legend ascribed to their woodland brethren."

"I… suppose I can see some degree of logic in that." Smim sounded dubious.

"Logical, maybe, but not *accurate*."

"Indeed. Why *do* you suppose the mountain fey share the sensitivity to iron?"

"I have no idea. Why don't you invite them over for wine or tea and we'll ask them."

"Do they *drink* wine or tea?"

"You can ask them that, too."

Neither said another word for long moments, either lost in thought or listening absently to the idle conversation or low snoring from the room's other quarters.

Until, finally, Smim spoke once more. "Tell me, Master…"

"Hmm?"

"How well does your plan hang together if you *never* ask Safia and Keva to aid you, for fear of their reply?"

In less humid climes, Nycolos's glare might well have ignited something nearby. "You know I'm permitted to club you senseless now, right?"

The goblin shrugged. "If that's part of the plan…"

Nycolos looked down at his feet, in part to hide the faint grin he couldn't quite suppress. Only when he'd wrestled it back under control did he speak again, his voice deathly serious. "I'm… not accustomed to making decisions without more information. Or with so little time to ponder them."

"Or that require you to trust others?" Smim added knowingly.

"Not others whom I haven't known for a long time, and who owe me no fealty."

The goblin offered no reply. He didn't have to.

It didn't *matter* what he was accustomed to, and Nycolos knew it. He hadn't the resources, the power, the *lifespan* to do things as he would prefer, as he once had. Time to accept that, at least for the time being, and behave accordingly.

No more waiting, then. Tomorrow. He would speak with Safia and Keva tomorrow, and deal with whatever followed.

———

"*Fire!*"

As alarms went, it was one of the last anyone wanted to hear from within a mine. A bracket holding a hanging lantern against the wall had given away, and at the worst possible time. It fell hard against the edge of the rock cart, splashing burning oil down both sides of the old wooden contraption. The vessel caught almost instantly, igniting with a sharp crackle and a dull *whoomp*. Flames danced high, and smoke swiftly accumulated in a swirling maelstrom around the ceiling.

Everyone, slave and overseer alike, dropped what they were doing and raced for buckets of sand or water to douse the conflagration before it spread. Or rather, almost everyone. Panicked and distracted, nobody noticed when one of the Firsts stepped back into the shadows of the corridor and disappeared into a side passage.

It would turn out, eventually, that none of the panic, and not even all the dashing about, was necessary. As bad as the situation initially seemed, the mine itself—and its workers, so long as everyone kept their heads—had been in little danger. When the cart had caught fire, it stood well distant from any of the wooden crossbeams that supported the weaker lengths of ceiling. Surrounded by nothing but earth and rock, the fire would have burned for a time, and the smoke could have proved dangerous to anyone who lingered, but barring the most unlikely stroke of ill fortune, it could never have spread.

In the soggy, smoky aftermath, workers and guards congratulated themselves on their efforts, offering prayers of thanks—depending on the faith in question—to God, gods, or the elemental spirits called *vinnkasti*, that what had at first appeared so disastrous had proved relatively benign.

All save two, a pair of slaves in particular, who exchanged furtive, guilty looks and shared hopes. Hope that nobody would ever learn it was they who had arranged and orchestrated the "accident"; that nobody would notice that someone had slipped away during everyone's distraction, and hadn't been present to assist in battling the blaze; and that whatever scheme Nycolos had involved them in would prove worth it and wouldn't get them, or anyone they cared about, killed.

———

Nycolos was far less concerned about anyone realizing he'd been absent during the fire. Since before he'd approached Safia and Keva to play their part in his diversion, he'd already worked out his excuse. The fire, he would claim, might have been a deliberate distraction, a precursor to another fey attack. Once he saw everyone else had it under control, he'd stepped aside to keep watch for just such a possibility.

No, he fretted as he stalked swiftly down the shadowed passage, his eyes transformed to golden, slitted orbs so he might find his way more easily in the dark, his only worry—highly improbable, if his allies had done their job well, but not impossible—was that someone might come looking for him too soon, before he was finished.

Still, this couldn't be rushed. He had to get far enough from the main tunnel even to start, and after that... They would come when they chose, *if* they chose. All he could do was call.

When they finally did, he nearly missed the signs. From the low-hanging ceiling above, a faint bulge in the stone abruptly developed shallow hollows that opened, closed, shifted, twisted, blinking eyes and smacking lips. A nose sprouted between them, little more than a crooked stalactite, and the first of the mountain fey gazed down upon him from above.

Others crawled from the walls, spindly fingers parting stone like curtains, or clambered from beneath the floor. Chittering and grinding, the sound of their words blending with the rumble of tiny earthen joints, they came; a pair, a dozen, a score and more. In seconds Nycolos found himself not merely unalone but surrounded. Forcing himself to remain calm and still—to refrain from transforming his skin to an armor of indigo scales, his nails to shredding talons—meant stomping hard on every instinct he possessed.

It was, he knew, only the flimsiest thread of curiosity that kept them from attacking, but it was a thread he counted on. It wouldn't do to be the one to sever it.

*"I am grateful you have come."* Again he felt the pain of forcing his mouth, and especially his throat, to speak their language. It was an unlovely tongue, full of harsh glottal sounds—some of which could only be made, at least by humans, while inhaling rather than exhaling—flowing without pause into prolonged chains of almost musical vowels. Combined with a dearth of concepts that most languages took for granted, such as tenses and notions of time, it was nigh impossible for anyone but the fey themselves to master.

A fact that clearly hadn't escaped the fey themselves. *"How do you learn our speech?"* one demanded of him.

Nycolos couldn't be certain, so similar were many of the so-called gnomes, but one near the forefront had height and proportion, wings and half-formed features, that *might* mark it as the same to whom he'd spoken earlier. For lack of any more propitious choice, then, he had addressed his greeting to that one in particular, and it was this one that questioned him now.

*"I am taught…"* He allowed himself one deep breath. Not only might the creatures react poorly to his answer, Nycolos wasn't entirely certain how he himself would handle it. He'd

shied away from speaking the name since he'd abandoned the body that had borne it.

"*...by Tzavalantzaval.*"

The roar of the fey was the rumble of a hundred tiny earthquakes. Their stone fingertips clashed and clicked together like a hailstorm of rock. Nycolos found himself bracing for an attack before he knew his body had moved.

"*The wyrm is our enemy!*" the gnome to which he'd been speaking cried. "*It kills us! Sends its servants to hunt us!*"

Nycolos straightened, nodding slowly. *Well, perhaps if you hadn't slaughtered my emissaries, if you'd consented to serve as the wyverns and the cliffside goblin tribes... Or at least hadn't tried to invade my home, steal what was mine, shattered and slaughtered my first clutch in a hundred years...*

He spoke none of these thoughts aloud, of course, saying instead, "*The wyrm is gone.*"

That, at least, brought some welcome silence to the echoing chamber. "*Dead?*" one of the other fey asked hesitantly.

*Not remotely, you wretched...!* "*I do not know. Perhaps. But many of Tzavalantzaval's servants flee. The goblin within the mines is another such.*"

"*Mines?!*" It was the first fey who responded again, enraged once more. "*Wounds! Gashes and gouges in our world!*" The others again grew agitated, rumbling and clicking. "*That you escape from our enemy gives you no right—*"

"*We do not intrude on your domain by choice!*"

Again the noise subsided. The fey said nothing more, but their gaze—already somewhat empty, thanks to the stiffness of their stone façade—showed no comprehension at all.

It was all Nycolos could do not to sigh, or to curse aloud at the uncomprehending gnomes. The mountain fey held no concept of government, of hierarchy. Most wanted the same thing, and acted accordingly. Those that didn't were left to do as they pleased. Rarely, if ever, was there conflict between or among them.

This would have been so much easier with the wyverns. If the mines were only several days travel further south, if he could have gotten outside and up into the foothills as easily as he'd slipped into this side passage, if he could have convinced the wyverns who he truly was...

All right, perhaps not easier. But less frustrating, for certain.

*"You wish the humans out of your domain. Some of the humans wish the same, but other humans—stronger humans—do not allow it. I have a plan that allows you to drive the humans away, with little battle, little loss of your own. But it works only if you do as I suggest."*

For a time the mountain fey rasped and grumbled among themselves, puzzled and untrusting. At last, however, the first one replied. *"We listen."*

Which was not, Nycolos noted, remotely any sort of promise to cooperate.

Still, it was a simple plan, all things considered; it should work. *If* they agreed. If he could get them to understand the necessity of timing, of waiting; of striking not just at the intruders within their mountain, but outside of it, in the outer world where they rarely traveled and for which they cared not a whit; of a handful of other details straightforward to most anyone else but utterly alien to the gnomes' way of thinking... it should work.

Nycolos idly rubbed at the pain in his chest, the true source of all his woes, and began—with great care and deliberation— to explain.

# CHAPTER FOUR

With the passing of the days, life in the Norbenus mines settled back toward normal, miserable as "normal" was. The soldiers never let down their guard, but they and the slaves ceased panicking at every sound and every shadow. Hopes that the gnome attack had been a one-time disaster, that no further assault would come any time soon, began to rise.

Only Nycolos, never certain that the mountain fey truly understood what he had asked of them, always wondering if this would be the day they somehow bungled the entire affair, remained on edge.

Still, nothing went awry, or at least nothing he could observe. His only other problem during those tense days—and more a nuisance than genuine trouble—came in the form of Safia and Keva. Both of his fellow slaves and potential friends remained furious, vexed by his refusal to explain in any detail what he had done with the time their diversion had granted him. Over and over they asked, and over and over he would tell them only to be ready to act when he gave the word. Smim alone, on whose silence Nycolos could utterly rely, was privy to the entire plan.

Less confident in it than Nycolos was, horrified at how much of it relied on not merely the cooperation but the comprehension of the mountain fey, but privy to it.

Another night fell. Exhausted and filthy, the slaves marched sullenly to their barracks, flopping out across their pallets while awaiting their meager evening fare. Nycolos and the other Firsts, save those who were overseeing the cooking in a neighboring shack, sat about the only table, playing a few rounds with a set of poorly carved handmade Suunimi dominos. Nycolos wasn't especially skilled at the game, having learned it only within the past couple of weeks, but he was fast improving.

He heard the first faint sounds of struggle—the clash of metal and stone, the shouts of frightened or injured sentries, from deep within the mine—long before anyone else, and he had steel himself to continue playing as though nothing was amiss. It wouldn't do to react too soon.

It didn't require long. Muttered conversation fell silent, ripples of quiet spreading through the barracks as first this group, then that, became aware of something happening beyond the walls. The Firsts looked up almost as one, listening with growing panic—or, in Nycolos's case, excitement—as they began to understand what they heard.

"We need to get to the guards!" one of the Firsts shouted as she rose from the head of the table. "Arm ourselves!"

Another, the man who'd been a close friend to Veddai and whose life Nycolos had saved, was shaking his head as though trying to dislodge it. "No! We're safe as long we stay out of the mountain!"

"I don't understand!" wailed yet a third. "They never come at night! There's almost nobody in the mines after dark!"

"No." Nycolos, too, had risen to his feet, though only after casting a meaningful glance behind him at Smim. "Not anymore. The gnomes won't hold themselves to the tunnels this time. They've come to understand that they cannot merely drive us out, that they must bring the fight to us out here, in our homes..." He couldn't keep a bitter, twisted sarcasm from tainting that last word. "...if they are to rid themselves of us."

The lot of them—and not just the Firsts, but many of the other slaves within earshot—stared in open-mouthed horror. "How do you know that?" the woman at the table's head whispered, her voice shaking, almost sifting, through quivering lips.

"Well... I explained it to them."

Veddai's friend died first, his face forever frozen in almost comical shock. With strength far greater than any normal man his size, Nycolos lashed out, driving his elbow into the man's throat, crushing cartilage and bone within. His other hand was less than half a second behind, cracking into another First's skull.

Slaves retreated from the table, some scampering and scooting back with heels and hands, not even taking the time to stand. Most of the surviving Firsts had yet to recover from their shock, but a few began to act. Two of them moved around the table toward Nycolos: one a woman with her fists raised, the other a heavily bearded man hefting a chair as a bludgeon. The First nearest the door turned and dashed for the portal, screaming for the armed guards stationed without.

She never reached it, and her scream died scarcely born. Smim leapt from behind, a hideous jumping spider, his spindly limbs clamping around her waist and shoulders. With a grotesque gurgle he latched his jaw onto the back of her neck, jagged teeth sawing easily through flesh and jarring on bone.

Nycolos delivered a fearsome kick to the edge of the table, sending the long wooden slab hard into the hips and stomachs of the Firsts standing across from him. Men and women fell, grunting in pain, and he knew none of them would be moving to attack or racing for aid—not in the moments it would take him to deal with the two who approached.

He punched hard with the palm of his hand, driving the oncoming chair back into the face of the man who carried it. Blood spurted and the First staggered, still in the fight but off his stride.

Nycolos spun, catching and then crushing the woman's fist as she struck. Her shriek of pain wavered as her body grew weak at the sudden shock, then died entirely as Nycolos reached forth his other hand, gripped her chin tight, and snapped her neck.

Another moment and he had wrested the chair away from the woman's companion; a moment after *that* was all the time it took for that chair to beat the life from the man who'd carried it.

Finishing off the remaining Firsts was even more slaughter and less combat than these had been. In the end, Nycolos stood upon the table, a bloody club that had once been a chair leg grasped tight in one fist, to ensure all the horrified slaves could see him.

Not all, it seemed, were as cowed as others. "What have you done?!" someone shouted from the far corner of the barracks.

"I killed the other Firsts," Nycolos answered. "I figured that was obvious enough I really wouldn't have to explain it in too much depth."

The goblin, wiping blood from his mouth on a scrap of tunic, sniggered.

"You've killed *all* of us! The overseers will never—!"

Nycolos shook his head. "The overseers are not your concern. The sounds of battle you've heard outside? The gnomes are coming. I spoke the truth earlier. They'll no longer confine their attacks to the mines. They're coming for everyone."

"Why?!" It was Safia who shouted now. "Why would you *do* this?"

"Because I've also made a bargain with them. Anyone who flees will be permitted to go unharmed."

The murmuring that had been growing as Nycolos spoke, an even mix of anger and fear, faded to nothing as the implications sank in.

"Where are we supposed to go?" another slave demanded. "The Outermark—"

"Is dangerous. It can be deadly. But it's not endless. Go with care, help one another, you've a good chance to survive. You can leave here, and live or die, you'll be free. Or you can stay and fight the gnomes at the side of the men and women who've made you into less than beasts!"

He leapt from the table and strode toward the door, Smim falling into step behind. "Do as you will. But I am leaving, and I will go through anyone who attempts to stop me."

Several of the slaves, Keva and Safia among them, gathered around him—some begging or pleading for a third option, some moving as though they would accompany him—but none stood in his path.

"You had no right!"

*That,* of everything he heard, dragged Nycolos to a brief halt, locking eyes with Safia. "I beg your pardon."

"You had no right!" she repeated, practically hissing. "Something like this? You should have talked to everyone first! We should have had a say in our own fate!"

"So the overseers could hear about it and move to stop us? So we could have our chance at freedom debated on, decided, ripped from our grasp by the cowards among us? No. I saw a chance—not just for myself, but for us all—and I took it. I allow no one, taskmaster or slave, to bind me. *No one!*"

"And is it any more just that *your* choice binds *us*?"

"Since nobody else was capable of offering us freedom? Yes."

"You could at least have told us," Keva interrupted before Nycolos could either storm off or continue the argument. "Safia and me. You roped us into this, and we helped because we trusted you. You could have trusted us in turn."

Nycolos blinked once, long and languid, the expression almost… reptilian. "And you, of course, would have told absolutely nobody."

"Of course!"

"You would never once have given into the temptation to warn even your closest friends of what was coming."

Keva's look of righteous indignation faltered. "Well…"

"And they, in turn, would not have warned any of *their* friends."

"I don't… I mean—"

"Word *would* have spread, Keva. And whether through cowardice, or greed, or simple carelessness, *someone* would eventually have let it slip to a First or an overseer. Where would that have left us?"

The smaller slave muttered something apparently directed either at his feet or the floor beneath them.

Still, before Nycolos had taken two more steps, Keva spoke up again. "So what are we doing now?"

Safia's lips twisted at that "we," but she said nothing to counter it.

"You," Nycolos said, "are going to get everyone else moving. Or run on your own, if you prefer."

"Shouldn't we stay together?"

"Smim and I are going to fulfill the rest of my bargain with the gnomes. You're welcome to come along and assist if you'd prefer, but…" He turned and looked pointedly at the corpses he and the goblin had left scattered about one side of the chamber. "I'm not convinced you'd care to be a part of it."

Without waiting for a response, or further interruption, he barged through the door and out into the struggle-filled night. As he'd expected, nobody but the goblin moved to join him.

———

The guards fought well, bravely—or perhaps desperately—but they had little chance. Their iron-studded clubs and similar weapons were effective, but they lacked the speed or sheer ferocity of the mountain fey. Even with the occasional lamp or torch, glowing atop poles throughout the camp, the night impeded them far more than it did the unnatural creatures from beneath the earth. Without the Firsts leading the other slaves to support them, they were greatly outnumbered, and none could spare even a moment's attention to try and learn *why* their workers had not yet appeared.

And, as they learned all too swiftly, they faced another enemy from behind.

Armed with a short blade taken from a fallen soldier, Smim crept through shadow and dirt, an invisible predator. Blood streaked sword and teeth, and his inhuman features had warped into an expression of savage glee utterly at odds with his normal demeanor. For a time, he allowed himself to be a goblin, and his heart reveled in the carnage.

For Nycolos, however, there was no skulking, no stealth. He carried no weapon. Standing tall, flesh hardened enough to turn away weak or glancing blows, he strode through the camp, daring anyone, everyone, to notice. Already a small band of guards, only just having forced themselves awake and climbed into their armor, had seen him coming and called to him for aid.

He had slammed into them, an avalanche of impossible muscle and razored talons, shredding two before anyone recognized him as threat rather than ally. He had made equally swift work of the remainder, taking only a single injury severe enough to penetrate his skin—a shallow slash across his left ribs—in the process. The exultation of that violence, of striking back not merely at collaborators but at the men and women who had dared to hold him, to call him slave, burned in his veins, searing away most of the pain.

Most, but not all—and even as another soldier crossed his path, fleeing an unseen foe and dying swiftly beneath Nycolos's black claws, he suddenly wondered.

If the wound wasn't deep, had not penetrated anywhere near the organs he dare not reshape, was it any different than armoring his skin, strengthening muscle, sprouting talons? Could he…?

The concentration required was intense. Not the change itself, no; rather, shifting that particular patch of flesh back to the form he'd initially chosen, when it was whole and healthy, while maintaining the claws, the inhuman durability and strength, that were alien to this human shape. Reverting here, but not there. Returning one tiny bit of his body to the human template while leaving so much of it… not.

Intense, but not impossible. His exultation flared higher as the wound closed, faded so that no scar, no sign beyond one extra rip in his tunic, remained.

He couldn't help it. He laughed, long and loud, the sound carrying over the clash of battle from within the mines and, growing ever nearer, various spots and patches throughout the camp itself.

The door to the equipment shed and armory, located just beside Justina's "office," burst open, revealing the taskmaster Rasmus and two of his soldiers. For an endless instant they gawped at the apparently maddened figure of their newest First.

Nycolos swallowed the rest of his mirth, but he allowed his face to remain stretched in an almost manic grin. "It seems things have gotten a bit out of hand, Rasmus."

"Where—where are the rest of my Firsts?"

"Hmm." Nycolos spread his hands in an exaggerated shrug, deliberately exposing his crimson-coated talons to the torchlight. "Where indeed?"

The taskmaster screamed an order, the two guards beside him advanced, raising their spears…

Uncaring, now, how much of his inhuman strength he exposed, Nycolos leapt.

Through the humid night air that strength propelled him, clearing more than a dozen feet. Passing between speartips brought to bear far too slowly by their startled wielders, he extended both arms.

Claws punched through flesh and skulls. Nycolos landed in a crouch before Rasmus, having dragged both soldiers to the ground with him. Accompanied by the crack of bone, he stood.

And nearly took a spear in the gut for his trouble. Only a desperate bound backward kept the blade from striking with enough force to slide clean through his toughened skin; he bled even as it was, though the wound was shallow. Say what one would about the taskmaster, the man had nerves iron enough they might have harmed the mountain fey. Obviously he was thrown, frightened, by Nycolos's powers, but just as obviously the dramatics had not intimidated him into freezing up.

They watched one another, circled a few steps. Rasmus's skin glinted in the lanternlight, pale and slick with sweat, but his hands remained steady. The spear flicked out, lizard's tongue-quick, faster even than Nycolos could grab it. Perhaps, if he augmented his body further still… But he wasn't certain he could push himself *that* far beyond the bounds of humanity, not without concentration that might distract him at a crucial moment. Later he would experiment with it, but for now he must make do with what he had. What he was.

He stepped forward, and the spear moved to intercept. The weapon thrust, and each time Nycolos sidestepped or parried with extended talons.

And then Rasmus grunted once, coughed up a mouthful of bile-tainted blood, and fell face-first with a limp, hollow *whump*.

"Did you get lost?" Nycolos sneered. "Should I have left you a map of the camp?"

"Sorry, Master." The goblin yanked his stolen sword free of the taskmaster's spine. "You appeared to be having such a grand time, I was hesitant to interrupt."

Nycolos moved to lift the nearest lantern off its post. "You have a peculiar notion of fun, Smim."

"Yes, Master. I haven't the faintest idea where I might possibly have learned such a thing."

"Oh, shut up." A quick toss with now-clawless human hands, a sharp shattering, and the storehouse from which Rasmus had emerged swiftly began to smolder.

"Yes, Master." Then, doing absolutely nothing of the sort, he continued, "Have we killed enough of the defenders to fulfill our obligation?"

"I thought you were enjoying murdering the people who'd enslaved you, Smim." Nycolos crouched briefly, hefting one of the fallen spears.

"Oh, very much so. But I'd even more enjoy being gone from here before the mountain fey conveniently forget that they're supposed to allow us to depart."

"Fair point. We're *almost* done. We've just one more stop."

Smim followed his gaze and nodded once. Marching almost in unison, the mismatched pair entered the structure nearest the now merrily burning storehouse.

Justina Norbenus stood within, dressed for travel, several chests and leather sacks lying at her feet. Coin and other valuables, Nycolos had no doubt. She was hunched over the desk, gathering selected ledgers, as they entered. She spun, straightening, at their sudden appearance, and just as swiftly relaxed, if only marginally, when she recognized them.

"Start loading these on the horses!" she ordered, gesturing at the gathered riches. "We have to get out of here!"

"Well," Nycolos mused, crossing his arms and otherwise moving not at all, "two-thirds of us do."

The mine owner froze, thoughts and questions churning almost visibly behind her slack expression. Her jaw gave a twitch.

"If you're contemplating shouting for Rasmus," Nycolos told her, "you might want to consider that you're far more likely to attract the gnomes. They have pretty good hearing."

"Also Rasmus is dead," Smim added helpfully.

"Also that, yes."

Justina's shoulders, indeed her entire body, slumped. Clearly it didn't even occur to her to doubt their claim. "You… You did this?"

"Some of it. The fey deserve their share of the credit, though."

"Why?!"

Nycolos felt his chin drop, his mouth gape, in utter disbelief. "You cannot have just asked me that!"

"It was never personal. We needed workers. Were you not fed? Given shelter? It's more than many people can—"

"Master?" The goblin's voice actually quivered with churning emotions. "May I please chew on her face now?"

"No."

"Stab her, at least?"

"No, Smim. We'll not be killing the Lady Norbenus today."

The vicious little creature had no opportunity to express his dismay, nor Justina her surprised and incredulous relief, before Nycolos struck.

With a low-pitched whistle and blur of motion, his scavenged spear flipped around so that it was the butt end, rather than the blade, that landed. A hideous *crack* flowed without pause into Justina's agonized scream as she collapsed, clutching at her now splintered shin.

"Can't have you leaving before the mountain fey find you," Nycolos explained, though he couldn't be certain his former "owner" heard or understood him through her pain. "They *really* don't want anyone intruding on their domain again, you see. So I explained to them the advantages of setting an unmistakable example."

He casually tossed the spear to clatter against the desk, landing halfway across the chamber. "I believe their intent is to see just how much of you they can turn to stone before you've died of the wounds, and then display what's left. I'm not certain, of course. They were still discussing it when I left. If that sounds too unpleasant, you can always drag yourself over to that spear and slit your own throat. I don't think you've the spine for it, since you've always had other people to commit your violence, but it's entirely up to you.

"In your next life, if you believe in such a thing, try to be a bit more selective in who you dare think to make your slave!" He could only hope, as his eyes turned gold and inhuman, the better to make his way through the dark of night, that she was coherent enough to notice it. "Come on, Smim. *Now* we're done."

With nary another word, he who now called himself Nycolos Anvarri vanished into the wilds of the Outermark, once more making his long way toward human civilization—and, with luck, the means to shed this pathetic lesser form, lesser *life*, he'd assumed along with his stolen name.

# CHAPTER FIVE

Conventional wisdom and tavern tales dubbed Tohl Delian the most heavily fortified city the continent of Galadras had ever seen. While some historians or sages might quibble with that claim, none could argue that the walls of this, the capital of Ktho Delios, were an awe-inspiring marvel.

Quarried from the nearby Aerugo Mountains, the stone walls averaged a dozen feet across and nearly three times that in height, though precise measurement varied. They sloped outward, boasted countless watchtowers and engine platforms. Rumor held that *thousands* of soldiers patrolled those walls or stood sentry within its towers—and many times that number of slaves, prisoners of raids and war, had given their labor, and often their lives, in the construction of that bastion.

None of which, the foreigner decided as she raised her gaze to that looming barrier for the umpteenth time in the last hour, made it even remotely beautiful. She'd never say so aloud, not in present company, but she thought it looked like some divine infant had used playroom blocks in an attempt to imitate a mountain.

She stood smack in the middle of a winding line of humanity, awaiting admission to the walled city, wrapped in layers of capes and shawls against the bite of Ktho Delios's autumn winds. Before such gusts the hems of her garments fluttered and flapped, as did those worn by every man and woman she could see, the tarps covering a variety of wagons, the tails and scraggly manes of mules, and anything else the weather could idly pick up and play with. It smelled of a bewildering combination of lush greenery and the coming winter snows, carried down from the peaks of the Aerugos.

In the distance—far from the ramparts, for the Ktho Delian military would never suffer a tree to grow near their walls—branches and leaves rustled their complaints against the growing cold. Atop the highest parapets furled and snapped the black banners of the Deliant, the military parliament that ruled Ktho Delios under an entrenched and permanent martial law. The dirt of the road, though packed down tight by constant travel, danced low in the wind, swirling around the ankles of all who waited.

Of all the visible world from where the foreigner stood, only the walls, ugly and dark, remained unmoving.

An old and battered wagon—driven by a burly fellow with the scattered burn scars of a blacksmith, and a curly-haired boy who might have been a nephew or an apprentice—*finally* made its way through gate inspection and trundled into the city. No surprise they'd been allowed through; the smell alone suggested they were hauling sacks of turnips or some other root vegetable, nothing to which even the most stringent sentinel would object. The entire line shifted forward several paces, the next entrant faced the guards, and the newcomer wondered if she would, in fact, still be young enough to walk unassisted by the time her turn came around.

The gate, when she did finally reach it, was a tunnel through the wall, a veritable maw: portcullis of heavy steel teeth, and enormous wooden doors, bound in iron, ready to slam shut into an impassible gullet. Although she couldn't spot them from here, she knew there must be dozens of murder holes, soldier-occupied alcoves, and additional layers of doors within. The soldiers who moved to bar her passage were hard of mien, cold of gaze; their mail and weapons well maintained, their tabards—black, sporting a tower of dusky hue only barely visible against the dark fabric—spotless.

"Your papers, miss."

With a feigned nervousness—not *too* much; it wouldn't do for him to think she had anything to hide—she passed across the sheaf of documents she had obtained, after careful questioning, at the border, and which had already been examined more than once.

The Deliant soldier glanced over them, taking in the various marks and shorthand that filled the carefully inked forms. Ironic, in its way, that the gate guards of Ktho Delian cities had to be fully literate, when so many of those passing through probably couldn't sign their own names.

"Your name is Tamirra Vallenfir?"

"Yes, sir. It is." Her name was, of course, nothing of the sort, but that was what the document read.

"Of Quindacra."

She nodded vigorously. "Oh, yes, sir. From the city of—"

"This mark here," he interrupted, "says that when you entered our nation, you passed through Tohl Khosar."

"Um, yes? I mean, is that—?"

"Tohl Khosar," the soldier continued, somewhere between instruction and accusation, "stands near the Kirresci border."

The woman calling herself Tamirra quailed. (*Not too much,* she reminded herself.) "I... I... Of course, sir. If I'd come through Suunim, I'd have had to cross the Aerugos. And the idea of coming up river, through Lake Orist..." She shuddered, hoping it looked as dainty—as weak—as it felt.

*And you already know all that, you arrogant, sanctimonious cockerel. You just want to see Tamirra squirm.*

"Hm. I suppose." Again he studied the documents, which she knew damn well he'd already fully read. She listened to the various creaks and mutters of the long line winding behind her, as well as the sounds of the city ahead, and tried not to tap her foot.

*He can't possibly engage in this nonsense with every traveler, or even every foreigner, who comes through. I'd have been waiting a week!*

"And why have you come to Tohl Delian?"

*It's written right in front of you! Is it just my blinding golden luck that you picked* me *for this sideshow?*

"Oh, I'm looking for a new home, somewhere I can set up shop. I'm a potter. Big cities always need pottery, don't they? And it's *ever* so much safer here than in Quindacra!"

That much, at least, was plausible. For all the downsides of life under the military cabal, petty crime was less common than in most other nations, particularly one struggling like Quindacra.

Less common, but not remotely unheard of—a fact the woman was counting on to complete her assignment.

*Assuming this jackass ever lets me through the gods damned door!*

"I don't see a wagon of pottery," the guardsman challenged.

"Well," she said, smiling, all but batting her lashes, and squelching every urge she had to reach for his throat, "I'm going to send for my stock if I find a place. I'd hardly want to lug it all the way here before I know if I'm staying, would I?"

That, at last, seemed to satisfy him. He pawed through the contents of her satchel, but she knew he would find nothing of interest there: several changes of clothes, some hemming and sewing tools for repairing said clothes, some basic toiletries, a smattering of coins. A few more idle questions, then, a few more marks on her documents, a reminder that foreigners could find themselves in substantial hot water if they violated curfew, gathered in large groups, or entered restricted areas, and finally, *finally* he waved her through.

As she strode by, a quick sideways glance into the small gatehouse built beside the wall revealed another pair of soldiers. They sat at a circular table, throwing dice, which wasn't remotely abnormal; but as the results came up, she saw one of them raise a finger, counting off the people still waiting in line.

The hassle, the extra questioning, the irritation? Bored soldiers selecting random travelers to give a hard time. It really *had* been dumb luck they'd chosen her.

*Thank you so much, Donaris. I'll have to remember to leave some stale crust or a handful of bird droppings on the altar next time I come across one of your shrines.* Just one of the many, many reasons the Lady of Luck was not high on her list of most honored deities.

She was, at last, inside the walls of Tohl Delian.

The city was precisely what one might envision, based on its reputation and defenses. Squat buildings, mostly stone, stood at attention alongside broad avenues. The roofs were flat, providing countless archery platforms in case of invasion; the roads were wide, perfect for moving troops and engines, yet twisted and turned without apparent reason so anyone unfamiliar with the layout would swiftly become lost. Other than the wealthy, who bedecked themselves in deep reds and blues, the people dressed primarily in drab hues and furs, an effect that managed to be strangely formal and unremarkable both. Hair was either cut short or plaited; beards neatly trimmed. Even among the common folk, the fashion held an unmistakable martial edge.

Conversation, even laughter, was ever so slightly subdued as compared to most other populations Tamirra knew. Few in Ktho Delios desired to stand out from their neighbors.

The regular patrols of sentries sporting the black Deliant tabards, peace-keepers and law enforcers, were a constant reminder as to why. But then, it wasn't really the uniformed soldiers, the guards one could see coming, that frightened everyone.

Adopting a similar expression and posture, one that screamed "I'm minding my own business!" she made her way along the avenue. Nothing about her stood out here, which was just as she preferred; lots of the citizens around her bore hair as black as her own, and while she was paler than most—nearly enough to suggest pure-blood Elgarrad stock, if not for those inky locks—Ktho Delios was, like most modern nations, a mixture of ethnicities. She'd chosen a foreign cover identity because it came with fewer complications in terms of forging and records, not because she couldn't pass if required.

If everything went well, according to plan and schedule, it wouldn't be required.

*And when was the last time* that *happened?* she asked herself, then refused to offer herself the satisfaction of answering.

Finding the place she searched for wasn't difficult. The hostelers and innkeeps knew how confusing their city could be, and competed fiercely for spots near the main gates. It took only a few moments of wandering and backtracking, as well as asking directions from an only moderately suspicious and reticent couple, for her to find it.

"Tiarmov's Inn." *Creative* and *evocative, isn't it?*

She picked her way through the common room, a cavernous wood-beamed chamber where men and women conversed, grumbled, occasionally guffawed, and kept to their own small groups, huddled over clear spirits so potent they made Tamirra's eyes water from ten paces. Nobody stared at her, but she felt any number of sharp, sidelong glances, and returned them in kind.

*They wonder if I'm what I seem. I wonder how many of them are...*

It would be far too easy to succumb to paranoia, a way of life in Ktho Delios, where any stranger might be an eye—or dagger—of the Deliant. It shouldn't matter to her if any of them were; she had no intention of doing anything to draw their ire.

Not where they could see, at any rate.

Smiling, she approached the burly, bearded barkeep who may or may not have been the eponymous Tiarmov, and who showed little interest in returning her cheerful expression. He made a quick check of her papers, just enough to ensure he wasn't about to harbor an unlicensed outsider, after which she secured herself a room, a small cup of wine—she wasn't about to risk the spirits—and a bowl of some kind of mutton-and-tuber stew.

Then she planted herself at a small table, refused to allow her expression to reveal what she actually thought of each bite of food, and waited.

And waited.

After which, there was more waiting.

*Something's gone wrong.* Even inside her own head, she couldn't muster the slightest twinge of surprise. *Of course it has.*

The barkeep cleared his throat and thumped a meaty fist on the counter. "Sun's going down," he announced in a vaguely bored, put-upon tone. "Don't forget that foreigners can't be out on the streets after dark without special dispensation." Then, grunting, he turned his attention back to his cups.

Was he legally required, as a hosteler, to offer the reminder? Or was he just trying to save himself the inconvenience of a visit from the authorities, if they had to back-check one of his guests? Either way, Tamirra hadn't forgotten the curfew, but it chafed. If something was amiss with the plan, with her contact, she'd prefer to be about the business of learning what it was.

Best not court trouble, though. Not yet. Grumbling internally, she finished off the drink she'd long been nursing and made her way to her room.

———

The following day allowed her to acquire a better feel for the city's ins and outs—or those of the nearby neighborhoods, at any rate—but proved equally useless as the first when it came to advancing her mission.

After a breakfast of sausage and some sort of cheese dumpling, which she greatly preferred to the prior evening's supper, and a couple more hours of waiting, Tamirra had decided to explore her surroundings. The morning streets were full of pedestrians, going about this business or that, and for a short time she could easily have been in any city, with only the fashions and accents separating it from one in Kirresc, Quindacra, or the other southern nations. People nodded to acquaintances, stopped to chat with friends, haggled with vendors, complained about the weather. She even received helpful if not always cheerful pointers when she asked, as her cover required, where she might best buy or rent a small property and set up shop.

But the illusion never lasted, shattered again and again by the arrival of yet another patrol. Normally in small squads but occasionally full-fledged processions, the soldiers of Ktho Delios marched along the thoroughfares, making their presence known. Warriors and watchmen, peacekeepers and government enforcers, each appearance reminded her anew that this was a martial nation, intolerant and wary.

Those soldiers rarely had to do much beyond letting themselves be seen—for they were *also* a reminder, to visitors and citizens alike, that the Deliant had *many* eyes and ears, and most were not so readily spotted as these.

Trained to observe such distinctions, Tamirra noted that while most of the Deliant soldiers wore either leather laminar or chain hauberks beneath their tabards, a select few—high-ranking officers, she imagined—augmented their chain with breastplates and other reinforcement. Once she even spotted a knight, mounted atop a massive warhorse, clad in an entire suit of overlapping steel plates—a recent invention by Ktho Delian armorers of which she'd heard but never before seen. It had to be hideously expensive to craft, thank the gods. She shuddered at the thought of the Deliant fielding any great number of soldiers so armored. It was hard enough to keep the damned nation contained within its borders already…

So she watched, and wandered; studied storefronts as though genuinely hoping to acquire one, and spoke to any number of citizens, most of whom were probably no more or less than they appeared. All the while she worked at memorizing twists, turns, and street names. Always she kept within a few blocks of the inn, checking back often, but nobody ever approached her, nor did she ever find any potential contact awaiting her return.

As the sun lowered and the temperature fell, she chose to risk a little bit more. Still in the guise of the hopeful shopkeeper, she asked helpful passersby or vendors about local crime. She hoped to unearth some idea of where she might go searching for her ostensible allies, assuming they didn't surprise her by finally showing up, though of course she couched her questions in general terms, inquiring as to which areas were safest, what sort of hassles a local merchant might expect, and so forth.

What she learned was that the openness and helpfulness of the Ktho Delians had sharply delineated boundaries, and she had just stepped over them. Smiles turned to frowns or suspicious glares. Men and women who'd been happy to chat only seconds earlier suddenly had business elsewhere, or had to see to other customers. A few actually tried to claim, in unconvincing mutters, that Tohl Delian *had* no crime to speak of.

It took until after the third such incident for Tamirra to understand. These people weren't afraid of the criminals, and they *certainly* weren't overly concerned what a foreign visitor thought of their city. No, it was that they couldn't be certain who she really was, or who else in the nearby throng might be listening. Doubtless the Deliant had strict laws regarding what sort of impression the people were *allowed* to give outsiders, what information they were and weren't permitted to offer. Just the sort of thing on which the nation's secret police might occasionally test its citizens.

If she was going to locate Tohl Delian's criminal underworld, she would have to go about it much more directly.

*If I didn't already despise this country,* she grumbled internally, *it would be remarkably easy to learn to despise this country.*

———

Now clad in a navy blouse and what appeared to be a black skirt, but was rather a pair of baggy trousers cut to *resemble* a skirt, the woman calling herself Tamirra prepared to face the many dangers of the Ktho Delian night.

Assuming she could even make her way out of the damn hostel!

Hours after sunset, the common room of Tiarmov's remained half full. Between residents who weren't permitted on the streets at night, and late-shift workers (with proper documentation, of course) who had come to drink, the place housed far too many observers for her to simply stroll out the door without attracting attention.

Out the window? Her room was on the second story, an easy enough descent, but also uncomfortably near the main avenue. The chances of being spotted climbing or jumping down, before she had the opportunity to vanish into the shadowed depths of the side street, were unacceptably high.

*Well, who says the window I use need be mine?* It might make getting back in a tad problematic, but she'd pay that toll when she came to it. After two nights, she couldn't afford to sit around waiting any longer.

She made her way down the hall, soft boots tapping almost silently against the uncarpeted floor, until she'd reached the far end. Slowing her pace only marginally, she listened as best she could at each door she passed. Conversation here; snoring there. And then, so far as she could determine, nothing.

Which could mean an empty room, either because it was unlet or because its occupant currently inhabited the common area downstairs. Or it could simply mean a quiet sleeper, or someone reading or meditating or any other inaudible pastime.

Her expertise lay in areas other than burglary, but Tamirra wasn't unfamiliar with the use of a lockpick. Straightening a pair of copper lengths that she'd worn as part of a larger bracelet, she reached down and began fiddling with the latch.

She had a bare instant to wonder if she'd caused that loud *click* or not when the door swung open and she found herself facing an older, doughy faced fellow. He froze in the midst of a yawn, his whole face widening in shock.

Tamirra looked up at him, gasped, and giggled. "This isn't my room!" Tightening her stomach, she forced a loud belch as punctuation, giggled again, and staggered down the hallway, listing like a sinking galleon.

The old merchant—not that she had the slightest evidence he was any such thing, he just looked to her like a merchant—grumbled something about drunkards, then slammed and audibly relocked his door.

*Shall I count the ways in which that might have gone better?*

She had to keep trying, unless some other plan came to mind, but the tipsy imbecile ploy would only work so many times. If she was caught a second time, she might wind up having to hurt someone—not an idea that bothered her to excess, but she'd prefer it be somebody who deserved it.

Fortune finally turned in her favor. The next silent room she tried was indeed unoccupied. After longer fumbling at the latch than she would have liked, she slipped inside, locking the door again behind her. Then she was across the room, kneeling on the bed and peering out between closed but ill-fitting shutters.

Here, back away from the larger byway, the street was poorly lit and currently unoccupied. Perfect.

Tamirra pulled open the window and shutters, slid out until she was seated on the sill with legs dangling, and carefully felt for footholds in the brickwork. The wall was smoother than optimal, but she was able to hang on well enough to pull the shutters to—only careful study should reveal that they weren't latched—and then she half slid, half dropped to the roadway.

Now she just had to wander around and get herself found by the right sort of people, while avoiding being found by the wrong sort. Should she happen to be spotted and stopped by a patrol, she could *probably* play the drunk and stupid foreigner, and get off with a night in gaol and a fine—or perhaps just an expensive bribe—but she had no guarantee. If the wrong officer decided she was a threat, or simply took a dislike to her, she wouldn't be the first person to disappear into the secret dungeons of the Deliant for the most minor of infractions.

Fighting the instinct to hide, struggling hard to adopt a posture that said "I have every right to be out and about at this hour," she made her way into the Tohl Delian night.

It was a balancing act, the lot of it. Avoid the main avenues, where the odds favored bumping into official patrols and were stacked against encountering the people she sought; but avoid, too, back streets so small or out of the way that her mere presence would raise suspicions. Other nighttime pedestrians either ignored her completely or watched her in sidelong suspicion until they had passed. None made any move to attract her attention.

She wondered, idly, how many of them were out and about legally, and how many were as anxious as she to avoid official notice.

More than once she heard the jingle of mail, carried on the chill breeze. Then she ducked into back alleys or the shadows around drab stone corners, hunched in the darkness until the Deliant soldiers were long past.

The blocks of squarish buildings, like rows of dull and graying teeth, looked very much the same wherever she went, and her unfamiliarity with Tohl Delian slowed her terribly, so that what should have taken only an hour or two dragged on. It was well after midnight when she finally found herself in what, to judge by the disrepair of the homes and the rougher cut to the garb of passersby, was one of the city's poorer districts.

Here, the night streets were dim indeed. Few streetlights shone, for many had been scavenged of their feeble reservoirs of oil. Above, the autumn overcast hung thick and ponderous; of the four moons, only Kalitarra and Perradan shone at all, and neither was at full. Still, she'd been wandering long enough, and the shift had been sufficiently gradual, for her vision to adjust.

Tamirra allowed her shoulders to slump, her stride to take on a nervous hitch, and continued on her way, choosing streets and turns largely at random.

For another hour or more she walked, offering herself as bait, with no results. The people, fewer in number now, ignored or feared her as they had before. Again she nearly bumped into a Deliant patrol, and again she hid herself rather than risk being stopped.

*Clearly the scum here are as paranoid as everyone else.*

She decided to sweeten the lure. She approached other pedestrians, now, rather than ignoring them, asking for help in a quavering, tear-laced voice. She was lost. She couldn't find her way back to her hostel, near the main gate. Oh, wouldn't someone take pity and help her? She avoided anything resembling a Ktho Delian accent, just to drive home her status as poor, helpless stranger.

Most recoiled, hurrying their steps, wanting nothing to do with her. A few mumbled half-hearted encouragement and vague directions while pointing back down this street or that.

Until, *finally*, she turned down a small alleyway and found herself confronted by a trio of rough, unshaven men.

"Couldn't help but overhear," one of them told her with a chuckle. "We can help you out, flower. But it'll cost."

"Oh!" She put a hand to her lips. "I… I don't carry much coin, but I'd be happy to pay what I can if you'd—"

They were moving closer, now, gathering around. Two had produced daggers—poorly maintained, she noted with professional disdain—and the third a club that had probably once been the haft of a larger of weapon. Not the most impressive of arsenals, but in a city where citizens weren't permitted to go about openly armed, they were intimidating enough. Or would have been under normal circumstances.

With a normal victim.

Their breath, as they surrounded her, was a miasma of garlic and spirits so cheap and so strong they might knock the lice off a man's head. It was enough to persuade her not to waste any more time here than she had to.

In half a heartbeat, she had a small dirk—sewing scissors, designed to be separated and reconnected to form a single blade—out of her belt and deep in the flesh between thigh and pelvis on the nearest thug.

She pivoted on one foot as he collapsed, screaming. Her open hand whipped out to snag the end of the second man's cudgel a split second before her heel connected hard with his sternum. He flew back, breath whooshing from his lungs, to slam against the nearby wall, leaving his weapon behind in her grasp.

The last of the trio reacted more swiftly than Tammria had anticipated, actually impressing her. He thrust with his dagger, fast and professional, as she came out of her spin. She twisted, sliding her foot back behind her, so the blow slid past. He stabbed out again. This time she parried with the edge of her empty hand, smacking into his wrist and knocking his blade out of line.

It left him open, and that was all she required. The club landed, hard—a swing, a thrust, another swing. His upper left arm, a rib, his right leg all cracked; probably bruised, possibly fractured. He gawped, gone pale to the lips, and a final rap to the head put him down.

Tucking the club under one arm, Tamirra knelt to retrieve his fallen dagger. A few steps and she crouched again, this time beside the man she'd stabbed. With a cold, merciless yank, she retrieved her own dirk—and promptly replaced it in the wound with the blade she'd just picked up. A final yelp and the robber passed out.

Her remaining assailant had only just regained his breath and hauled himself up against the wall. He tried to glare defiantly as she approached, but she could have bathed in the waves of fear spilling from him and they both knew it.

"Koldan Ovrach," she said, all doubt and helplessness gone from her tone. "And don't insult me by pretending you don't know who he is."

"What…" He cleared his throat, tried again without the shaking. "What about him?"

"Take me to him."

"What makes you think I know where he is?" he asked, sullen.

"Self-preservation."

"Huh?"

"You're only useful to me because I need to find him. And you want to live. Since living means taking me to him, you know where he is. It's a biological imperative."

After more quantities of sweat that were quite impressive given the weather, he swallowed once and nodded. "Follow me."

"You're a credit to your bloodline." Then, just as he took his first step, "If you're carrying a blade or any other weapon, hand it over. And trust me, if you make me search you, I *will* find anything you've got hidden, and make you very uncomfortable and bloody in the process."

He gave her a petulant glare—and a dagger.

"*Now* I'll follow you."

The route they took was not unlike that she'd used to get here, consisting of back roads and walkways, distant from the flow of nighttime traffic but not so obscure as to be innately worthy of suspicion. The man clearly knew not only where he was going, but all the tricks for arriving there unmolested. Not once did Tamirra so much as hear the distant jingle of mail or the drumming of marching boots.

She knew the brigand gave serious consideration to running. She'd have expected it even if it hadn't been obvious in the set of his shoulders, the stiffness in his steps.

"Third knot," she told him. Then, before he'd even completed the *wh* in *What?* she sent the dagger she'd taken from him winging hard down the block. It sank with a *thud* into the trunk of a small evergreen, quivering dead-center of a protruding knot.

The third up from the bottom, in fact.

"What was *that* about?" he demanded in a hoarse whisper. "Are you *trying* to bring a patrol down on us?!" She refused to answer until their course took them past the tree, whereupon she yanked the blade free with a cringe-worthy squeak of steel on wood.

"The small of a running man's back is a moving target," she mused as though the thought had only just occurred, "which makes it a harder shot. On the other hand, assuming a quick reaction time, it's also a *closer* target. Those probably cancel each other out, wouldn't you guess?"

He didn't actually *say* he got the point, but he never did try to run.

Their winding trek finally ended at a large carpenter's workshop, very near the city's south wall. She recognized its purpose by the larger equipment—pedal-driven lathes and saws, for instance—as well as the stacks of lumber, all of which were stored under an overhang outside. It was, Tamirra had to admit, a clever headquarters for a gang of thieves and smugglers. Nobody would question large deliveries moving in and out, smaller goods could be hidden amidst the lumber and furniture, and any late night activity could be explained away as craftsmen and—women catching up on their commissions.

The sight of their destination added a tiny bit of steel to her guide's spine. "Koldan… He, um, he's not fond of unexpected visitors, you understand?"

"Unless Koldan is even more of an idiot than I take him for, I'm not unexpected. Now go get us inside."

With a resigned sigh, he marched ahead and pounded a fist on the workshop door.

Nothing. He knocked again. And again.

Finally an irritated voice called out from within. "It's the middle of the damned night! Come back in the morning!"

As low as he could while still be heard, the thug hissed back, "I need to see Koldan!"

A narrow panel, hidden not in the door but among the bricks beside it, slid open. Tamirra couldn't see through it from her angle, but she figured about an equal chance of either a face or a crossbow lurking behind it.

"I remember seeing you around," the voice behind the wall said, "which is the only reason you're still breathing at all. But I don't think you've got any business with Koldan."

*That'll do.*

The brigand yelped as he was shoved roughly aside. "My name," she told the startled sentry, shedding the identity of Tamirra entirely, "is Silbeth Rasik. And perhaps you can ask Koldan why he appears to be neglecting *his* business with *me*."

# CHAPTER SIX

At some point in Tohl Delian's history, this spot had housed a public bath, or perhaps a steamroom, dug deep into the insulating earth. When it had closed, for whatever reasons and whims of business steered the course of such facilities, it had been locked away and largely forgotten, with the woodworking shop eventually constructed above.

Today, hidden behind a concealed entrance, it functioned as the heart and brain of Koldan Ovrach's criminal empire-in-miniature.

Silbeth leaned one hip against a support column and idly glanced over the balcony at the floor, and the sloping, tile-lined pits that were the former baths. Within one of those hollows, a cluster of men and women gathered around a table containing stacks of coins. Each disk of copper, brass, or silver—or, far more rarely, gold—passed from hand to hand. The first scraped a fine blade along the edge, stripping just a flake or two of valuable metal from the currency without any obvious alteration, slowly gathering those leavings into piles large enough to be melted down for actual use. The second and subsequent sets of hands counted and organized the coins by type, recording the totals in worn and ragged ledgers. In a second pit, older and more seasoned criminals debated the value of stolen goods, while the smugglers gathered in a third traced out Deliant patrol routes on rough maps and argued over how best to sneak shipments past the walls.

Or at least, she *thought* that was what they argued over. She couldn't be certain, in part because they kept their voices low even in the heat of their disagreement—as though afraid, even here, that the wrong ears might be listening—and in part because their boss was currently shouting loudly enough for all of them.

Koldan himself reminded Silbeth of nothing so much as a bear just emerged from hibernation—and not only because he smelled, to her mind, more animal than man. He was shaggy, his russet hair and beard longer and fuller than current Ktho Delian fashion, and his shoulders broad, but his features beneath that beard were surprisingly harsh, and his skin hung loose as though he'd but recently shed a great deal of weight.

If he had, however, it had resulted in no obvious weakness, either to his movements or his voice. Currently he bellowed at a gathering of his enforcers, demanding to know how an outsider such as she had even found his headquarters, to learn the name of the "traitor" who had led her here. (Her guide had, wisely, disappeared the moment the door guard had gone to deliver her name to Koldan, and she'd decided to let him go.)

Several other fierce-looking thugs watched over her, ensuring she did nothing and went nowhere without their leader's permission. She, however, after a few more moments of idle musing, decided she'd had enough with waiting.

"Perhaps," she suggested loudly, "you could leave off your tantrum until after we've concluded our business? I'm sure you'll have plenty of time to eat your subordinates after I'm gone."

Koldan went dead silent in mid-word, turning to stare with a twisted expression somewhere between fearsome and sickly. Then, growling, "You ought to learn yourself some patience, woman."

"I think I've shown quite an excess of patience, seeing as how you were supposed to contact me two days ago."

Again he growled, waving an arm at the people around him. The sound contained no actual words that Silbeth could make out, but clearly the others took some meaning from it. In a matter of moments they'd produced a pair of chairs—horribly mismatched but looking quite comfortable—and a small table to go along with them. The furniture laid out, the smuggler settled in one seat, gesturing for Silbeth to take the other.

By the time she sat, a pair of mugs had also appeared, seemingly out of nowhere. She took a polite gulp of the harsh spirits, managing neither to choke nor allow her eyes to water until they bobbed like tiny rafts, but otherwise ignored the drink.

"We had no way of knowing exactly when you were coming," Koldan said then, his tone flat. He was informing her of a fact, not making any sort of apology. "It was eating into my other operations, having to send someone across town to check Tiarmov's every day. If you'd waited, one of my guys would have found you there in a few more days. A week, at most."

"Absolutely not acceptable. This isn't a sightseeing sojourn I'm on. You were to make contact the day I arrived!"

"Tough. You're not my only project, Rasik, and I'll run my business as I see fit. Besides, it's done and you're here. Get past it."

Inwardly she seethed, and she hated to back down, to begin their dealings with even the slightest show of weakness, but he was correct at least in this: It was done. Nothing could be gained by pressing the issue.

"Fine. I'm past it. Let's talk specifics."

"I'm all ears." He smiled, almost a leer. She restrained herself from punching him until teeth were a distant memory.

"You should already have been informed that we're hiring you for your smuggling network, yes?"

The starving bear nodded. "You won't find better."

*Not for what we could afford to pay, anyway.* "You understand that this isn't just a matter of misdirecting a few gate guards? While I hope otherwise, it's entirely possible that the military proper or the Ninth Citadel will be hunting us."

Several of Koldan's people blanched. Even here, secure in their headquarters, overt mention of the Citadel, the Deliant secret police, was enough to trigger their paranoia.

Koldan himself, however, merely nodded a second time. "So I've been told. And am charging accordingly."

*I'll bet.* Silbeth gave a silent prayer of thanks that arranging that payment wasn't part of her own assignment. She could never have secreted that sort of coin into the city on her own.

"All you've got to do," he continued, "is tell me where, when, and what."

"Where is easy. If things go well, we'll just meet at Tiarmov's. If not, then here."

The tic in his jaw suggested he was less than thrilled with that latter option, but for the moment, he made no argument.

"When is trickier. Sometime in the next few days, but exactly when depends on how the rest of my efforts go. You may have to be patient and ready to go on a moment's notice." She sneered lightly. "More so than you were when it came to meeting up with me.

"As to what…" *If this lummox is going to cause me any problems, it's going to be now.* "It's not a 'what' at all. It's a 'who.'"

The surge of greed practically set the skin of his face to rippling. "Well, now, that complicates matters. It's a lot harder to smuggle out a person. Can't just stuff them in the nooks and crannies of a crate or what have you. We're going to have to renegotiate my fee just a—"

*How utterly predictable.* "We'll do nothing of the kind. I know what sorts of missives my employers exchanged with you when they hired you for this, Koldan. You knew this was a possibility when you agreed to their offer."

"A possibility. Not a certainty. Things change."

"Not *this* thing."

The gang lord made no overt move, but Silbeth would have to be blind not to notice the half dozen brigands closing from all directions on her side of the table. "I wouldn't think," her host taunted from behind his beard, "that it's in your best interests to be a stickler about this, Rasik."

Her reply was calm, soft, and utterly without fear. "And *I* wouldn't think that this is the sort of approach you want to take, or the impression you want to make, with the Priory of Steel."

The thieves and smugglers moving in behind her suddenly seemed deeply invested in their impersonations of statues and snowmen. Koldan scoffed, but it sounded forced. "You? Priory of Steel?"

Silbeth said nothing.

"Anyone could claim to be a member of the Priory!" he protested.

"Anyone could," she agreed.

"So I'm, what, supposed to believe that you are, just because you say so?"

Her answering smile was friendly, not remotely threatening, though she tensed beneath the table, ready to jump at anyone's and everyone's next move. "Yes."

A strained silence, as the smuggler pondered his options. Then he dismissed the others with a wave and leaned back in his chair.

"Fine. If I'd known whatever was going on was so important to somebody that they'd hire the Priory of Steel to carry it out, I'd have charged more from the start. But I won't renege on a deal that involves you people. I'd rather be your friend."

*Hardly likely. But be glad you haven't just made yourself our enemy.* "As would I," she lied blandly.

"This guy you're smuggling out of here," he said—in part, she was sure, to avoid letting her have the last word on the subject, though he did sound genuinely concerned—"he's not a witch or a conjurer of any kind, is he? Because dealing with state security or even the Ninth Citadel is one thing, but Priory of Steel or no, I am *not* putting myself in a position to pull the Inquisition down on my head. *Sure* as hell not for anything near to what your employer's paying me."

Silbeth felt certain that the reputation of the infamous Ktho Delian witch-hunting—and witch-*employing*—Inquisition was exaggerated, as much propaganda as reality. Still, she couldn't blame the man. "If he is," she said, choosing at this juncture not to correct Koldan's flawed assumption that the "package" was male, "it would be as much news to me as to you."

That, for the moment, seemed to satisfy him. "All right. Let's get down to details, then."

*And it's about gods damned time!* But at least she needn't worry about sneaking back into her room; at this rate, it would be *well* after dawn before she was back out on the street.

Scooting her chair closer, she began to lay out what she expected to need.

———

The housekeeper was a slight, blonde woman nearly as pale as Silbeth herself, clad in a woolen gray dress that buttoned all the way up to her chin. "I'm terribly sorry," she said, though her tone suggested she was anything but. "The Lady Povyar isn't available at this time. Perhaps you'd be so good as to try back another day."

Silbeth found herself reduced, if only briefly, to standing in the doorway and blinking. "I'm… Perhaps you misunderstood," she said finally, swallowing hard to melt the ice forming in the back of her throat. "My message is of the utmost importance, and Lady Povyar is *expecting* me."

"I'm sure it is. Nevertheless, my mistress is unavailable."

"I see." *Gods, what* else *has gone wrong?* "Have you any idea of when she might be able to see me?"

"I'm afraid not."

"Well, might I come in and wait?"

"I expect it could be some days. You'll just have to come back. Now," the servant concluded, "if that's all…?" Her tone, her posture, everything about her made it absolutely clear that the only acceptable answer was *yes*.

Yet... Worry, too, swirled within her. She did an excellent job of hiding it, burying it beneath the superior impatience that only the best and highest ranking of servants mastered, but it was present all the same.

Silbeth glanced swiftly around her. Located near the center of Tohl Delian, where many of the wealthy and aristocratic dwelled, the Povyar manor was nearly as large as Tiarmov's inn. A sizable lawn spread out before it, and the roofs of its several floors were tiered like a squashed wedding cake, but the home itself was made up primarily of the same drab stone as the city's other structures. A faint gilded trim around the windows and doorways were its only concession to aesthetic luxury—a trait shared, Silbeth had noted on her walk here, by most of the other larger houses and estates. It was as if people feared that the colors and decorations of affluence, but not the size of the homes, their property, or their staff, might draw the suspicions of the military authorities.

Fortunately for the current visitor, the Povyar staff was smaller than many—understandable, given Ulia Povyar's surreptitious activities—while the lawn, though not *huge*, was broad enough that none of the passersby on the street should immediately notice anything amiss in the doorway.

Silbeth began to turn away, then spun back toward the housekeeper before the shorter woman could shut the door. She closed the distance between them in a single pace, wrapping her left hand around the back of the servant's neck. The dagger, clutched in her other fist, pressed tight to the woman's wool-clad breast.

"Step back inside. I don't take you for an idiot, so I assume I need not spell out what happens if you scream?"

Eyes wide and glistening with sudden unshed tears, the housekeeper nodded and retreated. Silbeth followed, kicking the door shut with one heel. She caught a glimpse of lush carpet, hanging chandeliers, a broad sweeping staircase in a large room at the end of the hall to her left, but kept focused on the woman before her.

"You may not believe this," Silbeth continued, "and I've neither the time nor any particular interest in convincing you, but I'm on your mistress's side. I'm here to help her. The problem is, I don't know that *you're* on her side. She should be here. She should have known someone was coming. Something's very wrong, and you're standing in the way of my finding out what."

The dagger twitched by way of emphasis. The housekeeper sobbed once, and Silbeth couldn't help but sigh.

"Look, I don't want to hurt you, all right? Just tell me where Povyar is. For *her* sake."

"I *can't*!" If it had been any louder, it would have been a wail; as it was, it came out more as a whine.

Again the dagger twitched. "I said I don't *want* to hurt you. I didn't say I *won't*."

"She's been arrested," the housekeeper whispered, slumping. "Oh, *please* don't tell anybody! If this got out to Lady Povyar's circles, she'd be ruined! Please…"

The frost that had been clinging to the back of Silbeth's throat spread instantly through her veins, wrapping itself about her heart. *Arrested?* Gods, had all this been for nothing? Was she too late?

She left the housekeeper in the coat closet, bound with her own sleeves. The other servants would find her soon enough, but a few minutes was all she'd need to be long gone, on the off chance the woman actually chose to summon the authorities.

Maybe slightly more than a few minutes. She was dazed when she reached the street, her feet turning to carry her back toward the inn of their own accord, her mind racing and yet slipping, sliding, falling over itself on that inner layer of ice.

Leaving aside the political repercussions if and when the Deliant learned the full extent of Povyar's espionage, Silbeth's own mission was almost certainly a failure. So far as she was aware, nobody had ever broken out of—or into—a Ktho Delian military prison. Even assuming it could be done at all, it would require a massive team of experts, the best of the best, and months of preparation. There was absolutely nothing she could do on her own, no way she could—

"Good afternoon, m'lady. Lovely afternoon for a stroll, isn't it? Get the blood pumping, ward off the chill?"

Silbeth halted and turned, pasting "Tamirra" back over her features. "Why, yes. Yes, it is."

The pair behind her were a veritable portrait of the perfect Ktho Delian couple. He was clad in shades of gray and whites, formal without ostentation, his hair and beard neatly trimmed. Her dress was a bit more colorful, accented in crimson and gold, her own hair wound in ornate braids. She wore a cloak against the autumn breeze, while he sported a long overcoat, a relatively new product of Ktho Delian fashion.

Both of which, Silbeth observed, were more than capable of hiding an array of blades or other weapons that ordinary citizens of Ktho Delios wouldn't be permitted to carry. But then, she'd known from the instant they spoke to her that, appearances notwithstanding, this couple was by no means ordinary.

*They must have had the Povyar household under surveillance. And I missed it. I have seashells and grape seeds in my damn skull.*

The pair said nothing, just continued to smile. "Is... Is there something I can do for you?" she inquired with deliberate unease.

"Documents, please," the woman said.

"Oh! Oh, um, of course, just..." She fumbled at her satchel, eventually producing Tamirra's paperwork. "I think you'll find, that is, I'm sure it's all in order."

They barely glanced at the forms before the woman passed them on to the man, who stuck them in a coat pocket rather than returning them. *Well,* that's *not a good sign.*

"Is there a problem?" she squeaked. Internally, she was counting paces, first to that corner there, then past that second house down *there…*

"What is your business with Ulia Povyar?"

"I… I'm sorry, who are you, exactly? Why is my business *your* business?"

The couple offered her perfectly matching sinister smiles as they produced a pair of icons: tiny towers, smelted of copper.

*Ninth Citadel.* Not a surprise—she'd already figured as much—but still disturbing.

"Oh," she whispered.

"Povyar," the man prompted.

"I'm… looking for clients, for my pottery. I've heard Lady Povyar is kind and generous, someone it would be good to work for if—"

The woman scoffed. Her partner just shook his head, scowling.

"My dear," he said, "we're being as friendly about this as we can, but if you're going to lie to us, we'd be happy to take you somewhere we can have a more… private conversation."

"Oh, no. Oh, please don't do that!"

"The truth, then, and all of it. Your business with Lady Povyar. What you know about her. What she's involved in. Where we can find her. Everything!"

*Find her?* Silbeth's entire view shifted so sharply she almost stumbled. Why would they have to…?

*Of course!* Had the Deliant learned the woman was a spy, she'd have been tossed immediately in the deepest, blackest, dungeon they had, subject to all manner of dreadful interrogations. From the word "arrest," Silbeth had just assumed… But what if that wasn't what had happened at all? The Ktho Delian military might serve to enforce all the nation's laws, great and small, but they would not—could not—punish tiny infractions the same as major crimes. Local watchmen tossed petty troublemakers in local gaols, simple cells as different from Deliant prisons as a child's sling from a wall-shattering trebuchet. And in a bureaucracy as massive as this one, it was entirely possible, even probable, that the records of such minor violations—and their perpetrators—took ages to reach the higher authorities, if they ever did.

And that changed everything.

Silbeth ran.

They pursued, as she'd known they would. Their shouted commands to halt were almost perfunctory, though growing every angrier with each pounding step. She was a foolish, panicked foreigner in their minds, this chase an irritation. She was making their day more annoying, but hardly any more difficult, let alone dangerous.

Just what she needed them to think.

Pedestrians stared as she passed, their attention drawn either by her mad dash or by the shouts of her pursuers, though none moved to interfere. Nobody wanted anything to do with a stranger's troubles, particularly where the Citadel was concerned. Had she any choice in the matter, Silbeth would have happily skipped it, too.

Still she ran, her breath steady and even, searching, praying for a spot clear of those damned onlookers, just the briefest veil of privacy...

There! The manor at the end of the block boasted a fenced-in stretch of yard, probably a garden. That surrounding fence wasn't especially tall, more decorative than functional—unless meant to keep out stray animals—but it would hide what had to happen from public view.

Silbeth hit shoulder first rather than pausing to work the latch. Wood split and the gate flew open before her, rebounding hard and making the entire length of fencing shudder. She ducked to one side rather than continuing on as any truly panicked fugitive would have done, hands raised and ready...

Perhaps, under other circumstances, these agents of the secret police would have been more cautious, would have paused to clear the entryway before charging through it. She had their blood up, though, and their thoughts fixated on the notion of a terrified but harmless stranger who'd simply gotten into something over her head.

By the time either could have realized there was no sign of their fleeing target ahead of them, their steps had already carried them through the gate, and past the mercenary lurking in ambush.

Silbeth grabbed the nearest handhold, the hem of the woman's cloak, and yanked. The Ninth Citadel agent crashed to the soil with a gurgling gasp, landing hard on her back. Silbeth stomped down and felt something give. She wasn't certain what and didn't have time to look, for the woman's partner had already spun to face the surprise attack, whipping a wicked single-edged blade—built like a knife but the length of a short sword—from beneath his coat.

Just as swiftly she produced her own weapon, but the tiny dagger felt awfully lacking in comparison. Retreating a step, she took an extra second to unfasten her own thin cloak and set it slowly spinning in her left fist.

They circled, watching one another, late-season tubers crunching beneath their boots along the garden's edge. He stepped in, lunged in a quick feint, retreated. Testing, she knew, trying to determine how badly they'd underestimated the threat she posed—as well, perhaps, as buying time for his partner to recover.

Drawing this whole mess out, precisely what Silbeth couldn't permit.

She flipped the dagger around her thumb so she held it by the blade, cocked her hand back to her shoulder, and flicked the end of her cloak at her opponent's face even as she made to throw.

It was a desperate move, a foolish one, to release her only weapon against an armed foe. All he had to do was flinch aside or parry and she would be that much more at his mercy. The hem of the cloak blinded and bewildered him for only a split second, but not nearly enough to keep him from stepping from the dagger's path.

Except it had also hidden from him the fact that she'd *never released the blade.* The throw was another feint; she had, instead, reversed her grip once more, stepping in as he dodged a missile that had never flown.

Closing with one long pace, she smacked the dagger hard against the man's heavier blade, the speed and surprise of the strike more than sufficient to knock the sword, and the arm holding it, out of line. Another vicious slash, another quick step, and she was past him, leaving him to fall to his knees, blade tumbling to the earth as he clutched at his newly opened throat.

The woman staggered back to her feet, an impressive effort given how her right arm hung limp from an obviously broken and malformed collarbone. Despite her pallor and harsh panting, she'd reached back with her left hand to draw her own short sword, and glared at Silbeth with murderous fury.

Silbeth threw her dagger—actually letting fly this time— straight at that dangling right arm.

The operative twisted aside, barely avoiding the weapon, hissing with a new flare of pain, and that was more than enough time for Silbeth to scoop up the dying man's fallen blade. Now armed with a weapon capable of matching her opponent's, she advanced.

The Ninth Citadel trained their people well, but Silbeth was Priory of Steel. The contest would have been uneven even if the woman had been at her best. Injured and in hideous pain as she was, it ended in seconds.

It took Silbeth only a moment to scavenge the bodies, availing herself of a belt and sheath in which to carry her newly acquired short sword. She retrieved her dagger, and took both copper badges. She lifted the identification papers that went with them, though—as she didn't resemble either of the agents overmuch—they'd be useless if anyone of authority demanded to see them. She also reclaimed her own documents, of course.

After a moment's thought she took all other coin, jewelry or other valuables on them, in the hopes—slim as they were—that this might appear a robbery rather than a targeted assault. Finally, she stripped the man of his coat and slung it over her shoulders to hide the sword; it was a bit large for her, but not awkwardly so, and unlike the woman's cloak, dark enough to hide the stain of blood.

Another few moments, and she'd dragged both bodies behind a small shed that, she assumed, held the gardener's tools. It wasn't much of a hiding place, and she couldn't begin to conceal the upturned dirt and trampled vegetables, but if the owner didn't happen to examine the garden in any detail, it might buy her an extra few hours—maybe even a day or two, if Donaris truly smiled at her.

*Right, because she's been* so *generous this far*, Silbeth grumbled internally.

Well, whatever time she had was what she had. She crept through the garden gate and marched grimly down the avenue, praying she could locate Ulia Povyar before someone else unearthed her own crime and this entire gods-damned city went straight to hell.

# CHAPTER SEVEN

It proved a simple matter for Silbeth to learn where the local gaol could be found, and how to get there. The badge of the Ninth Citadel, and an imperious attitude to match, inspired a repulsive eagerness in anyone and everyone to cooperate. In her years with the Priory of Steel, never had she seen a more odious amalgamation of fawning, fearfulness, and barely concealed loathing.

She'd known the gaol itself wouldn't be much to look at, that it was little more than a holding cell for petty criminals the system could scarcely bother with, and a duty station for the sorts of soldiers assigned to watch over said petty criminals. Still she could only stare at it for a time, struggling to convince herself she'd come to the right place.

Proper Deliant installations, prisons included, were fortresses, towers and keeps and deep dungeons hunkered behind defensive ramparts. This? This was a brick of a building at an intersection amidst a number of warehouses and workshops, differentiated from its neighbors only by the bars on its windows and the tabard-clad soldiers at its doors.

Even if Silbeth could pull this off, she had no guarantee that Ulia Povyar was actually here. This was only one of a half dozen similar facilities across the city. It was, however, the nearest to the Povyar estate, and thus the best place to begin.

She steeled herself, forced her mind to stop counting the many disastrous ways the next few moments could go wrong, and stalked across the road.

One of the bored door sentries moved to bar her path. "Your business here?" he all but yawned at her.

Silbeth turned her best glower on him, an expression hammered into her through endless drills and practice bouts by the weaponmaster-monks of the Priory. Only then, when her sneer alone had brought him up short and snagged his full attention, did she present the copper icon.

"Your commanding officer," she snapped. "Now!"

He saluted and darted into the building. After a quick check to make sure the other sentries had all seen her badge and were properly cowed, she followed.

Passing through squared and narrow halls of stone, letting other soldiers—and sometimes their prisoners—step aside for her and her guide, Silbeth kept the mask of arrogance plastered to her face. She wanted no one to suspect just how nervous she truly was. The guards at the door were one thing, soldiers of low promise assigned an unimportant post. Could she assume the same of the man or woman in charge? Might someone demand identification beyond the badge, documentation that would instantly give her deception away?

And where did the Ninth Citadel stand in relation to officers of rank? That the common folk and the average soldier acknowledged her authority was no guarantee she had any genuine weight to throw around in this sort of place. What if—?

The broad-shouldered, slightly portly old officer—definitely not one of the Deliant's finest—rose from behind her desk as Silbeth and her guide burst into the office. Rather than waiting for an introduction, the fake agent again produced the icon of the Ninth Citadel, and while the commandant's nod of acknowledgement was composed enough, Silbeth missed neither the initial widening nor the subsequent tensing around the woman's eyes.

Still, best to test her authority rather than assume. "You," Silbeth said to the man who'd led her here. "Leave."

He glanced at his commandant, true, but obeyed without waiting for her to confirm the order. Although a brief frown indicated her displeasure, the officer made no objection to Silbeth barking orders.

*Excellent.*

"Welcome," the officer began. "Is there something I can—?"

"Ledger."

"I'm sorry, what?"

Silbeth exhaled the most irritated, and irritating, sigh she could manage. "Your ledger. You *do* actually record the names of the people you lock up here?"

"Of course! It's standard procedure to—"

"Then figure out your procedure for handing me the damn ledger!"

Biting back a snarl, the other woman rang a small bell and yelled at the first functionary to respond. A few more moments of fuming and glaring later, a young soldier delivered to them a heavy leatherbound tome.

Silbeth opened up and began flipping to the last several days'-worth of entries. The pages smelled of cheap ink and oily fingers.

"If you could tell me what it is you're looking for—" the officer tried again.

"Quiet."

The woman's teeth snapped shut sounding like the clash of a headsman's axe.

*There!* It was right there. She was here! *Thank the gods for that much, at least.*

"All right." Silbeth finally looked up. "I need every prisoner recorded on the lower half of this page..." She stabbed the paper with one gloved finger. "...to be released."

"What?! Are you insane? I can't just—"

"Immediately, Commandant!"

A fist crashed down on the desk, making a number of quills and a few stacks of forms, but not the massive ledger, jump. "I can't just let a dozen or so prisoners go at your word, dammit! I need to know what's going on!"

Was the woman just being stubborn? Prideful? Was this actually the limit of Silbeth's stolen influence?

A moment of study, then she turned and carefully closed the door to the office. "You understand that what I'm about to tell you is a state secret, Commandant?"

The officer puffed up like a mating peahen. "Of course."

Silbeth had to struggle not to laugh in her face. "One of your prisoners is Ninth Citadel. On a secret assignment. This arrest and incarceration is interfering."

"Oh. I… But… Why didn't he… or is it 'she'?"

The only answer Silbeth offered was to cross her arms.

"Well, why didn't she identify herself when she was arrested?" the woman asked, apparently choosing a gender at random.

"Do I need to explain 'secret assignment' to you?"

"Fine." The officer flushed, angry and embarrassed. "So why do you want the others released?"

"Because nobody—including you—can know who our operative is."

"But—"

"Commandant, these people are here for, what? Being raucous drunks? Brawling? Curfew violations? Petty theft? Please, by all means, tell me how punishing such hardened criminals and threats to society is more important than an ongoing Citadel operation against a genuine seditionist. I'm listening."

Another moment of pride, flaring almost brightly enough to blind, but the officer finally acquiesced. "I'll have them out before the afternoon shift is over."

"See that you do, Commandant." Silbeth was already at the door, flinging it open and determined to be gone before anything could go wrong, any suspicions could rise. "We appreciate your cooperation."

Even from the hall, over the conversation of other nearby soldiers, she could hear the other woman's disdainful snort.

———

Again she lurked across the avenue, loitering in the doorway of what, to judge by the scent and the coating of powder, was some sort of granary. After long and anxious minutes, a slow stream of un-uniformed men and women emerged from the gaol. She had a general description of the woman, so hopefully it wouldn't be too hard to spot—

Ulia Povyar stepped from the squat stone building and Silbeth's heart lodged in her throat.

The aristocrat and spy was the sort of beautiful more common to fairy tales than the real world. Skin of almost golden hue was accented by deep blue eyes and hair of a dark red normally seen only alongside far paler complexion. Her dress of emerald and gold, worn and wrinkled as it was by her days of incarceration, was a perfect complement, so that the overall effect was more sylvan or fey than merely mortal.

Silbeth felt her cheeks flushing, her pulse pounding, and actually slammed her hand into the edge of the nearby doorway, focusing intently on the pain.

*Knock it off, you idiot! Remember how badly everything went wrong in Muhdresh when you got involved with Ruval in the middle of that job, how badly that mistake cost you, cost* him…

Swearing at herself, the mercenary moved into the street, following a dozen paces behind Ulia until she was sure they were far enough from the gaol that none of the soldiers would spot them speaking.

"Ulia Povyar?" she asked, a formality more than anything else, as she fell into step alongside.

The other woman turned, and Silbeth ferociously ordered herself not to stare at her eyes. Her distraction wasn't so bad, though, that she missed the tightening in Ulia's lips, the tension radiating from her shoulders. "Yes, I am. And you?"

Her tone sounded almost… Resigned?

"The salmon are coming to Lake Orist awfully late this year," Silbeth observed.

Ulia stumbled at the code phrase, would have fallen if Silbeth hadn't caught her arm and steadied her. When she recovered and resumed her pace, those eyes glistened with unshed tears and her voice shook like the last fading reverberations of a church bell.

"Oh, God. Oh, thank… I thought you were one of *them*. I thought something must have happened, it'd been so long since I was told someone was coming…"

Silbeth squeezed reassuringly. "No, it just took a while for Kirresc to get everything in order. They started as soon as they got word that your cover was in danger, but…"

The aristocrat seemed more than a touch confused by the choice of words. "I'm not Kirresci myself," Silbeth clarified. "His Majesty couldn't send one of his own. Too politically dangerous if he were caught, yeah? So—"

Ulia looked almost ready to run. "You knew the pass phrase, but I can't believe they would trust—"

"A mercenary?"

"Well, yes."

"Priory of Steel."

"Oh!" Then, "I can see how that might have taken some time to arrange, yes. Um, how did you get me out of there, if I may ask?"

"You thought I was one of them?"

"As I said…"

Silbeth flashed the copper badge. "So did they."

Ulia swallowed hard and said nothing for perhaps half a block. Finally, she said, "You were almost too late. Getting to Tohl Delian at all, I mean."

"I can see that. You were right that you needed to get out of here. They were watching your house. If you hadn't been in gaol for whatever little…" Silbeth trailed off, her jaw dropping. "You got yourself arrested on purpose!"

Ulia smiled broadly. "I got 'drunk' and slapped an off-duty soldier. I figured they'd keep me for a few days. I'd have time to think, out of the way, and be out before word of my arrest reached anyone important. Maybe if I got *truly* fortunate, once it did, whoever suspected me would assume that no spy would be that careless and look elsewhere."

Silbeth smirked, though her heart abruptly wasn't in it. The patterns of foot traffic around them were changing; nothing dramatic, nothing overt, but enough to raise her hackles. "Maybe you're a lot luckier than I," she said, trying to study the avenue around her in every direction without a single obvious motion, "but in my experience, Donaris rarely grants anyone *that* much good fortune."

"Oh, I… don't believe the Empyrean Choir. I'm Deiumulin."

"Huh. I've never understood that. Only one god? Doesn't seem feasible to me. I mean, what if—?"

"Are you… Do you really want to have a theological discussion *now*?"

"I'm just trying to keep up the conversation," Silbeth admitted, "so we look nice and casual. Don't be conspicuous about it, but look around."

By now, she was certain, it must be obvious to even the untrained observer. (And she had no idea how much training Ulia, as a spy for Kirresc, actually had.) The street was more crowded than it should be, and many of the pedestrians were grim, nervous, in a shuffling hurry. Much of the throng was desperate to get somewhere—or away from something—and all were moving back in the direction Ulia and Silbeth had come.

"No panic," the aristocrat noted. "It's not a fire or any sort of disaster. Just something they'd rather avoid."

The women looked at one another. "Soldiers," Silbeth said.

"A lot of them." Ulia absently chewed on a loose lock of hair. "A simple patrol wouldn't be driving people to flee in these numbers. Do you think it's me? Did someone learn about—"

"No. You just got out. Word couldn't have reached them fast enough to have mobilized a large force. And *why*? Better to send out smaller parties to blend, figure out where you'd gone. No, this is something… Shit. Someone must have found the bodies. I thought I'd have more time."

"Bodies? What bod…" Ulia's face seemed almost to tarnish as the blood drained from it. "That badge isn't a forgery, is it?" she whispered.

"Afraid not." Then, at the woman's abject horror, "I didn't have a choice! They were about to take me in!"

"What do we do?"

"I have a way out of here, but it's going to be hard to reach at the moment. We need to get off the street, somewhere they won't find us. Let the first wave of soldiers move past, try to sneak through before the whole city's locked down in their wake. You know anywhere we can go?"

"I… I do, but…"

"Don't have a lot of time for 'but' just now, Ulia."

"We'll be putting other people in danger," she fretted.

"And how many people are in danger if you don't get whatever intelligence you've learned to Kirresc? To say nothing of what's going to happen to us if they catch us."

Ulia nodded, unhappy but steady, and made a beeline for the nearest side street.

———

"You're certain these people can be trusted?" Sibeth turned from the window, and the shutters through which she studied the busy street below.

Across the room—a private study, judging by the furnishings and the bookshelves—sat a small table with a pair of chairs. Over the back of one draped the long coat and swordbelt she'd acquired from the dead Ninth Citadel operative. In the other sat Ulia, idly swirling a glass of wine in one hand and picking at a plate of cheese and fruits with the other. The owners of the large house had invited the pair of women to join them at the dinner table, and Silbeth knew Ulia had been inclined to accept, but she'd insisted on privacy. Some time to rest, and to think.

And possibly to get away from the household's two children, whose presence made her gut twist with guilt over potentially putting them in harm's way, despite her earlier protestations to Ulia.

"Lady Salko is a friend," Ulia said after swallowing a mouthful of cheese. "Yes, I trust her. Besides, she and her husband are… sympathizers."

"Symp… They know you're a Kirresci spy?!"

"No! No, nothing like that." She paused, sipping from her crystal goblet. "A great many Ktho Delians," she explained, "dislike living under the Deliant regime."

"I would expect so!"

"A few are brave enough—or perhaps foolish enough—to engage in open sedition."

Silbeth grunted, wandered over to the table for a drink of her own. "I'd heard rumors, but nothing more."

"I'd be surprised if you had. The government spends a lot of effort suppressing word of such things—from its own citizens and outsiders both."

The mercenary pulled out her chair, sat, then nervously stood again and returned to the window. "And the Salkos are…?"

"Not seditionists, no. Sympathizers. People who support the resistance but lack the means, or the will, to act." Ulia shrugged. "I can't blame them. It's a hopeless cause. I just told them that I thought someone had accused me of financing the seditionists, and I—we—needed a place to stay for a few days until I could work out what to do next."

"I was there for that part," Silbeth reminded her.

"My point is, they won't turn us in."

"Mm." Silbeth wasn't entirely convinced, but she decided to let it lie. It wasn't as though she had any better idea where to hide. Again she returned to the table, forcing herself to sit and *stay* seated, at least long enough to eat a few bites.

"Anyway," Ulia said after then, "it's probably true."

"Eh? What is?"

"What I told them about the authorities suspecting me of sedition. I know they're on to me about something, but that doesn't mean they think I'm a spy. Probably they just think I'm a seditionist." She bared her teeth in what could only in the loosest of terms be considered a smile. "Not that it'll make any real difference if they catch me."

"Are the methods of Deliant torturers as nasty as I've heard?"

"I've not seen them myself, but I've never heard anything to make me doubt the stories." Ulia shuddered faintly, and Silbeth couldn't blame her.

"Well, then, let's not get you captured."

"Good plan." Ulia's smile this time was genuine. Silbeth stood and began to pace, forcing herself to think about things other than that glowing expression.

"Would the Salkos or any other sympathizers you know be more inclined to actively help us if they *did* know you were

Kirresci?" she asked. "I realize you can't just go about telling people, but—"

"No, I can't. But even if I could, it would make our situation worse. They still wouldn't turn us in, I don't think, but... Kirresc isn't well regarded by the seditionists, for the most part. Quindacra, Wenslir... None of the southern nations, really, save maybe Suunim."

Silbeth frowned, pivoted at the bookcase and paced back the other way. "I don't understand. I figured any enemy of the Deliant..."

"The pact," Ulia explained, referring to the treaty of mutual defense signed by most of the nearby lands, "may keep Ktho Delios largely confined to its current borders, but it doesn't do much to help the people here. Many of the resistance and sympathizers feel that the other nations don't really give a damn what happens to Ktho Delios's own citizens so long as the Deliant doesn't try expanding again."

"And they're probably right," Silbeth agreed with a sigh. "I hate politics."

"You and most sane people."

The mercenary chuckled. "Don't make assumptions about my san—" She froze as she reached the shutters, peering out between the narrow slats. "Ulia, there are soldiers on the street!"

Indeed, the avenue beyond was crawling with them, advancing slowly down the block, the evening sun casting their shadows out ahead as advance scouts. They approached slowly, pausing at each house. There the man at the front of the column would halt, hands held before him. Each time he would shake his head, and the soldiers would advance a few paces until they stood between two new houses, whereupon the process repeated.

Nor was it only this peculiar behavior that marked their leader as something other than a normal officer. His chain hauberk and breastplate were black, but what he wore over them…

"Ulia?" Silbeth had to ask, though she feared she already knew the answer. "What does a blue tabard signify?"

From the table behind her, she heard the clatter of a wine goblet dropped from shaking fingers. The answer reached her ears was a hiss, barely above a whisper. "Inquisitor!"

*That's what I was afraid of.*

"I don't understand. They've no reason to suspect sorcery in anything that's happened, so why…?"

"The Inquisitors aren't just witch hunters," Ulia told her, joining her at the window, shoulder pressed to Silbeth's own. "They're the only ones in Ktho Delios legally permitted to practice sorcery. The only ones the Deliant publicly admits to, anyway. They can be assigned almost any task, if it's deemed important enough."

"Something like finding the murderer of two Ninth Citadel agents?" Silbeth asked nervously.

"Yes. What do we do? They'll reach us in minutes!"

The mercenary's mind raced. While certainly no practitioner, she knew a little of magic. Several of the Priory monks and priests practiced mystical rites, enough so that she understood some basic theories. Almost against her will, she turned her head to study the coat that lay, innocent and unassuming, over the back of the chair.

Blood. She'd chosen the coat because its dark hue hid the blood that had spattered it during her struggle with its former wearer. That *had* to be how this Inquisitor had tracked them from the bodies!

But it was imprecise. It had only led him to the general vicinity, else he wouldn't need to concentrate anew at each house, would already have located her here.

"I have an idea," she announced. "You're not going to care for it, and the Salkos even less. But if we hurry, and if everyone does *exactly* as I say, and if the gods—or god—are in an abnormally giving mood today, we all might get out of this without spending the rest of our very short lives in a Deliant prison."

———

"Colonel! Colonel Ilx!"

The Deliant Inquisitor lowered his hands—slowly, though he wanted simply to let them fall—and composed his features before turning. The interruption was irritating, yet he couldn't pretend anything other than relief at the moment's respite.

It had been hours, now, since he had touched the blood of the dead man, etched the arcane glyphs into the soil around the bodies and summoned the essence of life recently spilled to guide his way. Hours in which he'd struggled to keep the feel of that life, those magics, in his head. He'd mentally redrawn the rune time and again to keep focused, and still it slipped away a bit more every time he stopped to feel for it. This interruption would make it that much harder, but the brief rest was welcome all the same.

He was a bit young for an Inquisitor, was Navirov Ilx, and wore a neatly trimmed mustache and goatee to appear older. He might have tried for a full beard, had not the burn scar across the right side of his face—not blatant, visible only up close or in bright lighting—prevented it. Age notwithstanding, however, none who witnessed his work, or had to stand before his determined and nigh unblinking gaze, could doubt that he had earned his accolades and more.

And right now, every iota of that determination was bent toward finding whatever criminal or enemy of the state had butchered two Ninth Citadel operatives. Navirov had no great love for the secret police, but still, such violations could not be allowed to stand.

"What is it, Private?" he asked once the soldier appeared before him.

The newcomer snapped off a salute. "You ordered me to find out if anyone had recently used Ninth Citadel authority to engage in any suspicious activity, Colonel," he began.

"Yes, I know. I was there. Spit it out, please."

"Yes, sir! A woman bearing a Citadel badge ordered the release of several prisoners from a nearby gaol, sir. No infractions of any importance, just petty transgressions."

"Hmm. You have the list?"

"Right here, sir." He handed over a page torn from a ledger, then pointed to a quickly scribbled and uneven line of ink. "Everyone from here down."

"Hmm," he repeated. "Yashir!"

A gaunt, severe woman with hair of blackest night and a coat to match—the only person in his entire entourage not clad in armor—stepped forward. "Yes, Colonel?"

He passed the page over his shoulder without looking. "Have your people been looking into anyone on this list?"

The Ninth Citadel operative scanned the paper. "This one. Povyar."

*Ulia Povyar?* Bit of a surprise, that. Navirov had met the woman a few times, at this function or that. She'd never struck him as a seditionist sympathizer. But then, one never knew, did one?

"Happen to know if she has any friends or relatives on this street?" The Citadel was rarely so forthcoming with their intelligence, but the loss of two of their own had changed the rules.

In the end, she had to send her own runner back to headquarters to look at Povyar's file, and by the time they identified the Salko household as their probable destination, Navirov could have already located it by picking up the lingering threads of his spell. Still, at least it was easier on him this way.

He ordered his people to surround the house, and to take up stations at the nearby intersections. Only then, flanked by several of his best soldiers and by Yashir herself, did he pound on the door.

It opened to reveal neither a servant nor Master or Lady Salko, but a small, formally clad boy of perhaps ten or twelve years. His younger sister, garbed in equal finery, stood behind him, a silk-dressed doll dangling from her fist.

Navirov dropped to one knee. "Are your parents here, son?"

The boy nodded, eyes wide and shining.

"Is anyone else here?"

"I don't know. They were."

"Who?"

"Two pretty ladies."

"And where are your parents now?"

"They…" The boy's lip began to quiver.

"All right." Navirov rose. "Take your sister to your neighbor's house. Run."

"Colonel—" Yashir began, voice hot.

"Quiet. Go, child."

They ran, hands clasped.

"You should have taken them aside for further questioning!" the woman from the Citadel snapped, livid. "Standard procedure "

"I do not interrogate children."

"You—!"

"I am stepping through that doorway now. Whether or not you're standing in it."

Yashir slipped aside, though the weight of her disdainful fury was nearly enough to slow his passage.

Navirov and his soldiers found the Salkos and their household staff, bound and gagged in the wine cellar. None had been too horribly mistreated; a bruise here, a contusion there, just enough to subdue them so they could be tied.

*Or,* he mused, *enough to make it look legitimate.*

He had no evidence of any such thing, and—regardless of what Yashir might do in his place—he wasn't about to arrest the victims of a seditionist on mere suspicion that their involvement was more than it appeared. He would, however, have a word or two with the Ninth Citadel, have the Salkos put under close surveillance for a time.

He found the stolen coat, as well, along with the copper badges and identification documents. They were buried in the hay of a cart being pulled behind an old sorrel mare trudging casually down a neighboring street. Since most Ktho Delians knew nothing of magic—certainly not enough to deduce that he'd located them via the blood on the coat—this raised a whole host of new questions.

"They cannot be more than minutes ahead of us," he shouted at his assembled unit. "Spread out! Send runners to nearby barracks with Povyar's description and get more people on the streets! Give them no opportunity to go to ground! Find them, surround them, and run them down!

"And above all… Something is going on here, something we don't understand. Something beyond mere sedition. So whatever happens, *I want them alive.*"

———

"Sure, I remember. Wasn't but a night ago you were here. Still," the sentry hedged from behind his viewport beside the door, "I really ought to check with Koldan before I just let you walk in here."

Silbeth shoved her own face against, practically *through,* the tiny window. When she raised her voice, though, it wasn't solely in an effort to intimidate the thug, but also to be sure he'd hear her over the sound of Ulia's desperate gasping. The spy remained upright only by leaning hard against the wall of the woodworker's shop, far more winded by the cross-city dash than was her Priory of Steel companion.

"Listen to me, you obtuse bastard! You think my friend and I just ran half of Tohl Delian for the exercise? We've got people after us! If they catch us, we're dead, and if we're dead, your boss doesn't get any of the *sizable* purse he's being paid for smuggling us the hell out of this wretched town! Now *open the gods damned door!*"

Between his snarl and his hesitation, she wondered if she might have overdone it, but the notion of costing Koldan his due coin obviously weighed on the man. "Who's after you?" he asked.

"I didn't stop to get their names! Rivals of yours, maybe?" Not *precisely* a lie…

Grousing to himself, the sentry hauled back the bolts. Silbeth darted inside before the door was fully open, dragging a still-wheezing Ulia behind her by the hand.

"I suggest you lock up," she said as she blew past him, not that she anticipated it doing any good. The pair had barely avoided search parties on numerous occasions, only just managed to escape them on numerous others. The Deliant soldiers knew their general area, and she had no doubt they would swiftly find someone who could be intimidated into revealing Koldan's hidden sanctum. As soon as the soldiers learned the notorious smuggler was based in the vicinity, it was the first place they'd look for the fleeing fugitives. Koldan was about to find a tidal wave of mail and swords crashing down on his head.

The fib that got her through the door notwithstanding, she never genuinely considered *not* telling the smuggler and gang leader what was coming. Disastrous as she knew the revelation could be, it would be even worse if they were caught unprepared.

He took it about as well as she'd had any right to expect.

"You gods damned stupid *bitch!* You had to lead them right *to us?!*"

"I had nowhere else to go, Koldan, and you—"

"We'll be lucky if we have time to get our asses out of here with a fraction of my money!" Indeed, his people were already in panic mode, gathering up the most portable riches and most incriminating of stolen goods. "You have *any* idea how much I'm going to lose, how much it'll cost to set up a new shop somewhere else? This could break us!"

"I understand. Obviously, what I said earlier about renegotiating no longer applies. I haven't a great deal of coin on me, personally, but I can arrange—"

"Oh, you'll arrange, all right. When your employers find out how much they owe me, you're going to wish you'd let the soldiers take you!"

For all Koldan's spitting fury—she felt the man's saliva speckling her face from clear across the room—Silbeth found her hackles rising at the reaction. He was proving too quick to forgive, and for what? So he could demand an unnamed reward that she hadn't even the authority to promise?

No. This was wrong.

"Very well," she said calmly, stepping aside as one of the smugglers stumbled past her carrying an armful of metalworking tools. "Shall we get going, then? Ulia, you should—"

"I don't think so," Koldan interrupted. "I have to oversee the evacuation, make sure we get all the most important stuff, and I'm not letting you two out of my sight. Besides, you're responsible for this, you can bloody well help lug the equipment!"

That was it, then. She could see the lie in his face, taste it in his words, knew what he had planned as surely as if he'd spelled it out. No way a man like Koldan stayed behind to "oversee" the gang abandoning its nest. He'd be one of the first gone, probably with the most valuable treasures stuffed in his pockets.

No, he wasn't running because he had no intention of trying to escape the coming soldiers; he was *waiting* for them. His only hope was to negotiate, to try and parlay something valuable into a monetary reward and a pass—or at least legal consideration—for his criminal activities.

"Something" such as, for example, a pair of fugitives wanted by damn near every department and division of the Deliant.

She and Ulia needed to find some means of slipping out from under Koldan's gaze, needed to be out of here before—

The heavily bolted portal, along with several chunks of the stone wall around it, blasted into the room in a hurricane of splinters, dust, and the dying remnants of the unfortunate door guard. Silbeth and Ulia had just run out of "before."

Silbeth had no idea what they'd hit the door with—portable ballista? Some sort of alchemical bomb?—and ultimately it didn't much matter. The first handful of Deliant soldiers poured through the breach, and she moved to meet them.

And as she ran, she shouted, loud enough for the others, soldiers included, to hear over the growing chaos.

"Koldan! Get your mistress out of here! I'll try to hold them!"

Even in the face of growing danger, the smuggler's confusion froze him. Ulia, however, was no fool. She must have seen the same potential for betrayal Silbeth had; the mercenary offered up a silent prayer of thanks when the other woman picked up on her cue, racing to Koldan's side and clutching at him like a storybook damsel in distress.

His frustrated, furious roar when he realized what they'd done—that the Deliant would never believe now that he hadn't been involved in Ulia's and Silbeth's crimes, no matter what he did or how he turned against them—was near as loud as the detonating door. He spun away from Ulia, drawing a broad-bladed fighting knife, and sprinted for one of his many hidden exits. Ulia followed, armed with a smaller dagger she'd filched from somewhere on the smuggler's body during her desperate cling.

Soldiers pursued them. Soldiers spread throughout the workshop, running down Koldan's people on the various levels. And then Silbeth couldn't afford to pay any further attention due to the soldiers converging on her as well.

*At least the Inquisitor hasn't gotten here yet...*

The trio facing her didn't seem especially concerned, Inquisitor or no, though they were professional enough to maintain their guard. And no wonder. Three to her one, their broadswords to her oversized knife, their chain hauberks to her unarmored flesh. This pale foreigner would have to be one of the greatest swordswomen they'd ever heard of to pose them any real threat.

Silbeth grinned, slipped to her left so they weren't all coming at her straight on, and attacked.

She twisted in midstep, allowing the first man's swing to pass her shoulder with a finger's width to spare, and slipped inside his reach. Her arm wrapped around his near the elbow, locking the joint as she thrust hard with the point of her knife. It punctured only shallowly through the sleeve of chain, but the tip digging into flesh, combined with her pressure on the elbow, was enough to break his grip on his own weapon.

Maintaining the lock on the man's arm, she threw her weight to one side, wrenching the limb from its socket and sending them both to the floor. He struck hard, crying out in pain. She rolled smoothly back to her feet, his fallen broadsword now held high and ready.

The other two were almost upon her and she retreated, cross-stepping and shifting direction at random, her sword moving in wide but controlled circles. Again and again they tried to flank her, only to find that she'd stepped just far enough aside that they couldn't. Again and again they struck, and each time she either pivoted from their weapon's arc or deflected the sword aside with her own.

Without warning or any obvious change in her stance, she abruptly leaned into a parry, deflecting one soldier's sword hard into the other's path. It wasn't much, would scarcely have scratched his hauberk even if he'd walked into it. Still, he saw a blade appear suddenly before him and raised his own to ward it off.

Silbeth's own sword followed a fraction of a second layer, punching through chain and burying itself deep in the soldier's guts. He slid from the blade with a groan and a hideous sucking sound to collapse in a spreading tangle of blood and entrails.

By now the first wounded soldier had regained his feet, drawing a heavy dagger with his one working hand, but he made little difference. Unable to fully defend himself and crippled by pain, he quickly fell a second time, and he'd not be rising again. That left Silbeth facing only a single opponent, and though the Deliant-trained woman was skilled, the outcome was never in doubt. After a few brief passes and parries, Silbeth almost casually danced through her defenses and split her opponent's skull.

She ran before any more of the Ktho Delian forces could converge on her, rushing to catch up with Koldan and Ulia. They hadn't gotten far down the escape passage: a squared tunnel with rough wooden bolsters, and walls dripping with condensation and slick mildew. They'd slain a couple of soldiers on their own, which was presumably why they'd not gotten much farther.

Koldan saw her approaching and drew breath to speak— perhaps to threaten or curse or command, or possibly all three at once.

Silbeth swung her stolen broadsword. The smuggler's head hit the floor with a wet smack, bouncing and rolling until it fetched up against the wall, lips still struggling to form those unspoken words.

Ulia stared, open-mouthed.

"He meant to betray us," Silbeth explained. "He still would have—to the Deliant, if he came up with a new way to do so, or just killing us if he decided we were no longer valuable."

"But…"

"He and I discussed detailed plans for sneaking us out last night. I know where to find the next person in his smuggling chain. If we hurry we might reach him before he hears that everything's gone ass-ward, or at least before he hears it was our fault. With any luck, he can get us outside Tohl Delian's walls."

"All right," Ulia agreed, steadying herself and stepping carefully over Koldan's body. "And then? We still have half of Ktho Delios between us and the nearest border."

Silbeth tried, and failed, to smile. "Then we improvise. And do a *lot* of hoping."

# CHAPTER EIGHT

The weeks it took to cross the unwelcoming reaches of the Outermark were, while perhaps not truly "hellish," certainly among the most arduous, most uncomfortable, and most exhausting of Nycolos's life.

The terrain was indifferent at best, often actively hostile. From the rocky foothills and cracked stone badlands around the mountains; the desiccated and frequently blighted grasslands beyond; the torrent of the Dragon's Tail; the vermin-spawning swamps where the Tail broke from the broader flow of the Dragon River. Every mile ate away their reserves, their strength, until Nycolos would almost have accepted the death that inevitably awaited if only he could resume his true form—and regain his wings—for a few glorious moments.

Nor was the land itself their only adversary. Late season storms lashed the open ground of the Outermark. Lightning scored deep lesions into the earth. Chilling rains pelted the travelers before accumulating into clinging puddles and sucking muck, yet never seemed to irrigate the earth much once they'd passed.

Plains wolves; the occasional bear; a circling speck high above, that might have been either wyvern or peryton hunting far from its mountain eyrie. Once, at the edge of the marsh, some form of monstrous toad-beast the size of a small horse, ambushed them. That, at least, was a battle that Nycolos's inhuman strengths had allowed him to win, and the beast, though ill-flavored, fed them for days.

On a handful of occasions, guards fortunate enough to escape from the mines and the mountain fey had caught up with them, seeking vengeance. Then, though it chafed Nycolos more fiercely than those storms, he and Smim would flee, or find some small shelter or woodland in which to hide, rather than face superior numbers in their fatigued state. So, too, had they been forced to avoid another, more vicious form of raider, as tribes of bog goblins discovered the many bands of slaves trudging across the region. Against these, Smim's presence was no buffer, for the slimy, peat-dwelling creatures bore little love for their cave-haunting cousins.

One twilight, as they hunted for a patch of halfway dry ground on which to bed down, they had stumbled across one of those goblin raiding parties at camp. The wicked things danced and cavorted around a fire, the light glistening on their algae-smeared and moss-clad bodies, stone-tipped spears and alligator-tooth-edged swords raised as high as their shrill, screeching voices.

Alongside the fire lay several dead men and women, stacked like logs, while another corpse rotated on a primitive spit, already lightly cooked by the flame's kiss. And though his hair had long since burnt away and much of his skin had followed, enough of the dead man's features remained for Nycolos, with his inhuman vision, to recognize the escaped slave Keva.

Nycolos's reaction had nothing to do with Keva, of course. That was just obvious, when Nycolos contemplated his choices in later days. He owed the man nothing, felt no affection for him. Rather, it was the frustration of the journey, all the pain and fatigue, the good fortune of catching so many goblins together and unaware. He just lost control, couldn't pass up the opportunity. It was about pride, about Nycolos himself.

Not about some dead slave Nycolos had barely known. That notion was just foolish. Nothing to do with Keva at all.

Unfortunately (or perhaps *quite* fortunately, if one happened to be a marsh goblin), Nycolos never launched his attack, whatever its motivations. Hoping to catch the entire tribe in one fell swoop, he had concentrated on his body, working to strengthen his gut, his lungs, his innards, the skin of his throat and his tongue, enough to bathe the lot of them in a gout of eldritch fire, as he'd done to so many of his foes of old.

But the only fire he'd felt burned within him as his entire body convulsed in overwhelming, maddening agony. He'd no idea of whether he was passing out or actually dying, and his final thought before the world and the pain faded was that he would welcome either. It had been hours before Smim had managed to shake him awake, and only—so the goblin told him—after dragging him for miles through the fetid swamp.

Piecing it together later, Nycolos knew he had gone too far, shifted too much of himself back. The cursed sliver, that tiny piece of enchanted steel, had recognized its prey anew, had begun to seek his heart. He must have reversed the process through sheer primal instinct before he'd gone under, turning his organs back to those of a mere human. Whatever healing he'd managed while a slave to Justina Norbenus had been brutally undone. His world was again one of constant torment, a soul-deep suffering that dogged his every breath, his every thought.

Despair might have overcome him then and there, he might have chosen to let himself die, but his ego would never allow it. Especially not with a possible salvation growing ever nearer.

So he had continued on, every step through the swamp the labor of a lifetime. He allowed Smim to support him, to help him through the roughest patches, though he burned anew at the indignity.

But finally, *finally* they stumbled through the last of the bogs to the banks of the Dragon River.

The broad and rapid torrent proved almost impassible. Even as he was nearly swept away, saved only by a convenient protruding rock and Smim's desperate efforts, Nycolos couldn't keep from smirking at the potential irony that the Dragon, of all things, might kill him. Trembling, more than half-drowned, too exhausted even to stand, they staggered and crawled out onto the opposite bank to collapse among the reeds.

And only then, his cheek buried in the muck, did Nycolos begin to truly realize: the Outermark was behind them. It hadn't stopped him, hadn't slain him, no matter how hard it had tried, how close it had come. They were past it.

He raised his mud-encrusted face and gazed into the kingdom of Kirresc.

It looked, from here, much like the rest of the world. Grasslands, more fertile than those in the stagnant Outermark, occasionally rolling, bedecked by sporadic patches of woodland. Nothing yet to mark it as a civilized land—by human standards, anyway—let alone the homeland of one Nycolos Anvarri.

They made camp amidst the reeds, fed themselves on uncooked fish, went to sleep shivering with the damp and awoke the same way. Then, yet again, they walked.

Aimlessly, at first. Smim had never been to Kirresc, while Nycolos had only seen it long, long ago, and only from high above. He possessed only the vaguest notion where they might be headed.

That had changed on their second day in the kingdom, when they stumbled across the highway. The broad dirt road suggested only a moderate amount of traffic, this far out, but it should lead them where they wanted to go.

The expressions of abject horror upon the first passersby they met—a farmer and several of his hands, hauling a late-season harvest to town—reminded Nycolos that, though the worst of the Outermark filth and sweat had been washed from him in the river, he was clad only in tattered rags. Also that Smim's presence would not go unremarked, or in any way welcomed, in these "civilized" lands.

When he and Smim moved on, the folks on the wagon were short some clothes, a pair of cloaks, and a sack-full of vegetables—and were, on the whole, grateful that those were all they'd lost to the pair of monstrous travelers.

So they had continued along the highway, Smim largely concealed by what was, for him, an oversized hood, Nycolos doing what talking proved unavoidable. They asked direction where they could, stole when and what they must, their pace kept infuriatingly slow by the twin necessities of pampering Nycolos's wound and finding shelter from the frequent autumn storms.

Until now, finally, on one late afternoon after days Nycolos had not bothered to count, they stood outside the walls of Talocsa, the great capital of Kirresc.

The place was a riot of colors that somehow wove themselves into a coherent whole even where they clashed, a tapestry of eccentric genius. Whitewashed and gleaming, the city's walls were just beginning to glow orange in the light of the setting sun. Above them rose Talocsa's towers and minarets, many built to almost house-like triangular peaks of umber shingles, others squared platforms with stone ramparts. Pennants in the many hues of the Kirresci noble houses saluted proudly, always overtopped by the golden eagle on crimson field that was the ensign of the royal house and the nation itself.

And while Nycolos could never have described exactly *how*, it seemed that the many sounds emerging from within those walls—of travel, of labor, of conversation, of laughter and tears and life itself—were of equally sharp colors.

The guards at the city gates, and those who walked the wall above, seemed of relatively good cheer, though it did not stop them doing their duty. Unlike some cities of which Nycolos had heard, they didn't halt everyone entering Talocsa, seeming to choose at random those whom they questioned or searched.

Well, not entirely at random. Dressed so roughly and traveling with a companion who shrouded his face, Nycolos correctly anticipated that he would be among those who were stopped.

The soldier who faced him sported a long mustache; Nycolos had already noted that, though clean-shaven faces were not uncommon, the majority of Kirresci men boasted either mustaches alone or beards of varying styles. Like his fellow guards, this man wore a hauberk of lamellar scales and an open-faced, slightly conical helm. He carried a sabre at his side, while long spears—some traditional, some of a curve-bladed style Nycolos had never seen—and short recurved bows leaned against the wall, within easy reach.

"You look to have had a hard time of it, traveler," the guard said, somehow sympathetic and suspicious at once.

Nycolos forced a chuckle he didn't feel. "You've no idea."

The answering smile was equally artificial. "Your business in Talocsa?"

"Coming home, actually."

"Indeed? And your name, sir?"

He gave some thought to lying. (Well, lying about the deeper lie.) It took him no time at all to decide not to bother.

"Nycolos Anvarri."

Oh, but he had the soldier's full attention now—and not *only* his. The nearby guards all stopped what they were doing to peer his way, as did many of the passersby. Against the constant song of the city, a bubble of silence seemed briefly to envelop the gate.

"Well," Nycolos said, shattering that silence like a mace to a mirror, "I'm pleased not to have been forgotten."

"Baronet Nycolos is gone," the soldier before him growled, hand dropping to his sabre. "He vanished many months ago."

"On a fool's errand!" an anonymous voice added from the growing audience, just loud enough to be heard.

"Now the errand is done," Nycolos said blandly. "And the fool has returned. Somewhat," he added, as though the admission were some great secret, "the worse for wear."

"You're a liar!" the sentry snapped, all but quivering in anger.

All trace of good humor vanished from Nycolos's features. "Be very careful what you say, soldier."

"And what of your companion?" another soldier demanded. "Why does he hide?" Before Nycolos could even think to respond, the armor-clad woman lunged forward, snagging the hood of the cloak and yanking it down.

"That was impolite," Smim sighed. "And unfortunate."

Everyone present recoiled, some even going so far as to hiss. Gloves wrapped around spears and multiple sabres slid from scabbards. "Goblin!" someone gasped, rather unnecessarily.

Nycolos unclenched his fists, fingers held straight, ready to sprout talons if no alternative option presented itself.

"Oi!" The voice fell on them from above, atop the wall. "What's going on down there?"

Looking up, Nycolos saw another figure—a woman, to judge by the voice and what little of her face he could see between the cheeks and nose guard of the helm. She wore a hauberk of chain rather than the simpler lamellar, but otherwise appeared no different than the other guards.

"Goblin, captain!"

"Are you serious?! There are no goblin tribes left in Kirresc!"

"That's not *entirely* accurate—" Smim began in a whisper. Nycolos elbowed him.

"He was trying to sneak into the city!"

"And this sort of entirely unwarranted reaction is exactly why—!" Another elbow.

"And who's this with him?" the captain shouted down.

"A liar and a fraud! Claims he's Baronet Nycolos Anvarri!"

A pause, then, "Hold them. I'll be right down."

The woman vanished from the parapet, leaving behind several archers, arrows trained unerringly on the two newcomers. Between them and the surrounding sentries, Nycolos had to admit he was in a great deal of trouble should the situation turn violent. Even if he could probably survive it, it wouldn't be easy, and he saw no way he could save Smim…

She appeared again, marching from out of the gate. This close, she was definitely female, and to judge by the dark shade of her face within the helm, probably shared a great deal of Nycolos's own heritage. (Or his current form's heritage, anyway.)

"I've met Baronet Nycolos a few times," she announced as she neared. "Even rode patrol with him once. I should be able to clear this up quickly en—" She stopped, studying him, working to focus through the wild growth of untamed beard, the months of hardship, the dust of the road.

Nycolos, who gazed right back at her, could pinpoint by the sudden dilation of her pupils the precise instant she succeeded.

"Oh, bloody hell!" She retreated a step, swept the helm from her head, and then—though not required or technically even proper for addressing a mere baronet—dropped to one knee. "Welcome home, Sir Nycolos."

An array of dropped jaws and gasps that threatened to draw the breathable air from around the gate was quickly followed by a series of salutes or kneeling, depending on the temperament of the individual in question.

*This… Oh, yes. This is how it should be. This is how it will be again.*

"Please, my friends, this is unnecessary. Rise."

They did, those who had knelt, while the others dropped their salutes. The glares of distrust and growing anger transformed into unabashed admiration, while whispers and breathless supposition raced plague-like through the onlookers.

"I apologize for the unseemly welcome, Sir Nycolos," the guard captain continued. "None of my people meant any disrespect—"

"Of course they did," he interrupted. Then, after a pause in which the others had only begun to cringe, he smiled. "Just not to *me*, exactly. An understandable confusion," he added magnanimously.

"Um, yes. Quite." The woman laughed, if a touch nervously. "It's only, nobody thought to see you again, sir. Nobody—forgive me, I mean no slight to your abilities—but nobody thought you stood any chance against.... Against a creature like…"

"Like a dragon?" It was an effort worthy of its own ballad that Nycolos kept the humor in his voice, kept the bitterness choked down where it roiled in his stomach like a bad meal. *He* should *have stood no chance, that damned, insignificant…!*

"A dragon. Yes. Is it… That is, did you…?"

"I won. That will have to satiate your curiosity for now, Captain. The tale isn't one I enjoy, and I've no intention of telling it more often than I must."

"Of course, sir," she agreed, though the bewilderment on her face belied her easy acquiescence. Understandable, Nycolos decided. To any of them, to these *humans*, merely surviving a confrontation with a dragon would be the boast of a lifetime. To *defeat* one? Surely he should be more than eager to spread that tale, shouldn't he?

But he could not bring himself to do so, not yet, no matter how out of character his reticence might be. The wound in his chest was not the only one that remained too painful.

Perhaps spotting his discomfort, even if she could not possibly have guessed at its true source, the captain snapped once more to attention. "Would you permit me to escort you to the palace, sir?"

"Oh. Yes, Captain." *Especially since I haven't the slightest notion of how to get there myself.* "That would be most kind of you."

"Not at all, sir. Um… Sir?"

"Hmm?"

"The, uh, the goblin?"

"Is with me."

The mutters and whispers this time were far less content, and even those who remained silent wore their disapproval in their expressions or their bearing. Nonetheless, the officer simply replied, "As you say, sir," waved a few of her soldiers to follow, and marched through the gate.

The colorful imagery of the city's exterior was easily matched, even exceeded, within. Most larger stone homes and structures boasted colored trim, intricately wrought iron fencing or upper-story railings, and—where space and wealth permitted—soaring archways. Even the poorer buildings, constructed of wood with shingled or thatch roofs, often sported brightly painted shutters, sills, and doorways. Many buildings of either construction were whitewashed.

And the pattern continued among the Kirresci people themselves. Men and women with skin and hair of every shade dressed largely in coats, vests, kaftans, robes, skirts, and similar long garments of almost every hue. From darkest black to forest green, sky or ocean blue to rich crimson, and almost always with lacing or embroidery of stark contrast, the garments announced to the world that these were a passionate, hot-blooded people who celebrated life.

None of which made the atmosphere of sweat, cookfires, and animal droppings any more pleasant, but then, one couldn't expect miracles.

Word of who marched through Talocsa spread before them. The return of Nycolos Anvarri didn't mean a great deal to the bulk of the population, but a significant minority—and certainly a great many of the soldiers and the city's nobility—were indeed shocked and fascinated by the news. Small crowds formed along the main avenue, if only to see for themselves if it were true, though many of the onlookers didn't seem remotely convinced by this bedraggled, exhausted vagabond of a man. A few more squads of soldiers, perhaps off or returning from duty, fell in with the guard captain. Nycolos had a small but significant entourage trailing around and behind him when Oztyerva Palace, the seat of Kirresci royalty, finally hove into view.

Except Oztyerva was no palace at all, no matter what the people of Talocsa had taken to calling it, but a fully fortified castle. The peak-roofed towers and high ramparts might be bright, the banners and sculpted eaves colorful, everything a shimmering ivory or crimson or gold, but it was every inch of it functional. An invader who thought their troubles over once they'd breached the city's walls might find themselves bogged down in a siege of months or years before this last and greatest bastion of Kirresc fell.

Thus the men- and women-at-arms assigned to guard the gates took their duties seriously indeed, and while they were equally as excited at the return of the prodigal baronet as anyone else, they were none too happy at the notion of allowing a "filthy goblin" into the palace grounds.

Even after several of the soldiers had personally identified Nycolos as being precisely who he claimed to be, their reluctance to accept his companion failed to diminish. Finally he announced, loudly and clearly enough for the entire courtyard to hear, "The goblin's name is Smim. I freed him from servitude to the wyrm. I have saved his life more than once on our travels, as he has saved mine. He has sworn fealty to me, and I have accepted his oath. He is my vassal. An attack on him is an attack on me. An insult to him is a spit in my face. And I will respond accordingly!

"Now, does anyone wish to challenge us?"

"What a fascinating interpretation of events," Smim muttered, softly enough that only Nycolos's enhanced hearing could possibly have caught the words. Nobody else spoke up, and the guards stepped aside, though many still wore expressions of deep misgiving.

The lawns beyond the wall were more palatial than the courtyard of a castle, with winding footpaths and marble fountains. And although that lawn required only a few moments to cross, a crowd had assembled on the broad palace steps by the time Nycolos and his entourage reached them. The great double door—gilded, but built of thick and reinforced wood that would frustrate all but the heaviest battering ram—stood wide, with courtiers in colorful finery and knights in the finest chain hauberks and heraldic tabards gathered to welcome Nycolos home.

The salutes were crisp, the cheers many, and he struggled to maintain a modest demeanor while accepting it all as his due.

"Oh, yes, indeed, Sir Nycolos. Welcome back." The voice cut through other nearby greetings and shouts, or rather those greetings and shouts seemed to recoil from the venom saturating the otherwise polite tone. "And I hear you've returned with a new vassal. Seeing him for myself, I have to say that, for the first time, I understand why someone would throw in his lot with yours."

She proceeded down the steps until she stood just before—and just one stair higher—than Nycolos. Hair and skin neither particularly light nor dark, her only outstanding features were the faint scar on her chin, her broad shoulders, and the intensity in her bearing. The sabre at her side boasted a well-worn hilt, shaped to her grip by long and frequent use, and she wore the chainmail of a knight, her red tabard sporting a rampant wyvern in black.

Nycolos would have wagered she'd never even laid eyes on such a creature in her life.

"Perhaps," she finished as she drew to a halt, "you should have remained with his people. You might have found your place among them more to your taste."

*At a wild guess*, the newcomer thought, taking her measure, *this is someone with whom Nycolos Anvarri doesn't get along.*

Having only this briefest of assessments on which to act, he chose the path least likely to reveal his ignorance of the woman while, to his mind, most likely to offend her pride.

He stepped around her without a word and continued up the stairs. To judge by the gasps of astonishment from nearby onlookers, and the hiss of fury from between her own teeth, he'd chosen accurately.

She lashed out as he passed, her fingers grasping his shoulder with such strength that he would have bruised had his skin been only as strong as a human's. "You *should* have stayed gone!" she spat angrily, keeping her tone low. "It matters nothing what deeds you claim to have accomplished while you were away! You disobeyed orders so you might run off and try to impress everyone. You've *handed* the position to me! Kortlaus is no threat, and after this stunt, you'll never be—!"

"Dame Zirresca!" Another stranger's voice, but this one boomed from the doorway with such force that Nycolos might have found it impressive even in his true form. Another armor-clad knight, this one far older and sporting a beard equal parts ash and coal, emerged from within the hall. "His Majesty has heard only the rumors that raced ahead of Sir Nycolos's miraculous return. Please go at once and inform him of their veracity."

The woman released her grip, snapped off a salute, and was gone without another word. Fortunately, Nycolos heard enough of the comments in the crowd to have identified the old warrior addressing him now.

He mimicked the salute he'd just seen, and which the city guards had directed his own way—right fist, clenched, held to his heart—and bowed his head. "Marshal Laszlan."

Orban Laszlan, Crown Marshal to the king and commander of Kirresc's armies, returned the salute. "I thank God for returning you to us, Sir Nycolos," he said, loudly and with what seemed genuine feeling. They fell into step, marching through the double doors and into the great hall of the palace—partly by choice, partly pushed along by the crowd that had grown impatient with hovering around the entrance. He continued, far more softly, "Oh, Nycos, you foolish boy. What did you hope to accomplish? You'll be fortunate to come out of this with your rank."

*Nycos?* Was he to have yet another name he must remember to answer to? How many did humans need?

Even stranger, both Zirresca and Orban had suggested that Nycolos's quest to hunt and slay the wyrm had been undertaken on his own, without the approval of his superiors. What did that mean? What *had* the man hoped to accomplish? What did it portend for his future?

The corridor passed beneath his tread as he pondered his answer. The carpet was lush, though trampled flat by the feet of years. Portraits, statues, and ornate sconces graced the walls between soaring arches of expertly crafted stone. The stairways were broad, yet wound tightly enough for defenders to lurk in wait against enemies climbing from below, and the windows, full of ornamental stained glass, were yet narrow and angled enough to function as arrowslits. Oztyerva was, indeed, an excellent blend of the decorative and the defensive.

"Have you at least brought it back?" Orban asked before Nycolos—Nycos?—could formulate a response.

And although he could hardly be certain, he had a grotesque, stomach-churning feeling, accompanied by a surge of agony in his chest and wrath in his soul, that he knew what "it" was.

"Marshal," he began hesitantly, "I—"

Again their conversation, and those of the people gathered around them, was interrupted. Again the guards—this time it was those assigned to the entryway of the royal court and throne room itself—objected to the presence of a goblin in their midst. And again Nycolos had to give a speech in which he claimed Smim as his oathbound vassal.

"You heard him!" Orban's bellow could have been, probably often was, audible clear across a practice- or battlefield. "Or do you deny the baronet's right to accept fealty from any he deems worthy?"

"Forgive us, Crown Marshal," the nearest of the men-at-arms begged. "It's not his right we question, it's just..." He waved helplessly, jogging his spear.

"Yes?"

"I... With your permission, I should at least obtain permission from His Majesty personally."

"Stay your post. *I* will go speak to His Majesty about the situation." Orban's scowl was dark indeed. "Among other things."

Ignoring the guardsman's salute, the marshal pushed past him, hauled open the double door just wide enough to slip through, and stormed inside.

Nycolos stood in the midst of a throng of strangers who believed they knew him, and waited.

"I anticipate a bright and joyous sojourn here, Master," the goblin commented, "replete with sunshine and celebration."

"I've no intention of remaining here any longer than necessary," Nycolos replied, squatting to whisper in Smim's ear and ignoring the odd looks directed his way. "I'm quite sure we'll be gone long before you've run out of sarcasm."

"Oh, thank you, Master. That was indeed my greatest concern."

"I thought it might be."

"Nycos! By the gods, it really *is* you!"

*Oh, who in hell's name is it* now*?!*

The man shoving through the throng was, like Zirresca and the marshal, clad in the mail and tabard of a Kirresci knight, though his ensign was a deep brown boar on a field of forest green. His hair and full mustache, its narrow ends reaching down past his chin, were the color of straw. He all but crashed into Nycolos, enfolding him in a crushing embrace.

"*Grgh!*" Nycolos greeted him.

Apparently feeling the violent flinch, the blond knight released him as abruptly. "Are you well?"

"Wound," he gasped, hand to the new surge of pain in his chest. "Not… quite healed yet."

"I'm sorry, Nycos. I had no idea."

Rather than screaming at him, as emotion demanded, Nycolos forced a smile. Clearly this was someone with whom he was expected to be friendly; best to play along with that. "No reason you should have. It's good to see you again, too."

The unnamed knight beamed, a second sun in miniature. "I want to hear everything! Every minute of your journey."

"Yes, I'm… certain you're not the only one."

That brought on a broad, almost conspiratorial grin. "I'm sure I'm not. Mariscal, in particular. She'll be overjoyed to see you again. And vice-versa, eh?" He actually elbowed Nycolos with that, though only lightly and carefully avoiding the injury.

Nycolos felt his own smile go a bit wan. Obviously he was supposed to know precisely what this fool was blathering about. *This may prove more difficult than I anticipated. Perhaps I should—*

The doors drifted open, an unfamiliar voice called his name, and the man who was currently Nycolos Anvarri had no more time to ponder the situation into which he'd gotten himself. Head held high, Smim and the strange knight each a pace or two behind him, he marched into the waiting throne room.

# CHAPTER NINE

The throne room, actually a grand hall, was precisely as Nycolos expected after what he'd seen of the city and of Kirresci culture. Great velvet curtains, trimmed in gold, overhung the walls between the hall's engaged columns. Several massive chandeliers cast their light across the chamber, growing ever brighter as they approached the thrones themselves. Of these there were two, seated upon a slightly raised dais beneath a canopy of royal purple. One was draped in black and, though well maintained, cleaned, and dusted, still somehow gave the impression that it had seen many years since its last use.

In the other sat His Majesty Hasyan III, King of Kirresc.

Even seated he was an imposing man—and must have been even more so in his youth—as well as a figure of sharp contrasts. His skin was dark, darker even than Nycolos's own, almost obsidian; yet his hair and beard were an iron gray, his robes of office white trimmed in silver and gold. Even his thin crown was of silver, so that only his ermine-lined cloak of wine purple added any real color.

Despite the empty throne beside him, the monarch was not alone atop the dais. Marshal Laszlan stood at his left, hand on the king's shoulder, leaning to whisper in his ear. So softly and so closely did he speak that even Nycolos had no chance of listening in. A pair of knights armed with shields and broadswords rather than the more popular sabres, royal purple tabards and cloaks worn atop their mail, stood to either side of the two old men.

Most of the throng that had congregated about Nycolos in the palace corridors were forbidden entrance, yet the throne room boasted crowd enough of its own. Nobles of greater or lesser rank had gathered by the dozens, as had various officers of the court, with more filtering in every moment. Most had assembled along the right-hand wall—or the left, if one were the king or atop his dais. A very few, however, stood upon the lower step of the dais itself. These, Nycolos assumed, were His Majesty's advisors and helpers. A handful of others stood along the left wall, and these bore sufficient resemblance to the king that they must be his children or other blood relatives.

The blond-haired knight moved to join the bulk of the gathered souls on the right, and thanks to the greetings he exchanged with several, Nycolos finally overheard his name: Lord Kortlaus, not another mere knight but the baron of someplace called Urwath.

Of higher rank than Nycolos himself, then, but the man had treated him as a friend and equal. Useful to know.

The knight Dame Zirresca was present as well, glaring his way with undisguised enmity and occasionally exchanging whispers with a young man beside her. And also in the crowd was a willowy, brightly-clad woman with coppery hair who also stared his way—not with Zirresca's anger but something more positive yet equally intense.

The "Mariscal" Kortlaus had mentioned, no doubt.

"Humans are complicated and bewildering entities, Smim," he muttered to his servant.

"There are ways to make them much simpler, Master."

"Not when they outnumber us this greatly."

A tall, gaunt man of middle years, stepped forward from his spot beside the dais and rang a small crystalline bell. The chime was hardly an overbearing sound, yet all conversation in the throne room ceased.

"His Majesty thanks you all for attending to his summons at such short notice," he decreed in a raspy but steady tone.

"We begin, as always, by seeking the blessings of the gods on our endeavor."

A second man, dressed in an ecclesiastical cassock of deepest blue, advanced. Built like a barrel and sporting a long, thick mustache but otherwise shaved bald, he would have seemed more appropriate in a smith's apron than priestly raiment. Nonetheless he intoned a long prayer, beseeching the many deities of the Empyrean Choir—with particular devotion to Inoleare the Guardian, patron of those who would rule with a just hand, and to Palanian the Judge—for their favor.

Perhaps because the priest spoke on behalf of not just the king but all who attended court, he acknowledged the other faiths in his prayer as well, naming the "one God" Deiumulos and the animistic Vinnkasti a time or two, but that his own devotion rested entirely with the Empyrean Choir was blatantly clear.

Nycolos, maintaining his façade, refrained from rolling his eyes or sighing aloud. *Humans and their gods…*

Finally the priest's benediction wound to an end, the gathered courtiers had all bowed their heads and intoned their proper amens. He retreated to the dais and the first man advanced once more.

"Thank you, Prelate Domatir." The priest nodded in acknowledgment, and the speaker continued. "Sir Nycolos Anvarri, please come forward."

*I'm already standing right here in the middle of the room, you protocol-obsessed primate!*

Nycolos approached, tried to estimate the proper distance from what he knew of various human cultures, and—hoping he wasn't about to prove himself utterly ignorant of details he should well know—dropped to one knee before the throne.

"Rise, Baronet Nycolos." His Majesty's voice lacked the power of the marshal's own thunderous bellow, but was even deeper of timbre. It was remarkable, at least for a human.

"First," King Hasyan continued, "we wish you to know how grateful we are that the gods have guided you home safely. Most of us had despaired of ever seeing you again." He smiled, then. "Though not all. Madam Balmorra told us you would return. We should have had more faith."

One of those who stood beside the dais bowed her head. An ancient woman clad in stiff finery, she appeared to be made entirely of wrinkles and leather with a tuft of cotton hair. "The stars never lie, Your Majesty. They told me Sir Nycolos had a part yet to play in Kirresc's tale." She turned then to Nycolos and smiled, cracked lips revealing a mouth that, belying her overall mien, still contained most of its teeth.

Nycolos, however, felt his shoulders tighten and his stomach twist. *A court astrologer?* That, he hadn't counted on. If her divinations were potent enough, might she discover his true nature?

Nothing in her expression suggested she saw anything but a battered young knight, returned from an arduous journey. He smiled in return and determined to keep close watch on this Balmorra.

"We have little doubt," the king said, "that your tale is a wondrous one. Ballads will be sung for generations of the man who bested the dread Tzavalantzaval!"

Several cheers erupted throughout the assembly, Kortlaus's the loudest among them. Mariscal's hand twitched at the wrist as though eager to reach out.

At the same time, it took all Nycolos had not to double over before everyone and retch—not merely for the pain of his wound, though it indeed flared in taunting mockery, but at the sound of that name spoken from human lips.

The name he'd been forced to abandon along with all, save Smim, that had been his.

As before, the man who'd first spoken rang his crystal bell, and the noise of the court subsided.

"Yet however great your deeds may have been," Hasyan told him, "you will suffer the consequences of your actions! To run off on your own with property of the crown, against the orders of your commander and without permission of your liege? When the court had yet even to decide what to *do* about the rapacious beast? This behavior does not befit a knight of Kirresc, let alone one who would be Crown Marshal!"

Again the crowd reacted. Kortlaus and several others muttered in discontent, and Mariscal frowned, deep and sorrowful. Zirresca, however, could not quite suppress a gloating smirk, and the nobleman beside her raised his brow as though studying some peculiar specimen.

"Rapacious beast" stuck hard in Nycolos's craw. True he had only recently awakened from a slumber of decades, had hunted beyond the bounds of the Outermark to sate his hunger, but he hadn't taken *that* much livestock or *that* many travelers from within Kirresc's borders!

Had he?

"Surely, Your Majesty," he risked saying, "the dragon was a threat worthy of our attention?"

"It was not your decision to make!" Marshal Orban roared at him. "As I told you then! Yes, we would probably have moved against the dragon, but when our attentions were not required elsewhere, and with a sufficient force! It was not your place to go haring off on your own, and that the gods' own luck was clearly with you doesn't excuse your behavior or impress me in any way!"

*Impress?* Nycolos abruptly felt the urge to scream. Had the bastard knight come after him, wounded him, destroyed life as he knew it for no greater cause than to make himself *look good?*

Had he been able, he would have roasted and split the life from each and every human in the hall.

It appeared the marshal might have more to say, but Hasyan reached out and laid a comforting hand on the man's own fingers, which still rested on his king's shoulders. Orban leaned in and again the pair exchanged quick, close whispers.

"My apologies," Orban said when he straightened again, far more calmly, "To His Majesty and Sir Nycolos both. I spoke out of turn, and some of these matters should be discussed in private."

"Begging His Majesty's pardon." It was the nobleman beside Dame Zirresca who spoke up. He was one of the few men present who went clean-shaven, and the light features of his bare face, as well as his red hair, suggested primarily Elgarrad descent. "Might I address Sir Nycolos and the court?"

The man with the crystal bell glanced at Hasyan, who nodded, then spoke. "His Majesty recognizes Andarjin, Margrave of Vidirrad."

"I thank Your Majesty. My friends, apologies if I am leaping ahead of the conversation, as it were, but I've a concern that I think each and every one of you must share, once you think about it.

"Sir Nycolos, where is Wyrmtaker?"

Again the wound in Nycolos's chest flared, as though the shard within heard the call of its name. "Shattered," he admitted, "in the struggle."

This time, Kortlaus and those others whom Nycolos took to be his friends and allies shared in the gasps and worried murmuring. Even Zirresca didn't seem happy at the thought, no matter that it would surely make her newly returned rival's position that much more precarious.

"Your Majesty," Andarjin said, palms upturned as though beseeching aid, "ladies and gentlemen of the court, I find this to be of far greater import than Sir Nycolos's unauthorized journey, or even his victory, impressive as it is. Wyrmtaker was but recently rediscovered, confirmed as anything more than a wishful myth. And now, as suddenly, it is lost to us.

Madam Balmorra? Rare as dragons may be, was it not you who prophesied that 'several' of the beasts would assault and bedevil our beloved kingdom in the coming years?"

"I believe," the astrologer replied, "that my words were 'make their mark on Kirresc,' not assault or bedevil."

The margrave waved a dismissive hand. "Hardly a meaningful distinction where these creatures are concerned."

*I could come to dislike this Margrave Andarjin with surprisingly little effort,* Nycolos fumed.

"Surely," the nobleman continued, "we ought to be contemplating the potential danger in which we have *all* been placed by the baronet's—error—before we consider the lesser infractions of his disobedience?"

*I foolishly took for granted the sheer convenience of setting someone aflame from great distances.*

Balmorra grunted, then said, "Or perhaps we ought at least hear Sir Nycolos's tale before we take this any further?"

"We agree," the king said before anyone might argue. "Sir Nycolos, if you please…"

Nycolos took a deep breath, then began with, "After an arduous but largely uneventful journey across the Outermark, I arrived at the mountains where I knew Tsavalantzaval made its home." He kept his expression neutral at the name, and at the use of "it," for he thought it improbable that the humans either knew or cared about the dragon's gender. "I began my climb in the foothills, where—"

"Apologies for interrupting," Andarjin said.

"And yet you'll do so anyway."

The margrave's face darkened. "Aren't you skipping over something rather important?"

"I took the sword," Nycolos said flatly. "I've never denied that. Nobody here has forgotten it, so your efforts to remind them are a waste. I see no cause to go into detail for your amusement." *Which is fortunate, since I haven't the first notion of how it was done.*

Ignoring the various shocked looks which suggested he had been rather more forward and impolite in his response than perhaps he ought, Nycolos continued his tale.

Fact and fiction melded into a single thread as he spoke, augmenting what he knew and was willing to tell with whatever sounded reasonable. And through it all, his memories flailed about his head like winged mountain fey, pounding at him with heavy fists.

He told them how Nycolos Anvarri had climbed the heights of the Outermark Mountains, wading with bloodied sword through multiple bands of cave-dwelling goblins and a small clutch of harpies, all agents of the great wyrm.

*How I watched in growing rage through my crystalline scrying pool as this boastful insect dared to invade my home and slaughter my servants...*

He spoke of how he had bravely fought and cleverly wound his way through the many traps and wards, both mundane and mystical, that guarded the labyrinthine passageways of the dragon's lair.

*How that damnable sword had somehow guided him past the traps of collapsing stones and hidden spikes, had dispelled the enchantments that would have incinerated the intruder in pillars of fire or summoned fists of stone from the cavern walls to crush the life from him...*

He told of finally finding Tzavalantzaval alone in a great cavern of monstrous stalactites and stalagmites, ledges and crevices, all told far larger than the entirety of Oztyerva.

*Not alone. He had physically restrained Smim and his other favored minions from attacking the knight in retaliation for the deaths of their goblin brethren, for he hadn't wished to lose his favorite servants, never imagining for even a second that he wouldn't soon be rebuilding his forces...*

And he spoke of the great battle, blade against claw and fang, armor against scale. Great gouts of flame burst from the dragon's maw, but the massive Wyrmtaker had split the hellish torrent in two as readily as it had the goblins. The beast soared from above, knocking stalactites from the ceiling, but Nycolos had readily rolled aside, and without its breath of fire, the dragon had no choice but to return to the ground and to fight. Talons and jaws and tail whipped about him, but Wyrmtaker granted him the speed and strength to meet each and every attack, until finally, *finally* the mystic blade had pierced Tzavalantzaval's chest, seeking the creature's inhuman heart—but how, in its death throes, the dragon's mightiest blow had shattered the blade that killed it into a blizzard of steel fragments, and badly wounded Nycolos himself.

*He still felt the pain, with every breath and every motion, of that hideous blade. His thrashing, though fraught with agony and a growing fear, had not been blind. He had sought to knock Wyrmtaker aside, rip it from his flesh before it could kill him.*

*He had failed, for when the blade shattered, it left a sliver of itself behind, a sliver still containing the magics of the sword. Even as it burrowed through him, seeking his heart, he had lashed out again, determined at least not to die alone—and without Wyrmtaker, Nycolos Anvarri had no means to stave off that blow. The knight had perished beneath Tzavalantzaval's claws, broken and torn asunder so that it was scarcely a slab of bone and meat that had smashed against the cavern wall.*

*And he only half-remembered those last, desperate moments. Clinging to life, the sudden revelation that it was only a* dragon's *heart the sliver of Wyrmtaker would seek. That if, with the last of his strength, he summoned his sorceries to take on another form, as he occasionally had in decades past, he might survive long enough to find a means of removing the deadly splinter. And that, if he were to gain access to the best chirurgeons or even healing magics that humanity might provide, then the obvious form to take was lying, mangled but recognizable, before his swiftly dimming eyes…*

"Smim," he said, gesturing to the goblin, "was one of the last survivors among Tzavalantzaval's servants. In gratitude for freeing him from his slavery, he helped me, bandaging my wounds and assisting me from the mountains. As he had nowhere else to go, I invited him to travel with me. The journey back across the Outermark was difficult, but… Certainly nothing worth telling in light of what came before.

"And so," he concluded, "we stand here before you now."

Not a word was spoken for long moments after he completed his recitation, though to his ears the hush was far from total. He heard the soft breaths of multiple scores of lungs, the shifting of arms and legs within armor, kaftans, and blouses. A great many faces stared upon him with pride and awe, and he was certain he was not the only one present to have noticed Mariscal's swift, almost triumphant grin.

Yet many of the nobles appeared moderately puzzled as well. No doubt his performance was imperfect; he must have omitted some style of speech, or failed to reproduce some mannerism, they were expecting. Well, so be it. He could perfect his guise only so far. Hopefully he and Smim would be gone long before any vague suspicions crystallized enough to become open questions.

For the third time, Orban and the king consulted in an intimate whisper. Afterward, the marshal spoke.

"Indeed a tale worthy of a minstrel's attention, as His Majesty suggested. And we have kept you more than long enough in the telling of it. Clearly you are fatigued, and— with all respect to your, ah, companion's ministrations—your wounds have gone untended for far too long. Retire to your chambers, Sir Nycolos. Rest yourself, while we summon a chirurgeon to attend you. Any further discussion can wait until you've recovered."

"Very kind of you, and His Majesty." Nycolos's thoughts twined and spun like agitated serpents—not least over the fact that he hadn't the faintest notion where his chambers might be. "I wonder if I might beg a favor of Your Majesty?"

Hasyan nodded for him to continue.

"I've been away a long time, Your Majesty. If you won't miss his presence, I would request Lord Kortlaus accompany me, that I might speak with him about all that's transpired in my absence."

"By all means."

Nycolos bowed, as did Kortlaus, and both made for the door. Mariscal seemed determined to catch his attention, but Nycolos offered her no more than a restrained smile.

Even as they departed, Smim tagging along behind, Nycolos heard the king dismissing many of the other courtiers and nobles as well. Clearly he wanted only his closest counselors present for whatever they would next discuss.

"You're sure you don't want to wait?" Kortlaus asked. "Greet, um, *anyone* more formally?"

"No. Should I?"

The baron examined him a moment, then shrugged. "Not if you don't think so."

*Damn humans! Make some sense!*

Hanging back a mere half step, allowing Kortlaus to take the lead without being obvious about it, Nycolos said, "So, tell me of the past months."

For a time Kortlaus's report involved little more than gossip, social or political competition between people Nycolos didn't know, or minor border skirmishes he cared nothing about. At one point the tales turned to several young suitors pursuing Margravine Mariscal, and Kortlaus seemed to expect some particular reaction from him, but other than learning the young woman's rank, he couldn't begin to imagine what he was supposed to have gleaned from that information. Again his friend appeared bemused, but said nothing as to why.

Instead, he focused the bulk of his attentions on studying his route, along this hallway, through those great doors, up that sweeping set of stairs. Although no longer in what he would dub the central keep, or whatever they called the main structure that was the heart of the palace, they had never stepped out of doors. The high, soaring corridors had taken him to what was partly another building, yet still a piece of Oztyerva proper. Nycolos knew enough of most human feudal and social systems to recognize that his title of "baronet," though minor, indicated he owned a small parcel of land somewhere. Why he and many of the other nobles appeared to have quarters here in the palace, he was uncertain. For use when visiting? Did something about their duties require them to dwell here, managing their lands via proxy? He would have to find out, so as not to give himself away with some foolish faux pas, but it would require reading or careful eavesdropping. He could hardly come out and ask, could he?

None of which meant there weren't plenty of topics he *could* openly discuss. And as they turned a corner into a second-floor hallway in what had to be a far wing of the palace, very near one of the corner towers, he did just that.

"Dame Zirresca didn't seem especially overjoyed to see me," he said with a shallow grin.

Kortlaus snorted. "She's been stomping about with her nose in the air for months. I think she'd all but convinced herself she'd already been declared Marshal Laszlan's successor. I wish I could have seen her reaction when she first got word you'd returned."

Indeed, Nycolos had guessed that was the situation the instant he'd been referred to as a knight who "would be Crown

Marshal." Equally apparent was Margrave Andarjin's desire to discredit him, though whether that was solely because he and Zirresca were friends, perhaps allies, or whether there was more to it, Nycolos couldn't guess.

She'd said something else to him on the palace steps, though, something about Kortlaus not being a threat.

"What of you?" he asked.

The baron's mail rattled as he shrugged. "Zirresca's never seen me as much competition. I think she believes I lack ambition, that my campaign for Crown Marshal is something I simply feel I'm due as the highest ranked of the three of us.

"I'm truly glad you're back, Nycos," he added with a broad grin, "but I still intend to be the one to prove her wrong."

*And more power to you. I intend not to be here.*

What he said was, "We'll see, won't we? Assuming His Majesty and Marshal Laszlan don't forbid it."

"Oh, they won't. You'll be chastised, given some punishment or other, but this is too important not to let our best compete for it. Especially if the rumors that Ktho Delios is mobilizing again have any truth to them..." He paused, chewing on either his lip or his mustache; from his half-pace behind, Nycolos couldn't quite tell.

"Nycos," Kortlaus said, far more seriously, "I don't know what your situation is with the Margravine Mariscal, why you haven't wanted to see her. But your position *is* a bit precarious just now. Leaving personal matters aside, you can't afford to lose any of the nobility who support your campaign over mine or Zirresca's. And she's still your loudest advocate."

"I... I won't." *Damn.* Again he was getting that odd, concerned look that could, with a gentle nudge, teeter over the edge into suspicion. "Kortlaus, the truth is, my journey back from the Outermark Mountains was far rougher, and my wounds bothering me worse, than I implied. I've no intention of avoiding Mariscal, and I'll speak to her when I'm able, I just… need some time first."

"Of course." The baron was instantly solicitous, gazing at Nycolos with a compassion that actually startled him. He found himself wondering, without any notion whence the thought had come, if anyone had *ever* looked at him that way before.

"You…" Kortlaus hesitated, glancing behind. "You truly trust the goblin?"

"The goblin is well within earshot and has a perfectly good name—" Smim began irritably. Nycolos cut him off.

"I do. Completely."

"Very well." Kortlaus turned. "You, uh… Swim, was it?"

"Smim, my Lord Curt-Louse."

The baron scowled, hard, but held his temper. "Smim, then. If you have it in you, I ask you to remain awake tonight, watch over your lord as he rests. Zirresca, for all her fuming, would not resort to dishonorable tactics now that Nycos has returned, but I'm not entirely certain I can say the same for the Margrave Andarjin. I'm probably doing him a disservice, but just in case… It cannot hurt to be watchful."

"On that, if nothing else" Smim said, "we find ourselves in absolute agreement."

————

Zirresca leaned against the cold stone beside a bust of Hasyan I, her arms crossed tight over her chest, struggling not to scowl at every courtier, page, or fellow knight who passed her by. The small stream of humanity exiting the throne room faded to a trickle and still she waited. Finally she leaned in to glare through the doorway.

Andarjin stood by the room's leftmost wall, engaged in animated conversation with a young woman. Her features were sharp, striking if not beautiful, and so traditionally noble that, along with her dark complexion, even a perfect stranger would have known her for a close relative of His Majesty.

Denuel Jarta, palatine to Hasyan III, rang his crystalline bell, summoning the woman to the king's side, and Margrave Andarjin at last departed from both her presence and the throne room.

"Are you sure you don't want to spend a bit more time in there?" Zirresca snapped as he emerged. "I haven't quite expired of old age yet!"

Andarjin raised that brow of his. "A bit testy are we?"

"Oh, just a bit, perhaps!" The knight forced herself to take a deep breath. "Sorry, Arj."

He smiled, gestured, and they began to walk the corridors of Oztyerva. "Concerned about Nycolos's return?" he asked, keeping his voice low.

"Shouldn't I be? Marshal Laszlan shouldn't be stepping down for a couple of years, yet. Plenty of time for Nycolos to recover from whatever setback his asinine escapade costs him! Gods almighty, Arj, he killed a dragon! That's going to overshadow whatever rules he might have broken, or whatever coarse company he's chosen to keep!"

"Possibly. You're still the better candidate, Zirresca. And whatever time he has, so do you. We'll prove it to everyone."

"Perhaps." Her scowl was back, now directed inward. "I reacted poorly to news of his return. My behavior on the steps was... unbecoming."

"Since when..." Andarjin held the rest of that thought while they split apart to hug opposite walls, allowing a group of oblivious and overly perfumed courtiers to pass between them, gossiping and giggling and nearly suffocating all who drew near, before coming together once more. "Gods, what a horrid stench! Anyway, since when do you care what Nycolos thinks of your behavior?"

"I care what *I* think of my behavior. Besides, we were in public."

"Perhaps, but—"

"What of Her Highness?" Zirresca asked, unwilling to speak any further of her own embarrassment. "Was she able to tell you anything of use?"

"Not particularly," the margrave replied, going along with the topic change. "She was fairly certain her father wanted to further discuss Nycolos's return and what it entails, but then, that was hardly a surprise." He smiled again, a mirror to his companion's frown. "Don't fret, Zirresca. Princess Firillia still supports everything we're trying to accomplish. If there's a word spoken in that council that we need to know, she'll tell me.

"In the interim," he added, halting at an intersection leading to different wings of Oztyerva, "I should go pen a letter to mother. I'm quite sure one of her agents here in the palace will let her know of Nycolos's return, but it would be inconsiderate of me not to inform her anyway."

"Well, we can't have that," Zirresca said, rather than any of the dozen questions she'd have preferred to ask—and which she knew Andarjin would never answer. Her Grace Pirosa, Archduchess of Vidirrad, ruled the largest of Kirresc's provinces and was, without doubt or competition, the most powerful and influential noble in the kingdom beside Hasyan himself. The knight often wondered just how much her friend's mother knew of her son's schemes and intentions, or whether she would approve if she did.

And Zirresca was just honest enough with herself to wonder, as Andarjin offered her a final wave and wandered off to his own chambers, if she refrained from asking because she knew the margrave wouldn't respond—or because she was afraid she wouldn't like the answer.

# CHAPTER TEN

Nycolos sat high in the stands alongside one of the many open fields that made up the back half of Oztyerva's grounds. He was clean for the first time in months and clad in genuine finery for… well, if one discounted natural scales, the first time in his very long life. Yet he radiated a cold hostility despite those pleasures, or the warming rays of the mid-morning sun. The many melees and jousts below, training for knights, palace guards, and even Prince Elias, scarcely registered in his mind. He was too preoccupied reliving recent events.

The remainder of last night, after Kortlaus had guided him to his chambers, had not gone well for him.

Nycolos had thought, when he first laid eyes upon his quarters, that this might prove the first truly comfortable night he'd spent since adopting this weak and ungainly body. As the bearer of a noble title, however minor, he was apparently entitled to a modicum of luxury. The canopied bed was decadently soft, the full wardrobe boasted every manner of outfit, and the dresser provided a mirror, a basin of clean water, and various toiletries and brushes in silver or ivory. The table bore a platter of fresh fruits, pungent cheeses, and cold meats, as well as a decanter of rich wine. A brass tub occupied one of the suite's several side rooms; it had already been filled, slowly warming over a layer of coals.

It was the merest pittance compared to what had once been his, what he deserved, but after the past weeks it was so inviting, Nycolos couldn't decide what to indulge in first.

And he had swiftly come to understand that things were not to go so smoothly as he might have preferred.

Smim, though proper and deferential as ever, had been irritable and unwilling to speak much. His master had finally wormed out of him that he was upset over the detail and apparent glee with which Nycolos had, during his recitation to the court, described the knight's slaughter of Smim's fellow goblins. The argument that this was the way a real human would have told the tale, oddly enough, did nothing to assuage Smim's ire.

Then, in the midst of that argument, and only just before Nycolos grew aggravated enough to *order* the goblin to move past it, had come a tentative knock upon the chamber door. Where he had anticipated the chirurgeon, however, he was faced instead with a small team of servants, maids and valets who all but swarmed him under as they poured into the room. His memory must be tricking him, but he swore their presence had made his chamber louder last night than the practice field was today.

Tired, uncertain as to custom and propriety, Nycolos had found himself efficiently stripped naked and herded into the tub. His initial instinct was to lash out, to fight, but they obviously expected him to accept, even relish, such treatment. So, though he found the entire notion demeaning, he reluctantly acquiesced. Once he was submerged, a trio of servants washed and scrubbed and combed until he was certain he must glisten like a new bronze statue while the rest went about tidying the chamber and absconding with the dust-encrusted outfit in which he'd traveled.

Pained by his injury, irritated at Smim and the fussing of the servants, and otherwise generally bewildered, Nycolos didn't really pay much notice to the procedure, or to the experience of being bathed by strangers. In retrospect, he could scarcely recall a moment of it, and it hadn't even occurred to him until later to wonder if, as a human, he was supposed to be somehow embarrassed by his nudity.

Only as he was being toweled dry by servants wielding soft and fluffy cloths did a new knock at the door signal the arrival of the chirurgeon: a straight-backed scarecrow of a fellow, clad in a stiff, dark tunic that buttoned up to his chin. Nycolos wondered how the man didn't find it ludicrously confining.

To him, as he had to no other, Nycolos admitted that a sliver of the weapon remained within his wound. The chirurgeon harumphed, and grumphed, and gave him a careful examination, poking and prodding at his chest until Nycolos nearly screamed in agony and had to restrain himself from taking the man's head clean off that reinforced collar.

And then, after all the study, all the poking about, all the pain, the chirurgeon's answer had been most unsatisfying. With the sliver so deep, he would need to consult with other healers, perhaps even seek sorcerous assistance, before it could possibly be removed, the wound properly treated. In the interim, take *these* herbs with every meal, keep the injury slathered in a salve made of *those*, and try not to engage in too much physical exertion. At which point, apparently in no way ashamed of his performance or lack of genuine answers, the man departed as pompously as he'd arrived.

Had he dared resume his proper form, Nycolos would have eaten him. Perhaps he still might.

Then, long after the servants departed and Nycolos finally began to stumble and grope his way toward slumber, had come yet another fist upon his door. He'd very nearly chosen to disregard it, but Smim answered before he could order him not to.

The young boy beyond, a page of some sort, had—after a momentary start, and fighting the urge to flee from the goblin—delivered a note from the Margravine Mariscal. It bore, in a flowery hand, a request that Nycolos meet for a brief conversation in "their garden, beneath the boughs of the quince trees."

Despite Kortlaus's earlier admonition regarding his supporters among the court, Nycolos ignored it. He wouldn't be here long enough to need any such support, and he was too fatigued to worry about maintaining appearances, or to care what sort of unimportant, human concerns anyone else wished to burden him with.

Closing the door in the page's face, he'd fallen into the bed and allowed the yielding, nigh-gelatinous mattress to engulf him...

The clash of blades dragged him from his reverie. On one end of the field, Kortlaus and two of his companions held a small mound of dirt against an assaulting force of four or five times their number. All were armed with dulled practice blades, primarily sabres and spears. Dozens of yards and several other faux skirmishes distant, Dame Zirresca dueled one on one with Prince Elias, oldest child and heir apparent of His Majesty, Hasyan III. The young man was a veritable giant, topping his father's own imposing height by nearly half a foot, yet his dark skin glistened with a sheen of sweat and, though clearly skilled, he was hard-pressed to defend himself against the far more experienced knight.

Each wielded a *szandzsya*, or as they were known beyond these borders, a Kirresci sabre-spear. A haft of two feet was topped by a gently curved blade of roughly equal length, sharpened on the crescent's inner edge. Although awkward in untrained hands, the *szandzsya* was a brutally effective weapon, cleaving armor and bone, crushing helms, or punching through mail—and that merely on foot. When swung from the back of a galloping charger, it was a veritable scythe of humanity.

Zirresca spun hers in a sword-like grip, both hands grasping the weapon near the blade, while Elias seemed to prefer a broader stance, fists further apart in a more traditional spear-fighter's hold. Nycolos, observing, found himself appreciating the weapon for its claw-like shape, to the extent he could bring himself to care.

"See, Master? Right there." Smim pointed a gnarled finger and Nycolos almost growled—or perhaps whimpered. The goblin had maintained a running commentary of the duels and skirmishes since they'd first sat down, and the wyrm-in-human-guise had kindled the faint spark of hope that Smim had finally wound down.

"This is precisely what I've been speaking of," Smim continued, clearly not having wound down at all. "She took the prince's legs out from under him and now she's just standing back, waiting for him to rise! What sort of combat lesson does that teach?"

"Human knights prefer to think of themselves as honorable warriors, Smim. Besides, I don't believe she'd do any such thing in a genuine battle. This is practice, after all, and he outranks her."

"Bah. Do you know what goblins call 'honorable' combatants, Master? We call them—"

"Food," both said in unison. "Yes," Nycolos continued alone. "I know."

"Even if this is training, even if the boy—"

"He's young, Smim, but he's a grown man."

"If you say so, Master. Even if the *young man* understands he shouldn't behave this way in a real fight, if all he's ever seen is his teachers pause to allow him to rise, who's to say he won't hesitate when the moment comes? This is foolish, the lot of it. And their armor? It—"

"You spent almost an hour pointing out the flaws in their armor, Smim. I don't actually need to hear it again."

"My point is," the goblin huffed, "I can think of a dozen ways to kill any one of these 'warriors.' Goblin children would never be instructed so poorly."

"Fewer than half of goblin children make it past the age of seven."

"Yes, but those of us who do know how to survive," Smim declared proudly.

Well, Nycolos couldn't argue with *that*.

"The humans can't be *so* incompetent," he pointed out, pausing to let a particularly loud flurry of steel on steel come to an end. "It only took one of them to kill me."

"Magic, Master. It was the power and protection of that damned sword, nothing to do with the wielder. Doesn't count."

*My chest feels as though it counts quite solidly.*

"And besides, you're not dead."

"Perhaps. I'm not yet certain this isn't just as—"

"Sir Nycolos?"

He turned and rose, bowing—as gallantly as he knew how—to the woman approaching across the stands. She wore flowing yellows and reds, the offspring of flower and flame, and peered at him from over a closed and folded fan which she tapped idly against her chin.

"My Lady Mariscal." He greeted her with a politeness he didn't feel. He might be unwilling to go out of his way to shore up friendships and alliances he wouldn't be needing, but no sense in deliberately damaging them, either.

She nodded, curt and unhappy. "I'm surprised to find you lazing about in the stands. You're not practicing with the others?"

"Chirurgeons orders, I'm afraid. I'm not to overly exert myself."

"I see." She seemed to be awaiting something. When it wasn't forthcoming, she cast a meaningful gaze, first at the lady-in-waiting she'd left some paces back—near enough for propriety's sake, far enough that she couldn't readily overhear their conversation—and then, with a faint moue, at the goblin.

*Ah.* "Smim?"

"Of course, Master. I'll just go somewhere else and be… somewhere else."

"Why don't you go keep the margravine's handmaiden company? We'd not want her to get lonely."

Smim smirked and scampered past the new arrival. The servant was professional and dignified enough not to flee, but she visibly recoiled and her *Eep!* was probably audible on the practice field below, despite the grunts and cries and the clash of blades.

"That is an unpleasant little creature," Mariscal sniffed once he was gone.

"Smim's not so bad. I wouldn't be here without him."

"If you say so." The tapping of the folded fan increased to match the beating of a nervous heart, then ceased. "Have I given you some manner of offense, baronet?"

"Uh, no, My Lady?"

"I was ecstatic to hear that you'd returned alive. I was so eager to see you."

"I, um." Nycolos hadn't the faintest idea why, but his instincts screamed that he trod the very precipice of dangerous territory. "And I you, of course."

"Then why are you acting this way?"

It wasn't a shout; the margravine was far too refined and self-possessed for that. Yet it clearly wanted to be.

"I…?"

"Surely you might have greeted me at court? Properly, chastely, as a peer and a friend, even if that's not—if nothing more?"

"I was… trying to stand before His Majesty and the others, to answer their questions. My fatigue, and my injuries—"

"Didn't stop you from insulting Margrave Andarjin, or spinning quite a lengthy tale, or interrogating Lord Kortlaus on the walk back to your chambers."

Nycolos could only manage a helpless shrug.

"And then later? My note?"

"I told you, Lady Mariscal. Exhaustion. Discomfort. I'd *just* returned from—"

"You could not even spare one moment? For me?"

Fists clenched now of their own accord. Nycolos still failed to understand what he might conceivably have done wrong. Was the woman insane? "Your message said nothing of this meeting being a matter of any urgency or importance—"

"It wasn't." Had she stood any nearer to him, he felt her tone would have frozen the humors in his body quite solid.

"Then why are you so troubled? We're both here, so talk to me now! Tell me what it is you wanted to say." He gestured down at the bench on which he'd earlier sat.

"I'm quite sure," she said, each word coated in frost, "that I cannot for the life of me recall what that might have been." She pivoted on her heel with an almost military precision and marched back across the stands, sparing him not one more word or glance. Her lady-in-waiting gratefully rushed to follow, leaving a smugly smirking Smim behind.

"What was that about, Master?" the goblin asked as he returned to Nycolos's side.

"I haven't the faintest—"

"Nycos!" Kortlaus appeared at the base of the stands, glaring upward in equal parts amusement and aggravation. "What in the name of Vizret's hell was *that*?"

"My, what an original question," Smim muttered.

"I'm sure," Nycolos said, dismissive and impatient, "that I've no idea what you're talking about."

"Oh, spare me. Are you trying to drive her away?"

*Would doing so negate the need for any more of these inane conversations?* "Not especially so."

"Then stop behaving like a donkey's arse and talk to the woman as if you value her a *little* more than your chamber pot!"

"I... What?"

"Oh, gods help him." Kortlaus's pious glance at the heavens neatly obscured from Nycolos his actual expression. "Get down here and grab a blade, you lackwit."

"I told you, the chirurgeon—"

"Yes, yes. I'll go easy on you." Then, in a stage whisper, "I'll make you look good before Mariscal's out of sight."

"Thank you." Nycolos's words were stiff as his spine. "That will not be necessary."

"Are you quite certain that injury was to your chest and not your head?"

"Leave the poor man be, Lord Kortlaus," Zirresca mocked from behind, where she'd stepped aside from her princely sparring partner. "Clearly whatever befell poor Nycolos in the Outermark has stripped him of any courage he possessed. Better that we've learned of it now than in an actual battle."

"Listen here, Nycos is injured and he's suffered through—"

But Nycolos was leaning forward over the bench as through straining against a leash.

"Master, no!" Smim hissed.

"I'll be fine, Smim."

"Yes, that's what concerns me."

Although the unhealing wound did indeed pain him, it was not the real reason Nycolos had avoided joining the others on the field that day. No, he'd meant to hide his complete ignorance of human styles and expertise in combat. That he could defeat any one of these foolish creatures one on one, even in this feeble body, he had no doubt—but it wouldn't be through besting them at their own arts.

His pride had been poked and scratched all morning, however: by his bitterness over his current state, his ignorance and defensiveness in the face of Margravine Mariscal's ire, and by the ridicule—however friendly—in Kortlaus's questioning and teasing. He allowed them to get away with such things, barely, to maintain his façade and because these were people whose friendship he might need until he was cured.

But Dame Zirresca? Who loathed him, and whom he was swiftly learning to despise in turn? He would take no more of that! If he revealed the limits of his martial knowledge here, what of it? What would they do? At worst they would assume his physical and mental state to be even more damaged than they had believed.

"Enough, Zirresca! You'll swallow those words, and maybe a blade along with them!"

The other knight recoiled, startled, then snarled. "Come, then!" She tossed her *szandzsya* end over end, tumbling over the stands. Nycolos snatched it out of the air with blinding speed.

As he bounded down the steps, Zirresca turned to Prince Elias. "May I, Your Highness?"

"Uh…" He hesitated, moths of doubt fluttering about his features. "I don't know about this, Dame Zirresca. I'm not so sure this is a good—"

"Nobody's going to be harmed *too* severely, Your Highness," she assured him. "Probably."

"I…" Already a crowd of soldiers and pages had gathered round, eager for the coming display, and Nycolos had reached the base of the stands. With obvious reluctance, the prince handed over his own weapon.

It was right about then, as Zirresca twisted to face him, that Nycolos registered the true nature of the foreign weapon he clutched. These were not the dulled, heavy practice blades Kortlaus and his partners had been using. Zirresca and Prince Elias had been training with live, razor-edged steel.

"First blood, then?" Kortlaus shouted, clearly desperate to at least put some half-sane restrictions on what was about to happen.

"Fine by me!" Zirresca agreed. Nycolos nodded, grunting.

They slammed together with twin screams.

Zirresca retreated before the sheer force of Nycolos's charge. Not with the controlled steps of any formal duel but at a near run, the combatants moved out into the field's center, their audience desperately stepping aside to clear them a path. His blade flashed in blinding arcs, driven not by skill but by an impossible, inhuman strength. If he could end this quickly, nobody should have opportunity to spot the deficiencies in his style.

She was having none of it. Her *szandzsya* spun almost like a baton in her two-fisted grip, constantly parrying even the fastest of Nycolos's strikes with either the blade or the thick haft. Where she couldn't deflect she pivoted away, sidestepping, always retreating. Whether or not she found her opponent's ferocity and near savage assault suspicious, she'd adapted to it instantly, allowing him to tire himself out while she avoided his clumsy, albeit powerful, blows.

Yet he *wasn't* tiring, would not tire for a good while. Even as he came at her Nycolos grinned, glorying in the power that was, if far less than he once boasted, still greater than she could ever expect. He hacked and thrust, utterly without finesse, driving her back, always back…

Zirresca must have recognized that he wasn't about to falter, that fatigue was not an ally on which she could rely. She broke the pattern of her retreat in midstep, lashing out with a low kick. Against a normal opponent, it might well have broken an ankle. Against Nycolos, it produced a jolt of pain and set him staggering, off-balance.

Her own sabre-spear whistled in a short arc that would have left an ugly gash across his chest. Nycolos hurled himself away, desperate to avoid the oncoming blade, and found himself landing hard on his back, nostrils filled with the scent of crushed grass, staring up at the bright blue sky.

Still Zirresca attacked, spinning, weapon sweeping around her and then upward, her first strike flowing smoothly into a second. Nycolos saw the *szandzsya* rise over him and begin its downward arc. Pushing with both heels, he slid himself across the grass and rolled to his feet.

His opponent's blade had plowed a furrow into the earth where he'd lain a heartbeat earlier. Zirresca retreated a step, shaking soil from the weapon, studying him with a narrowed gaze. He tried to mimic her earlier motion, spinning the *szandzsya* in both fists, but he knew he must appear awkward and slow in comparison. Indeed, he could hear puzzled mutters among the onlookers, wondering at his apparent ineptitude.

His face warmed as his embarrassment grew, though he was scarcely aware of it and would wonder only later what the sensation meant, if it was another human peculiarity. In the moment, he knew only that he had made himself look the fool, had potentially revealed an element of his deception, and had accomplished nothing in exchange.

Now Zirresca came at him and it was he who retreated. Her *szandzsya* struck first from one side then another, and even where he avoided the blade the heavy wooden shaft often knocked him staggering. He couldn't even pretend any longer, couldn't attempt to mimic what little technique he'd seen. He augmented his human form, allowing the muscles beneath the flesh to grow as swift and as strong as he could without becoming visibly unnatural, and even then it was only with the greatest effort that he parried Zirresca's attacks. Had it been a matter of pure skill, had he been as limited as a human, the struggle would be long over.

So be it. With what little corner of his attentions he could yet spare, he concentrated his innate magics on the skin he wore, hardening it right to the very edge of where it would take on inhuman hues or the texture of scale.

And not a moment too soon. Zirresca's weapon ended its spin in an underhand grip, held flat against her arm. She cross-stepped past him, twisting her body, dragging the inner curve of the *szandzsya* across his ribs and his left arm. She halted, facing him, butt of her sabre-spear planted, forcing her quickened breathing to slow, presumably so that she might accept his concession or perhaps lightly mock his clumsy efforts and his defeat...

Nycolos managed not to laugh aloud, but couldn't suppress a nasty grin, at the expression on her face when she saw she'd drawn no blood.

His first blow, unexpected and oh, so swift, struck the weapon on which she leaned, knocking it aside and staggering her. He stepped in and delivered a swift punch to her midsection, doubling her over, and then yanked her *szandzsya* completely away with that unoccupied hand. A final blow, again with the butt end of his sabre-spear, sent the knight flying. She landed hard, hissing in pain, hand rising to what must surely have been a bruised if not fractured collarbone.

Standing over her, Nycolos tossed aside his own weapon. With hers, he deliberately, even contemptuously, reached down and poked just the very tip of the blade against her jaw, drawing a tiny squiggle of blood across the faded scar on her chin.

"I believe this means I win," he told her.

Her glower of overwhelming hatred would have done one of his own kind, his *true* kind, proud. "I hit you. I know I did!"

He lifted an arm to reveal the gash in kaftan and tunic but not skin. "Clearly you were mistaken. Perhaps you need more practice."

"You son of a—!"

"Sir Nycolos Anvarri!"

He looked up, only noticing that every man and woman present had stared at him in various degrees of bewilderment and dismay—perhaps even disdain—now that they were looking away toward the source of that shout. He, in turn, followed their gaze, and frowned.

*Where the hell had he come from?*

Marshal Laszlan stomped across the field, heavy-footed, as though the grass had recently offended his mother. His face bore a ruddy tint beneath his bristling beard.

"Is this the man I've trained for years? The man I permitted to vie for my office? I am ashamed of you, Sir Nycolos, and so should you be!"

The *szandzsya* creaked, wood threatening to split, in his grip. "Marshal—"

"No. I don't want to hear it right now. I've seen pages just come of age fight with more proper form than you've just displayed here. And your behavior! I've no idea how you could *possibly* have bested Dame Zirresca, incompetently as you wielded that weapon…"

The woman, clambering to her feet with the assistance of several friends and Prince Elias himself, growled low in her throat.

"…but to show such disdain for a fallen opponent—"

"So," Nycolos interrupted, that act itself drawing gritted teeth from Orban and gasps from several of the others, Kortlaus included, "it's only permissible to show such disdain for an opponent *before* battle? Convenient that you arrived late enough to miss the insults she cast in my teeth before blades entered into it."

Jaws dropped and eyes widened. No one could believe what they were hearing from him. Although he was quite certain the act was rude in and of itself, Nycolos departed without awaiting further word or permission from the Crown Marshal, determined to be gone before he could make his situation more dire still.

Smim fell in behind him, but while Nycolos could sense, could literally smell, the disapproval radiating from his smaller servant, the goblin wisely chose to keep his own counsel for a change.

---

As a knight of the realm and gentry in residence at Oztyerva Palace, Nycolos was entitled—and, more often than not, expected—to dine with His Majesty, along with a veritable throng of other nobles, courtiers, advisors, favored guests, and so forth. (It was an invitation that, as had been made politely but explicitly clear, did not extend to his goblin retainer.) On his first night back, nobody had looked for him to attend, not as exhausted as he had clearly been. Tonight, however, was another story.

A story that could have most kindly been dubbed a farce, and more accurately a disaster.

The dining hall was the same carpeted, buttressed, and portrait-adorned stone as the bulk of the palace, and occupied primarily by an enormous table of finest wood.

No, tables, plural. One, smaller and standing upon a slightly raised floor, seated the king himself, his offspring, and his closest advisors and honored guests. The other, lower and much, much longer, was for everyone else, seated in strict descending order of rank, from nearest the royal family to farthest.

Nycolos, having squeezed himself into dark and stiff-necked formalwear that nearly made him claustrophobic, had deliberately arrived as late as he could without giving offense. The near breach of propriety drew some disapproval, but far less attention than he might have attracted had he been unable to find his proper seat. As everyone else had already arrived, however, it was simple enough to estimate roughly where he would fall, as a baronet, and then choose appropriate open setting.

He planted himself upon well-cushioned velvet, unfolded his napkin and tucked it into his collar as the others had done. It was the last thing he managed to do wholly right that evening.

Domatir Matyas, the court prelate, rose to speak a blessing over the meal, over His Majesty and his guests, just as he'd done over the court gathering of the previous day. Thankfully for Nycolos's swiftly waning patience, this prayer was shorter than the prior.

Then the servants brought out the first course, an array of pickled fish and hen's eggs served on a bed of vegetables so heavily spiced one could practically taste them from the kitchen. The dishes were wood, far more practical than the crystal, ceramic, or precious metal one might expect in a royal dining hall, though the silver utensils and glass goblets more than made up for it. The table manners and customs, too, were a peculiar combination of fine and functional; Kirresc's was a culture that celebrated its joy in good food and drink, yet also bound itself in custom. Noble etiquette was, perhaps, less convoluted than in some other nations, but what rules there were must be observed in every detail.

And it was here that Nycolos made his first blunder. Oh, not with his manners in and of themselves. He was quite careful to study the men and women about him, to note their every move. He learned swiftly enough that knife and fork never switched hands, that both must be laid down before a drink was lifted to his lips, that hands never dipped below the table nor elbows rested atop it, that platters were passed always with the right hand, that the silverware was laid *thus* to indicate one was finished with his dish but *that* way if one awaited a second helping, that one always requested a dish or seasoning from a servant even if one's fellow guests could easily pass it along, and so on and so forth.

Irritating, particularly to one who had once been accustomed to eating whole cattle and the equivalent as a cure for peckishness, but hardly impenetrable. No, his error was in being caught staring at those around him. Some flinched away, some boldly returned his examination, but all seemed to take it as tacit permission to openly discuss amongst themselves what had already been on their minds: Namely, the events of that morning and Nycolos's mental and physical state in general. Their conversations, ranging from hushed whisper to arrogant proclamation, rang out over the clatter of dinnerware.

The rampant supposition grew wilder and, in its own way, more entertaining as the appetizer course concluded, the dishes and scraps removed and replaced with vinegar-drenched salads by the serving staff's well-practiced sleight of hand. Nycolos had taken a bad head injury, some theorized, one that had transformed his entire personality. He suffered from the dragon's dying curse. The goblin was a tribal shaman and held the knight in thrall with foul witchcrafts. Tivador Valacos—one of the youngest knights in attendance and son of Amisco Valacos, Judge Royal of Kirresc—even suggested to his dinner companion, in a low murmur, that perhaps Tzavalantzaval had not been slain at all, and that Nycolos either labored under the wyrm's evil influence or was burdened by the guilt of his lies and disgrace.

That was one theory that, however inaccurate, Nycolos had to find some means of quieting. He wanted nobody dwelling on the possibility of the dragon's survival.

Not that he could find any willing conversationalists with whom he might readily change the topic. Kortlaus seemed to be having difficulty meeting his gaze, and reddened anew each time he tried, clearly embarrassed for his friend and utterly uncertain of what, if anything, he might do about it. Margravine Mariscal wouldn't even try, refusing to so much as glance his way, maintaining polite interest in her neighbors' chatter while absently chasing errant cabbage around her plate with a fork that hadn't touched her lips that evening. Zirresca, on the other hand, refused to look anywhere *but* his direction, clenching her knife so hard her arm trembled, glaring with hatred hot enough to overcook any dish carelessly set between them.

Even the royal table provided no succor, no relief from the constant scrutiny. Orban whispered, as usual, in His Majesty's ear, and while Nycolos could hear nothing of the conversation, he didn't think it arrogant to assume he might be its subject. Hasyan's other friends and counselors watched either Nycolos or their liege himself, and Princess Firillia studied the newly returned knight with a frank and oddly contemplative pity. Nycolos had to set down the goblet he'd just lifted, filled with a sour cherry wine, lest it shatter in his fist.

Only Prince Elias, of them all, seemed largely oblivious to the ubiquitous disquiet, or at least to the source of that unease. On occasion he would raise his head, perhaps seeking to pinpoint a nagging wrongness, but otherwise remained contentedly focused on his meal.

It was between the salad and the main course—a slow roasted and heavily flavored stew of mutton, by the aromas wafting from the kitchen—that Nycolos's well of patience ran dry and he made his second error of the evening.

"If I'd known I was to be the night's entertainment," he announced during a brief lull in the conversation around him, "I'd have prepared a performance for you all. Juggling, or perhaps an amusing ditty."

A few words choked off with quick gasps, the clatter of knives and forks laid down, and then silence save for the crackling and popping of the torches.

"Sir Nycolos," Denuel Jarta berated him from the king's table, "this is unseemly."

Kortlaus rose with a scrape of chair legs. "Begging your pardon, palatine, but has not the behavior of this entire gathering been unseemly tonight? Sir Nycolos deserves better than to be gossiped of this way."

Several people voiced their assent, Mariscal—albeit somewhat reluctantly—included. A few others looked down at their plates, properly chastised. Prince Elias leaned over to Prelate Matyas, who sat beside him, and loudly whispered, "What's going on?"

"Later, your Highness."

Most of those at the lower table, however, seemed unapologetic. "While I certainly intended no offense," young Tivador began, "after his disgraceful behavior this morning, I hardly think Sir Nycolos has any right to expect—"

"No, my Lord Kortlaus is quite correct." Margrave Andarjin also stood, seeming oblivious to Tivador's shock—and to his friend Zirresca's, who looked ready to strike him for defending the man who'd humiliated her. Andarjin bowed at the neck, first to the baron, then to Nycolos. "Our behavior tonight, *my* behavior, has undeniably been inappropriate, even offensive, and for that I apologize.

"Indeed," he continued, turning in place to face each diner in turn, "we owe Sir Nycolos a debt we can never repay. He set out a brave and faithful knight of the court, to rid Kirresc, and other nations of Galadras besides, of a great threat. That he obviously gave the best of himself in the execution of his duty—his health, his honor, his dream of someday serving His Majesty in any greater capacity—is a sacrifice that should be revered, not mocked. I thank you, Sir Nycolos, and I am certain that in this I am not alone."

Nycolos knew it would be yet another mistake to stack atop all the others, that it would only encourage further talk and speculation, but the other option was open bloodshed. Ignoring Andarjin's disingenuous smile, Zirresca's ill-concealed gloating, the helpless pain of Kortlaus and Mariscal, and the growing whispers of everyone else, he pushed back his chair, forced a "With Your Majesty's permission" through a portcullis of clenched teeth, and stalked from the dining hall.

# CHAPTER ELEVEN

"Inhale. Good. Now hold that as long as you're able and for God's sake, try not to flinch."

Nycolos obeyed, swallowing a grunt of pain at the pressure that deep lungful of air put on his unhealed wound. A second helping of grunt followed the first as the woman, too, prodded at that tender spot.

Lady Ilkya resembled nothing so much as a tree struck by lightning. Tall, gaunt of frame, spindly of limb, dark of both complexion and demeanor. She had little patience for the foibles of those less intelligent than she, which she believed was almost everyone, and was almost as lacking in sympathy for the discomforts her patients endured. Nycolos found it a particularly galling attitude, not merely because of the pain he suffered beneath her ministrations, but because he'd been forced to wait in this damn nest of squabbling nobles and petty rivalries and—and *humans*—for almost a week before she arrived!

But she was also, Hasyan's chirurgeon had assured Nycolos upon summoning the knight to his own suite of chambers, which included his operating theater, the single greatest healer he had ever met, versed in methods both mundane and mystical.

That latter had sent a frisson of nerves through Nycolos. As she pressed her fingers around his wound, however, muttered invocations and slathered him with herbal and alchemical salves, then sniffed at the aromas they'd produced, he grew convinced that any mage-craft she knew was indeed limited to the medicinal arts, used solely to augment her own learned skills. Ilkya was no true sorceress or witch, and highly unlikely to sense that the body he wore, and which she now struggled to treat, was not originally his own.

Besides, this was why he had come to Kirresc, why he had assumed the form of the man who had nearly slain him: to acquire just this treatment. For the promise of freedom, to have that cursed sliver of blade excised from his breast and be allowed to take on his true shape and his true name, he would risk, and endure, far worse. Even through the agony as her magics warmed and chilled the intruding steel, as she poked beneath the skin and deep into muscle with needles and probes, as the discharge of putrefaction burst from his flesh and dribbled in warm rivulets down his torso, he couldn't quite keep from smiling at what was to come.

Then, as if she'd sensed his earlier worries, "You don't happen to know any mighty sorcerers, do you?"

It was a half-breathed mutter, one he wasn't certain he'd been meant to hear, but it set his mind to racing. Or perhaps, imagining a near future in which he'd returned to his old body and his old life, his thoughts had already been inclined toward memories of that life.

*Ondoniram.* Oh, Tzavalantzaval had met many a practitioner of the occult in his time—human, fey, dragon, and other— but none had possessed half Ondoniram's right to the title of wizard. The old man had been longer lived than some of Tzavalantzaval's own cousins, and potent enough to challenge the wyrm himself. Until Nycolos Anvarri and Wyrmtaker, no human had come so close to slaying Tzavalantzaval as Ondoniram once had.

But the ancient mage was long dead, and wouldn't likely have been inclined to help Nycolos now even had he not been.

Which train of thought, as a dog chasing its tail, finally circled back around to the start. With a sudden spike of fear,

Nycolos voiced the question that *should* have been his very first thought. "Why do you ask?"

The old stick of a human stepped back, carefully wiping each of her tools clean with a wine-soaked rag, then placing them—in their precise order, of course—in the pockets of a deerskin case. "I can treat your injury," she informed him. Her tone was haughty, matter of fact, yet she wouldn't *quite* meet his gaze. "The infection should be gone within weeks, the pain greatly reduced, even absent more often than not. Your body will heal around the sliver, rendering it unlikely to cause you any further harm. Within months, I doubt you'll have cause to often recall it's even there."

"But…?" *No. No, no, no, no, NO!*

"But," she admitted with a long-suffering sigh, as though *he* were at fault for thwarting *her*, "the fragment is too deeply embedded, too near your organs. Without magics far more precise and more potent than anything with which I'm familiar, it would be…"

*Don't you dare say it, you filthy, ignorant little primate! Don't you dare think it! Don't you dare!*

"…impossible to remove without killing you.

"I'm sorry, Sir Nycolos," though she didn't sound very sorry at all, save maybe to have found a challenge she couldn't best, "but I'm afraid you're simply going to have to live with it."

---

In a distant wing of the palace, Andarjin of Vidirrad and Dame Zirresca lazed about a sitting room that was one small portion of the margrave's vast suite. As heir apparent to the greatest duchy in the kingdom, currently dwelling within Oztyerva to learn the ins and outs of his Majesty's court—as was traditional for all firstborn sons and daughters of Kirresc's high nobles to do for several years—he was entitled to a standard of living not much below that of the royal family themselves.

Servants came and went, ensuring that the decanter of fine drink on the table remained no less than half full, and satisfying the dictates of propriety by never leaving their young lord and his female guest alone together.

They were, however, well trained to remain out of earshot when not needed, and to make a point of never hearing a word spoken even when they could have. Not that either Andarjin or Zirresca had spoken at all in minutes.

"Come on, now," the margrave finally said after a particularly large sip of the pear brandy they currently enjoyed. "You know I'd not offend you for the world, Zirresca, but this sulking isn't remotely your best look."

"You weren't there, Arj!" she snarled, twisting the goblet between two fingertips. "You didn't see it!"

"No, but seeing as how I've heard the tale nigh unto a dozen times now…"

"I want him destroyed! I want him cowed! Beaten! I want—!"

Yes, yes, he'd heard *that* a dozen times, too. "Zirresca," he said with far more patience than he felt, "Nycolos isn't a threat. He's not even an obstacle. You want him destroyed? He's doing a magnificent job accomplishing that on his own, wouldn't you say?" He took another swig. "You should try actually drinking some of this, you know, instead of just spinning it about. It's an excellent vintage."

The knight's grunt was unamused.

"You need to calm yourself," he continued more seriously. "Prove yourself more patient than he. He really is demolishing what little regard, and what little chance at the position, he has remaining. We should let him flounder, and focus our attentions on Lord Kor—"

An imperious knock on the suite's front door silenced him. Since his private guards stationed in the hall wouldn't have permitted anyone without official business or sufficient rank to disturb him, Andarjin waved at one of his servants at the room's periphery. The man bowed his head and departed.

A few exchanged words, muffled by the cold stone walls, and then he returned a moment later. "Her Highness," he announced, "the Princess Firillia."

Andarjin rose, of course, as did Zirresca, then joined the various servants in a series of deep bows.

"Oh, get up, you two." Firillia swept into the room, clad in a golden gown that contrasted beautifully with her complexion but wasn't quite formal enough for court proper. Her attendants filtered in behind her, joining Andarjin's at a polite distance.

The princess took a place at the table, straddling the chair in a casual and most unladylike pose, and poured herself a brandy before any of the servants could draw near enough to do it for her.

"My dear," Andarjin said, seating himself beside her, "there are people here who would be glad to wait on you, myself incl—"

"Don't fret over it, Arj. I promise, I'm capable of pouring a decanter with my own two dainty hands. I've known how for, oh, at least a year or two, now. You pick up all *sorts* of skills observing the royal court."

Zirresca snorted, then politely hid her grin behind her glass.

Andarjin's own chuckle was, perhaps, a tad forced. He waited until Firillia placed one hand on the table, then gently laid his atop it. "To what do I owe the honor, your Highness?"

"I assume the two of you are speaking of Zirresca's campaign?"

"Indeed, yes."

"And perhaps of Sir Nycolos?"

The knight's smile perished of natural but swift causes and toppled from her face.

"Yes," the margrave confirmed. "I was just telling Zirresca that Nycolos is doing splendidly at sabotaging himself, and there's no need for us to be all that concerned with—"

"You have *no* idea."

That certainly got *both* their attention. "Has something happened? Is that why you've come?"

Firillia took a deep draught, then set it down. "I'm not all that fond of pear brandies," she admitted. "I much prefer plum or apple. But this isn't bad."

"Your Highness, *please...*"

She laughed, then. "Sorry, Arj. Just having a bit of fun with you." Her expression sobered quickly. "Though in truth, it's nothing to laugh at. It's going to cost us hundreds of *zlatka* to replace the tools and furniture he destroyed, and Lady Ilkya has declared that she will never again work, or so much as set foot, in Oztyerva. Gods know how long it may take, or how many additional *zlatka*-worth of gifts, for her to reconsider."

Neither of her two companions seemed entirely able to follow. "Are you saying..." Zirresca eventually asked. "That is, Nycolos *attacked* her?"

"Not... specifically," Firillia hedged. "Apparently, whatever news she delivered, he didn't care for it. As I've heard it told, he seemed to go mad. Hurling tables, shattering tools, even taking doors off their hinges. He made no *deliberate* move to harm her or the others, but she was nearly crushed under a bench, and a number of the guards who subdued him suffered contusions and even a few broken bones."

"I should go look in on them," Zirresca mused, her expression a study in contradictions. "Make certain they're taken care of."

Andarjin, for his part, was smirking openly. "I'm sure they will be. But yes, you should make an appearance." If he noted Firillia's brief flash of disdain, or that she chose that moment to remove her hand from his, he gave no sign.

"What happened to him out there?" Zirresca asked, for all that she well knew nobody could answer. "Nycolos was always impulsive, but this sort of temper..."

"Why should you care?" the margrave sneered.

"Far safer to know, wouldn't you think? If only to anticipate whatever else he might do, or in case Kirresc is ever, gods forbid, threatened by another dragon? Besides, whatever else I might think of him, Nycolos has always been a strong warrior, and loyal to his liege. He would be—or would have been—useful, once he'd accepted me as Crown Marshal."

"Bah. Perhaps. Still and all, it's better this way. It certainly makes the road forward easier for you, and thus for all of us. That's worthy of some small celebration, no?" Chortling, he reached for his goblet.

And it was then, as he faced her, that he felt, and begin to wither beneath, Princess Firillia's frosty mien. "This sort of gloating," she informed him, "is not becoming in a man who would be king."

Andarjin physically recoiled. "Who, then? Your brother? I am by far the better candidate—!"

"So you've convinced me, Margrave, otherwise I'd not be here at all. But I've made you no vows yet—of any sort—and Kirresc has others I might choose to support, or who might be enticed to support *me*."

A moment of burning, prideful anger, then Andarjin dropped to one knee. "You're right, of course, your Highness. My love. That was inappropriate of me. I humbly apologize."

Zirresca looked away, made deeply uncomfortable by the whole spectacle.

"You're not wrong, for all that," Firillia said, utterly failing—deliberately, no doubt—to address the issue of whether she'd yet elected to forgive Andarjin's impropriety. "If we're to assist Zirresca in succeeding Orban as Crown Marshal, we're probably better served in focusing on Lord Kortlaus. I truly don't think Nycolos is likely to prove any further competition."

————

The following days made Nycolos long for a return to the dreary, painful exhaustion of his slow hike across the Outermark. At least then, he'd seen a possible dawn at the far end of the impenetrable darkness. Then, he'd had hope.

None but Smim could possibly understand his reaction to Lady Ilkya's pronouncement. None of them understood that it wasn't enough to treat the trauma around the splinter of broken blade, wasn't enough that it should soon cease to bother him save under the worst of circumstances. How could they?

But Nycolos understood the repercussions. No matter how much healing, how much scar tissue wrapped the cursed thing, as soon as his heart became that of a dragon it would again begin to move, to seek, slowly digging through whatever his body might place in its path.

Returning to who he was, what he was, meant death. And Nycolos sincerely wondered, now that he faced not merely weeks or months as a human, but perhaps the rest of his life, if that death might be worth it.

He ceased to shave, to bathe or allow himself to be bathed, even to eat save when the ache of hunger grew intolerable. He rarely appeared where he was expected—at court, on the field, at his Majesty's table—and as his foul disposition and even fouler stench grew ever more offensive, fewer and fewer objected to or even commented upon his absence.

"What can I do for you?" Margravine Mariscal had asked, nearly begged, standing in his doorway one afternoon. He had ignored messenger after messenger from her, and even her own pounding at the portal. Only when she'd ordered several palace guards to force the door had he deigned to open it, and then only because he wouldn't be able to lock the world out if it were damaged.

She seemed unsure what to do with her hands, intertwining her fingers and nearly wringing them one moment, fists clenching in anger the next. Her tear-sheened eyes drifted from his ever more gaunt and unwashed face to the wreck of the chambers about him. When they once alighted, however briefly, on the goblin who stood back in the far corner, Smim could only shrug.

"What can you do?" Nycolos repeated, his throat a heap of gravel.

"Yes! Anything!"

"What can you *do*?!"

And damn if he didn't nearly tell her. After all, why not? What had he left to lose? He almost blurted the entire story, almost shouted it in her face, daring her to understand what he was and what he'd lost. How eager would she be to help him then?

Almost, but he did not. It wasn't worth the effort, wasn't worth the pain.

"You," he told her, "can leave. Me. *Alone!*" He didn't *think* the slamming door had actually struck her, but he didn't care enough to open it back up and be sure. The sound of her fading steps meant she was well enough to walk away, and that would suffice.

What few people had been making an effort ceased calling after that. Kortlaus still tried to strike up conversations whenever Nycolos appeared outside his quarters, but each time he found himself ignored, and slowly his attempts grew more and more perfunctory, until they were scarcely more than a polite nod and a "Good afternoon." Mariscal uttered not another word to him, though he knew she watched his every move. Once, even Prince Elias had approached him as he'd wandered one of Oztyerva's various gardens, this one made up primarily of poppies, peonies, and tulips.

"Sir Nycolos."

"Mm. Your Highness."

"Listen, I… I can't, that is, I obviously have no notion what's troubled you so since you came home…"

"Obviously."

"You've been through something I can't possibly understand," the earnest prince bulled on. "But I know you're a good man, Nycos. And I know you don't want to be hurting people the way you have been."

"You're absolutely right, your Highness."

"Good! I'm glad to—"

"You *can't* possibly understand. With your permission?" Not that he'd waited for it before stomping on his way.

And so it might have continued, Nycolos further and further isolating himself until he was nothing but a hermit in the midst of the palace, friendless, shunned by all and without purpose or meaning.

The day things changed was a holy day, though Nycolos hadn't heard, and didn't much care, to what purpose. This observance in particular was sacred not to the followers of the many gods of the Empyrean Choir, but rather to the monotheist Deiumulin. They accounted for a minority of the nobles and servants in the palace, and indeed of the Kirresci populace, but it was a sizable, significant one. As such, while they carried less weight and held less influence than the Empyreans, a few of their holiest days were granted official status.

Today, then, was a time of pious ritual and sermons for some, and a day of feasting and freedom from work for a great many others. Smim convinced his master to leave their chambers, however briefly, if only to acquire some food to bring back. This was, after all, an opportunity for unusual dishes and finely prepared fare that wouldn't require him to tolerate the presence, and the unforgiving disapproval, of the king's table.

The mismatched pair were returning to their quarters—Nycolos carrying plates heaped with cuts of roast boar, braised in garlic butter, Smim balancing a pair of bowls full of a sharply scented paprika-heavy venison-and-vegetable goulash—when they turned a corner of the winding stone passageways and found themselves face to face with a group of young knights and other gentry.

These were led by Sir Tivador and some of his friends, and while the young knight was normally of a more polite, well-bred disposition, today an excess of drink, the presence of so many peers, and the general disdain in which courtly gossip held Nycolos, all conspired against his better nature.

In all fairness, though, it was one of Tivador's companions—a slender, blond-haired young man, baronet of something or other, whose names and lands Nycolos could not have cared about less had he been fully unconscious—who started it all. "Has Sir Nycolos actually emerged from his den? Perhaps even beasts have a limit to how far they're willing to foul their own nests!"

Caught up in the spirit of things and the sniggers of his friends, Tivador then chimed in. "I imagine he's simply run out of rats to hunt. Poor fellow. It must be difficult learning to live as a goblin with only the one instructor."

More sniggers. Nycolos ignored them and continued walking. Smim followed, but as he passed, he couldn't help but comment, "As he clearly hasn't seen one *human* worth modeling himself after, perhaps one ought not blame him if he's elected to give being a goblin a try."

Consternation rippled through the small crowd, a low grumble spreading like a spilled chamber pot, as drunken minds processed the insult. They pursued, gathering angrily around the pariah knight and his goblin cohort.

"Filthy beast!" Tivador spat. "You've no right even to be here, much less to eat so well. That food was prepared for Kirresci, for *people*, not animals!"

Had he held himself to words alone, he would have been just fine. Had he chosen to knock the bowls from Smim's grasp, still he would probably have suffered no consequences. In his slightly pickled fury, however, he darted ahead and wildly smacked aside the plates Nycolos had carried, sending boar and juices spraying over the walls, the carpet, and the unwashed and sullen baronet himself.

Nycolos never could remember snapping, that endless instant where rage and humiliation overwhelmed the near fugue through which he'd trudged for days.

He saw the world through a sheet of hot white, illuminating the stone and the humans around him more brightly than any torch. He felt flesh giving beneath his knuckles, twisting under his fingertips; lifted men without effort to send them hurtling along the corridor, cracked bones in his grip, pried several dislocated teeth from the meat of his hand.

Shouts and screams, impacts and footsteps, echoed in his ears, and he failed to recognize that he was in the midst of them, even adding to them. Only a single voice, shrill and inhuman, uttered slow, calming sounds amidst the incomprehensible cries, but he could not, initially, make them out.

"Master… Master… Sir Nycolos… Master…"

And then, far, *far* more softly, so that it was nearly lost in the chaos even to his preternatural hearing, "Tzavalantzaval…"

Nycolos's vision gradually cleared. Sir Tivador and his compatriots lay or crouched throughout the hall. Many were curled in tight balls around this injury or that, while others faced him with bloodied jaws, swelling features—and half-naked blades. None were armored or as fully armed as they might have been on duty, but light sabres and the occasional arming sword or heavy dagger would prove deadly enough. None had fully drawn steel, as of yet, but only because Nycolos had halted his own advance.

And there was a peculiar weight dangling from his fists.

*Smim.* The goblin gazed calmly at him, despite the fact that Nycolos's talons had ripped through his tunic and drawn shallow furrows of blood on his chest, holding him aloft.

*Talons?* He had no recollection of sprouting talons. And he realized, with a start, that it was only because Smim blocked their view that the others hadn't spotted them.

Carefully he put the goblin down, transforming his fingers back to human with a moment's effort. "Thank you," he mumbled gracelessly.

"You're welcome, Master. I couldn't allow you to kill them—"

"You. Couldn't *allow*?"

Smim winced, clearly aware it had been the wrong thing to say. "Poor choice of words, Master. What I mean is—"

"You do not *allow* me to do anything, Smim!"

"I know. I meant—"

"Besides, what's the difference? What matter if they know that—"

"You're distraught, Master!" Smim *must* have been desperate, if he dared interrupt when Nycolos was already irritated. Then, again more softly, "There are still good reasons for keeping your secrets. Besides, I've developed a hypothesis as to why you've been, well, behaving as you have. You—"

Nycolos shoved him away in disgust, glaring equally at him and the watching—and often moaning—knights. "You're so concerned with my behavior, are you? These ladies and gentlemen seem to share your concerns. Why don't you talk it over with them?"

He marched through the thick of them, slowly, hoping somebody would attack or try to stop him. When nobody did, he turned the nearest corner without looking back and made for the doors, determined to leave all of this—the knights, the court, Oztyerva, even Smim—behind.

———

He wandered without destination or purpose through the streets of Talocsa, just another tiny segment of first this crowd, then that one. The entire world danced slowly about him, or so it seemed: the people to every side; crisp dead leaves and the hems of kaftans, coats, and skirts below; the lowering autumn clouds, leaning listlessly on the minarets and flagpoles above. Nycolos ignored them all, and the leaves and clouds, at least, politely did him the same courtesy in return.

His fellow pedestrians were often another matter altogether.

Oh, many paid him no mind, seeing—if they noticed him at all—just another passerby, perhaps a holiday reveler or one of the many citizens who, for reasons of obligation or necessity, could not afford to take the day away from his labors. Quite a few others, however, couldn't help but note the rich cut and fabrics of his wardrobe, marking him as the upper class. Of course, as soon as he drew even remotely near, his overall slovenly appearance, unshaven and unwashed whiskers, and the rank stench of those clothes—which was grotesquely mixed with, and not remotely masked by, the fresher odor of pork greases and gravies—conflicted wildly with that initial impression. Thus did the people who took any notice of him swiftly draw away in confusion and distaste, all of which suited Nycolos's mood well enough.

Still, the open revulsion and accompanying whispers grew to irritate him. They were unwanted attention, and an even more unwanted reminder of the universal disdain under which he'd been crushed throughout Oztyerva Palace. Without conscious intent, then, and despite lacking any real sense of the city's layout, Nycolos made his way toward poorer, rougher parts of town by moving in the direction of least overt disapproval.

The clothes grew less refined, more elegant fabrics giving way to meanly dyed wools and worn leathers, their colors drab compared to what had come before. Gaps appeared in the paving stones, and entire side streets were nothing but dirt. The buildings grew smaller, more dilapidated, the whitewash filthy and peeling where it wasn't entirely absent. More and more of the passersby were laborers, and those who *were* celebrants appeared more frequently drunk, reeking of cheap wines and beers. The ubiquitous stench of refuse left to rot, chamber pots emptied from upper story windows, and unwashed laundry permeated the wood, the earth, the people, so that even the fiercest storms could never wash it away.

And Nycolos, as he'd hoped, looked—and smelled—far less out of place, though his garb still attracted the occasional wandering glance.

Perhaps, despite his filth, someone would take those clothes as impetus to try to rob him. Wouldn't *that* be fun? He found himself rather looking forward to the prospect.

When he did find some trouble—after hours of random wandering, as the sun grew sleepy and faint, and the wind began spreading flower petals of a frosty chill across the path of the coming night—it wasn't actually directed his way.

The thumps and cries, rattles and threats, emerged from a gap between two slumping, wood-walled shops that would have had to raise its standing in the world to qualify as an alleyway. Almost too narrow to traverse without turning sideways, it led, to judge by the echoes and the shadows visible beyond, into a small and otherwise isolated courtyard.

Enticed by no genuine concern or even much curiosity, but simple boredom, Nycolos went to take a look. He squeezed through the opening, stepping over a splintered crate and a puddle of half-dried mud that smelled to have been formed of drunkards' urine rather than water.

The courtyard, too, was full of garbage and other refuse. Broken barrels, old pans, shattered bottles, and heaps of rot that had once probably been the leftovers of various butchered cuts of meat lay strewn about, creating a repulsive and possibly even injurious carpet. Crows and other scavengers squawked overhead, circling low in the overcast sky or perched atop nearby buildings, watching and waiting that they might return to their meals.

Meals they'd abandoned because various portions of said garbage were trying to kill one another.

Nycolos couldn't begin to guess what the grudge might have been about. He watched, leaning against a filth-encrusted wall, as five greasy, sloppily dressed men cursed, laughed, and spat while pounding a sixth bloody. Even though he could see that at least a couple of them wore long knives under their coats, none had drawn them. Instead they wielded rusty chains, broken boards, or—in one instance—a jagged rock. He might have thought that they were only looking to beat their victim, rather than kill him, except that the blows they landed were brutal, savage.

Oh, they meant to kill. They just meant for it to take some time.

The sixth man, who didn't look too different save for the fresh blood staining his beard and his clothes, writhed on the ground, arms wrapped over his head. His own weapon, a sharply curved knife, lay in a heap of filthy rags just beyond his reach. Not, at this stage, that it would do him any good even if he could reach it.

Nycolos observed for a moment, turned to go back the way he'd come, and stopped. He had no business here, no reason to care what was happening or why. But... He burned within, roiling with fury and frustration. Hadn't he just been hoping for an excuse to lash out? Why shouldn't this suffice just as well as if the attack had been launched against him personally?

Furthermore, something about the beating, about the deliberate cruelty of the thugs with their clubs and chains, reminded him of the overseers in the Norbenus mines. It was not a memory, or a comparison, likely to endear these men to him.

Grinning broadly and rolling his shoulders, once more letting his innate magics flow through him to firm up flesh and strengthen his limbs, Nycolos stepped openly into the courtyard.

The nearest brigand turned his way, mouth opening—no doubt to utter some threat, some command to leave and to forget what he'd seen. Nycolos never knew, because he gave the fool no chance to speak.

A massive leap launched him across the courtyard, over a dozen feet from a standing start. Detritus shattered and mud spattered beneath his boots as he landed, nose to nose with the astonished thug. The knight's fist struck with the force of a battering ram, fragmenting ribs and driving pieces of bone deep into the softer organs beneath. Gasping, choking as one lung grew fat and bloated with blood while the other deflated, the first of Nycolos's prey dropped to a thrashing heap.

The dying man's nearest companions charged, one swinging his makeshift club, the other dropping his chain to scrabble for the dagger at his belt. Nycolos stepped in, blindingly fast, and caught the wooden board halfway in its arc toward his head. Wood crunched in his grip. With his other hand he stabbed outward, stiff-fingered, snapping the weapon in two, and then plunged the broken end deep into his attacker's shoulder. The man toppled, shrieking wordlessly as he clutched at the thing now protruding from his flesh.

The third brigand's dagger came in low, thrusting at Nycolos's stomach. He should have been able to dodge aside, more than fast enough to avoid the strike, but his anger and the sheer exultation of letting loose had him preoccupied, less alert than he ought to be.

It didn't matter.

He hadn't strengthened his skin to the point of sprouting scales, so it wasn't the armor it could be. It was tough enough, however, that, combined with his last-second twist, the blade merely traced a shallow line of blood through fabric and filth, rather than plunging into his guts.

Nycolos pounced, almost cat-like, hands landing on his attacker's chest with his full weight behind them. Both went down, hard, but after a series of sharp *cracks*, only one returned to his feet.

The remaining three men—two standing, corpse-white and shaking, the third peering up through a mask of drying blood—seemed paralyzed. Nycolos could have walked over and slaughtered them with no more effort than pulling a book or a dish off a waiting shelf.

But what fun was that?

"Run."

The upright pair obeyed. Not *wholly* mindless from shock and terror, they broke in opposite directions around the courtyard, clearly thinking that, in the time it took their hideous assailant to chase down and maul one of them, the other might escape into Talocsa's busy streets.

Nycolos laughed, long and loud; crouched and sprang backwards, a leap more impossible even than the one that had started the fray.

He all but soared, spreading his hands and allowing reptilian talons to sprout from his fingertips. He struck the wall beside the narrow alleyway, nearly fifteen feet above the ground, and *lodged* there, claws dug in behind him so that he clung to the building like some impossible lizard.

The faster of the two thugs, who had nearly made it to the mouth of the alley, froze beneath him, staring upward. The sound he made was low, primal, somewhere between a sob and hysterical laughter.

Withdrawing his grip and shifting his fingers back to human, Nycolos dropped before him, hefted him with both hands around the man's neck, and hurled him into the path of the other fleeing brigand. Both went down in a clatter of limbs, and Nycolos dove after them.

Again he was the only one to rise.

He looked long and hard at the injured survivor, the victim of the other five, wondered if it would be wiser to kill him, too, then shrugged. Let the man talk. What did it matter? He started to turn away.

"Thank… thank you, stranger."

"Hmm."

"Name's Xi… Xilmos."

It wasn't the introduction that arrested Nycolos's exit, but the fact that the man had forced himself not merely to rise, but to stagger near enough to stretch out his hand. That, after what he'd just seen, was an act of courage if nothing else.

Imitating the human greetings he'd seen, Nycolos clasped Xilmos's forearm. "Nycos." He'd never grown used to that shortened version of the name he'd adopted, but he wanted no chance, however small, of being recognized for who he was. Or rather, who he had recently pretended to be.

"I'm not sure what I saw back there, Nycos, but I owe you. They'd have killed me, and not clean."

"So I noticed." Then, as he had nothing better to say, "What was their grudge with you?"

"Those bastards were Fletcher Street Wolves. I'm White Knife." He seemed to expect Nycolos to know what those names meant, so the disgraced knight just nodded.

"They jumped me on the street, shoved me back here," Xilmos continued. "If you hadn't showed up—"

"Yes, we've established that part already. Well, Xilmos, if that's—"

"Come with me." The criminal—for Nycolos had put together that much, if nothing else—wiped away a gobbet of blood currently matting his thick mustache. "Let me introduce you to the guys. Maybe you want to work with us some? Fighter like you could turn this whole thing around for us, and I wager Samsa could more than make it worth your while."

Again he'd started to turn away, and again he halted. *Why not?* Oh, he didn't see himself joining Xilmos's little gaggle, but it *was* growing late. He'd exerted himself a lot today, his chest wound ached... It wouldn't hurt to find a place to bed down for the night, take a fresh look at his options in the morning.

"Very well, then, Xilmos, I'll hear your Samsa out. Lead the way."

# CHAPTER TWELVE

Well, Master Tzav—that is, Master Nycolos had really made a right steaming heap of mountain goat scat out of this whole situation, hadn't he?

Smim sat tucked against the cushions that formed one corner of the divan, long spindly arms wrapped about his knees. He managed somehow both to sulk and skulk while so seated, as only a goblin could, and had anyone in Oztyerva seen the bestial twist to his jaw, the jagged teeth bared in frustration or the jaundiced, homicidal slits through which he glared about the suite, they'd most certainly have killed him on the spot, the protection and parole of Sir Nycolos notwithstanding.

He would, honestly, have almost welcomed the attempt. The snap of a tendon between his teeth or the spongy collapse of a windpipe beneath his deceptively powerful fingers might cheer him up.

Right until someone shoved something sharp and cold and generally unpleasant through his belly, of course. Which might just happen anyway, if the master didn't pull himself together and stop trying to make an enemy of every man, woman, and child in the palace.

Nor did it help that Smim hadn't the faintest notion of where the master had gone, or when—*if*—he might return.

*Gods of the deep, what a disaster.*

The goblin unfolded, almost uncoiled, from against the furniture and scuttled across the room toward the table. He found the various fruit brandies so popular among the humans of Kirresc to be the pinnacle of revolting, enough to bring bile to the back of his throat—give him well fermented cave lizard squeezings any day!—but just at this moment, the notion of getting blackout drunk was so enticing that he'd gladly choke down an entire decanter of the vile stuff.

Master wasn't here to object, and it wasn't as if he'd anything better to—

He twitched and froze, all but canted sideways, one shoulder tensed far higher than the other, at the sudden tapping on the chamber door.

His first crazed thought—some might have called it paranoid, but as a goblin currently stuck dwelling within a hive of humans, paranoia was hardly unwise—was that his earlier worries had manifested, that they'd come to murder him while Nycolos was away. Just as swiftly, though, he calmed. Rather unlikely that such an endeavor would begin with a polite knock, and anyway, they shouldn't yet be aware that Nycolos was missing. It wasn't as though the man had spent a great deal of time in public lately.

*Just ignore it. They'll go away.*

More tapping, more insistent than before.

*They'll go. Any minute now.*

Tap tap.

*Go away!*

"Open this door!" Margravine Mariscal somehow made herself heard through the heavy wood despite scarcely raising her voice above a whisper. "You open this door right this instant or I'll have the guards break it down!"

Smim sighed deeply, strode to the door, and opened it with an extravagant bow. "You seem awfully fond of that particular threat, my Lady. Do you suppose they'd actually do it?"

She swept into the room in a flurry of scarlet and gold, scarcely glancing at him, though whether that was a sign of distraction or merely her surprised repugnance at the unkempt state of the chamber he couldn't say. "With my rank and title, they'd have little choice but to obey. Where's Nycos?"

"I fear the master is out on a personal errand. If you wish me to tell him you called, or deliver a message, I shall be delighted—nay, honored!—to pass along—"

"Oh, stuff it, you obsequious little toad."

"As you wish. If my Lady would just enlighten me as to what, precisely, I'm to stuff, and where—?"

"I'm actually glad he's not here," she admitted. "It saves me from making up excuses. I want to speak to you."

That, finally, caught Smim sufficiently by surprise to shut him up.

Mariscal found a chair that met her standards of cleanliness, and planted herself in it. Then, after a moment and a cloudy expression, she rose and moved to the table, poured herself a drink, and returned to her seat. Apparently doing it herself was less offensive than having the goblin touch the goblet she meant to sip from.

*I should tell her I pissed in it, the haughty snot.*

"Smim, was it?" she asked, idly swirling the brandy.

"It was. Indeed, it still is."

"I apologize for my earlier words. You've been nothing but a loyal servant to Nycos, and you deserve better treatment than that."

Shocked to the core of his being, Smim found himself so completely paralyzed he actually wondered, for a maddened instant, if he might have died.

"What happened to him out there, Smim?"

*Oh, shit.* And just like that, he could move again. "You... heard his tale, my Lady. When he addressed the court. He—"

"Yes, yes, I heard all that. It explains nothing! This man who's been brooding and snarling about the palace isn't my Nycos, though!"

*You've no idea. Also, "my Nycos"? Interesting…*

"Something is *very* wrong. I don't know what he was like when you met him, but this, this isn't him!" She swallowed once, continued. "Something happened to him, something he won't tell me—us. So I need *you* to tell me."

What was he to say? That the dragon who'd taken the man's form was in deep mourning, deep despair, for the death of his only hope? That the notion of a life trapped in an inferior form among inferior beings was eating away at Nycolos's soul?

Or what of Smim's own theories, that there was more to the master's suffering and behavior? That Nycolos was behaving sullenly and temperamentally, even immaturely so? Smim had slowly grown convinced that the master was battling not merely his circumstances, but his *body*. The thoughts, the feelings, the urges and needs that lurked in the minds and roared through the blood of all humanoids, that peaked in adolescent years, that all adults—human, goblin, and other—had spent their lives learning to deal with? These were all brand new to Nycolos, who had only a few months' experience with them. Frankly, that things hadn't gotten much worse much sooner was a testament to the master's iron will.

Put a sparrow's soul within a wolf's body, how long would it take for the sparrow to become a predator, or cease trying to fly? How long would that conflict rage? Yet that was a far nearer match, in many respects, than what Nycolos must now struggle to reconcile.

None of which, even had he been utterly certain, even if it were more than his own hypothesis, could Smim possibly tell the woman.

Mariscal had read meaning in his pause, however, in his posture. "You *do* know something!" she declared, leaning sharply forward.

"Obviously, Master Nycolos did not reveal *every* detail of his—our—journey," the goblin said carefully. "Nor of our tribulations. If he chose not to speak of something, however, we must trust that he has his reasons. Or at least I must. I suppose you're free to trust or distrust whatever you choose."

"Smim—"

"But it is not my place to reveal his secrets, if any. I'm sorry, my Lady."

"I could *make* you talk, goblin. We have methods, techniques. We prefer not to resort to such measures. They're... unenlightened. But that doesn't mean we *won't*. And I imagine his Majesty would prove far less reluctant where a creature such as yourself is concerned."

Smim felt his stomach turn over, his knees turn liquid, but he forced himself to remain steady. "And how do you imagine the master would react to that, when he learned of it? When he heard you had such little regard for his friendships, and his word, that you did that to me when he has already declared me a vassal under his protection?"

Mariscal squeezed and bunched a handful her skirts in both fists until it seemed the wrinkles and creases were indelibly pressed into the rich fabric. Then she rose and made to leave, halting only as she reached the doorway.

"There are those in Oztyerva," she said without looking back, "who believe *you* are somehow responsible, in whole or in part, for the change in Nycos. That you have some hold over him, or serve someone who does."

"So I've heard," Smim said.

"I don't believe that's so," she admitted. "But if I'm wrong, if I learn there's the slimmest truth to it, or discover evidence to *suggest* that it's true, I *will* have you put to slow torture. Your death will be long and ugly, and damn the consequences. You understand?"

The goblin swallowed, hard, and hoped she hadn't heard it. "I do."

She was gone. Smim lunged for the door, slamming and latching it, and then sank to the floor with his back against the portal.

*I've no idea where you are, Master, but it will be far better for the both of us if you aren't gone long.*

———

The group's gathering spot—it didn't seem worthy of so grandiose a term as "headquarters"—was a back room in someone's house. A cheap, ramshackle structure standing alongside a filthy street among other cheap, ramshackle structures, it hunkered against the chilly breeze and faint drops of a late night shower. Nycolos guessed it belonged to the White Knife leader, a squat, pale-skinned, tattooed woman named Samsa, though he supposed it could just as easily have been one of the other members' home.

The White Knife, as he had picked up from Xilmos on route, and then from everyone else's hushed conversation once they'd arrived, was a small gang of criminals. Thugs, robbers, occasional purveyors of illegal goods, pimps and prostitutes, and so forth. Unimportant and unimpressive, but apparently worth fighting over, as the White Knife currently waged a territorial war with a rival band of riffraff calling themselves the Fletcher Street Wolves.

None of them had been thrilled to see Xilmos show up on their doorstep with a stranger, though his tale of how "Nycos" had saved his life seemed to soften their distrust. Not entirely, though, and in no small part because they refused to believe some of the more outlandish details.

"Swear to us," Samsa had demanded, "that you won't reveal to anyone what you learn here."

"Or?" Nycolos had asked, his tone amused.

"Or you're a dead man."

She and the others had recoiled at his cold laughter, and gone off to the other end of the room to discuss further. Nycolos, who could of course hear every word, had brushed aside a stack of dirty clothes, on which had lain a small collection of cheap jewelry—stolen, no doubt—and sprawled tiredly across the sagging, beetle-eaten old cot doubling as a sofa.

He eavesdropped for a time, chortling to himself when Xilmos argued that the White Knife should try to entice him to join them—Nycolos couldn't even *begin* to imagine what they had to offer him, beyond a place to sleep for the night—and then rolled over to face the wall in hopes of drifting off.

And he'd almost done just that when a particular overheard word made his eyelids snap open.

"I'm sorry," he said, turning over once more to face the others. "But who are these 'Creeping Dragons' you're speaking of?"

"How in God's name did you *hear* that?!" Samsa demanded, her tone shrill.

"I told you he had some kind of magic!" Xilmos crowed, though he frowned right after. "But how've you never heard of the Creeping Dragons?"

"Just accept that I haven't and answer my question."

It was Samsa who did so, albeit uneasily. "The Creeping Dragons are... I guess you'd call them a thieves' and smugglers' guild, but bigger. They operate in a bunch of cities, in a couple different kingdoms."

*Creeping Dragons. The Dragon River. What* is *it with humans and that word?*

*Although I suppose we* are *impressive...*

"And their involvement in this is what?" he pressed, though he'd already begun to lose interest again.

"The Wolves are trying to prove themselves worthy of working for the Dragons," Xilmos said. "Maybe even take over managing their interests in Talocsa."

*If the Fletcher Street Wolves are as unimpressive as you silly creatures, I doubt that's probable.*

"We think that's why they were willing to grab Xilmos in the middle of the day like they did," one of the others chimed in.

"And why they're so eager to finally get us out of the way," Samsa said.

*Because you lot are such a threat.*

At a whisper and a nudge from Xilmos, she added, "And why we could really use someone with your talents working with us. *If* you can really do what he claims you can."

Nycolos hadn't yet decided whether to explain that he had no intention of throwing in his lot with theirs, or whether to simply laugh in her face again, when the faintest scrape from above caught his attention. It was barely there, far too soft for anyone else to have heard.

He cocked his head, focusing, and now that he made a point of listening, he sensed this was no mere animal, no branch swaying against the rough shingles in the wind.

"I would wager," he said, "that's *also* why they're creeping around on your roof right now."

He'd give them credit for this much: Nobody hesitated, nobody asked how he might possibly know or pelted him with inane questions, nobody panicked. Everyone present either rose or dropped, as appropriate, into a fighting stance, producing small blades and similar weapons from the folds of their clothes and all corners of the room. Several sidestepped so they stood back to back, while others leapt atop or crouched beside the furniture, well away from the door and the boarded windows.

Perhaps the White Knife didn't consist solely of idiots after all.

Whether they'd heard their prey readying for battle or because their timing was simply that dramatically appropriate, the Fletcher Street Wolves chose that moment to burst inside. Some had crept up on the house from the streets, others swung down from the roof on frayed hempen rope, boards and shutters cracking inward before their bootheels. They looked... Well, they looked, to Nycolos, like the same sorts of unimportant street thugs as their White Knife rivals. The only difference was the mantle of grey-dyed fur each of them wore on their shoulders, presumably a badge of membership. Their enemies were probably meant to assume those were wolf pelts, but Nycolos spotted, and smelled, much dog and other animal fur, with only a few traces of genuine wolf to be had.

He never did learn, nor did he much care, how they'd found the heart of the White Knife, a secret Samsa and her people had kept for years. The Wolves outnumbered their enemy, but not by much; the battle might, had this been a normal night, have gone either way. The scourge of Fletcher Street had not, however, come alone.

When every member of the White Knife present had turned to face the enemies barging in through the windows, the door to house shivered and cracked, sundered by a single mighty blow. The man who stood beyond was one of the largest humans Nycolos had seen in all his many centuries, topping seven feet in height and *still* abnormally broad of shoulder. Muscles bunched visibly across his chest as he spun, in one hand, a great double-headed axe that most people could scarcely have lifted with two. The grin that split his wild beard was savage indeed.

They called him the Black Bear, Nycolos would later learn: an infamous killer-for-hire who had learned to fight as a gladiator-slave in the slum-cradled arenas of Mahdresh. The White Knife could never have gathered the resources to hire him, and the Wolves shouldn't have been able to, either. The Fletcher Street criminals must have gone all-out, pouring everything they had into one lightning-swift strike to take down their rivals and impress the Creeping Dragons. The Bear's appearance alone set several of the White Knife to trembling, to lowering their blades as though they'd lost all hope of fighting back.

Nycolos roared and leapt to meet him.

The two ferocious shapes met in the center of the chamber, White Knife and Fletcher Street Wolf alike scrambling from their converging paths. Met, and it was Nycolos, much to his astonishment, who came out second-best in that initial clash. He felt himself hurtling back, a sharp and pounding ache in his ribs, to crash against the cot he'd so recently vacated.

It wasn't that the Black Bear was stronger than he. So far as he knew, no human could be, though this one came closer than most. The man was fast, remarkably so, but again he was only human. No, he was clever, cunning. Nycolos had been so focused upon that massive blade that he'd never seen the kick coming.

And it *hurt*. A lot. Anyone else would be dead, or at least bleeding to death on the inside, ribs crushed, organs battered. Had the blow impacted against Nycolos's old wound, jarring the sliver in its cocoon of scarred flesh, he might have been, too.

As it was, he stood from the overturned cot, brushed himself off, and nodded to the Black Bear. "First round to you."

Gasps sounded from both gangs, and the behemoth's expression grew uncertain.

He took the opportunity granted by that instant of hesitation to concentrate on his chest, allowing the skin beneath his tunic to harden beyond anything remotely human, taking on a deep wine hue and the consistency of scales. His goal was solely to guard his lingering injury; for the rest of his body, he didn't bother. No, he didn't want the people here to know of his abilities, but more to the point, against a direct blow from that axe, no protection he could manage in human shape would suffice. His only defense was not to get hit.

The skirmishes that had begun between White Knife and Fletcher Street Wolves ceased as everyone in the room stepped back to watch, knowing full well that victory or defeat—life or death—hinged on what was about to happen between the outside champions of both sides.

The axe whirled in great but swift arcs, first from this angle then from that, horizontal, diagonal, vertical, each capable of punching deep into Nycolos's body or taking off a limb. For a time he merely avoided the cleaving blade—and the sporadic punch or kick or grab, now that he was wise to the Bear's tricks. He ducked, weaved, twisted aside, drawing upon his impossible speed, watching for his foe to fall into a predictable pattern or reveal an exploitable weakness in technique. Furniture shattered beneath the axe as they moved about the room, Nycolos slowly giving way, but never was the impact enough to slow the killer's momentum, and no opportunity appeared.

So he'd simply have to make his own.

When next the Black Bear lunged and the axe whistled near, Nycolos didn't just flow aside but leapt back, hard. His momentum carried him several steps from his foe, to land beside the circled audience of criminals.

He spun, fingers closing tight on the tunic and belt of a startled Fletcher Street Wolf. The young thug drew breath, but the gestating words or shout or scream never saw birth.

Nycolos jumped yet again, kicking his legs over and out, spinning flat and horizontal in the air, dragging the other with him. At the height of that spin, he released the Wolf, hurling him away.

Perhaps the Black Bear meant only to protect himself from being flattened by the flying man. Or maybe, not caring which faction the living projectile might belong to, he'd sought to cut him out of the air. Either way he brought his axe in line, but lacked the time for a full swing. The Wolf died, split upon that massive blade, but not fully bisected. Lodged in muscle and bone, the weapon required an extra heartbeat or two to recover, to raise and ready to strike once more.

All the time Nycolos required to close.

A second pair of fists closed on the haft of that monstrous weapon, two fearsome tugs in opposite directions holding it as still as if it supported the weight of the sky itself. Nycolos was the stronger; the Bear was the larger, exerting greater leverage and holding the better placed, more secure grip.

They glared, watching, never blinking, sweat breaking out across reddening faces. The audience around them, and it seemed even the chamber itself, all held their breath. Each time one of the combatants took a step, hoping to break the stalemate, the other followed, maintaining the struggle. Sporadically the weapon would shift, half an inch closer to one combatant or the other, and then surrounding lungs would remember to breathe in quick, explosive gasps.

The Black Bear was indeed cunning, but he was unaccustomed to a foe like Nycolos. More to the point, this axe was his weapon, an ally by his side and a tool he had wielded through countless battles and equally innumerable murders. The answer to their struggle, which seemed so obvious to Nycolos, either never occurred to him, or he couldn't bring himself to do it.

Nycolos could. He simply let go.

The giant stumbled at the sudden lack of resistance, off balance and unable to catch himself. Nycolos stepped in behind those massive blades, reached out, and twisted, hard and fast.

The snap of the Bear's neck was an detonation that filled the confines of the room and echoed in the skulls of everyone watching.

Nycolos plucked the axe from the dead man's grip before the body hit the floor. He hefted it thoughtfully in one hand. "You run," he said, "and you die before you reach the window or the door. Weapons down."

He was clearly addressing the Fletcher Street Wolves, but many of the White Knife obeyed as well. Just in case.

"Which of you is the leader?"

One man, one of the few whose pelt was actual wolf hair, reluctantly raised a hand—only after the eyes of many of his subordinates had turned his way.

"Good." Nycolos nodded, then moved to loom over the man. "Only loyal members of the White Knife are going to leave this house alive today. You understand?"

Even through his fear, the man scowled. "I don't—"

The Black Bear's axe sank through flesh and into the floor. Nycolos booted the puzzled head out of his path like a child's ball.

"Which of you is the leader?"

The former leader's second—now in charge of the Fletcher Street Wolves—assured Nycolos in no uncertain terms, despite the violent quaver in his voice, that he absolutely understood what was being asked of them, and was the first to swear obedience to a somewhat stunned Samsa.

Nycolos himself wasn't entirely sure why he cared. He owed nothing to, and had no real affection for, the members of the White Knife. Maybe it was just that they'd offered him a roof, however unselfless their reasons, while the Wolves had tried to kill him?

Ultimately, he supposed it didn't matter.

"You just got a lot bigger," he said to Samsa. "Take your new influence—and perhaps this man's shaggy head—to your 'Creeping Dragons.' Maybe you can assume the position the Fletcher Street Wolves had hoped for."

Samsa gazed at him in absolute awe, an attitude mirrored by almost everyone there. Nycolos basked in it, buoyed by it, felt worth something for the first time in days.

"Join us," Xilmos said, voice cracking. "With you, we can do anything. We might not even *need* the Dragons!"

A rumble of assent circled him, skipping across the broken furniture. Samsa frowned briefly, then seemed to come to a decision. "I'll step down." Everyone fell silent once more. "Lead us, if that's what it takes for you to stay. I've worked long and hard to command the White Knife, but I'll follow you, gladly."

Somewhere, deep within his soul, Nycolos wanted to say yes. It was a lowly life among lowly creatures, even as humans went, but he had, if only from them, the respect and the fear and the prestige he was due. He could start with them, perhaps build it all up to something greater, acquire some measure of comfort…

Only one thing stopped him, a single thought.

*I earned their awe, their reverence, so easily. So swiftly. Who else might I win over, then, with a modicum of effort?*

For the first time since the Lady Ilkya's unwelcome diagnosis, he felt a stirring of purpose, felt as though he had an inkling of how to build a life—a *human* life—that, until he could locate the magics required to heal himself, to resume his proper form and place, he would find tolerable. Even worth fighting for.

"Thank you, Samsa, but no. Keep your station. And know," he added the lie easily, for benefit of those Fletcher Street Wolves who might harbor doubt and resentment for their new situation, "that I will watch over you when I can.

"But I have somewhere else I have to be, and some tasks I've put off for far too long."

# CHAPTER THIRTEEN

The water was hot, soothing. The heat seeped into his flesh, relaxing muscles that had grown sore and weary with constant tension, easing the pain of aches and bruises. He had enjoyed such experiences before, soaking his older body in an underground hot spring deep beneath his mountain lair. It had never occurred to him that a man made experience might come near to matching it, and he hadn't relaxed enough in any of his prior baths to discover otherwise.

That new relaxation, unfortunately, carried with it a number of other fresh discoveries which were, in turn, making it much harder to *stay* relaxed.

It wasn't the sickly grey tint to the water or the slight oily sheen that the various soaps and perfumes couldn't entirely hide. No, he'd expected that. He'd not washed in weeks, had known he was filthy—a fact that nearly prevented him from being allowed back into Oztyerva by guards who initially assumed he was some greasy vagabond or, at best, a drunken gentleman in the midst of some dishonorable revelry. Nor was it the clumps of loose hair floating within that ever less cleanly pool, trimmed from his neck and cheeks by meticulous servants.

No, it was, through no fault of their own, those servants themselves that chipped away at his composure.

Perhaps because the experience had always before been so alien to him, and he had only viewed his humanoid body as a short-term, temporary impediment, he'd never paid much attention to the experience of being bathed by a small gaggle of strangers. Now, however, he felt the stroke of every brush, the wet heat of every cloth, and—most distractingly of all—every slip of a soap-slickened hand or finger against his own skin.

Each such touch was a jolt of miniature lightning, nearly enough to send him leaping from the great brass tub, only getting worse as the careful scrubbing progressed to ever more sensitive spots. And the servants were thorough cleaners indeed.

His heart pounded. His whole body tensed. His breath caught. And when he felt other, more dramatic reactions occurring below the waterline—to say nothing of the sly glances among two of the servants, suggesting they had noticed, too—the bewilderment and embarrassment became too great.

"That's enough!" he snarled. "You're... Thank you for your assistance, but it's no longer required. I'll finish up on my own."

"But, Sir Nycolos—"

"*I said leave!*"

They fled, leaving him to fumble and fidget with the various brushes and oils until he felt he was probably clean enough to suffice. He actually welcomed the extra time and concentration required; it enabled him to calm himself.

He emerged from the bathing chamber wrapped in a silken gown belted loosely at the waist. Smim awaited him, tapping spindly fingers against the back of the sofa on which he sat.

"That, Master, is *entirely* what we were talking about."

"What do you mean?" Nycolos ran a towel over his hair and beard, then realized with a grunt that he'd have to comb them all over again.

"The sort of behavior that you're going to have to alter if you plan to earn back, or enhance, your respect and position in the court."

It was the first thing they'd talked about upon Nycolos's return, even before calling for the filthy knight's bath. He had explained how he'd felt when receiving the adulation of the White Knife, and how he'd realized that, if he could accomplish the same here, he might yet build a lifestyle worth having until he could find new answers to his circumstances. With enough of the nobility looking up to him, he might even obtain a fair amount of power and greater physical comforts.

All of which began with putting himself back in the running for Crown Marshal.

"They're just servants, Smim," he protested. "Not the sorts of people I need to impress."

"Which does not change the fact that certain expectations regarding your own demeanor are universal, Master. And servants are known to gossip."

Another grunt. "Fine. I'll… better prepare myself for next time."

He allowed the towel that had scoured his head to fall in a heap, then moved to the table and poured himself a glass of sour cherry wine. He found he preferred such drinks to the far sweeter brandies that were so well loved in Kirresc, though both were slowly growing on him.

"So," he continued, raising the goblet to his lips, "where do you suggest we begin?"

"We should probably start with your apologies, Master."

Nycolos froze mid-sip. When he did finally swallow, he'd forgotten the wine; he was just clearing his tongue for speech. "What. Apologies."

"Um… To Lord Kortlaus? Lady Mariscal? His Highness? The entire court? If you're to repair the real Nycolos Anvarri's friendships, regain your standing in everyone's sight—"

"I'm sure I can make it clear through my actions that my poor behavior is behind me. Once I've impressed them enough, they'll have forgotten all about—"

The goblin's head shook so fiercely it almost unscrewed itself. "That's not how humans work, Master. Oh, you'll have to do all you say as well, but after the sort of offense you've given to—well, pardon me for saying it, but *everybody*—you cannot simply expect them to welcome you back, or give you a chance to prove yourself changed."

"So you're saying an apology might not even work if I *did* offer it!"

"It might not, no. But it remains necessary."

The goblet shattered against the far wall, leaving a splotch that made the stone appear to bleed. "I have never apologized to another living creature in all my life!"

"Well, that *is* the sort of behavior you can get away with as a dragon, Master, but as things stand—"

"And even if I ever *were* to… to apologize for my behavior to anyone, it would be to an *equal*. Not to a bunch of *humans!*"

Smim just waited, watching.

"What?" Nycolos finally demanded.

"Master, if you're to have even the slightest chance of making this work, the first thing you're going to have to do is alter your thinking about this 'bunch of humans.'"

"Meaning?"

"Meaning you're going to have to treat them as though they *are* your equals. In pretty much every imaginable respect, save where your rank and title make an alternate case."

Nycolos scowled in indignant horror. "I cannot possibly be expected to maintain such… such a farce!"

"If it's too much to ask, Master, you can always return to those hooligans you've spoken of. I've no doubt they'd take you back in a second, and would almost assuredly never demand an apology of you for anything. If you think you could be happy with what that sort of life can offer you, I'll start packing right away."

The nearest chair creaked in protest as Nycolos slumped hard into its embrace, head in his hands. "This is going to be a lot more difficult than I thought, Smim."

"Of that, Master, I have absolutely no doubt whatsoever."

———

"Kor—that is, my Lord Kortlaus?"

"Sir Nycolos."

Nycolos had found his friend—or sort-of-friend, or ex-friend, or ostensible friend—after nearly two hours of searching. They met not in Kortlaus's quarters, the dining hall, the chapel, or even the training fields but in a random corridor of Oztyerva where they had, by sheer chance, finally run into one another.

Now that they stood face to face, Nycolos rather wished his search had remained fruitless.

"It's... I'm glad I was able to catch up with you."

"Oh? Well, here I am." Then, perhaps deliberately reminding himself of his manners, the baron added, "It's good to see you cleaned up and presentable again. Many of us were more than a little concerned."

"Yes, well... That's rather what I wanted to... That is..."

*Get it together, you gibbering cretin!* Nycolos snapped at himself. *Just a few simple words. Not that difficult!*

His sense of pride, sulking obstinately in the corner of his soul, seemed to disagree with that assessment.

"Kortlaus, I... Would like to apologize. For, uh, my recent behavior."

"All right." Kortlaus crossed his arms, waiting.

"Um. So, I apologize for that behavior. It was inappropriate."

"Yes."

It would have taken some form of incontinence or similar loss of bodily control to make the subsequent pause any more awkward.

"Is that it, then?" Nycolos finally asked. "I mean, can we move past this now?"

Still the baron's expression didn't so much as shift. "*Is* that it?"

"I..." *What the hell else did the man want?!* "I suppose it is."

"Then no, Nycolos, I don't believe we can move past this. If you'll excuse me."

Nycolos watched his receding back disappear down the

hallway, melding in amongst the other passersby. Only then did he realize that Smim had emerged from where he'd waited around the corner to stand at his side.

"That could probably have gone better," the knight observed wryly.

"It almost had to have, Master. It's rather a remarkable achievement that it went *this* poorly."

"Smim…"

"No bloodshed, though, nor any references to incestuous or anatomically impossible ancestral relations, so I suppose an argument could be made that it wasn't quite as bad as it might have—"

"That will *do*, Smim."

"Yes, Master."

They walked, wending their way upstream through the veins of the palace. "What's the matter with him, anyway?" Nycolos finally asked, waving his arms in exasperation and nearly striking a passing page with an armful of parchments in the process. "You said I should apologize, and I apologized."

"Um. By a strict definition, yes, Master, you did. But—"

"Are you suggesting my apology was flawed somehow?"

"It lacked… substance, Master. And sincerity. And emotion. And—"

"So I'm to, what? Humiliate myself further? Abase myself? To *them*?"

Smim cringed beneath the weight of multiple passing stares. "Please, Master, keep your voice down." He took Nycolos's heavy sigh as assent, and continued. "I realize that you've been in a dark mood, Master, and that you never expected to be forced to maintain your current shape for any length of time. But—"

"Am I to be regaled with another of your intricate theories, Smim?" He had not been remotely taken, and certainly not convinced, with the goblin's hypothesis regarding the link between his mental state and his unfamiliarity with the urges and influence of his human blood.

Smim bulled ahead, his words nicking themselves and bleeding on the jagged edges of his clenched teeth. "But were you paying any attention at all to the humans around us? Surely you must have seen a *few* apologies on which you might model—"

But he was already storming ahead, was Nycolos Anvarri. He remained distraught over his circumstances, though he was gaining control over that emotional maelstrom. He remained irritated that he must lower himself to treat these people as peers. And although he would have denied it, even to himself, he still flailed in the tide of human sensation and emotion and need, precisely as Smim believed.

Thanks to his current state, he had already decided that Smim was mistaken about this, too: It was just an apology, simple and straightforward. How could he possibly need *help* with that? How could one do it *wrong*?

No, the problem was with Kortlaus. The baron was being unreasonable. Nycolos just had to find someone more rational, someone who truly, deeply wanted to patch things up.

Fortunately, he knew precisely where to locate such an individual. Margravine Mariscal would be overjoyed with any sort of apology from him, and to hell with Smim's nitpicking!

―――

Nycolos staggered back from the door, head ringing with more than the sound of its abrupt slam. His eyes blurred, watering with the unexpected shock and pain. One of the nearby guards, stationed in the hall outside the margravine's chambers, passed him a handkerchief to wipe away the trail of blood that trickled from his door-battered nostrils.

"T'ank you," he said, offering it back.

"Keep it, sir."

Smim awaited him some yards down the corridor, making no effort whatsoever to hide his knowing smirk.

"Perhaps," Nycolos said, carefully prodding at his aching nose, "it might be wise for me to rethink my apologies. Maybe try to observe a few before making another."

"What a marvelous notion, Master. I couldn't have said it better myself. *Sooner*," he added with only a perfunctory effort at lowering his voice, "but not *better*."

"Are you quite through, now, Smim?"

"At this rate, Master? I can only doubt it."

"You are starting to *truly* irritate me, you know."

"I'm sorry, Master. Oh, there! See! One perfectly good wild apology."

Muttering to himself in the language of dragons, Nycolos made for his quarters, a non-bloodstained tunic, and perhaps five or six stiff drinks.

———

Days passed, very nearly another week since Nycolos's return from his overnight sojourn into Talocsa's seedier underbelly. In that time, he attempted no further conversations with either Kortlaus or Mariscal, save for exchanging the necessary pleasantries should he happen to pass one of them in the hall or meet them while he was on duty. Nor had he yet attended any of his Majesty's dinners, so that—despite his newfound reputation for isolation and the fact that nobody really wanted him there—people had begun to talk.

But he had not, in all that time, been idle.

Nycolos tackled the basics of his responsibilities as a knight of Kirresc, standing ceremonial guard for hours at a time, overseeing the ledgers and records of the tiny parcel of land that was his, as baronet, to manage. By playing up his lingering wound and the chirurgeon's earlier orders, he avoided any of his more arduous duties, including training and practice, anything that might give away his ignorance of things he ought to know. That, too, was beginning to wear, and he knew his excuses would not long suffice.

For that, he was prepared—for that, and so much more. Nearly every waking hour not consumed by his official duties was spent in careful observation of Oztyerva's men and women. He studied their combat training, despite his own lack of participation, quickly picking up the basics of the local fighting styles. He watched people's manners, their interactions, and—wherever possible—their apologies and amends. Now that he no longer held himself above such concerns but instead immersed himself, a drowning man struggling to learn to swim, his self-education proceeded swiftly.

And where the knowledge he wished to acquire was less overt, where stealth and sneaking were of greater use, he had Smim. For all their initial objections and lingering revulsion, the court, the aristocrats, and the servants had slowly grown accustomed to seeing the goblin in their midst, running this errand or that for his liege. Now that his mere appearance didn't put people on their guard, Smim went to work. He lingered, he hid, and above all, he eavesdropped, absorbing all manner of gossip and semi-open secrets but with a particular ear toward the various political factions and rivalries that could be found in any and every capitol.

Tonight, finally, Nycolos was ready—or, if nothing else, he was ready *enough*, and had decided he could afford to put this off no longer.

In the hours before evening, he rehearsed his performance with Smim, touching on everything he knew he must convey. He ruthlessly squelched his prideful inner objections, and what portion he could not suppress he channeled instead into those details of his story that he believed a real human, the true Nycolos, would have found intolerable. Done properly, it would make tonight all the more convincing. Done wrong... Well, he simply wouldn't do it wrong.

Preparing himself through intense mental effort and several glasses of wine, he called for his servants to bathe him thoroughly until his dark complexion practically shone; to comb any lingering tangles from his hair, and trim his beard back to a thin, stylish length; to oil and perfume his body until a casually sniffing hound might not recognize him as a living mammal.

With their assistance he donned his most formal garb: supple boots of leather, tightly laced; sky-blue tunic with trousers of black; burgundy kaftan with fine gold trim. He even belted on his scabbard, wearing his finest sabre not because he anticipated needing it, but for the extra air of ceremony it conveyed.

He left a wake of gossiping pages and gentry behind him, as he'd known he would, but he paid them no heed. And then, finally, he arrived at the entrance to the dining hall and waited for one of the servants to announce him.

Everyone already seated turned his way, and all were clearly shocked not merely to see him, but to see him in his current state. Some were better at hiding it than others, but more than a few stared openly or began to whisper against the cheeks of their neighbors at the table.

The rest of the guests filtered in over several minutes, adding their own gazes or lowered voices to the throng, until finally Denuel Jarta called for silence so that Prelate Domatir might offer the usual suppertime prayer.

Nycolos waited until the invocation was complete, then rose from his seat before the servants could begin to serve the appetizers. He bowed, first to the table around him and then, far lower and more extravagantly, in the direction of the royal table.

"If it please his Majesty," he said, "I recognize that this is somewhat irregular, but I beg permission to address my king, and this assembly."

The hall grew so silent that everyone present could hear the steam rising from the servants' waiting platters. Several of the gathered nobles and officers leaned unconsciously forward, eager to listen—Marshal Laszlan chief among them, though not without a quick word in the king's ear.

"Speak, Sir Nycolos," Hasyan answered. "You've our permission."

Nycolos didn't begin instantly, instead walking past his dinner companions to stand before the royal table itself, where he dropped to one knee. "Thank you, Your Majesty. If I might… I've no grounds to ask favors of anyone, after the past weeks, but I beseech you to send the servants and guards from the hall, for just a few moments. What I've to say is… not merely difficult, but humiliating. I would keep it among my peers and my betters, if you'll permit it."

That required a bit of discussion between the king, the Crown Marshal, and the other counselors and advisors, but again—perhaps sensing the importance of what was to come—his Majesty acquiesced. After a polite scramble, the room was cleared of everybody not of noble breeding or high office.

Only then did Nycolos rise once more, take a deep and steadying breath that was only partly theater, and begin.

"Many of you were present in the court, the day I returned and told the tale of my journey to the Outermark Mountains and my battle with the wyrm Tzavalantzaval. The rest of you have, I am *quite* certain heard the same tale—probably several versions of it—from those who were there.

"It will also come as news to none of you that my behavior since that day has been inexcusable. Rude. Boorish. Unbefitting any human being with a sliver of pride, let alone a man of my station."

Several of his audience were nodding or otherwise silently voicing their acknowledgment of his assessment. A few, Lady Mariscal included, kept their faces down, examining the table rather than looking his way.

Balmorra Zas, court astrologer to Hasyan III, also nodded, but she wore the faintest traces of a expectant smile, as if she'd known this was coming. And perhaps she had.

"If any of you have done the math," Nycolos said, "you might have noted that, even allowing for the vagaries of travel, my story leaves several weeks, even up to a couple of months, unaccounted for. Perhaps, if you noticed it at all, you assumed that time was eaten by a variety of minor pauses and inconveniences, and by the difficulties of traveling while injured.

"Some of it was. My wounds were—*are*—more severe than I let on in court. Only the chirurgeons have known how much so. I didn't wish people to worry, or to look on me with... pity."

A very few expressions had lost some degree of hostility, and Mariscal finally looked his way, though most faces still wore masks of neutrality at best, and often dislike. Thus far, what he had said might elicit some measure of sympathy, but still explained little of his behavior.

Nycolos took another deep breath, returned to his place long enough to pour himself a small gullet-wetting drink.

"It was just after I had slain the dragon and lost Wyrmtaker, no more than several days later. My injuries were at their worst, and I had survived even that long only with the help of Smim. And then someone found us. A wagon, deep in the Outermark where few honest travelers have cause to go.

"It was no rescue. We were found, and we were taken. By Mahdreshan slavers."

Gasps, of horror and of sudden fury, sounded around the table. Kortlaus's skin flushed with deep anger, and Mariscal dropped the spoon she had been toying with.

"We were kept, caged, with many others. And then we were sold, traded off like beasts. Smim and I spent... I'm not certain how long. Weeks, if not more, at forced labor in an Ythani mine, in the northern Outermark Mountains."

A dozen nobles spoke at once, voicing their outrage, but Nycolos raised a hand. "They treated my wounds, enough that I was able to work, enough that I was worth the pittance of food they offered.

"We were worked to exhaustion. Whipped frequently. It wasn't the pain of the lash, you understand. Pain, I can tolerate. But to be treated as less than a beast, after—however close, however painful—the greatest victory of my life? A man of my station? It was intolerable, it was... dishonorable. Humiliating.

"I grew paranoid. Many of the slaves would turn on one another, in hopes of currying favor with the overseers—several of whom were, themselves, all too eager for any excuse to dole out punishment. Danger lurked in the mines, as well, for Tzavalantzaval was *far* from the only inhuman creature to dwell within the Outermark Mountains.

"I survived, in part, thanks to what few friends I had. Smim, yes, but several others amongst the slaves as well. Friends I lost, friends I couldn't save, once we finally escaped and fled into the Outermark. Nor was our escape even of my doing, for we merely took advantage of an attack on the camp by some of those creatures from within the mountain's deepest caves."

Half truth, half lies; details he omitted, or altered to fit the narrative he needed to convey. And yet, as he spoke, Nycolos felt a small portion of the weight he carried lift from off his shoulders, from within his gut and within his soul. Telling the tale aloud, even an obfuscated and twisted echo of it, was a balm on a hurt he had not realized he still bore.

"I was..." His voice didn't crack—he had more control than that—but it definitely flexed a bit. "I was ashamed. I didn't feel I deserved my freedom, didn't feel I had done all I should for those who had stood by me in my suffering. I didn't... remember how to trust. Didn't know how to regain my pride. And the result, well, was what you saw of me over the past weeks.

"I wasn't ready to return, to resume my life here. I'd forgotten how. I should never have inflicted myself upon all of you, not in that state. And for that, as much as for my behavior itself, I can scarcely begin to apologize."

Mariscal wept openly as the magnitude of what he had endured sank in, as did several others who had been close to Nycolos in one way or another, or who were particularly tender-hearted. Others, voices raised or trembling with fury, spoke of retaliation against Ythane for daring to treat a knight of Kirresc so—and none seemed angrier on his behalf, surprisingly, than Dame Zirresca. Kortlaus stood, his chair almost tipping over, and wrapped his friend in a crushing embrace, one that Nycolos forced himself to return for a span before gently extricating himself.

He slowly walked back toward the royal table, briefly clutching hands with many of the diners who reached out to him as he passed, or exchanging nods and kind words. Everyone, it seemed, was horrified and deeply sympathetic. Sir Tivador shamefacedly apologized for his drunken actions of the festival day, and Andarjin expressed his own condolences for Nycolos's travails.

Finally the knight dropped once more to one knee, but this time at a slight angle. Rather than facing his Majesty directly, he seemed to be kneeling to the narrow space between the king and Orban Laszlan.

"Crown Marshal, my behavior has reflected poorly on myself, and on my suitability for the position I've been striving for. If you wish me to, I will withdraw my candidacy for your office."

Baron Kortlaus, still on his feet, instantly moved just behind and to one side of the kneeling knight, then lowered himself next to him. "Marshal Laszlan, Your Majesty. As one of Sir Nycolos's competitors for the office, I ask that he permitted to continue his efforts, and to prove his sincerity."

"That's quite noble of you, my Lord," the palatine, Denuel Jarta, said. "But you're also well known to be a friend of Sir Nycolos, and I'm not certain that your recommendation in this matter is entirely—"

The hall erupted in a new round of murmuring as Dame Zirresca stood from her chair. Although her face was a flickering candle flame of vying emotions, her pace was steady and sure. She, too, knelt albeit on the other side of the table.

"As the other of Sir Nycolos's competitors," she announced, her tone steady and more than loud enough to carry, clearly and unmistakably, "I, too, ask that he be allowed to resume his efforts. Please, Marshal, don't ask that he withdraw his candidacy. Not after all we've just heard."

Nycolos was grateful, in that moment, that he must remain in his current posture until the king granted him permission to rise. Had he not been staring intently at the floor, he knew he couldn't possibly have hidden his shock at the woman's support.

Orban and King Hasyan conferred in their hushed tones. Finally, the king commanded all three to rise.

"Speaking up on Sir Nycolos's behalf does each of you credit," Orban said in his booming voice. "Please return to your seats." Only when they both had done so—Kortlaus laying a brief hand on Nycolos's shoulder as he stepped away—did the marshal continue. "Sir Nycolos."

The knight straightened his shoulders. Whatever was about to occur, he felt confident that—for the first time in weeks—he'd done himself proud. It felt good to be working toward something again, rather than moping about, however justifiably.

"You have much to atone for, baronet. Not only your behavior since your return, but your unauthorized departure in the first place, to say nothing of taking—and *losing*—Wyrmtaker."

"I do," Nycolos agreed without protest.

"You'll be doing penance and enduring punishment for some time. You understand this? You accept this?"

"I welcome it, Marshal Laszlan."

"Excellent. Then let everyone present know that while you have a difficult road ahead, Sir Nycolos, if you can navigate it with the poise and honor for which you were once known, and if you can show us that you have learned from your experiences, you remain in consideration for the office of Crown Marshal when the day comes for me to step down."

Again everyone spoke at once, but Nycolos was heartened to realize that, from several segments of the table, that susurrus was punctuated by applause and even a few vigorous cheers.

"You've fallen behind, son," Orban said more softly, "but you're not out of the race."

Nycolos bowed low, and swept back to his chair, again clasping several hands on his way. Palatine Jarta called for the meal to (finally) commence, and the evening took a few steps back toward normal.

He returned Mariscal's radiant smile, exchanged a few light comments with Kortlaus, but he knew well not everyone present would be pleased with this evening's turn of events. Several supporters of other candidates scowled his way when they thought he wasn't looking. He half expected to see the same from Margrave Andarjin, but saw only the man's usual polite expression.

Or rather, that was *almost* all he saw. For an instant, the façade slipped, and Nycolos caught the briefest glimpse of the anger stirring beneath it—not when Andarjin looked his way, no, but when he turned once to face Zirresca.

*Dissention in the ranks, is it? I believe I have just the right fellow in mind to peek into that...*

———

"What in the name of Straigon's missing jawbone is *wrong* with you?"

"First," Zirresca said stiffly, "I'll thank you not to swear by that name around me, or anywhere within Oztyerva's walls. And second…" She glanced meaningfully at the fingers clasped with almost bruising intensity around her bicep, pressing the wrinkled sleeve of her gown into her skin. "Because you're my friend, Arj, I'm going to offer you a chance to remove your hand from my arm before I remove it from yours."

Andarjin's mouth worked in silence, and it seemed as if the breeze of the thoughts whirling within was audible each time his lips opened. He was, however, wise enough to withdraw his hand, and he even managed a shallow smile.

"You'd threaten a margrave this way, Zirresca?"

"Not just any margrave. Lucky you."

He chuckled, however forced. "I apologize. I shouldn't have grabbed you. But we *do* need to discuss what happened at dinner." He began to pace, though the small sitting room didn't allow more than a few steps each way.

For her own part, Zirresca took a seat at the table. "And were your own expressions of sympathy so empty, Arj?" She sounded almost disappointed.

"They were expected. It would have been unseemly not to offer them. And anyway, no, not empty. What Nycolos endured was truly unfortunate. But acknowledging that is a *far* cry from supporting his return to the marshal's good graces, or from sabotaging your own campaign for the office!"

Zirresca leaned over the table. "I've sabotaged nothing. I'm still the best candidate, and I still intend to be the next Crown Marshal."

"But—"

"And even beyond his status as my rival, I've never much liked Sir Nycolos. You know that. But I would not wish what befell him on my worst enemy, and I will not stand in the way of a once-honorable man who seeks to regain that honor.

"Besides, I want to best him fairly and without doubt. It will strengthen my own position when I become marshal, and it will make him more likely to accept his defeat and the requirement of serving under me."

"You becoming Crown Marshal is too important for our plans to leave to chance, Zirresca! We should be taking every advantage we can!"

"Me becoming Crown Marshal is too important for cheats or shortcuts, Arj. I will do it properly, and I won't dishonor myself in the process."

"We—"

"Shall we take the question to her Highness? See what Princess Firillia thinks, whose viewpoint she approves of?"

"No." Andarjin's scowl once more transformed itself back into his traditional polished cast. "That won't be necessary. It is, after all, already done. For good or for ill."

"Yes. It is."

*I suppose*, Smim mused, ensconced and all but invisible in the deep shadows of the window alcove high above the arguing pair, *it was too much to hope that they might feel the unnatural urge to explain these plans of theirs in exacting detail.* Still and all, he'd learned much, more images to weave into the ever-growing tapestry that was the political and social landscape of Oztyerva.

At this rate, he might even learn enough to keep the master from stumbling blindly into something that, lingering draconic sorceries or not, might get him killed.

——

With each day of autumn's passage and the steady approach of winter, the garden had grown less and less colorful. The best efforts of the palace groundskeepers, even with the tiny sprinkling of magic that rumor suggested they practiced, could only slow the inevitable deterioration. Blossoms were smaller, limper, less fragrant; leaves and stems browner; birds less frequent and less vocal in the denuded trees.

But here was where the margravine had wanted to meet, on a granite bench tucked away between fading crimson tulips—her favorite flower—on one side, and a marble statue of a centaur on the other. So here was where Nycolos, eager to rebuild bridges despite his bewilderment with certain aspects of the conversation, sat.

"...genuine than your *last* attempt at an apology," Mariscal was saying. Having dismissed her ladies-in-waiting to stand far back, she leaned eagerly toward him from her side of the bench, both her hands clasped around one of his own. Yet there remained a fragility to her expression, however delighted. Even Nycolos, no expert on human interaction, recognized the need to tread carefully.

He wished, with hidden chagrin, that he understood more about this relationship he apparently had with Mariscal. His interactions with Kortlaus never seemed this fraught!

"I wasn't ready to... admit to everything then," he said haltingly. Then, sensing without entirely knowing how or why that she would welcome hearing such a thing, he added, "Once I had decided, I... I thought seriously of coming to you with the whole story first. But I wasn't certain you'd see me, and... Well, I was even less certain I could bring myself to relive it more than once. I'm sorry."

Mariscal's grip on his hand tightened fiercely. She started to lean even closer, seemed to catch herself at the last minute. "It's all right, Nycos." Her words quavered in the air between them. "I'm just so glad you finally *did* speak of it. Whatever you need, whatever it takes to help you heal, I'll do. You know that, right?"

"Of... of course." Was it just nervousness, confusion over his situation and fear of another social misstep, that had his heart beating as it was?

"Tell me," she said, sitting up straight and clearing her throat, "what duties has the Crown Marshal assigned you, now that you're... working with him again?"

"I'm to handle some of the beginner training. New recruits, pages, young children of the nobility. How to properly hold a sabre, basic parries and cuts, and whatnot."

Mariscal's lips turned in a deep frown. "That is beneath you, Nycos. Insulting, even under the circumstances. I'd like to have a word with—"

"No, it's all right. I volunteered. I thought it a good way to prove I'm willing to take whatever steps I must to regain the court's confidence, while still performing a useful task."

Also—and in fact, foremost in his mind—had been the theory that this would permit him to learn by watching others even as he was required to teach only the bits of human and Kirresci martial skills that he had already picked up. That this would be a way to hide his own unfamiliarity until he could correct that deficit. For obvious reasons, though, he didn't share that particular reasoning with the margravine.

"That's... That's brilliant, Nycos! Kind-hearted, humble, and yet perfectly suited to beginning your road back to Laszlan's favor!"

"Um. Thank you?"

Her cheeks had grown flushed, her gaze taken on an almost dreamy cast. "I haven't felt this hopeful since the day you returned! I feel like you can actually do this. You can make things better—and when you're Crown Marshal, they'll be better still. You'll have your high office, and our differing ranks won't matter any longer. And then..."

"Yes," he said, struggling to match her smile. "And then."

He found himself suddenly, almost desperately, wishing Smim were here—but he couldn't decide whether he needed the goblin to explain to him what was going on, or to protect him from it.

# CHAPTER FOURTEEN

Earth trembled, songbirds scattered, and dust billowed like a parting sea beneath the rolling thunder of iron-shod hooves; a stormfront of flesh and bone and steel surged along the road and the surrounding grasslands. The knights and soldiers of Kirresc, their powerful steeds shortening the miles with each distance-chewing stride, charged after those who had dared intrude upon their lands and prey upon their people. Crescent blades bristled, scythes to reap the lives from these foolish foreigners. And in their vanguard, half-standing in his stirrups, nostrils choked with acrid equine sweat as he and his warhorse both broiled in their armor beneath the high midsummer sun, rode Sir Nycolos Anvarri.

After months of lesser duties, of simple instruction, of standing meaningless posts, of every bit of scutwork not utterly beneath his station, all in the name of proving himself a changed man from the boorish brute who had returned from the Outermark, this was his first assignment of any significance— though it had still been meant to prove uneventful. All the knights of the court took their turn at leading long-running patrols along this border or that highway, a symbol to the soldiers that the gentry, the nobility, the king and his court, stood with them.

Here, though? Not two dozen leagues from Talocsa itself? This was a quiet stretch of border, a line on the map that few crossed with ill intent. Nycos knew full well that being sent here, while a sign of his improving status, had also been an indication he wasn't yet to be trusted with anything of import. He should, at worst, have been required to put the fear of the gods into a few tariff-dodgers trying to scoot around border stations on the main roads.

Then a group of bandits and raiders had crossed that line from Mahdresh, looting—and in one instance, burning—several border towns on the Kirresci side.

Nycos had learned much in those months, and he knew precisely how such an event would play out diplomatically. Kirresc would angrily demand Mahdresh keep tighter control of their criminal element. The Mahdreshan government would apologize profusely, but point out that their impoverished society hadn't the resources to deal with crime within the city-state proper, let alone at the edges of its outermost territories. Never mind that many in the Mahdreshan government were wealthier than that government itself, that it was an open secret their people lived in poverty because of their rulers' greed. There was simply nothing they could do, and they *certainly* couldn't devote what few resources they had to protecting so powerful and prosperous a nation as their neighbor.

It was, Nycos fumed, an even bet as to whether someone in Mahdresh's upper echelons was actually getting paid off by these selfsame raiders.

But so be it. Mahdresh wouldn't police its own? Nycos and his soldiers were more than happy to do the job, and now, as their trained steeds slowly closed the gap between them and the fleeing brigands on their smaller, weaker mounts, was near time for them to send a message of their own.

The raiders had fled off road, pounding across the lightly forested grasslands that stretched for miles in every direction—a mistake that Nycos was more than happy to ensure they paid for. True, had they remained on the highway, they might have found themselves trapped between the oncoming knights and the Kirresci border station, but that station would also have served as a clear demarcation between the two sovereign lands.

Here in the wild, that line on the map did not so readily translate into real life, and the Kirresci pursuers could see no border that would obligate them to break off their hunt.

One of the raider's horses stumbled—not severely, just a brief loss of footing on some bulge or depression hidden in the knee-high grasses—but enough to slow. Nycos kicked his heels into Avalanche's side, but the warhorse scarcely needed the prod; he had already lengthened his stride, snorting his excitement, at the smaller beast's stagger.

Screaming something unintelligible, face slack with fear, the bandit turned in his saddle, raising a heavy broadsword to face the oncoming attack. It made no difference.

Nycos rose in his stirrups, snapping his *szandzsya* to the side with lightning speed born equally, now, of months spent in practice and muscles enhanced just a touch beyond human. The unsharpened outer edge of the sabre-spear smacked the heavy sword partway along its arc, knocking the thicker blade out of line. Then, the shaft braced along Nycos's arm and against his back as he swept it outward, the weapon connected with the raider's neck.

Between the rigid grip and Avalanche's pounding pace, flesh and bone didn't even slow the blade's passage. A few rogue drops of blood from the sudden geyser spattered across Nycos's kaftan, as well as the chain hauberk and reinforcing breastplate beneath, but otherwise he was gone without so much as a hint that a man had died in his passing.

Up ahead, the Mahdreshan raiders had altered course, guiding their own mounts slightly leftward toward a large copse of trees whose thick boles and even thicker foliage broke the rolling monotony of the grasslands. Many such tiny oases of woodland speckled the region, eventually growing into genuine forest—but that was many leagues distant, east of

Talocsa. Here, a copse this size was the closest cousin to forest the land offered.

Did the Mahdreshans mean to hide within? That was beyond desperate, a foolish and utterly futile gesture. The copse, though larger than many, was too small for concealment, could buy them a few extra minutes, at most. Turn and fight? The boles would prevent the soldiers of Kirresc from mounting a charge, yes, but the raiders remained outnumbered by opponents both better armored and better trained.

No, something about this didn't feel right. Nycos's instincts—both those of his current form and those remembered from his earlier, predatory life—tapped insistently at the back of his head and along his neck, their demands for attention speckling goosebumps across his skin.

He raised a fist, the entire company slowing to a brisk canter at the signal. Several of the troops tossed questions or complaints back and forth to one another, worried about letting the brigands escape, but Nycos's second-in-command on this patrol, a gruff veteran with graying hair, immediately rode to his side so they might speak despite the lessened but still overwhelming drumbeat of the hooves.

"Sir Nycolos," she began with a sharp nod.

"Captain Rahdel."

"You're sensing it too, then, sir?"

"Indeed. They're up to something."

"Yes, sir."

"Any thoughts as to what, Captain?"

"Not much of use. I might suspect an ambush in the trees—I don't see how they could have sent word ahead, but I won't swear they didn't—but it seems too obvious. And unless there's a *lot* of them, the copse wouldn't provide them particular advantage over us."

"And if there *were* a lot, they probably couldn't all hide there."

Her frown deepened. "No. We'd best figure it out swiftly, though, sir. Else they really are going to escape us."

Rahdel was right; the raiders were rapidly pulling ahead. Nycos didn't much care for the idea of breaking into another gallop without figuring out what trouble or trick awaited them, but it was a risk he would take if no other option presented itself. At least the Kirresci warhorses could close the gap again, charging over the relatively flat grasslands...

Nycos cocked his head. The flat, breeze-kissed, *knee-high* grasslands.

He strove to listen, but even with his hearing magnified to supernatural extremes, he couldn't pinpoint anything beyond the horses, the voices, the distant calls of bird and beast, the rustling of those grasses in the faint summer winds. It didn't matter, though, not really. He was sure, or at least sure enough to act.

"Archers," he ordered.

Although she must have been running over with questions, the soldier never hesitated, nor did she ask any of those questions save for, "Target, Sir Nycolos?"

He told her, and she practically lit up with understanding. "I should have thought of that," she muttered, before turning to bark a few quick commands to the soldiers behind.

Perhaps a third of the company unslung recurved bows from where they hung upon their saddles, aimed high, and loosed. A small swarm of arrows buzzed through the air, angry wasps hunting prey, to plummet point first into those gently dancing grasses to either side of the trampled path left behind by the Mahdreshan bandits.

Shooting blind, it was no surprise that none of the Kirresci archers actually hit anyone. Their sudden volley had all the effect Nycos could have hoped for, however.

It drove the brigands' own archers, who had lurked prone in the high grasses waiting for their targets to draw near, out into the open. Panicking at their premature discovery, they rose—to their knees, if not their feet—and began to shoot back.

Against armored soldiers, who had once more spurred their mounts into a furious charge and whose own more experienced bowmen and –women now had visible quarry at which to aim, they had no chance. Two of Nycos's people fell, true, arrows finding or punching gaps in their hauberks of chain, and for that the enraged knight would see Mahdreshan blood fed to the dry and thirsty soil. Yet in exchange for those two lives, all seven of the enemy who had lurked in ambush perished beneath either Kirresci arrows or Kirresci hooves.

The fleeing fugitives redoubled their efforts, now, but it was only a matter of time. Their weaker horses tired, wheezing and foaming. With every step the soldiers neared. Nycos didn't doubt that they were technically within Mahdresh-claimed territories by the time they caught up, but again, lacking any obvious markers, who could say for sure?

And in the moment, who cared?

As any cornered animal, once the bandits knew escape was no option, they turned to fight. Spears and heavy chopping swords flew free to clash with *szandzsya* and sabre. The anger, the desperation, and—in one or two instances—the indignation in their features suggested the raiders were well aware this was a fight they could not win, yet neither were they going down without a struggle.

All save one. He and he alone continued in his flight, whipping at his steed with vicious but controlled strokes. Fear drove him, yes, but not the outright panic Nycos would have expected from a man abandoning his comrades to certain death.

*Hmm.*

"Archers!" he called over his shoulder. "I want that man off his horse!"

Then the two opposing forces came together in a deafening clash, and he had no more time for contemplating any foes but those he faced personally.

Avalanche lived up to his name. Hundreds of pounds of dense muscle and chain barding slammed, screaming, into the enemy. The first brigand fell, his steed broken and driven into the dust by the living boulder upon which Nycos rode, and already Nycos was after the next.

Most of the soldiers had hefted their shields as the lines met, guiding their mounts with their knees, laying about with sabres or with *szandzsya* spinning in one-handed grips.

Not Nycos. Leaving his shield hanging from the saddle, he clutched to the horn with his left hand, fist so inhumanly tight it deformed the leather. So anchored he slid his left foot from the stirrup and leaned far out to the right, his sabre-spear whirling. The first spin severed the arm of a Mahdreshan who had thought himself beyond the knight's reach; the second opened the screaming bandit's chest.

Another came at him in a charge, hunched low behind a lance slightly thinner but easily twice as long as the *szandzsya*. Clearly the brigand assumed him an easy target, off-balance and lacking a shield.

Confident that none might spot the impossible details in the chaotic melee, Nycos reached out with his own weapon quicker than a striking serpent, knocking her spear aside so the lethal tip passed him harmlessly by, then leapt from his already precarious perch. Inhuman muscle and bone propelled him, fast and far, so that his own armored body collided with hers as swiftly as the galloping horses themselves. He felt the bandit simply *give*, bones crumbling at the impact. Her spear fell to the grass from limp fingers, and only her feet, wedged in the stirrups, kept the dying raider from following suit. A quick shove solved that problem, then Nycos twisted and sawed at the reins, turning the wildly frantic horse about. He whistled for Avalanche to return to him, hoped the horse could hear him over—

A second, smaller spear—hurled, not thrust, albeit it from close range—slipped in beneath the cuirass he wore and punched through the chain hauberk protecting his sides.

And there it stopped, the impact jarring him in the saddle and sending a jolt of pain through his body. Bruising, but otherwise inconsequential. He smiled broadly enough for the stunned young brigand who had thrown that spear to see the gleam of his teeth even through the ventail of Nycos's helm.

Not that the man's shock lasted long, as one of Nycos's soldiers appeared behind the paralyzed fellow and brained him with a flanged mace.

*That*, though of course none knew it, was why Nycos rarely bothered with his shield: Not out of "high-born knightly arrogance," as some of the lower ranks whispered when they thought he could not hear, but because he trusted to his sorcerously hardened skin to stop most blades or bludgeons already slowed by his armor.

He found, as Avalanche trotted to his side, that his charge, and the leap that followed, had carried him clear through the small mass of the enemy. He stood now beside that copse of trees and, looking beyond them, could just see the fleeing man some distance across the plain.

He was, indeed, escaping now on foot. One of the Kirresci archers had taken his horse out from under him. An impressive shot, that. Nycos owed the company a round of drinks when they got home.

"Sir Nycolos!" Rahdel rode up beside him as he swung himself back over Avalanche's saddle. Her helm looked to have absorbed most, if not quite all, of a nasty blow. The rim was bent inward along one side, and even as he watched, she unhooked the ventail—a "veil" of chain that protected the lower face—from one of the cheeks and the nasal guard, pushing it aside so she could spit a mouthful of blood and dust.

"Are you injured, Captain?"

"Nothing serious." She waved back at the remnants of battle. "We cut most of them down on our first pass, sir. It's just cleanup, now."

"Good. See to it that everything's secure and then come after me!" Without waiting for acknowledgment, he spurred Avalanche forward. The beast sprang eagerly into a run, so that Nycos felt as though the whole world had lurched beneath him.

It was, in his current life, the closest he could come to recapturing the joy of flying. He would never admit it, but he loved the aggressive creature for that.

The cluster of lush greenery flashed by, and once again there was only grass and the occasional lonely bole. Avalanche's hooves tore divots in the gently rolling waves of earth, clumps of sod and individual verdant blades launched back in a veritable wake. In seemingly no time at all they had swept by the bandit's dying mount and closed inexorably on the man himself.

He spun, revealing shaggy beard and sun-reddened skin—and a compact crossbow, an intricate weapon not often found in the hands of Mahdreshan criminals.

Nycos leaned even as he hauled Avalanche's reins violently aside. The warhorse twisted, nearly tumbling end over end, then screamed as the powerful weapon *thrummed* and steel glanced off steel with a piercing screech.

Now the mighty beast *did* fall, in a roll that might have crushed Nycos's leg had he not yanked it from the stirrup at the last second. He found himself lying awkwardly beside Avalanche, his legs resting atop the horse's heaving side. From here he couldn't see the barding that protected his mount's chest and head; knew the bolt hadn't penetrated, but not how badly the armor had been crushed, or how much damage the impact might have inflicted. A hot rage burned in his gut, and he tried to roll aside so that he could stand.

A sharp tug at his shoulders and his waist stopped him cold. He might have pulled his leg aside in time, he realized, but both his kaftan and his sabre, sheathed at his side, were pinned by Avalanche's massive bulk. His hand was empty. His *szandzsya* must have been thrown aside when he fell.

And from yards away, he heard the grunt and metallic *click* as the raider cocked the crossbow for a second shot.

Nycos roared upright, reaching down to snap the buckles off his belt and ripping himself free of the tattered kaftan. The bolt drove itself through that fabric, deep into the soil where he'd lain a heartbeat before. Rolling with the momentum of his lunge, Nycos dove over his fallen horse, reaching out to yank his remaining weapon clear of the sling by which it hung from the saddle.

His *szandzsya* was yards away, his sabre pinned beneath Avalanche, but no need to rely on his claws as of yet (nor to damage his gauntlets, in ways that would prove troublesome to explain, in the process). Nycos rose, a vicious warhammer held ready in two fists. He rotated it slowly, deliberately showing off both sides of the weapon's head: the four-pronged bludgeon first, then the curved steel raptor's beak of a pick, either one capable of obliterating armor and bone.

The brigand dropped the crossbow, impossible to load for a third time with Nycos so near, and drew his sword. Although very gently curved, much as a Kirresci sabre, this was not the same sort of weapon. Thicker and heavier of blade, this was meant to hack and to chop where the sabre sliced; forged for power, not finesse. In his other hand he produced a small buckler from the back of his belt, then lowered himself ever so slightly into a shield-first stance that looked—to Nycos's admittedly inexperienced eye—far more disciplined, far more *military*, than one might expect from a Mahdreshan thug.

Nycos advanced around the horse with equal care, grass bending and crunching beneath his tread.

His foe knew what he was doing. He swayed aside, away from each tentative swing of the warhammer, or else brought his buckler around to intercept. The tiny shield couldn't absorb the force of even a moderate blow, not from the crushing head or beak, but the man never blocked directly. Always he angled the shield so the hammer slid away, or slapped it aside with the thick steel edge.

He proved equally adept with the chopping blade, swinging and spinning the weapon in a smooth flow. He let the weight and momentum of the sword handle the brunt of the work, putting his own muscle into it only to change direction or recover from a missed slash.

Where Nycos advanced, the other retreated, trying to entice the knight to step into his weapon's arc. Where Nycos feinted, his opponent never faltered. No matter how Nycos struck, with whichever end of the hammer's head, the brigand wasn't there, or else his shield was. Once or twice he even parried with his heavier sword, a tactic that made Nycos nervous. The blade was no axe, it *probably* lacked the power to chop through the warhammer's fat wooden haft—but Nycos didn't care to rely on "probably."

Around they circled, stomping rough patterns into the grass. And in so doing, Nycos grew careless.

It wasn't that he forgot his inhuman might or the other advantages his dragon's sorcery could invoke. No amount of time trapped in a human body could cause that. He did, however, grow unconsciously wrapped up in the notion of defeating this opponent with the skills he'd mastered, and with the only slightly exaggerated strength and speed he'd already bestowed upon himself. Perhaps, in the back of his mind, he was testing himself, seeing if he was learning as swiftly as he believed himself to be.

He *was* a fast study, was Nycos; since autumn, he'd learned more of Kirresci martial arts and weaponscraft than most humans could have picked up in four or five times as long. What he yet lacked was experience, and so when the duel fell into a pattern—beat by predictable beat, step-following-parry-following-strike-following-step—he failed to take note.

His enemy did not.

A slip to one side where Nycos expected a step back; a change of direction, a slash of the blade; the crunch of rending mail.

Tearing pain shot through Nycos's side, not much above where the spear had failed to injure him earlier—but this time, there was no such failure. Not even his toughened skin had saved him, not from a cut so fiercely and expertly delivered. He felt the sick sensation of metal sliding through meat, the hot rush of blood escaping the wound, welling up through links in the chain, drenching the padding and clothes beneath.

Which wasn't to say his armored hide had done him no good. The cut was agonizing, nearly driving him to his knees, slowing him, weakening him. But any other man would be dead, organs lacerated, maybe even his spine severed.

And Nycos decided he was through testing himself, through fighting human to human.

He had practiced, these many months, mastering new tricks and learning how to more easily and more swiftly invoke the old. Skin closed over the wound, not healing it completely—it had gone too deep into muscle, too near his organs where he dared not reshape himself—but preventing further blood loss. And then that skin, and indeed his entire body, turned rigid, coming over with a pattern of deep amethyst scales. Power surged through his limbs as an instant's focus transformed those muscles into something never meant to be contained within the human form.

Howling in fury, Nycos sprang at his horrified foe.

Now the warhammer flew through swift, sharp arcs, impossible to predict, nigh impossible to *see*. Blows that should have sent him stumbling when they missed instead flowed one into the next as he recovered, dragging the weapon back into line through sheer main strength.

Perhaps the raider knew that he could not possibly outrun his monstrous assailant if he broke and fled, or perhaps he simply never had the opportunity to try, but he stood and fought to the end. It was a sign of his skill and determination that it took as long as it did—almost fifteen whole seconds, from the moment Nycos dropped the facade—for that end to come.

By the time Captain Rahdel arrived with half the company a few moments later, Nycos had cleaned blood and brain from his weapon and caused his body to revert back to, if not fully human, then near enough that no observer would note the difference. He even, with a growl of pain, forced the wound to reopen, so he might have it properly treated without raising questions.

He was kneeling beside Avalanche—who, Nycos was delighted to learn, had only been stunned and perhaps concussed—when he heard the captain's familiar "Sir Nycolos! Are you all right, sir?"

"I've been better, Captain." He rose, indicating the bloody rent in his armor. "But I'm a damn sight happier than the other fellow."

The captain shouted an order, and one of the soldiers dismounted and began digging bandages, poultices, and the like from his saddlebag.

"The others?" Nycolos asked, wincing as he worked at removing his breastplate and hauberk.

"Sweeping the grasslands, making sure we didn't miss anyone. They'll be joining us shortly."

"How many?"

"Four dead, sir. Only one of the wounded I'm concerned we might lose. Everyone else should recover well enough."

Four. Not bad against a force of raiders this size. Not great, and not part of his report he looked forward to making, but not bad.

"I don't—" Nycos winced as the soldier slathered some sort of herbal concoction over his wound. "I don't think the man I chased down is just another Mahdreshan raider, Captain."

"Sir?"

"He hasn't been on the road as long as the others. His face is still sunburnt. He's not been out here long enough to get weathered. And he's not quite as filthy. And I'm not convinced he's Mahdreshan at all."

Rahdel started. "How can you tell that, sir?"

What could he say? The man didn't especially look Mahdreshan, but in cultures as racially mixed as most nations of southern Galadras, only about half the people, on average, really resembled any particular nationality. And somehow, Nycos didn't think the truth—that he'd given the man a good sniff with his unnatural senses, that his sweat was different, that he didn't smell as though he'd spent the last months or years eating the same stuff as the others—would go over well.

"Just a hunch. Fighting style, little details like that."

"Hm. Well, you may be onto something, sir. I had a few of the soldiers searching the fallen, see if we could figure out whether they were part of a larger band, maybe even find something the damn Mahdreshan government couldn't shrug off. Didn't come up with anything in that regard, but Valladi found a sizable pouch in the saddlebags of the man we think was their leader."

"Yes—ow! Be careful with those bandages! Ahem. Yes, Captain?"

"Pouch was half full of silver *zlatka*, Sir Nycolos."

"Kirresci minted?"

"Yes, sir. But that'd be an awful lot of raw coin for these bastards to have gathered from a few border towns, wouldn't you think?"

Nycos pointed a thumb at the man he'd killed, and several of the soldiers hopped from their horses to look him over.

"Yes, sir!" one called back. "Pouch full of them!"

"So either Mahdreshan bandits are paying good silver for an outsider to travel and pillage with them…" Captain Rahdel began, her tone making it quite clear what she thought of *that* hypothesis.

"Or this man paid them," Nycos mused, "to… what? Strike certain villages? At certain times? As an escort? Or a diversion…"

He chewed it over and decided he abhorred the taste.

"Gather the company," he ordered. "Sound horns if you have to. Anyone still scouring the plains, call them back. As soon as this torturer-in-training is finished jabbing at my wounds with acid and sackcloth—"

"It's salves and bandages, sir," the soldier piped in, not looking up from his work.

"—acid and sackcloth, we're making an early camp. We all need rest, and I want us mounted up and on our way to the nearest border station by dawn. Oh, and I want that body— clothes, weapons, pouches, all of it—wrapped up and brought with us. Something rotten's going on here, Captain, something beyond a few savaged villages. I want to see if anyone's heard anything from home while we've been out here."

---

The stations and checkpoints sitting astride the roadways on Kirresc's northwestern border were symbolic at best. Oh, they had their gates, their small shacks where guards could watch the highway without sun or rain or wind beating on them, the larger cottages further back where they bedded down and entertained themselves in their off hours. Yet the terrain for scores of leagues was grassland or sparse forest, without natural barriers larger than a few rolling hills or gentle streams. A fence ran for miles from the road, but it couldn't possibly encompass the whole border. It was easy enough to travel around, even easier to climb if one were traveling without horse or cart.

Open. Exposed. Vulnerable.

And the reason that Kirresc's government put up with the lies and gameplaying by Mahdresh. Better to deal with their regular irritations than to risk the city-state and its territories withdrawing from the treaty of mutual defense against Ktho Delian aggression. So precarious was the political balance that the loss of even a single ally could spur Ktho Delios to action. Better occasional Mahdreshan bandits crossing that wide-open border than Deliant legions.

Nycos and his company had tethered their horses to a length of that fence and now stood in what shade they could find, waiting on the station's commander. The anxious knight, still pained by his wounds—a sharp, fresh ache from the new, a dull throbbing reminder from the old—leaned against the guard shack. On occasion his attention wandered to Avalanche, who cropped unenthusiastically at the sun-baked grass, but so far as Nycos could tell, the warhorse had recovered from his close call. If anything, the beast seemed vaguely embarrassed by it all.

With that concern fading, then, and being in no mood for idle chatter with his soldiers, Nycos found himself gazing down at his helmet, which he held in both hands and slowly rocked from side to side, watching the partially unhooked ventail flow and scrape across the steel bowl of the helm in an almost liquid fashion.

A peculiar bit of armor, that, though Nycos was certainly no expert. Originally, or so he had learned, the heavy chain hung from all sides of the helm, protecting the back of the head, the neck, even draping over the shoulders of the wearer. Now that Kirresci armor and metalwork had advanced, now that solid steel protected much of the head and neck, now that chain hauberks often had reinforcing bands or breastplates, the chain portion of the helm guarded only the wearer's face—part of the nose, the mouth, the chin. It was effectively a compromise design, offering less protection than a full faceplate, but cheaper and easier to produce, far lighter, and—of greatest import to the wearer—far less constricting of breath or vision.

None of which was immediately relevant, but pondering such minutiae made Nycos more comfortable in his efforts to fit in, present himself as more knowledgeable than he was. And it passed the time.

Time, of which the commander on whom he waited had already taken too much. That was all right, though. Unlike his underlings, who could only stand and grouse impatiently, Nycos overheard bits of shouting from inside the small house that served as a barracks. The woman wasn't keeping them waiting deliberately, she was trying to figure out precisely what had gone wrong.

And who was to blame for it.

She finally emerged from the structure, mail jangling, boots all but stomping. An older woman of iron in hair and posture, she might have been Rahdel's sister if not for her far paler complexion.

"Sir Nycolos."

"Commander."

"I apologize for the wait. And for the... miscommunication."

Oh, but he knew that look, had seen it many times on many faces in the past months, that combination of shame and fury. One of her subordinates, whoever had bungled things, was going to get more than an earful.

"Messengers were dispatched to all the border patrols in the area," she explained stiffly. "They had your routes, your schedules. They successfully located all the others, I don't know *how* they could have missed you."

"We *were* somewhat off course, pursuing the raiders, commander."

"Yes, yesterday. Maybe the day before. The runners should have found you a week ago."

"Well, never mind how, for the moment. Just tell us what's happening. Your men only gave us the very basic gist when we arrived."

"Yes, sir." The station commander made herself relax, if only a little. "I haven't been told all the details myself, of course. But apparently one of the Oztyerva Palace servants was caught passing information on to an outside party who Marshal Laszlan believes to have been a foreign agent. This man fled Talocsa before he could be apprehended, and we were instructed to watch for him, try to locate him before he could cross the border."

One man, along the entire border with Mahdresh? As likely find a specific tick in a pack of stray dogs. Still…

"You have a description or a portrait of this man, commander?"

She handed him a rolled parchment.

"Any word on which nation he was spying for?" he asked as he unfurled the image.

"Not that I heard, sir. I don't think they knew."

"Hmm. Captain!"

Rahdel appeared almost immediately at his side.

"Does this look like the man I killed to you?"

She peered at the sketch, frowning. "You can never be too sure with these, but I'd have to say no, sir."

"That's what I thought, too." He allowed the parchment to curl itself back up, then tapped it thoughtfully against his chin.

"It wouldn't make sense for an escaping spy to ride with the raiders, anyway."

"A diversion, then? The man with them was a comrade, using the raiders to draw our attention while the spy escapes?"

"Seems most probable, doesn't it? It was probably overkill—I doubt we'd have had much luck finding a single fugitive—but still, it fits."

"And the failure of the messengers to inform you, Sir Nycolos?" the commander asked. "Also due to enemy action?"

"No, I don't believe so. Assuming it wasn't just bad luck…" He didn't finish the notion aloud, but assuming it *wasn't* just bad luck, it felt *personal*.

"Captain Rahdel, take over the company. You've only a few more weeks out here, I'm more than confident you can manage."

"Yes, Sir Nycolos. And you?"

"I am making an early return to Oztyerva. What happened out here needs to be reported, in-depth—and what's happening back *there* needs looking into."

"I'm sure they have people doing just that, sir."

"Yes, I'm certain they do." He smiled, though he knew the officers, ignorant of his unique talents and abilities, would take it for arrogance at best. "But they don't have me."

# CHAPTER FIFTEEN

Nycos strode through the stone halls of Oztyerva, grateful to be out from under the midsummer blaze. He had come to fully understand, over the last month or so, why—for the many followers of the so-called Empyrean Choir—the sun god Alazir was among the most highly respected and revered deities, but not widely beloved. How, he wondered for what was far from the first time, did normal humans, who could not magically adjust their bodies to better deal with the heat, learn to stand it?

He nodded or smiled or spoke his greetings to those he passed, accepting their own in turn; a dramatic change indeed from earlier days! But so, too, had things changed while he was away on his border patrol. An undercurrent of worry, of suspicion, flowed beneath even the friendliest exchanges. Gazes lingered too long, or flickered away uneasily. Steps were stiff, as though everyone were self-conscious about some unseen observer. Armored soldiers, always present in the palace corridors, now appeared in greater numbers than Nycos ever remembered seeing, standing sentry or marching patrols where none had been deemed necessary before.

Whatever espionage or intrigue had occurred here, King Hasyan and his advisors clearly took it seriously. Nycos increased his pace, sweeping toward the throne room, and if his speed and his bulk weren't sufficient to clear his path, the intensity writ large across his features certainly did the job.

When he finally stepped into the great hall, beneath the watchful gaze of several guards, he realized he would have to move aside, stand with the bulk of the gathered nobles and await his turn to speak—although Marshal Laszlan did acknowledge his arrival with a quick nod from beside the throne. Many waited to address the king, including Dame Zirresca, who must have only just returned from her own patrols along the northern border with Ktho Delios, but it was not to any of them that his Majesty currently spoke. No, the king and his advisors atop the dais were engaged in conversation with two figures Nycos knew by appearance and by name, though he was only passingly familiar with either.

One, an old and dark-skinned man in a flowing robe of purple and gold, could almost have been a male version of the physician, Lady Ilkya. He had the same gaunt, spindly limbs and age-roughened features. The other, a round-faced, sandy-haired woman of middle years, wore a blue gown, silver-trimmed, of an almost but not quite Kirresci cut.

Ambassadors, both—Aadesh Kidil of Suunim, and Leomyn Guldoell of Quindacra.

Nycos had entered in the midst of Leomyn's response to whatever the king had just asked her.

"…official response," the ambassador was saying, cooling herself with a folding fan that perfectly matched her gown, "would have to be that Quindacra would never stoop to spying on, or infiltrating the palace of, our neighbors and good friends of Kirresc. I might even have to go so far as to take offense that you would even suggest such a thing, Your Majesty."

"I see," Hasyan replied with surprising good humor. "And if I were to utter a royal command that you provide your *unofficial* response, Ambassador Guldoell?"

She returned a sad smile and as much of a shrug as her formalwear allowed. "Then I would tell you, Your Majesty, that I'd be the last person to know if we *were* spying on you. They don't tell me anything that might cause conflict between my loyalty to King Boruden and my duties as envoy to your court. Frankly, they don't trust me that much."

Was Ambassador Guldoell always this open, this dismissive of her own position? Nycos had been present in court for very few meetings with the emissaries of other nations, as he'd remained focused on learning what he needed to know of Kirresc itself. He'd have to ask Smim if the goblin knew more about this than he did.

"And you, Ambassador Kidil?" Hasyan asked. "What have you to say if I ask whether the spy we unearthed recently was Suunimi?"

"I say," the old man replied with a friendly grin, in a voice even deeper than the king's own baritone, "that if we truly needed to learn something from Kirresci you wished not to tell us, we have far more efficient and subtle ways to go about it."

From many, it would have been a grossly disrespectful remark, but Aadesh had been Suunim's ambassador to Oztyerva Palace for decades. He and King Hasyan knew one another well, were even friends so far as their positions and political duties would permit. Thus, his Majesty simply laughed.

Nor was it an idle boast. Even before he'd become human or cared much for their borders, Nycos—Tzavalantzaval—had known of Suunim's importance. It was there, so history and legend would have it, that the Cennuen people first landed on Galadras after sailing across the treacherous Arrendic Ocean. Suunim was the womb of today's civilization on the continent, the birthplace of philosophy and modern government. They boasted the greatest archives, libraries, schools—if it could be known, people said, it could be learned in Suunim, and travelers came from all over not only to study, but to share new discoveries.

It meant that Suunim had people loyal to it—to what it stood for and to its institutions and history, if not its government—all over southern Galadras. Further, the archivists there were said to have mastered some of the greatest divination magics known to humanity. The astrologies that Balmorra Zas and people like her practiced had been born and developed within that nation's borders.

So when Aadesh Kidil claimed that Suunim need not rely on clumsy methods of espionage to learn what they wished, he might have exaggerated, but his words contained some measure of truth.

"Father?" It was Princess Firillia, standing along the opposite wall with her brother Elias and several royal cousins and favored servants, who spoke. "I understand that we must consider all possibilities, but are we not dancing around the most obvious culprit?"

It didn't require Nycos's enhanced hearing to pick up the name "Ktho Delios" among the many mutters and whispers sparked by her comment.

"In fact, we are not," Hasyan told her. "Ambassadors? Thank you for your time. Should I learn anything regarding this incident that I believe has bearing on either of your nations, I will of course inform you immediately."

Aadesh and Leomyn bowed and made their departures. Only when the courtroom doors had thudded shut once more did his Majesty continue.

"We have just summoned Dame Zirresca back from patrolling the Ktho Delian border, where she was—among other duties—assigned to watch for any evidence of buildup or other military activity. Zirresca?"

"Your Majesty." She advanced, knelt briefly, then spoke. "Unfortunately, I can only report that my observations in that regard are inconclusive. I witnessed a great deal of troop movement, border patrols, and military exercises—but that's normal for Ktho Delios in any but the coldest winter months. I cannot say I saw anything to suggest they're any *more* active than normal.

"Nor did my patrols discover any hint of the spy escaping over the northern border, though of course with so many leagues of wilderness to cover, the odds were ever against us locating him."

"You wouldn't have caught him anyway," Nycos announced. "He didn't go north." Then, with sudden realization as every gaze turned his way, he knelt. "Apologies, Your Majesty. May I—?"

"Of course, Sir Nycolos. Rise, and speak."

He did so, advancing to the center of the room. "I have reason to believe," he began, "that the fugitive you sought actually fled north*west*, across the Mahdreshan border."

"And you let him go?" Zirresca demanded. "You let him escape you? What sort of—"

"I did not 'let him go,' because I never encountered him. As you pointed out, finding one man in that much wilderness? Nigh impossible—especially since I was not even aware we were hunting for him."

"You weren't—?"

"Sir Nycolos," Orban Laszlan interrupted, "please tell us why it is you believe our spy fled that way, if you didn't see him for yourself?"

So Nycos offered his report, leaving nothing out: the raiders, the outsider among them, the silver *zlatka*, and the peculiar failure of the runners to find his company on patrol, to deliver the news of the escaping spy, when they managed to contact all the others.

"It's not hard proof," he acknowledged as he wound down. "The outsider *could* have been paying the bandits for some other purpose. But it certainly all fits."

"It does," Orban mused. "A pity you found no evidence on the man to suggest who he served, whether this operation was Ktho Delian or... well, anyone else's."

"No, Marshal. But I did bring the body and all his belongings back with me. Perhaps others, with a more thorough examination, might find something I missed."

"Very good thinking, Sir Nycolos!" Hasyan said. "And well done, reporting this to us so swiftly. We are well pleased. We're about done here for the nonce anyway—my advisors and I need to discuss all we've learned today—so go take your ease, clean off the dust of your travels. We hope to see you at supper tonight."

Nycos bowed, offered Orban a friendly smile—and a second one to the faintly scowling Zirresca, for good measure—and made his way toward the exit through the slowly dispersing crowd.

———

"I'm not a man frequently given to prayer." Margrave Andarjin sounded steady as ever, but his hand shook just enough that filling his goblet was proving difficult. "But I could see my way to offering multiple paeans to Neras if she'd be willing to turn her attentions to Nycolos damned Anvarri!"

"Bit of an overreaction, isn't that?" Zirresca, lounging back on the sofa, sipped her own drink. "He discovered that someone might have been using the Mahdreshans to cover the spy's escape. It's *good* for us to know that."

"And it's another victory in the eyes of Laszlan and his Majesty. He was supposed to be out of the way and wasting his time on a meaningless patrol!"

"It's a victory," Zirresca acknowledged. "Hardly the end of the contest, though. It's unfortunate he was the one to make the discovery, yes. I'll manage."

"But—"

"Did *you* find anything on his housebroken goblin while I was away?"

Andarjin sighed, pulled out a chair, sat, stood again almost immediately and wandered to the far wall. There he leaned an arm against the stone, peering into his wine as though seeking answers there. "Nothing. He actually had the creature managing his estates while he was away, and so far as my people can tell, it didn't make a single error! It's been polite, it's kept out of the way. Many people are still unhappy having it around at all, but it's given us no excuse to violate Nycolos's protection. I understand it's even become *friends* with a few of the servants."

"Hmm." Zirresca seemed equally fascinated with her own beverage, swirling it about in the goblet. They'd hoped to somehow use the goblin to weaken her rival's position, to indicate that he was unsuited to the office, but... "I suppose we'll have to drop that line of attack, then."

"We're having to drop a lot of those. He's recovering much faster than I anticipated, Zirresca."

"He's still behind. Anything on Lord Kortlaus?"

"No, he's not returned from his own patrol yet."

"Nothing regarding his... *relationship* with his subordinate?"

"No," the margrave repeated. "If there was anything to those rumors, the baron kept it from influencing his behavior in any way his soldiers noticed. Nothing but positive reports, if uninspired. I can handle the baron politically, if it comes to that. I'm telling you, Nycolos is the greater threat. He's the one we need to worry about."

"I never argued it," Zirresca said.

Silence again, as Andarjin returned once more to his chair. "It could have been worse for us, I suppose," he acknowledged. "At least Nycolos didn't capture the actual spy. *That* would have been a feat impossible to downplay."

"Yes, but as we both mentioned in court, the odds of finding one man along an entire..." The knight froze at a sudden, horrid thought. She sat upright, pulling herself from the deep embrace of the cushions. "Andarjin? Please tell me you're not the reason the runners failed to find Nycolos's company!"

She took his instant of hesitation before opening his lips to respond as answer enough.

"For the gods' sake, Arj! That's practically treason!"

"Oh, nonsense. Maybe a messenger simply got a little bit lost while tracking a patrol route. Even *if* such a thing were to happen deliberately, what difference would it make? You said yourself Nycolos had precious little chance of actually finding the man. Besides, nations spy on each other all the time. I'm quite sure this one particular operative learned nothing that his government—and we have no reason to believe it's Ktho Delios, as opposed to one of our ostensible allies—couldn't acquire some other way."

"I am not remotely satisfied with that answer," she said, "and I don't believe her Highness Firillia would be, either."

"Zirresca, what are you thinking of—?"

"I'm not going to tell her anything. This time."

"Thank—"

"But you're going too far, Andarjin. It needs to stop. I *will* be Crown Marshal, and I will support you and Princess Firillia over Prince Elias, when the time comes. But I will not dishonor myself, and I certainly will not endanger Kirresc, to do it!"

"But of course, Zirresca. Nor would I."

"So long as we understand each other."

*Oh, yes,* Smim noted silently from his by now familiar spot in the alcove above, lying flat to avoid casting a visible shadow in the last rays of the setting sun. *I think we all understand each other very well.*

———

"Well," Nycos said, voice echoing from the depths of the bath, "isn't *that* a fascinating tale?"

"I thought you might think so, Master," Smim replied from the adjoining chamber, where he currently straightened up after the knight's breakfast—a task that appeared to consist, for the most part, of gulping down every scrap of leftovers like a starving hyena. "The question," he continued around a mouthful of breaded and spiced liver sausage, "is what you wish for us to do about it."

Nycos allowed his head to sink beneath the warm water as he pondered. After retiring from court last night, the fatigue of the long, hot patrol had caught up with him. Since neither Kortlaus nor Mariscal were available to talk—the margravine was off visiting her father's court, though she was expected back any day—he'd bothered with only a quick dunk in tepid water, to wash away the worst of the dust and stink, and then taken to his bed. Fast asleep when Smim returned from his regular bout of eavesdropping, he'd only heard the goblin's report this morning, first over breakfast and then during a far longer and more luxurious bath. (He had, of course, dismissed the servants after they'd refreshed and heated the water, rather than allowing them to bathe him—in part so that he and Smim could speak in private, but also because he remained uncomfortable with his body's reaction to their ministrations.)

"We," he said, upon coming up for air, "are going to do nothing for now."

He couldn't help but chuckle softly at the audible pause in the goblin's chewing, followed by a hard swallow. "Pardon, Master? Nothing?"

"It's useful information, Smim. And we'll definitely want to keep an ear on Andarjin."

"Oh, if only I'd thought of that while you were gone, Master."

Nycos ignored the sarcasm with the ease of long practice. "But for right now, we've no proof of any wrongdoing. It's your word against theirs, and we both know who comes out ahead in *that* contest. It might even give them the excuse they want to act against you."

Dishes clattered as Smim began to collect them from the table in the suite's main chamber. "On that subject, Master?"

"Hmm?"

"We ought to discuss giving me a formal title."

Nycos paused in the midst of reaching out, fingers brushing the ceramic vial that held the mixture of soaps and oils he'd come to prefer for his beard. "Pardon?"

"There's a status, a pecking order, even among the servants. It's based largely on the rank of masters and employers, but our own official positions do enter into it. My impression is that some of them, and even a few of the nobles, would be more comfortable around me if they knew how to categorize me. And that might make them more liable to speak to me."

"I see. And what shall we call you, then? My palatine?"

"Seeing as how you have neither a royal household for me to oversee, nor a kingdom in which I might serve as your official voice and surrogate, I think not, Master. Besides, I'd rather not give Jarta reason to request my execution. Being without a head might make it more difficult to listen in on conversations."

"I can understand how it might. 'Seneschal' would seem to be out for many of the same reasons. Any suggestions?"

Somehow, despite the goblin being in the other room, Nycos knew that Smim shrugged. "Most of your brethren have squires serving them."

"Am I training you for the knighthood, now?" Nycos asked in amusement, running the soap through his facial hair. "Sir Smim, the Goblin Knight?"

"Pah! I'm certain there must be worse ideas, Master, but it might require more than the two of us working together to come up with one. Although," he added with an audible smirk, "it would be amusing to see everyone's reaction to the notion."

"In any case, we'll figure something out. I don't see that there's any rush to—" Nycos fell silent for an instant at the abrupt pounding on the door. "See to that, would you, Smim?"

He listened as the goblin's footsteps crossed the room, then ducked under the water once more to wash the soap from his face. The lingering scent of breakfast, when he emerged, was for some reason stronger than the bath oils.

Due to the draft from the open door, maybe.

"Sir Nycolos!"

The messenger, a young palace page, stood in the doorway to the bathing chamber, Smim hovering behind. Clearly something of import, then, if the goblin had allowed the boy inside rather than insist he wait for Nycos to dry off, dress, and come to him.

"Yes, what is it?"

"I'm to tell you that runners have reported a foreign delegation approaching Talocsa, sir."

"Um... All right? And?" Kirresc received envoys and ambassadors from most of the southern nations on a regular basis, and Nycos himself wasn't much involved with international—

"It's Ythani, sir."

The knight was out of the tub like a breaching orca, sending a geyser of water across the ceiling and the floor. "My clothes, Smim. Now!"

"Yes, Master!"

"And Smim?"

The goblin halted in mid-spin. "Master?"

"My sabre, as well."

———

It would be inaccurate to say Nycos had never seen the throne room so crowded—in fact, a great many of the lower ranking gentry and servants who normally formed the ever-present audience along the right-hand wall were notably absent—but it had certainly been some time since he had observed so many of the land's highest and most important assembled here all at once.

The king, of course, sat in state upon his throne, Crown Marshal Laszlan as ever at his side. Present, too, were the

Palatine Denuel Jarta and Prelate Domatir Matyas, also hardly unusual. Hasyan had also, however, gathered to him the astrologer, Balmorra; Amisco Valacos, Kirrisc's Judge Royal; and a small entourage of other politicians and military leaders, several of whom Nycos had never before seen save in passing. Even the king's offspring, their Highnesses Elias and Firillia, stood amidst the group at the dais, as advisors, rather than in their customary spot along the other wall.

Nycos found himself standing beside Zirresca, who offered him a polite if frosty nod of greeting. Nor were they the only knights of the realm present. In fact, the entire front row of those waiting along the wall was made up of men- and women-at-arms. The other nobles, margraves and counts and barons, stood behind them. Nycos wasn't entirely comfortable with Andarjin at his back, even though he knew the man was too clever to do anything violent or foolish, but he did appreciate the need for a show of strength.

He heard many footsteps approaching from beyond the hall doors, and a symphony of voices that were not all Kirresci. The other accent sent a scurry of centipedes down his spine; his shoulders tensed hard, bunching the lines of his tunic. He could only hope that the kaftan he wore over it hid his discomfiture.

Messengers had run back and forth between the palace and the approaching delegation long before they arrived, as would have been standard, so Nycos was unsurprised when Denuel Jarta stepped forward, even as the massive doors swung open, and announced, "Haralius Carviliun, emissary of honored Ythane!"

*Honored.* Nycos wanted to spit.

The man at the head of the contingent boasted the same pallid skin and sharp, smirking features as Justina Norbenus once had, though not so alike as to suggest any familial relation. His thinning hair was a pale yellow that didn't much stand out from his flesh, and he wore a burgundy robe of office with a golden sash. His guards and assistants halted near the entrance, moving to stand along the back wall, while he alone advanced.

Only when he stood a few paces from the dais did he make obeisance, a peculiar combination of a low bow and a brief kneel, his fist clasped to his breast. "I greet his Majesty, Hasyan III, in the spirit of warmth and friendship. I am humbled. You do me great honor by allowing me to appear before you." His timbre was soft yet powerful and carrying at once.

Somehow, Nycos thought it would take more than an audience with royalty to humble this man. Possibly an ancient invocation, or an act of divinity.

"As you do us," the king replied with equal formality. "We are overjoyed to receive the greetings of our dear friend Praetor Anurius, and his senate, from whom we hear far too infrequently."

A very polite and political way of saying *We have no ambassadorial ties or treaties with you, we rarely have anything to say to one another, what the hell are you doing here?* Nycos had to choke back an amused snort.

It was a question that would go unanswered for some minutes, however. First there were additional exchanges of pleasantries, regards from this ruler to that noble, expressions of affection and honor that were such patent nonsense in both directions it was a wonder Prelate Domatir didn't combust where he stood. Then, of course, nothing would do but to discuss political matters in the world that could impact both nations (of which there were few) and the various possibilities for trade agreements and other economic treaties (of which there were even fewer).

Finally, at just about the point where Nycos worried whether the shortened lifespan he could expect while in human form might not be enough to see him through this interminable charade, Haralius at last got down to the meat.

"I do have one other matter I must discuss with Your Majesty," the envoy said, each word all but marinating in reluctance. "I hate to bring up something so unpleasant during the first real conversation our peoples have had in so very long, but I fear the issue must be addressed."

"Of course. You have our complete attention."

"It has to do, Your Majesty, with the murder of one of our highest and most revered citizens."

Hasyan frowned. "We are deeply sorry to hear of that, emissary."

"Yes, well. It was, it is my sad duty to report, not merely her death alone, but that of a great many others, honest workers and craftsmen all, who labored under her at the mine she owned in the Outermark Mountains."

Nycos felt it then, surging, raging beneath the surface of his skin, of his heart, as it hadn't for months. The fury, the fire, the searing hatred for all that had been done to him and all who were responsible. No matter its source—his resentment of the direction his life had taken, the pain of his experiences and the wound that would never heal, Smim's foolish ramblings about the alien influence of human blood and brain upon his soul—he had forced it back. Through iron will and careful thought, self-examination and constant practice, he had pushed it deep, extinguished all but its faintest embers, until he had almost forgotten, save in his darkest or angriest moments, how it had felt.

No more. It roared in his mind, shrieking at him to lash out and damn the consequences, to salve his pride in the blood of those who had wronged him and to *dare* these mewling, insignificant primates to protest his actions!

Had he tensed? Growled? Was it something less material, a change in his breathing or his attitude visible only to another warrior? Whatever she'd sensed, Zirresca placed a hand before him—not touching, but ready to hold him back if necessary.

"Steady on, Nycolos." Her gaze remained straight ahead, at the yammering Ythani fool, and her lips barely moved with the whisper. "I'm sure he more than deserves whatever you've got in mind, but trying it here and now won't help anyone."

That she spoke at all was, he knew, not out of any affection for him, but rather concern over the political repercussions of any ill-conceived violence. Nevertheless, he grunted his thanks and worked at taking deep, calming breaths.

So he listened, quivering with repressed emotion, as Haralius told his tale. He spoke of mangled, bloody bodies, brutally slain and left strewn about the mine and its surrounding camp, including the deeply lamented Justina Norbenus herself—although, Nycos couldn't help but note, he made no mention of the unnatural wounds that would have been left by the mountain fey. The envoy spoke, as well, of many months and many Ythani soldiers, searching the mountains, the rocky hills and the badlands, the wilds of the Outermark, in a desperate hunt for survivors. How they had found mostly lingering scraps—a length of torn fabric caught in a thicket, the remnants of an old and long-cold campfire—or, on occasion, bits of human bone, picked clean by scavengers. How, after battling fearsome beasts and marauding goblins, they had successfully located barely half a dozen survivors, guards or escaped slaves who had managed to flee the massacre and survive the many hardships of the Outermark.

And how each and every one of those survivors had offered sworn testimony as to precisely what had occurred.

"It grieves me terribly to say it, Your Majesty," Haralius concluded, hand to his heart, "for I dearly dislike the notion of bringing you pain at such a nascent stage of what I hope will be a new brotherhood between our nations. Yet I am sworn to the truth—and the truth is that, by the descriptions offered by every witness, the attack on our mine, this massacre of innocent Ythani citizens, was led by a knight of Kirresc."

The volcano within Nycos's soul erupted, refusing any longer to be suppressed. It was all he could do, required every ounce of will he possessed, to keep his outburst partially contained, to resort only to bellows rather than blades—or worse.

"And what of the rest of the tale, you lying worm?" His shout was a gale to shake the chamber. "How this knight who supposedly 'led the attack' was enslaved in the depths of your mine! How *many* of your slaves, he included, were waylaid, taken by no legal or moral right! How they were beaten like beasts, how this Norbenus was a criminal and a monster, and how she and her torturers died, not at the hands of any intruder, but in self-defense as these poor souls made their desperate escape! How—!"

"Sir Nycolos! Stand down!" Many voices called to him as one, but it was, as always, the battlefield-spanning cry of the Crown Marshal that penetrated. Nycos found that he had stepped forward without realizing, that not just Zirresca but several in the crowd had reached out to haul him back. The Ythani guards had dashed from their posts by the door to surround the envoy, each ready to draw the thick-bladed short sword hanging at their waist. Only their own restraint, the knowledge that pulling steel in their host's throne room would instigate far worse, kept their fists empty.

"Really, Your Majesty," Haralius said, his tone unconcerned save for a touch of disappointment, "is this Kirresci courtesy? Am I to be subject to shouted incivility and slander? We use only the most respectable of slavers, known throughout Ythane, Mahdresh, and beyond. Men who would never stoop so low as to acquire merchandise by *any* illicit means, let alone violence. Frankly, I would be insulted on their behalf were I not already offended on mine—and my deceased countrymen's.

"I know not who you are, Sir Knight," he continued, now turning toward a fuming Nycos, "but you have no right, and it would appear no honor. And I wonder if what we are seeing here is, mayhap, the outpouring of a guilty conscience?"

Nycos straightened, statue-rigid. Firmly he brushed aside the many hands that held him, then—internally wincing at but otherwise ignoring the livid expression on Marshal Laszlan's face—directed his next words toward the king.

"I beg your pardon, Your Majesty." He was honestly faintly amazed at how steady a tone he managed now. "I believe it would be best for all concerned if I were to absent myself from the remainder of this discussion. By your leave?"

Hasyan nodded, saying nothing. Nycos bowed and, equally wordless, made for the door, ignoring the glares every one of the Ythani soldiers cast his way in lieu of their weapons. Palace servants hauled the great portal open before him, slamming it shut again behind, and Nycos was more grateful for his Majesty's forbearance than he could have expressed.

Now, if nothing else, he could find himself somewhere private before the violence came. Now he could avoid humiliating himself further, and could ensure that only objects, rather than people, broke beneath the wrath he'd thought to have mastered.

# CHAPTER SIXTEEN

For the third time in less than twenty-four hours, Nycos found himself approaching the throne room.

He'd been summoned back, as he'd known he would be since he'd taken his leave so abruptly and with the bare minimum of civility toward his liege. The moments immediately following that departure were a crimson blur he could scarcely recall. He had no notion of how long he'd stalked the halls of Oztyerva, conflicting urges waging brutal war within him.

Ultimately he'd decided not to return to his quarters, instead passing the bulk of the afternoon in one of the palace's most distant and most isolated gardens. There, once he'd determined he was truly alone, he'd allowed himself to run amok, purging the worst of his wrath in a paroxysm of violence. Whole bushes were uprooted and left strewn about, soil-encrusted roots dangling like the entrails of slain soldiers. Several of the smaller trees, which even his strength could not wrench from the earth, had instead been mauled, whole stretches torn asunder by inhuman claws, leaving behind a disturbingly sweet-smelling abattoir of bark and sap.

Presumably, when the groundskeepers discovered it, they'd assume a wild animal must have somehow wandered onto the property, though the walls and the gate guards should make that impossible. Maybe they'd even launch some sort of hunt. He decided—later, when his thoughts had emerged from the fog and reassembled themselves in some sort of order—that it might make a good exercise for some of the younger soldiers.

He also recognized, not just later on but even in the moment, if he were being honest with himself, that the whole tantrum was silly. Immature, childish, and very much not in keeping with either who he once was, or who was supposed to be now.

Maybe Smim had a point, damn the little creature.

Again the great doors swung open before him, and Nycos forced his mind back to the present. The hall was less crowded than it had been. Not only was the Ythani contingent no longer present—doubtless making themselves comfortably at home in Oztyerva's sumptuous guest quarters—but well over half the bystanders had been dismissed as well. Only his Majesty's advisors and particularly high-ranking nobles remained. It meant, at least, that Zirresca wasn't here to see him berated. Then again, as both a margrave and as the heir apparent to Kirresc's most powerful archduke, Andarjin *was*, so his rival knight would probably hear every word of it regardless.

Well, so be it.

As was customary, Nycos approached the dais and then dropped to one knee, speaking only after receiving permission to rise. "I apologize for taking so long to respond to your summons, Your Majesty," he began. "I was walking the halls, and I fear I did not make it easy for your page to find me."

"And do you feel that is the only breach of decorum worth discussing, Sir Nycolos?" It was not the king, but Orban Laszlan, standing beside the throne with one hand on his Majesty's shoulder, who spoke.

"I certainly acknowledge that my outburst was inappropriate."

"'Inappropriate' is the word you'd choose? Not 'undiplomatic'? 'Offensive'? Possibly 'damaging to your king and country'? You've been doing marvelously over the past months, Sir Nycolos, but this is an unfortunate, and worrying, step back."

"In the face of that Ythani bastard's lies? His effort to paint me as the villain after all I endured? I think 'inappropriate' *is* sufficient, Marshal. Or are we to allow the insults to flow in one direction only?"

"In this court, such insults and falsehoods are *not* yours to answer!" Orban bellowed. Then, less vehemently, "Ythane enjoys throwing their weight around, as the only remaining vassal state of Tir Nalon. They know well that, despite generations of quiet, the elven empire still has a reputation for both great power and unpredictability. This? They've merely turned what happened in the Outermark into an excuse for rattling sabres. They can be assuaged with a diplomatic apology and a modicum of… restitution."

From the low grumbles to his right, Nycos could sense that he was not the only one present displeased with that particular resolution. "You mean a bribe they can extort from us, and an admission of wrongdoing that was never committed."

"Sir Nycolos—"

"I will offer Ythane no apology, Marshal Laszlan. Under any circumstances."

"Even were I to order you to do so?"

The knight bowed his head. "I am your loyal soldier, but this is a matter of personal honor, not a military concern. No."

"And if your king commands it?"

Nycos looked up, his expression stricken, helpless to answer. To refuse a royal command… Well, Hasyan didn't seem the sort to declare such minor disobedience treason, although he surely could, but it would permanently besmirch Nycos's honor, and probably obliterate any chance he had to succeed Orban. Yet, how could he possibly bring himself to—?

It was the king himself who saved him. "Fret not over that impossible choice, Sir Nycolos," Hasyan said, reaching up to squeeze the fingers that Orban had laid upon his shoulder. "I'll not be giving you any such order."

"Thank you, Your Majesty." Nycos bowed, low and sincerely.

"Amisco?" Hasyan called.

Kirresc's Judge Royal stepped to the front of the dais, the heavy fabrics of her robes and cape of office sliding audibly against one another like heavy leaves in the wind. "Your Majesty."

"Please work with Denuel to draft a message of condolences and apology worded to contain no admission of guilt admissible in any court—Kirresci or, to the best of our understanding, Ythani. Make no mention of Sir Nycolos by name, either. We'll send that to the praetor and his senate along with a small token of restitution."

"Of course, Your Majesty."

Hasyan leaned back in his throne, uncomfortable though it must have been, and then met Nycos's eye. "You still object, Sir Nycolos?"

"We owe them no apology, Your Majesty, and we *certainly* owe them no gold. This is extortion, pure and simple, and we're giving in to it. This—forgive me, Your Majesty, for saying so— makes Kirresc appear weak."

"Sir Nycolos!" It was the palatine, Denuel Jarta, who spoke now. "It is inappropriate for you to question his Majesty's decisions, particularly in the presence of—"

Prince Elias stepped forward. "I think he's right, though. Why should we pay Ythane a single *zlatka*? It makes no sense, and it's humiliating."

"Your Highness..." Jarta spoke with the tone of a man repeating the same lesson or explanation for the umpteenth time. "Sometimes it's better, in the long run, to pay a small amount in gold and pride now than to suffer greater expenses later."

Elias looked as though he desperately wanted to disagree, but wasn't remotely sure of where to begin.

Nycos decided it was as good an opening as any. "Your Majesty, your Highness, Palatine, perhaps I'm too close to the issue to see the larger picture. And I assure you, I mean no disrespect, I simply wish to understand. We have no financial or diplomatic ties with Ythane. We share no borders with them. What future costs are we avoiding by conceding to these baseless demands?"

He took a risk even asking, he knew that. Everything he'd learned of Hasyan III over the past months suggested that this was a monarch who welcomed discussion, so long as it did not cross into disobedience or insubordination, but he'd never seen said discussion quite reach the point of open questioning as he did now. Further, it was just possible that he was outing himself as ignorant on a matter that he, as Nycolos Anvarri, should already be familiar. His genuine lack of comprehension conspired with his anger to make him ask, however, and he could only hope that selfsame anger, the fact that this was personal to him, would excuse any apparent gaps in his understanding.

"We *do* trade, and share a border, with Mahdresh," Judge Valacos pointed out. "And they have substantial economic ties to Ythane."

"Ythane also controls a length of the Dragon River," his Majesty said, picking up the thread. "Without which we lose one of our primary routes to points north. We don't do a *lot* of travel or trade with the frontier towns or the Vingossa tribes, but little doesn't mean none. To say nothing of the religious significance of the Vingossa Plains to Kirresci citizens who worship the Vinnkasti.

"And," he continued before Nycos could object, or point out that those concerns—while perhaps genuine—were awfully minor, "there are none of us who can predict with certainty how Tir Nalon might react to any open insult given their vassal state."

"It's my understanding," Nycos said carefully, "that the Bronze Empire has remained almost entirely quiescent regarding anything beyond their borders for generations."

"It has," Marshal Laszlan said. "But the elves don't think as we do. They're ageless, and not remotely human. Who can guess what drives creatures such as that, or what might give them reason to stir?"

Nycos could have offered a unique perspective on such questions, but chose, for obvious reasons, to refrain.

"The ultimate point to all this, Sir Nycolos," the king told him, "is that we determined some time ago just how far we would humor Ythane's posturing, to what extent and how often we could tolerate their pushing before risking their threats, and the unknowable hazards posed by their fey masters. As much as I know it stings at your pride—and not just yours; you're foolish if you don't believe we feel it, too—the current circumstance, and the amount of gold we feel confident will satisfy them, falls within the 'worth paying them off to avoid the hassle' category."

Although his teeth ground so fiercely he feared the next words he spoke might prove jagged enough to draw blood, Nycos bowed his head in acquiescence. In his Majesty's intonation, and perhaps in the admission that his pride, too, was wounded, Nycos heard the unspoken message that any further challenge or questioning of the issue would not be welcome.

At least he wasn't alone in his distaste, even if none of the others had reason to take the matter as personally as he. None of Hasyan's advisors seemed any more thrilled about the decision than the king himself, and the expressions many of the gathered nobles directed his way suggested approval of the challenge he and Prince Elias had raised, and even sympathy over his own history with Ythane's rich and powerful.

Andarjin's gaze, too, lay heavily upon him, but in *that* nobleman's features, Nycos could read nothing at all.

———

The attack came out of nowhere, unheralded and unexpected. And Nycos, playing right into their hands, could not have made it much easier for them if he'd tried.

After court had adjourned, and following a polite appearance at dinner—where his tightly wrapped caul of frustration had allowed little of the conversation to penetrate his ears, and made even the most delectable foods taste of ash—he had chosen once again to spend some time walking Oztyerva's winding passageways. In his current mood, he preferred the constant motion, aimless wandering through arteries of stone, to the conscious thought that would be required were he to settle down to the peace and quiet of his quarters or engage anyone in prolonged discussion.

He might have made an exception, to the latter, for Kortlaus or Mariscal, but as both were away…

Night had fallen, as night always does. Servants wandered about, lighting a few additional torches in their sconces or lanterns in their brackets. Traffic thinned as gentry and staff alike took to their beds, until Nycos shared his route with only sporadic guards or messengers. By keeping to less busy portions of Oztyerva, far from the living quarters, he managed to create for himself the illusion that he walked, isolated and alone, through some long-abandoned labyrinth.

An illusion shattered by the sudden pounding of charging feet.

They numbered a dozen, easily, spilling out of the corridors to either side as Nycos passed through the next of countless intersections. Each was hooded or masked, and wielding a wooden cudgel: axe handles, old table legs, quarterstaves, bludgeons of every kind. Their choice of weaponry suggested that their goal was not to kill, but that hardly meant their intended victim was in for an easy time.

The first blow struck the arm he hastily raised to protect himself. The slight toughening of his skin—which he had adopted as his norm, a compromise that allowed him to appear and to feel sensation as normal, while still offering some degree of protection—prevented the bone from cracking, but only just. Pain surged through the limb, a jolt of man-made lightning, and he felt his grip grow numb, the arm hang limp.

The abrupt ferocity of the attack staggered him, stunning him for a split second. A second cudgel struck him across the back of his skull. Blazing stars and streaks of black flashed across his vision, a wave of nausea nearly swept him from his feet.

And then he learned that one of his assailants carried a tool other than a wooden bludgeon.

Someone hurled themselves at him, leading with a shoulder, so that Nycos flew backward, lips split and bleeding, to slam against the wall. The masked figure who had struck him followed just as rapidly, crushing him between flesh and stone. Nycos felt a cold pressure on his wrists, a sudden resounding click…

They'd manacled him. The steel cuffs pinched his flesh, but far worse was that they boasted only a short length of fat chain between them, allowing mere inches of slack.

Clubs struck again and again, pounding his gut, his sides, his legs, until Nycos crawled on the floor like some low beast, his body seizing up in agony. The acrid, metallic scent of his own blood mixed in his nostrils with the stench of his attackers' sweat, a heady amalgamation of exertion, anger, fear. And still the rain of blows continued, not just cudgels now but kicks as well.

Kicks…

He remained aware enough to recognize that these were no Kirresci boots or shoes striking him. Here, at their level, he could see the leather strips that, wrapped and tied, formed the basis of Ythani sandals.

His Majesty's advisors, it appeared, had been mistaken regarding how easily the bastards would be satisfied for the deaths of their countrymen.

But then, for all the pain, the deep aches, the contusions and bruised bone, Nycos had no intention of letting them off so easily either.

A quick tug at the chain convinced him that he'd never break the thing. Had his arm not been numbed, weakened—had he the necessary concentration to focus—he might have strengthened his muscles enough to do so. Now it wasn't possible, certainly not without transforming enough to reveal himself as something other than human. Similarly, without giving himself away, he couldn't armor himself enough to shrug off their attacks, though he *did*, through great mental effort, thicken his hide a small amount. It didn't end the torrent of pain, didn't keep vessels from bursting beneath his skin or bones from flexing beneath the worst impacts, but it took the edge off.

And he still had a few tricks available to him.

Nycos had learned well and painfully, in his struggles to cross the Outermark, that he could never again breathe the fire that had been his birthright; that transforming his innards so much would invite the shard of Wyrmtaker to once more seek his heart.

But he'd had months in which to experiment, to learn the precise extent of those limitations. To learn he could manipulate the interior of his mouth, of his jaw, transforming just a trickle of saliva into the alchemical fuel that had, in his true body, been a vital ingredient of that fearsome conflagration.

Tucked into a ball as any human would have, trying to protect his most vulnerable spots from the storm of wood, Nycos struggled to focus, pouring every ounce of will into ignoring the pain until he felt things shifting beneath the flesh in his jaw. Then and only then did he allow his mouth to gape open, a viscous mix of blood and spit to wobble obscenely from his lips and splatter down upon the chain. A few quick passes with his tongue added to the solution, spreading it evenly across the steel links.

One last effort, putting everything he had into a surge of inhuman—but not *too* inhuman—strength. Nycos lunged to his feet, hurling himself upstream against the battering current.

He bowled two of his attackers over, deliberately stomping on the knee of one and exulting as it shattered beneath his heel, shoulder slamming the other across the hallway. At a half run, half stagger, he lunged down the corridor, not seeking escape but simply the nearest torch, crackling away in its sconce, unconcerned with the violence being perpetrated yards away.

Nycos all but fell against the stone, shoving the glistening, fluid-coated chain into the open fire.

The sheen of dragon's saliva ignited in a blinding crackle, so bright he had to look aside, so hot that—even with his arms fully extended—he felt a painful searing in his forearms and short length of his hair burn away.

Just as swiftly it was gone, the tiny amount of fuel expended in less than a heartbeat, but with it, the supernatural heat had melted wide portions of the links that bound him.

He turned to face his enemies, mere steps behind him, held the manacles up high where they might see the mangled, misshapen chain. He saw their apprehension, unsure how so brief an exposure to the low flame of a torch could have done such damage. Well, let them wonder.

Showing bloodstained teeth in a fearsome grin, Nycos tugged and the damaged links parted.

The torch crackled. The man whose knee Nycos had broken moaned in torment. Everyone else breathed aloud, fast and heavy, trying to determine how dramatically the circumstances had just changed. Several eyes drifted to the sabre at the knight's side, grimly certain that he must unsheathe the blade at any moment.

Indeed, Nycos dropped a hand to the hilt. Everyone facing him tensed, their attentions drawn involuntarily to the sword.

He charged, without drawing, and slammed his fist hard into the concealed visage of his nearest foe. Teeth gave away beneath the burlap mask, ripping bloody holes through the fabric. Several would have ended up embedded in Nycos's knuckles had his skin been that of a normal man. He loosened his fingers for an instant, clenched again, and when he withdrew his hand the mask came with it. He wanted a good look at these Ythani vermin who—

Except, despite the evidence of the sandals, the battered face staring back his way wasn't Ythani at all. Not only was it darker than the normally pale citizens of that distant nation, it struck in Nycos's mind the faintest chord of recognition.

The rest of his assailants surged forward in a single tide, determined to beat him down once more, remaining confident in their greater numbers.

Still Nycos chose not to draw his sabre. Furious as he was, he repressed the urge to slaughter those who would dare heap such indignities upon him. Too much was happening here that he didn't yet understand. Instead he snatched the axe handle from the man he'd just pummeled, letting the fool collapse and moving to meet the others. With his other hand he hauled the torch from its sconce, holding it near the base, letting the smoke and cinders plume as he waved it with deceptive languor at his enemies.

Had they known what they were about, had they all been able to come at him at once, those numbers might have made the difference—or at least forced Nycos to resort to feats of strength or endurance he could never have passed off as human. With his back to the wall, however, and the fallen man a partial obstacle to one side, they could approach only four or so at a time without stumbling into one another's way. And between Nycos's months of practice and the degree of strength and speed he *was* willing display, four at once… was not sufficient.

He struck hard, fast, and he aimed for the joints. He twisted, stepping inside the first man's reach and snapping an elbow with one swift blow. A vicious parry when another club swung his way, nearly knocking the weapon from impact-numbed hands, then a strike downward at an exposed hip, sending the foe limping away.

He turned, stepped, constantly moving but always keeping the wall behind him. The torch protected his open side—not so well as a shield, perhaps, but nobody was eager to approach the blazing brand and risk seeing their clothes or their hair set aflame. They learned quickly to stay away from Nycos's spinning bludgeon, too, but that hesitance left them unable to make any attack of their own.

Again the hall echoed with a sudden rush of footsteps, but any fears Nycos might have had regarding additional enemies were swiftly allayed. A small bevy of palace servants, their attention drawn by the sounds of battle, came racing around the corner, nearly stumbling over each other as they skidded to a halt.

"Sir Nycolos!"

"Stay back!" he called. "Fetch the guards!" While several of the new arrivals froze, shocked at the tableaux, one woman instantly pivoted on her heel and ran back the way she'd come, skirts held high.

Desperate, now, the ambushers made one last rush, perhaps hoping to catch Nycos distracted by the servants. He met their charge with his own, the axe handle whirling more than fast enough to crack a skull, to break an arm or leg and drive the bone through fragile flesh.

When that weapon cracked another man's club clear through, and a vicious thrust of the torch left a blackened blotch of flesh across a carelessly outthrust arm, the assailants finally had enough. Turning tail, pausing only long enough to hoist their wounded comrades from the floor, the lot fled back the way they'd come.

"Sir Nycolos?" The servants approached, now, timid and hesitant. "Are you all right, sir?"

"I'll live. Thank you."

He leaned hard against the wall, aching legs barely propping him up. He allowed the cudgel to drop, listlessly handed the torch to the man nearest him and pointed, with a grunt, at the empty sconce. Then he could only stare down at the broken manacles about his wrists and hope the guards wouldn't take too long to produce a key that fit them.

Oh, he'd given some thought to pursuit, but the throbbing and pounding of the punishment he'd endured, while less than might be expected, was sufficient to slow him down, to make him think that additional conflict was not a wise choice just now.

It was also unnecessary. As soon as the servants had rounded the bend, the sight of them had been sufficient to jog his memory, to give him a context for the face he'd recognized.

The bastard was, himself, an Ozteryva servant! Oh, not part of the regular palace staff, not someone who dwelt on the grounds, but one of the extra gardeners hired on during the spring and summer months. Nycos didn't know his name, didn't know where he lived, but none of that would stop him. He could track the man down if necessary. More to the point, merely knowing who he was told him much.

Namely that this ambush hadn't been conducted by the Ythani delegation at all. He was merely meant to *think* they had, thanks to the timing and, especially, the footwear.

And he could think of only one man in the palace who had both the means and the motivation to orchestrate such a deception.

———

"To what end, though, Master?" Smim asked, carefully wrapping Nycos's salve-smeared arm. The heavy bandaging would not merely compress the limb, hopefully reducing any swelling, but also tied it firmly to a length of wood, immobilizing it. Nycos winced, and already worked at mentally reshaping it back to its earlier, uninjured form—a process that, though far faster than waiting for it to heal naturally, would still take longer, and leave him in rather more pain, than he would have preferred. "I don't doubt that it was the margrave behind this, but what do you imagine he hoped to accomplish?"

"I think *Ow!*" Nycos recoiled as Smim shifted his attention from the arm to the split and battered skin around the knight's lips. "Watch it, goblin!"

Smim stood back, holding fingertips coated in salve up before him. "You were the one who insisted I not call any of the servants or a physician who would actually know what they were doing, Master."

"I don't want them to know how bad the injuries are."

"They're not nearly so severe as one might expect, Master."

"Yes. That's what I don't want them to know."

The goblin nodded. "Wise. It does mean, however, that you're going to have to tolerate my own tender ministrations. Which will go a lot more smoothly and swiftly, especially around your mouth—which currently looks as though a particularly excitable mule trod upon an overripe plum—if you were to find it in yourself *not* to shout at me every other breath. Master."

"You," Nycos grumbled, "are not a born healer, Smim."

"I will try to contain my sorrow, Master."

A few moments of silent prodding and slightly less silent wincing followed, until Smim had finished applying the herbal balm to Nycos's mouth and had moved on to a badly bruised shoulder.

"I think," Nycos said then, picking up the thread of their earlier conversation, "Andarjin probably felt he'd discovered a way to tilt at two targets at once. He despises me, of course, for potentially standing in Zirresca's way. He's also furious at Ythane, and he's no happier about King Hasyan's choice to assuage them and pay them off than are the rest of us, even if he understands the expediency of it.

"So, this attack? Either it gives his Majesty cause to send the Ythani packing for the violence and insult done to me, and thus to him, as their host—or, perhaps, it might have encouraged me to respond with insults or even bloodshed, thus shaming the court and doing severe damage to my standing. And no matter which way that goes, I'm badly beaten enough that I'm working at a disadvantage for months. Or at least would be, if I were what he thought me to be."

"My own guess was similar," Smim said. "What do you intend to do about it, Master?"

Nycos sighed, deeply, irritated at the weaknesses inherent in both his human form and his current position. "I'm uncertain what I *can* do, Smim. We've no proof of any of this. Andarjin's not that careless."

"We could track down your gardener, Master."

"I've been trying to decide if it's worth our time. We could probably force him to talk, but it would be his word against Andarjin's. And that's *if* the margrave approached him personally, which I tend to doubt. At best, it would prove a small conspiracy. People might make their own assumptions, but it would point no solid fingers at any culprit. A lot of work for, at best, a small smirch on Andarjin's reputation in the opinion of only a portion of the court."

"You're assuming we'd have to rely on his word. He might have proof."

"I am assuming that, yes," Nycos told him. "We both know how likely it is that Andarjin left a provable trail."

"You know, Master," Smim suggested with an artificial nonchalance that instantly had Nycos worried, "we don't actually *need* proof of anything. There are ways he could be handled that wouldn't lead back to—"

"No."

"But—"

"No, Smim."

The goblin sighed. "You're taking this whole affair awfully casually, Master."

"Don't mistake me. I'm furious. The very instant I have solid cause to move against Andarjin and tear his world down around him before picking his heart out through his ribs in tiny, quivering gobbets, I will. But I won't undo everything I'm working for, or my chance at as comfortable and powerful a life as this feeble body offers, by throwing away all I've learned since we arrived.

"Besides," he added hesitantly, "just at this moment, my standing with Marshal Laszlan is on uneven ground at best. He was far angrier over my unfortunate outburst earlier than his Majesty was. I'm lucky he's so loyal to the king. I imagine I'd be in for some punitive duties, otherwise."

"Yes." Smim chuckled, his tone snide. "Loyal."

Nycos peered at him, confused. The goblin, despite obvious effort, could not help but laugh.

"Master, I recognize that you've been away from the palace far more often than I—and, further, that the ways of humans are *vastly* different than those of dragons. But we simply *must* work on your powers of observation and comprehension where people are concerned."

"If you're quite through amusing yourself," Nycos said, clear in his tone that he did *not* feel similarly, "perhaps you would care to explain?"

"His Majesty and the Crown Marshal are not just liege and vassal, Master, or even friends."

"Meaning?"

Smim spoke as if to a child. "They're a couple, Master. Lovers."

Nycos stared. Blinked. Continued to stare.

"Oh," he said, some few years later.

It was, indeed, a notion with which dragons were unfamiliar. The wyrms were capable of affection for one another, on those rare instances when they met without instant territorial conflict, but nothing more. When the mating urge came upon them—at the pinnacle of a cycle lasting many decades—it was sheer biological impetus, one that overpowered all but the most intense loathing and drove them together with whatever fellow dragons were both compatible and available.

The idea of linking sexual activity with emotional intimacy, or any purpose beyond breeding, was utterly alien—as was the concept of romantic love itself.

"And… this is known?" he asked finally, because he had no idea what else *to* ask.

"Not widely discussed, Master, but yes. It's something of an open secret among the court. Since he's already produced heirs from a legal marriage, there's no cause for anyone to object. Some few feel he engaged in this relationship too soon after the queen died, but that was long enough ago, now, that it's rarely brought up."

Again Nycos could do little more than blink, trying to wrap his mind around such foreign notions. "Humans are peculiar, Smim."

"No arguments from me, Mas—"

They both turned toward the door, wondering—and then swiftly realizing—who could possibly be knocking at this hour.

Smim politely showed her in, offered her a drink which she didn't refuse so much as fail to notice. Then, without waiting to be told, he stepped out into the hall to join her lady-in-waiting (who had never really gotten over her habit of looking down upon him as though he were a particularly squishy bug she'd found in her breakfast). He pulled the door to but not quite shut, granting his master a modicum of privacy.

The injured knight, who had risen to his feet, waited as Marsical slowly crossed the chamber between them, avoiding the intervening table almost by accident.

"Welcome home, my Lady."

"Oh, Nycos…"

"It, ah, looks far worse than it is."

"Sit down."

"I—"

"Sit!" It wasn't much of a shove—clearly she was concerned about other wounds she couldn't see—but it got her point across. Nycos allowed himself to fall back into the sofa.

"You have balms and salves?" she asked him, casting about the room.

"I assure you, Smim's already tended to—" Well, *that* expression might have changed his mind even had he still worn his original body. "Over there," he pointed, giving in.

She scooped up the various bowls and tins, planting herself beside him and carefully daubing at the most obvious of the lacerations on his face. Nycos gulped down a sigh that he felt would go unappreciated just at this moment. *What is it with this woman?*

"I actually arrived last night," she said softly, running a finger across his cheek. "I wanted to tell you that I'd heard of what happened on your patrol, and to congratulate you on discovering the spy's arrangements with the Mahdreshans, even if you couldn't catch him."

"You did?" He spoke carefully, unwilling to jar her hand against various sore spots. "I had no idea…"

"Smim told me you were sleeping, that you were fatigued from your travels and making your report to his Majesty. He even permitted me a brief look, though he wouldn't let me stay."

"He trusts you more than most," Nycos said with a faint smile, "but to him, you're still just another human."

"You'd drifted off atop your blankets. I knew you must truly have been exhausted, so I didn't insist he let me wake you."

"I appreciate the consideration."

Mariscal dipped another finger in the salve, then gently leaned his head forward to rest on her shoulder so she might treat the angry contusions on the back of his scalp. He felt the warmth of her skin through her blouse, the flutter of her pulse along her neck. Further, he found himself gazing down inside her neckline and wondering with a flash of near panic why this particular view should strike him as particularly enticing. He almost welcomed the dull wave of pain as she prodded at the injuries, trying to locate them beneath his hair.

"I also heard of the argument in court this morning, the lies they—" Her arms tensed, breath caught; the pounding of her heart grew fast and violent. "Was it them?" she demanded, lifting his head with both hands. "Did those Ythani bastards do this to you?"

"Um, what? I…" Nycos's world spun, a maelstrom of confusion, of pain, of sensations and urges for which he had no name and even less ability to cope. "That is, I was supposed to *believe* it was them, but…"

It hit him, then, all at once. Mariscal's overly emotional state, the abrupt switch from her deep concern and need to care for him to her rage at those who'd attacked him—but more even than that, their interactions over the prior months, the closeness punctuated by periods of offense and anger over what he had thought of as quite minor slights.

Only because he had now been primed to consider human relationships in that context, because of the conversation he had just concluded with Smim regarding King Hasyan and Orban, did Nycos *finally* understand.

*She wants us to mate!*

It was too much. Countless clashing human emotions, none of which he knew how to handle; the vast array of conflicts and intrigues he struggled to navigate every day; the memories of Tzavalantzaval's last few clutches, and the tragedies that had befallen them… It crashed over Nycos in a frothing wave, until he truly felt as though he were drowning.

"Are we actually working to figure this out?" he blurted—panicked, angry, unthinking. "Or are we just wasting time with more of this foolish mating ritual?"

He wondered for a brief and horrid instant if the woman had actually died. She stopped breathing. Her skin paled to a sickly grey, not unlike broken and sun-bleached wood. Two dawning suns of pure crimson rose to burn in her cheek, equal parts embarrassment and fury.

"How dare you?! I have stood by you, I have excused every one of your mistakes, your insults, because of all you've been through. But I will *not* be treated this way!"

"I'm sure there are many rooms in this palace where you wouldn't need to worry about that, aren't there?"

She said nothing more, only rose and, her hands shaking but her steps steady and firm, walked slowly from the chamber. Her lady-in-waiting cast Nycos a single withering glare before falling in behind her mistress.

Nycos looked at the goblin, who stared at him in despairing astonishment from the doorway.

"What?" Nycos demanded.

Smim went to bed.

# CHAPTER SEVENTEEN

Nycos deliberately arrived late to court the next morning, having permitted and even encouraged the servant who had delivered his summons to assume he still recovered from his injuries of the prior night.

In fact, his wounds were already partly healed, thanks to the effort and shapeshifting magics he directed their way. None could doubt that he had taken a beating, but any observer would assume it could not have been terribly severe, or else must have occurred at least a week gone by. Even his arm, though far from perfect, was recovered enough that he could go several hours without any binding or sling.

When he did finally head toward the room, again clad in his most formal attire and with sabre hanging at his side, the knight still chose to wait a time before approaching the great doors and the guards beside them. From down the hallway he could hear voices raised in what the diplomats would call "emphatic debate" and others would call "screaming argument," and he could not help but grin. He had long pondered how to handle the coming events, and it was only to his benefit that emotions ran hot.

Finally, head high and shoulders straight, he strode toward the men-at-arms, who swiftly hauled the doors aside.

Voices faltered as both sides of the argument became aware of his arrival. Everyone, Kirresci and Ythani, turned his way, observing his approach, and curious whispers were his heralds. He nodded with rigid formality to Haralius Carviliun and his entourage, offered a more sincere greeting and even an open smile to his fellow knights, nobles, and servants along the wall. He forced himself not to linger on Margrave Andarjin, though he did note a brief flicker of curiosity from the man—presumably because Nycos appeared far healthier than he ought.

He halted, dropping to one knee before the dais. "Your Majesty. Apologies for my tardiness."

"Understandable given the circumstances, Sir Nycolos. Are you well?"

"Well enough, Your Majesty. Somewhat stiff and sore, but I've had worse. I should be fine."

"We are glad to hear it." He motioned for the knight to stand. "If you would be so good as to take your place with the others?"

"Actually, if it please Your Majesty, might I address the court and our honored guests? I have news of direct import regarding the current… discussion."

Hasyan, Orban, Denuel Jarta, and Amisco Valacos frowned almost in unison, doubtless leery of letting him speak to the Ythani delegation, given his outburst of yesterday. King and Marshal engaged in a hurried exchange of whispers, with occasional input from the others. They came to a decision swiftly, however, and it seemed that the attack on Nycos had bought him some leeway.

"Very well, Sir Nycolos," Hasyan said. "Speak. But take care."

"Of course, Your Majesty." He half pivoted, so he might address either the royalty and advisors on the dais, the assembled gentry along the wall, or the Ythani, all by merely turning his neck this way or that. "I couldn't help but pick up on the essence of your conversation," he began, "as I approached the throne room. Although I imagine I might have guessed at its nature, even had I not overheard."

Not that *anyone* could have missed it, at that volume. Between the witness accounts and Nycos's own broken, incomplete report, a flurry of accusations had awaited Haralius and the others when they'd approached the throne that morning. The envoy, of course, had angrily refuted every one of them, even going so far as to accuse witnesses of perjuring themselves in order to slander Ythane. The argument had, from that point, pursued the obvious course.

"Having had the night to recover," Nycos continued, "and to think back on the events of the evening, I have come to the conclusion that Oztyerva has been sullied."

Haralius looked fit to burst. "How dare—!"

"Not by you, emissary."

The man slowly deflated, gawping.

"No, by a criminal conspiracy directed, at least in part, *against* our Ythani guests." He hoped nobody heard how near he came to choking on that final word. Before anyone could speak or begin to ask questions, he went on explain how the Ythani sandals and other details were meant to lay the blame at the delegation's feet, but how the one face he'd seen clearly wore Kirresci features, and the voices he'd heard boasted the local accent.

That he'd recognized the man specifically he did *not* reveal, instead playing up those other signs far more than he'd actually noticed.

Dead silence reigned as he concluded his observations. Not a man or woman present could doubt him. He would never level such accusations—charges that could dishonor the entire Kirresci court, if only by association, and work to the benefit of those who had enslaved and insulted him—were he not certain.

The Ythani envoy himself broke that silence, his voice shrill. "And what do you propose to do about this… this insult and threat to myself and my people?!"

Nycos almost laughed aloud. Haralius couldn't have played his part any better if the two of them had planned it together.

"The envoy is quite right, Your Majesty. Clearly, until we can guarantee him the safety and hospitality we promise all our guests, until we can determine who his hidden enemy may be and why they've done this, he and his compatriots are in danger every moment they remain here. For the sake of the newly reforged bond of friendship between our nations, I suggest, in the very strongest of terms, that they be granted the protection of the best and most trustworthy soldiers we can muster and escorted to the border without delay. Let them return home, where they can rest in comfort and, above all, security, until we know it's safe for them to return."

From atop the dais, Orban replied, and though he kept the smirk from his face, it managed to escape via the faint gleam in his eyes. "I believe Sir Nycolos is quite correct. Our first concern *must* be the safety of our honored guests. I know just the soldiers, trustworthy to the last. With Your Majesty's permission?"

Hasyan wore a matching glimmer of mischievous approval. "By all means, Marshal Laszlan. Haralius, my abject apologies for what has occurred, but we *will* keep you safe until you've reached our borders. No matter what."

"I…" The man was trapped, and he knew it. He'd demanded his hosts act on his behalf, and so they had. Unless he wanted to accuse the court, and King Hasyan himself, of collusion, he had to believe the danger was genuine. Nor could he legitimately demand the recompense they'd discussed earlier while Kirresc mobilized soldiers for his own protection, not without appearing wretchedly ungrateful and quite possibly exposing his motivations, and his entire mission, for the gold-digging they were.

He could only scowl, furious but helpless, as the king's own personal guards quickly rushed him and his delegation from the hall, that they might swiftly and immediately pack for their well-protected journey home.

"A splendid suggestion, Sir Nycolos," Hasyan said when the Ythani were gone and the hubbub quieted once again. "Well done."

"Thank you, Your Majesty." *Of course, that is only half the problem solved.*

"What of the conspiracy itself?" Amisco, the Judge Royal, asked from beside her sovereign. "Have you any notion as to who might be behind it?"

*And there is the other half.*

"I have found no sign or proof of that, Judge Valacos," he answered carefully. "But I do believe we must launch a thorough investigation."

"With you leading it, Sir Nycolos?"

"I know that you've your own investigators," he told her, "but this not merely an internal crime, but also an act against another nation. So I do feel that the Crown Marshal ought to have a representative assisting with the investigation, someone who holds both social and military rank. However... No, it should not be me. *Must* not, in fact. My own personal history with the Ythani would taint the results. Any findings or secrets uncovered must be beyond any doubt.

"No." Again he turned to face the gathering along the wall, in part to study the reactions he hoped his pronouncement might elicit. "I believe Dame Zirresca should conduct the investigation."

The other knight visibly started, then stepped to the fore of the assembly. "Why?" she asked—a perfectly understandable question, given their circumstances.

"Because this is larger than our competition, Zirresca. Furthermore, when word reaches Ythane that it is one of Marshal Laszlan's presumed successors looking into this—and we all know that word *will* reach them—it will go that much further toward convincing them we take this seriously. I might have preferred Lord Kortlaus," he admitted, or rather pretended to admit. "But he's yet to return from his own patrols, and this can't wait. That leaves you."

"Very well," she agreed slowly, turning her attention to the dais. "If it please Your Majesty and the Crown Marshal to accept Sir Nycolos's counsel, I'm quite willing to take this on."

"We shall talk it over with our advisors," Hasyan replied, "but it seems sound thinking to us. Your efforts will not go unappreciated, Dame Zirresca—nor your suggestion and willingness to step aside, Sir Nycolos."

Both knights bowed. Zirresca wore a moue of faint suspicion, but Nycos fully expected that. No, it was the face of Magrave Andarjin that Nycos was interested in—and though the man kept his expression largely neutral, it was the growing chagrin he couldn't *quite* hide in which Nycos exulted.

For now, in addition to his bewilderment over the knight's apparent lack of severe injury, and his fretting over how much Nycos might know of his involvement, the margrave found himself maneuvered into a political trap. He couldn't possibly permit Zirresca to discover that he was behind the ambush. For all her flaws, Nycos was quite certain that his rival would never have gone along with such a plan. Andarjin would have to work against her, hide evidence, lead her astray—and in so doing ensure that she failed in her task, thus weakening her own campaign for the office of Crown Marshal.

It was, Nycos proudly decided, a political maneuver worthy of Andarjin himself.

He only wished, and grew irritated at himself for wishing it, he could discuss all that just occurred with Mariscal.

———

"Hello, Smim."

Despite himself, the goblin jumped, though he swiftly regained control and carefully shut the door. Nycos, stripped to the waist and reclining on the sofa with a glass of cherry wine, couldn't help but snicker.

"Greetings, Master. I thought you would be longer at court."

"What I had planned for the Ythani didn't require very long. Where have you been?"

"Oh, just running various errands and—"

"Smim?"

"Master?"

"I know you very much better than most people you lie to."

Smim offered a rough, phlegmy sigh and planted himself in a chair by the table. "Yes, Master. I was visiting Margrave Andarjin's chambers."

Had either of the two beings involved in the conversation been human, that might have led to a wide variety of questions and clarifications. What had Smim hoped to accomplish? Didn't he know Andarjin, too, would be at court, leaving nobody to spy on? Had he hoped to search the chambers for evidence of the margrave's misdeeds? If so, how had he planned to conduct any thorough examination without leaving any sign of intrusion?

But Nycos asked none of these, for he knew the goblin would already have considered all of that, and decided on an alternate course of action. And he knew, too, how Smim's devious and sometimes vicious mind worked.

"I told you I didn't want you taking any steps against Andarjin!" It wasn't a roar, for that might have been overheard by someone in the hall beyond, but Nycos easily made up in vehemence what he lacked in volume.

"I know, Master, but… That is…"

"But you thought you knew better. You thought my decision was too soft, too *human*. You thought you were protecting me from myself."

Smim hung his head. "Yes, Master."

"Listen to me, Smim." Nycos carefully placed his glass down on the floor, so that hands trembling in repressed anger would not shatter it. "I don't want Andarjin killed because I don't know what the political repercussions would be. For the court in general, and for me in particular. Our dislike for one another, and his support for my chief rival, are well known. An investigation, even without proof, could be more damaging than Andarjin is. *That's* why I told you not to act!"

"I understand. Forgive me, Master."

"We'll see." Nycos's scowl grew even deeper as he glanced down at his beverage. "Poison?"

"Yes, Master."

"You know that others often share his wine, don't you?"

"Mostly Zirresca, and if she died, too, it would hardly…" Whatever Smim saw in Nycos's expression, he clearly realized he'd best not finish that thought.

"Do I need to take steps, Smim?"

"No, Master. This was meant to be a gradual thing, to look natural. Even if Andarjin drinks the entire decanter himself, a single exposure to the poison shouldn't be fatal, though he'd grow quite ill for a time."

Nycos growled something. "Stop disobeying me 'for my own good,' Smim. I don't appreciate it. If it happens again, I might have to make that lack of appreciation more explicit."

"I understand. I'm sorry, Master."

It was Nycos's turn to sigh. "If you feel you *must* do something, why don't you try to find out more about the gardener who attacked me? See if he can lead us to… What, exactly, does that expression mean, Smim?"

"The man doesn't know anything of use, Master."

"You've already done that, too."

"I… Yes, Master."

"I don't want to know."

"No, Master."

———

"I cannot *believe* you spoke to her like that!" Kortlaus—finally returned from the east and his own patrol—spun his *szandzsya* in a wide arc, then retreated several paces across the open field.

"Yes," Nycos growled, taking a quick and largely useless swipe with his sabre and then moving to follow, "so you've told me. Time and time and time again. Have you any plans to *stop* saying it any time soon?"

The baron's answering grin, a mix of genuine good humor and simmering anger at his friend's foolishness, was visible through the chain ventail of his helm. "As soon as I can force myself to believe that even you could be *that* stupid."

Nycos snarled and lunged, feinting with his sword one way, arresting the blow and thrusting from another—and then doubled over, gasping, as Kortlaus's sabre-spear slammed, hard and bruising, into his hauberk-protected ribs.

"And that," Kortlaus said, extending a helping hand, "is why I insisted on full armor *and* blunted practice weapons. You're *clearly* not at your best right now, Nycos. Distracted."

"I wonder what with," the other answered through pain-clenched teeth. He accepted Kortlaus's assist, then ripped his own helm from his head, gasping for air and sweating in the baking summer sun.

Around them, the field was a small sea full of currents and whirlpools and islands of other training combatants. Individual duels such as his and Kortlaus's took place between clashing rows of soldiers in massed formation, which in turn took care not to cross over into the archery range. At the far end of the field, several chain-clad mounted knights with lances longer and straighter than *szandzsya* tilted at one another, less for practice than for sport and to show off for the less experienced squires. All was a deafening cacophony of voices and steel and pounding boots and more heavily pounding hooves, so that Nycos and Kortlaus could speak freely without risk of eavesdroppers.

"Seriously, Nycos," the baron said, voice raised only just high enough to be heard over the clamor, "what were you thinking?!"

"I've told you, I wasn't! I was still recovering from the attack, in pain, my thoughts on trying to figure out what had happened and who was behind it. I was preoccupied, and just sort of—blurted it out."

When Kortlaus had returned from patrolling the borders with the nation of Wenslir and the purportedly haunted ford of Gronch, he had gone straight to the throne room to make his report. There, too, the baron heard of all that had transpired in his absence, so by the time this morning came around and he finally had the chance to speak with his friend, he already knew of current events.

Which left their conversation free to focus on more personal—and, for Nycos, far more humiliating—topics. At this stage, he'd rather have been discussing the actual assault and the beating he'd suffered. It might prove less painful.

Kortlaus planted the haft of his weapon in the grass and leaned against it, catching his breath. "You've attempted to make things right, I assume?"

"At every opportunity!" And so, indeed, he had. Distraught as he'd been, it still hadn't taken Nycos long to understand the damage he'd done to a valuable alliance—and, though he was less inclined to admit it, to realize that he missed the margravine's companionship. "I've gone to her door multiple times," he continued, "but she won't speak to me. Her servants tell me she 'wants time to think.' I've sent messages, gifts. I even made another public apology at dinner once. I swear I'm becoming more known for those than anything else I've done. 'Sir Nycolos Anvarri, Knight of the Apology.'"

Irritated as he was, he couldn't quite repress a grin at his friend's chuckle. Kortlaus's laugh was infectious. He grew morose again swiftly enough, though.

"It's been weeks, and she still turns the other way if she so much as sees me in the halls. I've no idea how to fix this."

"Nycos, are you certain you *want* to fix it?"

He could answer that only with an eloquent blink. The baron sighed, then gestured with his helm, suggesting they resume their practice. Nycos crammed his own back on his head and raised his sabre.

"What I mean," Kortlaus said, launching a few probing thrusts with the sabre-spear, "is that your behavior toward Mariscal hasn't been the same ever since you returned from the Outermark. You've been friendly enough, but… little more."

Nycos sidestepped, dodged again, then slapped the *szandzsya*'s tip aside with his own blade and lunged. Kortlaus pivoted so the sabre scraped by, barely nicking his hauberk, and the pair began to circle. "Go on," was all Nycos said, since he didn't believe *I barely know how to recognize human romantic overtures!* would be a well-received reply.

"No matter how determined Mariscal may be to keep things prim and proper until you've acquired a station more her equal, few in Oztyerva are ignorant of how the two of you feel for one another." Kortlaus feinted, then launched a brutal kick to catch his opponent as he dodged, but Nycos didn't fall for it. "Or at least how she feels for you, and you *did* for her. But the relationship, what little the two of you show of it, has been decidedly—"

He scarcely managed to bring the haft up to parry a sudden slash from Nycos's sabre, and received for his trouble a closed fist to the helm that Nycos knew must have made his head ring. "Decidedly one-sided," he finished a bit woozily.

Nycos took advantage of the opening and stepped in, trapping the *szandzsya* between his arm and his ribs. Even as he struck at Kortlaus's chest, however, the baron twisted, hurling Nycos aside with his own weight and the leverage provided by the spear. The knight struck the grass, rolled, and came back to his feet just in time to parry a thrust to the belly. "What are you suggesting?" he demanded.

"Oh, for the love of..." Kortlaus retreated, planted his weapon in the ground in a signal to end the match, and once more took off his helm. "Nycos, you *know* how much appearances and propriety mean to her, how much she's bent her own rules fraternizing with you even as openly as she has! You know that she's thrown her entire support behind your campaign to become Crown Marshal in part so you can be together openly, as equals! And you know you were lucky not to have permanently alienated her during your, um, period of adjustment when you first returned. Your lack of warmth since, and then your asinine behavior that night? Knowing all that, you *have* to have known, on some level, how she'd react!"

"You're suggesting," Nycos said, tossing his own helmet to the grass, "that I don't *want* to be—involved—with Mariscal any longer." Somehow, that notion was more disturbing coming from someone else than it had been when confined to his own thoughts.

"Had you asked me months ago, I'd have sworn on something holy that you would never feel that way, but it's certainly a viable interpretation of your behavior."

"What do you think I ought to do?" Nycos asked carefully.

The baron burst out laughing. "I think you ought to remember who you're talking to, and ask someone whose interest in the opposite sex hasn't been dead and buried for over a decade. Men are just as crazy-making, but at least I understand where they're coming from." His laugh trailed away into a subtler grin. "Sir Jancsiv and Sir Tivador are supposed to be popular with the young noblewomen, you might ask them.

And rumor has it Prelate Domatir was quite the ladies' man before age and ecclesiastic duties slowed him down."

His grin, too, slowly faded. "Nycos, you can ask all the advice you want—from me, from anyone else, from the gods themselves if they somehow deigned to listen." He bent down to lift up his friend's helm and hand it back to him. "None of it means a damn if you don't know what you want to accomplish."

What *did* he wish to accomplish? His day-to-day life might well be easier, certainly simpler, if he needn't worry over the romantic pitfalls and personal implications of a relationship with the margravine. Further, on an intellectual level, such entanglements held no interest or appeal. If they crossed his mind at all, they struck him as a silly waste of effort, a time-sink without any value to offset the cost.

Then again, the pull *wasn't* intellectual, was it? However much he tried to ignore it, Nycos's human body, blood, and heart had their own concerns regarding which they refused to consult his nominally draconic mind. He felt no deep love, no burning passion for the woman—he might be ignorant of these creatures' urges, but he knew enough to recognize that much. He *was* drawn to her, though, by an affection, an attraction that, while mild, remained unmistakable. The notions of cutting her from his life or of deeply hurting her were bearable, but unpleasant. He'd prefer to avoid either, if feasible.

And of greater importance were the benefits to his plans. He needed all the allies and influence he could acquire if he were truly to advance his station, to become Crown Marshal—or any other high office—and Mariscal was both the highest ranking and, at least until lately, the most determined and invested, of those potential supporters.

If he retained even a small chance of salvaging that relationship, then, wasn't it the wisest course of action, regardless of what emotions were or were not intertwined with it?

"What I want," he said slowly, after obvious thought, "is to win her back."

Kortlaus studied him carefully, then nodded. "We've a couple of hours before I'm to make my full report to his Majesty's council. I'll go speak to her."

"Um. I mean. You can certainly try, but I told you she's been unwilling to see me. I don't know that she'll be inclined to speak to you *about* me, either."

"Yes, I know. But you can't do it. You'll damage your cause if you ignore her request for time to think. I can use the excuse that I just got back to try to find out what's going on, and make it clear in the process that you want to make things right while respecting her wishes. Later on, we'll discuss other possible avenues of approach." Kortlaus leaned his *szandzsya* over his shoulder and headed for the racks on which the practice weapons were stored. "We're going to have to find a way for you to make your sincerity clear, Nycos. Without you being able to speak to her."

"And how would I do that, exactly?"

"I have no idea. But we're both reasonably clever fellows. We'll come up with something."

# CHAPTER EIGHTEEN

The council chamber stood within one of Oztyerva's central towers, rounded on two sides to follow the contours of the outer wall. The light from several arrow slits and a large oil-burning chandelier shone down upon a circular table on which was laid out a detailed and brightly inked map of southern Galadras. The king's usual group of advisors were gathered about that table, along with his two children and nearly a dozen knights and military officers. Also present were Ambassadors Kidil and Guldoell, and a tall, middle-aged man whom Nycos had never met before. He wore stiff, formal tunic and trousers of a style long out of fashion in Kirresc, and had been introduced as Kholdoun Razmos, ambassador from Althlalen.

The emissary of Wenslir would have attended, had she been in Talocsa at the moment, while the Mahdreshan ambassador was currently away due to the tensions that recent raids had caused between that nation and Kirresc.

Although far smaller an assembly than that normally found in open court, it was almost too large for the room to comfortably manage. "Quite a few kaftans, tabards, and other outer garments had been shed in a futile attempt to escape the heat of so many bodies crammed together. Nycos, as one of the lower-ranking attendees, was stuck at the back of the group, where he could see mostly shoulders and hair, with only an occasional glimpse at the map.

*But at least Zirresca is stuck back here, too, equally frustrated and looking for any excuse to snarl at me. So that's good.*

"...did not encounter unexplained or hostile activity ourselves," Kortlaus was saying, repeating and expanding upon the report he'd offered his Majesty the previous day. "We did, however, come across a large timber camp that had been utterly slaughtered and razed by *something*."

"Bandits?" one of the other knights asked.

"I suppose it's possible, if you can tell me what in the gods' names they might have been after. Raw lumber?" Before the other could respond, the baron continued. "We did meet with a Wenslirran border patrol one evening. We stopped, took our supper, and made camp together. They assured me that they *had* seen overt signs of activity within the shadows of Gronch, not two weeks past."

Princess Firillia frowned. "The people of Wenslir are good neighbors, but they've always been superstitious zealots. Ah, no offense, Domatir."

Prelate Matyas offered a stiff, shallow smile. "Probably none taken, your Highness. I'll let you know for certain when you finish that thought."

Several of the attendees chuckled, if a touch nervously. Wenslir was the second oldest of what were now considered the continent's civilized nations, behind only Suunim, and its many temples were widely considered the birthplace of faith in the Empyrean Choir on Galadras.

"Right. My point is, they take the forest's title of the 'Ogre-Weald' far too seriously. They'd attribute *anything* that happened in and around Gronch to monsters or haunts or what have you."

Nycos cleared his throat from the chamber's far side. "You don't believe in the creatures of Gronch, your Highness? Are they so much more difficult to countenance than, say, elves or the mountain fey?"

"Oh, I don't doubt there are inhuman things dwelling in that forest, Sir Nycolos," she said, her tone that of a teacher to a child. And no wonder, as more people of the modern era agreed with her belief than didn't. "But the sorts of nightmares the stories claim? Or in such numbers? Pure fairy tale."

Considering that Nycos knew for absolute fact not only that such "nightmares" were very real, but that they weren't the worst horror dwelling in the Ogre-Weald, it was difficult for him not to scoff. Instead, determined to remain polite, he said only, "If we treat the report Lord Kortlaus has passed along to us as fairy tale and you're wrong, Highness, it'll be too late to do anything about it."

Firillia's scowl returned, even deeper, but she inclined her head, acknowledging the point.

"We should indeed keep an eye on Gronch." It was Aadesh Kidil, the Suunimi ambassador, who spoke—perhaps unsurprisingly, as his own nation, like Wenslir, shared a border with the kingdom-sized Ogre-Weald. "If the beasts within are agitated, it could prove a distraction for us at a most inconvenient time. I think, however, that we need to remain focused on the reason we've gathered."

Rumbles of assent made their way around the table.

That reason—as was so often the case for assemblies of this sort—was Ktho Delios.

Dame Zirresca's patrol may have detected no abnormal activity near the edges of Kirresc, spotting only standard Deliant military drills, but word filtering down from various border towns—not just Kirresci, but Suunimi and Althlalan as well—was rather more disturbing. According to *them*, Ktho Delios was moving large forces of troops to various staging grounds only a few leagues from the border, sometimes under cover of darkness. It wouldn't be the first time that nation had engaged in such exercises without anything coming of it, but it always made the other kingdoms nervous. Nor would it be the first time such alarms had been sounded and then proved false, but rarely from so many communities at once.

When combined with rumors of several new up-and-coming officers making ripples in the Deliant power structure, officers who just might be pushing for a chance to prove their military prowess, it was more than enough to make *all* the southern nations sit up and take notice.

"I'm not entirely certain," King Hasyan admitted, dropping the "royal we" in this less formal gathering, "what else we can do, beyond posting lookouts and remaining wary. I can't imagine why Ktho Delios would think it viable to move against any of us now—nothing's happened to weaken our treaty—and I'm *certainly* not going to risk precipitating war by striking against them first when we've no idea what they're doing."

"There's wisdom in all of that," Ambassador Razmos said. He spoke with the tone of a man faintly distracted, as though thinking on other matters, yet he never appeared lost or to have missed anything of relevance. "But it wouldn't be the first time they've tested that treaty. And as Althlalen is arguably most vulnerable and furthest from any potential aid, no matter how well intentioned the rest of you may be..." He shrugged. "Well, you can imagine how 'wait and see' may not be our first choice of responses."

The Quindacran ambassador, Leomyn Guldoell, thumped a hand on the table. "I do understand, but what would you have us do? Any sort of gathering of forces along the borders might provoke the very incursion you fear!"

"It's easy for *you* to counsel patience!" Razmos snapped back. "You don't share a border with the bastards! You're in no immediate—!"

Denuel Jarta, Hasyan's palatine, interrupted. "The simple truth is, ladies and lords, that we lack sufficient information to take *any* substantive action. Until we know more, watching and waiting may not be the most satisfying or even the most prudent course, but it's all we can do."

"I'd hoped," Hasyan said softly, and the whole room quieted so the attendees might hear, "that we'd *have* that information by now."

"Your Majesty..." Jarta and Marshal Laszlan cautioned in unison.

"Oh, hush. There's no reason to keep it secret any longer. The whole operation clearly failed." The king sighed. "I had managed, my friends, to get a spy into the upper echelons of Ktho Delian society. No direct access to the Deliant, but she had several *indirect* channels of information. And in fact, she signaled some time ago that she'd learned something of import, that she needed extraction."

The silence was tense, now, quivering. So far as anyone here knew, it had been well over a generation since any of the southern nations had placed an operative so deeply within the ranks of their common enemy.

"I don't know what happened," the king confessed sadly. "I never heard from either my agent, or the one sent to retrieve her. Obviously such operations are unpredictable, but this was *months* ago. I... have to assume they didn't make it."

Immediately the room erupted again: into theories and wild speculation over what the spy might have learned, a list of horrors that might have befallen his Majesty's operatives, worries over what the Deliant might do if they had silence who the spy answered to. And that, of course, brought the argument clear back around to the same empty guesses about Ktho Delios's current plans, if any, and what the treaty nations ought to be doing to counter those hypothetical plans.

Nycos, though, found his thoughts returning to earlier bits of conversation. Maybe it was because he knew the many horrors of Gronch, the many nightmarish varieties of so-called "ogres," were real. And perhaps his own experiences using "monsters"—wyverns, perytons, goblins, and the like—set the wheels of his mind turning in directions diagonal to every man and woman around him.

"Lord Kortlaus." The near-bellow, a battlefield tone he'd learned from watching the Crown Marshal, cut through the hubbub and dragged the chamber once more into silence.

"Um, Sir Nycolos?"

"Did the Wenslirran soldiers say *when* the increased activities in and around Gronch had begun?"

Several others in the gathering groaned, sighed, or otherwise indicated in no uncertain terms how they felt about a return to the prior, and *clearly* less urgent topic.

"Not specifically," Kortlaus replied after a bit of thought. "I got the impression it had been fairly recent, though."

"Awful timing, isn't that? For us, I mean. Awfully *convenient* for others."

"Yes, yes, Sir Nycolos," Ambassador Razmos snapped. "We've already acknowledged it's problematic, that we need to keep an eye on the Ogre-Weald. But it's hardly—"

Nycos raised an interrupting hand. "Are we quite certain," he asked, cold and implacable, "that Ktho Delios hasn't *deliberately* stirred up the creatures of Gronch as a means of keeping us distracted?"

Mouths opened. No sound emerged.

"Considering the Deliant's distrust toward practitioners or creatures of sorcery beyond their control, I would think their inquisitors and military witches are probably as near as anyone to being experts on the unnatural beasts of the world. Who would know better how to aggravate them, agitate them, to keep our attentions on the Ogre-Weald while they reposition their forces?"

Orban whispered, quickly and fiercely, into the king's ear, until the monarch nodded his agreement. "My friends," his Majesty said, "I think we all need to give some thought to Sir Nycolos's theory. However likely or unlikely it may be, we must at least consider the impact it would have on our decisions. Given that, and as we've been at this for some while now, this seems as propitious a time as any for a break. Get some air, ask the servants for whatever food or beverage you might wish, and we'll reconvene in, say, an hour? Good."

People dispersed, the movement and the opening of the door sufficient to send a welcome draft through the chamber. First a few, then the greater portion of the assembly, filtered out into the hallway, making their way toward this refreshment or that. A handful approached Nycos, Kortlaus included, doubtless wishing to question him further on his theory. All fell back, however, when Prince Elias drew near. His Highness wore a peculiar expression on his clean-shaven and deceptively young face.

"A word in private, Sir Nycolos?"

Now what might *this* be about? Nycos had precious little notion what the prince might have to say to him, and frankly almost as little interest, but it wasn't an invitation he could refuse. With a polite bow, he allowed Elias to lead him to the far side of the room—hardly isolated, but now that the throng had scattered, as good a spot as any. There remained every chance a few stragglers might overhear, but if that didn't bother Elias, it wasn't going to bother Nycos.

And if it simply hadn't occurred to the somewhat simple-minded royal scion, well, it *still* wasn't going to bother Nycos.

"How may I be of service, your Highness?"

Now that they stood here, the prince seemed unsure how to begin the conversation, instead idly running a finger along the inner contours of an arrow slit in the wall beside them. Finally, a faint flush coloring his already dark complexion, he took a deep breath and spoke.

"Nycolos, the idea of war with Ktho Delios—however unlikely—has got me thinking recently."

*Well,* something *had to.*

"At my father's age, well, he may have many good years left, gods willing, but he will not sit on the throne forever, and a catastrophe like war can only hasten that time. I'm…" Another breath. "I know that I'm… not the most intelligent fellow in the room most of the time."

That took Nycos aback. Not the revelation itself; that was hardly any great secret. That the prince had the self-awareness to recognize it, however, was news.

"There are many," he continued, "who wish that my sister were the elder, so that it would be her responsibility to rule after father is gone, rather than mine. Some days, I agree with them. I wouldn't be entirely surprised if some hoped to take steps to make that happen."

"You fear assassination or revolt, your Highness?" Nycos asked, startled.

"No, nothing so dramatic, just… If Firillia *wanted* the throne badly enough, the support of enough of the nobility could basically force me to abdicate, or else have the blood of civil war stain *my* hands."

"And will you let them do that?"

"I hope not to let it come to that." Elias's features turned grim. "For good or ill, I *am* the king's first born. This is my duty, my responsibility, and I will not surrender it lightly. And that, Sir Nycolos, is where you come in."

"Do I?"

"If I cannot count on fully grasping every issue brought before me," the prince said bitterly, "then I need advisors around me whom I can trust *absolutely*. To help me understand, or—when it's time for me to make the important decisions—to guide me on the right course of action even where understanding eludes me. You've developed something of a reputation, you know."

Nycolos couldn't help but smirk. "Several, I would imagine. Might you narrow it down for me, your Highness?"

Elias blinked, then chuckled. "In this case, I mean a reputation for speaking out, sharing ideas or opinions even if it's not entirely the, uh, polite or expedient thing to do. I need that. I need someone in my circle of advisors to be blunt, without worry over whether it's proper to say what needs saying."

The knight almost reeled. He had little patience for foolishness, thought of Prince Elias as little more than an occasional irritation and didn't relish the idea of spending more time with the man. On the other hand, it was an opportunity to climb the ladder of power and influence that didn't rely on his success in becoming Crown Marshal, as well as the chance to keep an ear on the sundry goings-on within the palace—and perhaps the kingdom at large.

"I… am honored, your Highness."

The prince's eyes lit like torches. "Does that mean yes?"

"You understand that I cannot ignore my duties as a knight of Kirresc, or to your father? That, until you are king—some time away, one hopes—those have to come first, and I can offer you my counsel only when it does not conflict with my responsibilities?"

"Of course, Sir Nycolos. I would expect nothing else."

"Then I believe I'm your man, your Highness." *And may all your human gods help me. If nothing else, I'll have plenty of practice being patient.*

"Wonderful! And thank you, truly."

"Actually, your Highness?" He spoke before the prince could step away, before the thought had even fully formed. "Perhaps there's something you might be able to help me with, as well."

"Of course, Sir Nycolos. What do you need?"

What *did* he need? Was it even doable? Would it help if it were? He knew, now, that no single grand gesture would solve his problems with Mariscal—but one might just cool her anger enough that she would speak with him again. He could figure out the rest from there.

"Is it true," he asked slowly, ideas stalking one another through his head like ravenous wolves, "that the chief gardeners here make use of magics in their craft? I suppose I ought to know that," he added, "but I've never really had cause to pay them much heed."

Whatever Elias had been expecting to hear, this clearly was nowhere even in the same general vicinity. "I... Well, I mean, yes. Only a very little bit, to keep up appearances when the weather doesn't cooperate or the like. I don't really understand the specifics."

"That's all right, your Highness," Nycos told him, grinning. "I don't need you to understand. I just need you to give a royal command or two for me."

———

It took a great deal of doing, far more than Nycos had anticipated. At every step of the way, the groundskeepers protested. It threw their entire decorative scheme out of balance, required backbreaking labor as entire bushes were carefully uprooted and moved. The season was wrong. This wasn't how the few arcane tricks they'd mastered were meant to be used!

And those tricks were few indeed. Those rare gardeners of Oztyerva who practiced any such magics knew only a few minor invocations, recipes of occult significance or spell-paeans to the Vinnkasti of flowering vegetation. Like healers such as Lady Ilkya—or, indeed, the overwhelming proportion of Galadran mystics—they were dabblers at best, hedge wizards and alchemists who knew only enough in the way of eldritch secrets to enhance and expand upon their more mundane labors.

A genuine sorcerer could have done what Nycos requested in a matter of days. A true archmage of old, such as his long-dead foe Ondoniram, would—had he deigned to perform so frivolous a task—have accomplished the feat in hours, perhaps minutes.

For the poor, beleaguered gardeners of Oztyerva, it required *weeks*. More than once, Prince Elias would almost certainly have given in to their complaints, their protests, their near begging, had he not felt indebted to Nycos as his newest ally and advisor. Nycos took merciless advantage of that sense of obligation with barely a modicum of guilt, spurring Elias onward when his enthusiasm flagged, and slowly the garden, one particular patch of color and greenery on the winding palace grounds, evolved.

And so, finally, more than a month after the process began— and during which, it must be noted, Kirresc and the other allied nations had indeed increased their surveillance of Ktho Delios but taken no other action—the sun dawned on a late summer morning. The sky shone a cloudless azure, the towers of Oztyerva gleamed, and beneath them all, directly below many a window but particularly that of Margravine Mariscal, the earth bloomed with fire.

Prodded and sustained by the hard work of many and the magics of a few, a vast array of tulips, normally quite out of season this long after spring, opened to greet the day. The wide-spread petals were a brilliant scarlet, save in their center where a deep golden hue outlined patterns in far darker, almost coal-like crimson. The result was as though the garden had sprouted hundreds of individual fires, each frozen in time for a few precious days before the harshness of the season would doubtless hammer them down.

People gathered at the windows, drawn from all over the palace by spreading word. For many it was merely a touch of beauty before they went about their business, perhaps a whim of the groundskeepers or one of the royal family.

Some, however, understood their significance. They recognized those fiery colors as a match for the garb often worn by one particular margravine, and some were even well enough acquainted with her to know that this particular tulip was her favorite flower. These people, at least, could have no doubt that the wonder in the garden was a message intended specifically, personally, for her.

Nor could they doubt who must be responsible for that message. That rumor, too, spread through Oztyerva, until even people who had heard only the barest inklings of the tale gazed at Nycos with a touch of respect or a knowing smirk.

Mariscal failed to attend the nobles' supper those next several evenings, and when Nycos stopped by her chambers to ensure she was well, he was still refused entry. The margravine's lady-in-waiting, however, greeted him politely at his knock, and apologized that her mistress wasn't feeling up to company, rather than reminding him that he wasn't welcome.

It was, Nycos decided, an adequate start.

———

"...of anything new," Zirresca concluded. "Everyone's still arguing over what to do about Ktho Delios, if anything, or Gronch, if anything. Or whether they're related."

"Idiocy!" Andarjin snapped, briefly clutching his stomach in pain. "The idea of any link at all... Why does anyone listen to a word that man says?!"

Zirresca seated herself at one of the small tables, where she'd earlier been poring over and making notes on a potential plan for moving small squadrons of soldiers into northern border towns. Picking up a nearby quill, she scribbled a quick thought, and then shrugged. "I find it highly unlikely, myself, but it's worth considering."

"Bah!" The margrave slammed his cane into the wall—he'd been using the walking stick since falling ill last month, though he'd recovered enough that he scarcely needed it any longer—shaking the dust of old mortar loose from between the stones. "It's asinine."

"If you say so."

Andarjin snarled something obscene and unkind, snatched a goblet from the cabinet—setting several of the other crystalline vessels rocking precariously—and poured it full to overflowing with the nearest decanter to hand, hoping to settle his churning gut. "And you! You couldn't bring me any more details? 'Everything's the same.' Not helpful, Zirresca!"

"So attend court yourself, Arj. You're well enough again, most days."

"Most days, yes! Today I wasn't!"

"So today you get 'everything's the same.' I promise you, if anything of import had occurred, I would tell you."

"*I'll* decide what's important, Dame Zirresca!"

Slowly, meticulously, the knight stacked and straightened the parchments she had been examining. She laid them to one side, placing an inkwell atop them at the corner so they wouldn't drift apart at the next opening of the door or passing of a body. Then, careful to make no noise, she scraped her chair back across the thin carpet and stood.

"Very well, then, *my Lord*. I most humbly offer *my Lord* my counsel, if he would do me the honor of hearing it?"

"Zirresca…"

Apparently she took that as permission to continue. "If you would be king, *my Lord*, it is not enough that you be clever, or educated, or cunning. You must also *behave* as a king."

Andarjin bristled to do a porcupine proud. "I *do* behave as…" He stopped, took a breath. "Well, I normally do. I admit these past weeks have been… trying. My illness—"

"A king needs to know how to hide his weakness. I sympathize with your discomfort, but you cannot let it influence your behavior this way, *my Lord*."

"Stop calling me—!"

"People are watching you, you know. Watching how you handle this. People such as her Highness."

Andarjin went pale and stiff as petrified wood. "What has she said?"

"She's said nothing about it to me specifically, but... You know that Prince Elias has been gathering a circle of advisors? That he's openly admitted to them he needs their help if he's to keep informed, to be able to make wise decisions when his time comes?"

"I'd heard rumors. What of it?"

"Princess Firillia was taken aback that her brother showed such self-awareness, and could put aside his pride enough to seek aid. I have every reason to believe she still thinks she'd make a better queen than he would a king, and that she still feels the support of Vidirrad—your support, and your mother's—is integral to making that happen without violence.

"But it's the only time since we first discussed the possibility, when we were all barely more than children, that I've heard from her even the slightest doubt, the tiniest inkling that perhaps her brother might make an acceptable sovereign after all. This is *not* the time to give her any cause to doubt you, Arj. Any at all."

Andarjin turned, carefully placed his drink on the table, and then bowed. "I apologize for how I spoke to you, Zirresca. And your guidance is wise, as usual. Thank you."

Behind the conciliatory smile he offered her, however—a smile that she faintly returned before going back to her report—the margrave's mind raced. First that damned Nycolos, and now the royal idiot? How many people who should have been nothing were going to stand in his way?

He'd always had other plans, more dangerous and desperate plans, in case his current efforts failed to yield fruit. It wasn't time to execute any of them, not yet, but he needed to sit down, review them, perhaps start preparing to make sure everything was in place. He needed to have options ready if there was *any* chance his pursuit of Princess Firillia, or her need for him, was under threat.

Any at all.

# CHAPTER NINETEEN

Summer faded, the days growing ever more pleasant and the nights increasingly chill. Leaves turned. The breezes passing through Talocsa came thick and redolent with the flavors of the harvest, the healthy aroma of felled grains and fresh crops and the heavier, less delightful odor as the leavings slowly rotted back into the soil.

And with the cooling of the season, the sporadic gentle rains that presaged the fiercer and colder weather to come, the bright blue skies ever more frequently flecked with grey, came his Majesty's tournament.

Held yearly, save in times of war, it was a period of celebration, of competition, of parley and politics and planning. Nobles and their retinues came from across Kirresc, and even from other lands, for while Hasyan's was not the only tourney to be held in the nations of southern Galadras, it was certainly the largest. Men and women challenged one another to all manner of martial competition, of course, but for many this was merely an excuse, a spectacle to be enjoyed while engaged in other, more pressing matters. Treaties and trade agreements were signed, marriages and alliances arranged, rivalries renewed, battle plans orchestrated. Nobles and gentry who dwelt nowhere near one another reestablished old acquaintances or met one another for the first time. Offspring were introduced to those peers among whom they would one day take their rightful place.

Musicians and entertainers, who had competed all year for the opportunity to perform at the tourney, made or broke their careers over the span of this hectic fortnight. Crafters sold wares enough to equal many months of normal business; hunters and cooks ran themselves ragged. Many of the common folk took a few days off work, some to watch the matches, others simply to enjoy the festive, holiday air. Restrictions on public drunkenness were relaxed (within reason), while both the larders of Oztyerva and the private hunting grounds of the king himself were briefly opened to all who wished to partake. (Again, within reason.)

For the servants who had to keep everyone happy and everything flowing smoothly, for the guards assigned to keep the peace, and for Denuel Jarta—who, as palatine, was responsible both for overseeing the arrangements of all visiting dignitaries and for effectively managing the kingdom while his Majesty attended the tournament and a thousand different meetings—these two weeks were sheer misery. For everyone else, they were supposed to be a delight.

Nycos hadn't the first notion what to make of it all. He understood, intellectually, the need for knights and other warriors to practice their skills among the best Galadras had to offer, to feel as though they were noticed; the need for various nobles of various kingdoms to hobnob amongst themselves; even the need for the populace to have occasional opportunity to celebrate and escape their daily drudgery. For all that, though, it *felt* like nothing but a waste of energy, a chaotic and cacophonic mess that occasionally reached the level of physical discomfort.

That might have been the dragon within him talking—he, as with most of his kind, generally preferred solitude and periods of long rest between bursts of activity—but the fact that he was stuck as a human right now didn't mean he had to enjoy it.

Such were his thoughts in general, and had been throughout most of the tournament thus far, but they were *not* his thoughts at this instant. No, at the moment, his head was full only of a dull pain, a flicker of embarrassment buried beneath the ashes of indifference, and the rich, heady smell of churned mud and horse manure.

Slow and aching, Nycos began to haul himself up from the dirt in which he'd landed, hard, only to find that his opponent—a fellow Kirresci knight, albeit from the court of Duke Gostav of Janu-Vala rather than here in Talocsa—had already dismounted and now held his sabre to Nycos's throat.

"Yield!" the mail-clad warrior demanded from behind a mustache so thick it could have adorned the end of a broom.

Nycos nodded tiredly. "I yield."

The other grinned, sheathed his sabre, and reached down a gauntleted hand. Keeping his grumbles internal, Nycos clasped it with his own and allowed himself to be helped upright.

"That was a nasty fall, Sir Nycolos."

"You wield a nasty lance, Sir Oclan." He winced, flexing and rotating a sore shoulder and struggling to fake his opponent's good humor. "Best hope we don't meet again in the melee, though. You'll find me a far less easy opponent on foot."

"I look forward to finding out." Oclan raised a finger to his helm, then turned to march from the list, accompanied by the cheers of his friends and the blaring of trumpets.

Nycos watched him go, then headed the other way, letting the pages and grooms chase down Avalanche.

He had barely passed between the stands, raised tiers of benches from which audience members could watch the jousts, when he felt the brush of soft fabrics and a small hand almost, but not quite, touching his own. "What happened, Nycos?"

He shrugged, still walking. "I don't have much use for the lance. If I'm fighting from horseback, I far prefer the *szandsya*, or just my sabre. I have… not been keeping up practice with it as much as I probably ought. My hold on it was just a hair out of line, and Sir Oclan took full advantage."

"It looked painful," Mariscal said, gently mocking and genuinely concerned all at once.

"It wasn't fun, but it's not bad. I'm fine."

"I'm glad to hear it." Again her fingers just barely caressed his own without lingering. "You *should* find time to practice with the lance more, though."

"Yes, and I'm quite certain I'll be hearing that from Marshal Laszlan as well, only louder. Care to join me? He'll likely be a *tad* politer with you present."

"Are... If you're sure you want me there?"

Much had improved between Nycos and Mariscal, but they still shied back around the edges of their interaction, each worried—albeit for different reasons, with different motivations—that an ill-chosen word might set things spiraling off in the wrong direction once more. It was yet another drain on Nycos's patience, something else to tug at his attentions during what was already a nigh overwhelming time.

Right now, she sounded almost timid, doubtless surprised that he'd want her to witness him being reprimanded. For Nycos, however, more concerned with settling that situation and solidifying her status as an ally than with emotional attachment, to show her that he relied on her was far more important than any potential moment of humiliation.

"I'm sure, my Lady."

He *did* have to admit to himself, however reluctantly, that her smile made him feel just a little bit better.

The pair meandered between various fenced-in competitions, around and among rows of food vendors, dodged wandering jugglers and jesters. Nycos found a minced meat pie in his hand with no memory of purchasing it, and found it gone a minute later with only the lingering spice on his tongue to remind him of eating it.

He *clearly* recalled, however, passing by a small melee— three warriors on three—that set him to scowling. One trio consisted of Kirresci soldiers, young but skilled, chosen for their teamwork and swordsmanship. The other...

"Why are they even permitted to be here?" he asked, not so much objecting as genuinely curious.

Now Mariscal did take a solid grip on his hand, perhaps half afraid that he would dash off and do something foolish. "We aren't actually at war," she reminded him. "And I'm quite certain Jarta and Marshal Laszlan both have any number of eyes on them."

Nycos continued to watch the black-tabarded soldiers of Ktho Delios wielding their heavier broadswords against the sabres of their Kirresci opponents, but allowed Mariscal to guide him past.

He wondered what intelligence those men and women might be able to provide, if only the methods required to extract that information wouldn't ignite the very conflict King Hasyan and the other southern monarchs sought desperately to avoid. *Perhaps someone whose affiliation with the court can't be proven ought to pay them a visit on their journey back home...*

Those thoughts, and others of a similarly vicious nature, occupied him until they'd crossed the great fields behind Oztyerva and their destination hove into sight.

The royal pavilion, not quite a tent and not quite a gazebo but some peculiar offspring of both, stood atop a small hill overlooking those fields. From here, the most important and impressive of the contests played out within view, allowing the king and his guests to observe the best parts of the tourney from luxury. Servants moved in and about the various daises and platforms, providing a never-ending array of refreshments, while several dozen of the king's bodyguards stood post to ensure the safety of their liege. The fact that this shelter was so distant from the doors of Oztyerva bestowed upon it—and his Majesty—an air of vulnerability despite those guards, an impression meant to foster trust and mutual goodwill.

The hidden hatchway to a collapsible tunnel leading back into the palace ensured that said perception of vulnerability was just that: perception.

At this time, his Majesty was indeed in attendance, along with several of his court, a number of visiting dukes and counts, and Ambassador Kidil. Most were watching a one-on-one match between Sir Tivador, son of the Judge Royal Amisco Valacos, and one of the Suunimi envoy's countrymen. The tall, slender foreigner wore leathers dyed in deep reds and emeralds that shone against the dark of his skin. He fought with an elongated shield and a short spear that might have resembled a *szandzsya* save that its blade was leaf-shaped and dual-edged. His tumbling, acrobatic style of battle stymied Sir Tivador, whose own sabre-spear never came near to connecting.

Aadesh Kidil smiled broadly at Nycos and Mariscal as they pushed their way beneath the overhang that kept rain, sun, or wind from disturbing the audience within. "Zeyaash," he boasted proudly. "The nephew of an old, old friend of mine. It appears this year's single combat champion will be Suunimi, Sir Nycolos."

Nycos grinned back. "Perhaps because I haven't faced him, Ambassador."

The laugh in response was booming. "I believe your custom is that anyone of rank may challenge the final victor, is it not? Feel free to do so when Zeyaash wins. Do not worry," he added, a mischievous twinkle in his eye. "It will be a duel on foot. We Suunimi do not favor fighting from horseback."

The humor in which the jibe was offered made it impossible to take real offense. Mariscal snickered; Nycos merely grumbled and moved on. He *did* wonder just how rapidly word of his unfortunately swift unhorsing had traveled, though, since the lists in which he'd ridden were not readily visible from the hilltop.

His Majesty sat ensconced in a massive wooden chair, cushioned in purple velvet, far enough from the edge to rest in the shade without cutting off his view of the proceedings. He only half watched, however, engaged as he was in laughing conversation and reminiscence with one Duke Ishmar of Hesztilna.

Slightly older than the king himself, Ishmar had been a close friend of Hasyan's since they'd been youths, learning the ins and outs of politics in the chambers of Oztyerva. He was far paler than his Majesty, his beard almost brittle, his skin showing the faint fleshiness and sallow tint of a man who enjoyed his wines and spirits perhaps a touch more often than was strictly healthy. His laugh remained hearty, however, his mind sharp, and his company welcomed by most of the court on those rare occasions when his duties to Hesztilna permitted him to visit.

And welcomed, in particular, by his daughter, the Margravine Mariscal.

She and Nycos wended their way through the guards and servants to stand before the duke and the king. Nycos knelt, while Mariscal moved straight to her father and kissed him on his bristly cheek.

"My dear!" he greeted her, moving his goblet to his other hand so he could wrap an arm briefly around her. Then, without hostility but without much in the way of affection, either, "Sir Nycolos."

"Your Grace." He had no notion whether the duke approved of his relationship—or "potential relationship," at any rate—with Mariscal. Presumably, Ishmar would be a bit happier with it if and when Nycos attained the office of Crown Marshal, but it was yet another complication for which the knight had little comprehension, and even less patience.

He wondered, at times, if Smim was right and he should just forget this whole concept of intimate relations. He didn't want to hurt Mariscal, nor did he want to surrender his greatest supporter, but human entanglement and courtship were *maddening*.

His Majesty took something between a sip and a swig from his own drink. "What are you doing here, Sir Nycolos? Aren't you supposed to be at the lists?"

"Ah…"

"He was, Your Majesty." Orban Laszlan appeared from deeper within the pavilion. His tone was stern, but his expression far milder than Nycos had feared. "It seems, however, that our honored knight has been less than industrious in practice with the lance of late."

Nycos grinned sheepishly. "It's true, I'm afraid. My attentions have been elsewhere than the joust. I—"

He fell briefly silent as a gasp of awed appreciation flowed through the audience, both here in the shelter and across the stands beyond. On the grass before them, Zeyaash had leapt into the air, kicking out with both feet and twisting over a sharp slash of Tivador's blade. The Suunimi warrior landed on one foot, continuing the momentum of his spin and sweeping the knight's own feet from under him. By the time Tivador had even realized he was on his back, Zeyaash's spear-tip hovered inches from his face.

The officiants called the match in favor of Zeyaash, to loud cheers and jeers alike, and the two combatants moved aside to rest and recuperate so the next pair of contenders might take the field.

"I've been caught up in other practices," Nycos continued during the brief lull. "I'll show you when the time comes for the dueling champion to accept final challenge."

The king nodded. "Ambassador Kidil seems convinced Zeyaash will be that champion."

"He's probably right," Orban warned. "He's very, very good, Nycolos."

"Well, I'll just have to be—"

A trumpet blared, announcing the start of the next match. Only those who had already won a significant number of duels or melees were invited to contest here, beneath the watchful gaze of the king himself, so whoever appeared would be skilled indeed, and well worth observing.

"We present to you," the herald's voice rang out over the field, "the Lord Kortlaus, Baron of Urwath!"

Cheers and applause—some from Nycos himself, glad to see his friend having advanced so far in the tournament. Kortlaus stepped out into the grassy arena, clad in his finest reinforced chain hauberk, sabre held high for the crowd to see.

"And his opponent, Silbeth Rasik, of..." The herald's pause was brief, nigh unnoticeable, as though he were faintly startled by whatever bit of information had been passed on to him to relay. "...the Priory of Steel!"

Now the audience reaction was one of wonder, a wave of murmurs that formed a slow whirlpool around the field. Although it wasn't uncommon for mercenary guilds or martial organizations to participate in the Kirresci tournament, it had been quite some time since the Priory had bothered. Most of the citizenry had heard tales of their prowess, some doubtless exaggerated, and they were eager indeed to see what this Silbeth Rasik could do.

The king's guests and even guards were no more immune to that draw, leaning forward or craning their necks for a better view. Hasyan himself had grown suddenly intent—and not just intent but somewhat distracted, as though pondering questions to which few present were privy.

It was neither his Majesty's reaction, however, nor any particular curiosity over the Priory of Steel that held Nycos spellbound, rapt in open fascination. No, those might have drawn his initial attention, but what kept it, snagged like a fish wriggling on a hook, was the woman herself.

No mere physical attraction, this. The pale brunette, clad in worn mail and an old, mismatched cuirass, was handsome enough, but not remarkably so. Many of the palace's noblewomen, not least Mariscal herself, were easily her superior if physical beauty was all Nycos had sought, but of course he rarely even noticed such things. No, it was something about the way this Silbeth moved, held herself; her steady gaze, her every fluid step.

The creature that Nycos had been, that still lurked within his heart and soul, recognized a kindred spirit, a fellow hunter, when it saw one.

"Wonderful!" Mariscal appeared at his side. He hadn't even noticed her approach or her presence until she spoke. "It's been a few years since a woman was tournament champion. I know Lord Kortlaus is your friend, Nycos, but I think I'm cheering for her."

He scarcely heard, but he knew, without the faintest sliver of doubt, that the margravine would not be disappointed. Kortlaus didn't have a chance. The baron might not have been the greatest swordsman in the land, but he was an experienced knight of Kirresc. That alone made him better than most who dared take the field against him. Today, however, Nycos was certain it wouldn't be enough.

Kortlaus raised his sabre, twisting his body so that his torso was concealed from his opponent behind his round-topped, kite-shaped shield. With a faint hiss of metal on leather, not unlike the whisper of a soft breeze, Silbeth drew her own sword, narrow and straight, long of blade and of grip so that it might be—but didn't *quite* have to be—wielded in both hands. And indeed she held it in one fist, her other wrapped around the handle of a small steel buckler.

The officiating herald called for the two challengers to begin. Kortlaus advanced, slowly, smoothly. Silbeth waited, the tip of her blade weaving tiny curls in the air.

And then she proved Nycos absolutely correct. The fight was over almost before he had a chance to cheer for his friend—which didn't matter since, in his fascination with watching Silbeth, he'd utterly forgotten to do so.

They came together, and though the greater length of her blade allowed Silbeth to strike first, she made only a few tentative prods, tip of the sword glancing off Kortlaus's shield. The baron, in turn, took the opportunity to move inside her reach and make a few quick attacks. She sidestepped the sabre once, deflected it with her buckler, ducked the third stroke, and retreated.

Disappointed mutters sounded here and there, members of the audience wondering when the fabled skill of the Priory might show itself. Mariscal herself made a small *tsking* sound.

Nycos swallowed a laugh. *Wait for it…*

The sabre sliced through the air, and Silbeth parried with her buckler. Again, and she dodged. Kortlaus lunged, shoving with his shield, and she pivoted away. He swung the sabre once more…

Just that suddenly, the woman was a blur; Nycos wasn't sure how much the others, with their mere human senses, actually saw of what happened. Silbeth swayed sharply backward so that the baron's blade swept past her, his arm crossed diagonally before his chest for the barest instant, and then she snapped upright.

The edge of her buckler came down, hooking the lip of his shield and dragging the two opponents together. Her sword came up and across, the blade resting against his throat. The weight of her body slamming into him knocked him off balance, and she extended a foot to catch her heel behind his.

And like that, they froze. Kortlaus couldn't attack, for his sword arm was pinned between her breastplate and his own shield. He couldn't straighten, with her leaning into him. He couldn't step backward to catch his balance without tripping over her boot. The hilt of her sword pressed against the side of his neck kept him from sliding or pivoting to his left, and the blade would begin to cut into his throat were he to drag himself across its edge to the right.

An unorthodox clinch, to say the least, and not one just anybody had the speed and precision to master. Half the audience was on their feet, astonished, trying to figure out what precisely they'd just seen.

"Yield, my Lord?" It didn't take Nycos's senses to hear that. Her voice carried nearly as far, as clearly, as Marshal Laszlan's would have.

"I'm not entirely sure what just happened," Kortlaus rasped, chagrined but with good humor, "but I think I'd better."

The herald announced Silbeth's victory, a trumpet sounded, and the Priory warrior stepped back so the baron might regain his balance. They exchanged salutes and abandoned the field to a wave of applause and acclaim.

Mariscal said something, then, but Nycos, still enraptured, caught not a word of it.

———

The last few days of the tournament were a bit of a blur for Nycos. He still had duties to perform, and he saw to those with as much haste as he could manage. So, too, did he have various social obligations—though fewer than he otherwise might, as Mariscal spent long stretches with her visiting father—and he rushed through those as rapidly as propriety would permit.

The rest of the time, he watched.

He learned a lot, then, of human martial arts and, to a lesser extent, their various cultures. He watched a twelve-on-twelve melee in which nine fighters essentially sacrificed their chance for victory rather than defend the trio of despised Ktho Delian soldiers with whom they'd been matched. In group melee and individual duels, he witnessed his fellow Kirresci knights in victory and in defeat. He studied the axe-wielders and staff-fighters of Althlalen; the knights of Quindacra, modeled after but never *quite* so well trained nor so well equipped as those of Kirresc; religious crusaders and masterless mercenaries both out of Wenslir, one of whom fought with a most peculiar style, a flanged mace in each hand. Even a handful of tribal warriors from the Vingossa Plains made an appearance, putting on astonishing displays of mounted archery, then fighting on foot with hatchets and sickle-shaped swords, calling battle-prayers to their animist Vinnkasti spirits.

But it was all quite secondary. Whenever she was competing, Nycos's attentions were entirely on Silbeth Rasik.

It would have been dishonest of him to insist that she was amazing at *everything* she set her hand to. She was a fair archer, but hardly an expert, and never reached the final rounds of that competition; and while her skills at unarmed combat were significant, she lacked the mass or strength to overcome a few equally skilled but larger wrestlers in the tourney's final days.

Even in defeat, however, she was impressive, well worth watching, for still she moved with that almost unnatural grace, a fluidity and clarity of purpose that spoke directly to his soul in a language Nycos recognized yet couldn't begin to comprehend.

He was, in a word, fascinated, and he could not articulate why.

And that? That was when she *lost*, wielding a bow or an empty fist. Put a blade in her hand and she became something greater, something for whom "defeat" seemed an alien concept. Men and women, Kirresci and foreigner, experts in sword or spear or axe or whatever weapon one cared to name… Some lasted longer than Kortlaus had, a few even made their fights a near match, but none could conquer her.

Until, as the sun passed noon on the tournament's last day, and a moist, cooling autumn gust swept across the fields, leaving brief shivers in its wake, the many duels culminated in what was—barring any challenge by a noble competitor—the final one-on-one match. The *only* match to which the prior duels could possibly have led. Nycos, the entirety of the royal pavilion, and every member of the audience waited in breathless silence as the herald made his announcement.

Silbeth Rasik of the Priory of Steel, against Zeyaash Viruk of Suunim.

The first moments of the contest were a blur of whirling steel, striking limbs, clashing shields. Zeyaash was everywhere, lashing out with spear, foot, fist, spinning and twisting, always in motion. Silbeth was less acrobatic but no slower, her own blade and buckler always in place to deflect an attack no matter how exotic, her own boots and gauntlets landing blows where opportunity allowed. The song of steel was an unbroken ring, less a series of impacts than a single, tremulous note.

They met, parted, came together once more, a dance in which even the war god Teslak must have found beauty and grace.

Just as swiftly, it very nearly ended.

Zeyaash, shield tucked tight to his side, spear moving in tight arcs before his body, stepped in and whirled the haft of the weapon at Silbeth's head. Even as she smacked the attack aside with the flat of her sword, he was spinning, crouched, shield abruptly extended to sweep her ankles. Again she saw the attack coming, easily hopped over it.

But the Suunimi warrior continued his spin, leaping into the air. Feet pinwheeled upward in a devastating kick, and the outer edge of his boot cracked hard across his opponent's face.

The audience members came to their feet, Nycos among them. It was a brutal blow, powerful and well aimed. Silbeth staggered, toppling, and every soul watching must have believed the duel was ended then and there.

Silbeth came out of her backwards roll, springing back to her feet and grinning through a mask of blood. Unable to avoid the massive kick, still she'd managed to turn with it, transforming what could—*should*—have been a stunning blow into a merely painful one. The entire crowd roared with excitement as she wiped the blood from her eyes with the back of a gauntleted hand and the two opponents advanced again.

Another series of clashes, dodges, parries, ripostes, and then it truly *was* over. Using her buckler, Silbeth smacked aside another thrust of Zeyaash's spear, knocking it wide. At the same instant, she leaned left and kicked, turning her entire body horizontal save for the one leg on which she stood. The heel of her boot shoved his shield in the opposite direction, leaving his body open if only briefly. Her sword whistled, slicing the autumn air, and crunched into the raised leather collar that protected the man's throat.

It didn't quite penetrate, but nobody—Silbeth, Zeyaash, or the officiants—doubted that it *could* have, had she wished it.

The herald sounded his trumpet, the Suunimi bowed, and the crowd once more roared in a single, unbroken voice.

As for the victor, she waved once to the crowd and then knelt, planting her sword blade-first in the soil and leaning heavily upon it, catching her breath. Her lowered gaze scanned the crowd, however, as though seeking someone particular.

Nycos blinked, startled, as her eyes locked on his and ceased moving.

Relying on his rank where it proved sufficient, and on his size and armored elbows where more forceful measures were required, he pushed his way through the milling throng to stand before her. She rose as he approached, her expression mildly amused.

"You know me?" Nycos asked, struggling to be heard over the ambient clamor.

"I might ask you the same. You've been watching me for three days." Then, at his expression, "I pay attention, and not just to *obvious* opponents."

"Um." Somehow, in all his fascination with observing her, Nycos had never given any thought as to what he would do or say should they actually meet. "You're very good."

Her lips twitched. "Why, so I am! How did *that* happen?"

Was he blushing? He still didn't know this damned body well enough to know if that was what the faint warming in his cheeks actually meant. "I've been considering challenging the champion," he told her, trying to regain some measure of dignity.

"I've not been declared champion yet."

"Formalities. You just won the final match. It's just a matter of his Majesty making the declaration."

"And you've the right and rank to challenge, my Lord…?"

"No lord. Sir Nycolos Anvarri."

Her eyes grew wide, then came alight. "The dragon slayer?"

*Not exactly.* "So they call me." He grinned at her. "Does that make you nervous?"

"Not at all."

"And why not?"

"I'm no dragon."

Nycos laughed, loudly enough to draw puzzled looks from several of nearby observers. "Your opponents might argue differently."

She returned his grin, but her expression swiftly turned serious. "Please tell his Majesty that I must speak with him when the tournament has ended."

"All you need do is defeat me," he said, still chuckling. "The king addresses all the tournament champions at the end of the final—"

"I need him to speak with me in private."

The sounds of the crowd receded and Nycos grew tense, swaddled in a caul of suspicion. "Why would you need that? Why would you expect his Majesty to agree to something so unheard of?"

"Just tell him… Tell him the salmon were even later than expected this year, but they've finally reached Lake Orist."

She vanished into the milling throng before Nycos could voice even the first of the many, many questions he suddenly needed to ask.

# CHAPTER TWENTY

As he was not an utter fool, Nycos recognized that the bizarre statement as a signal or a code of some sort. It was a fact that left him with more questions than answers. Who was this Silbeth Rasik? What connection had she with King Hasyan? If they had some prior interaction or communication, why choose to make contact through so roundabout a method as fighting her way to the tournament's championships? Why ask a knight of the realm, rather than any one of the hundreds of soldiers or servants present, to deliver the incomprehensible message?

It left him both suspicious and utterly bewildered, two emotions of which Nycos was rather emphatically unfond.

Unfortunately for his burning curiosity, his Majesty seemed disinclined to clarify. He merely nodded thoughtfully when Nycos explained the conversation and delivered the message, dismissing the knight with a curt thank you before sending a page to go find and retrieve the Crown Marshal. Nycos wandered away, growling to himself.

Late afternoon brought a chilly autumn drizzle, less real rain than a haze of droplets squished tightly between clouds above and earth below. Grass, guards, stands, and stalls all shimmered in the wet. Pennants hung limp, clothes clung to shivering skin, and a good portion of the audience decided that they didn't actually need to stay for the last few performances, challenge bouts, or closing ceremonies. Smim, after a quick check of his master's chainmail and other accoutrements, delightedly wished Nycos good luck and headed back toward their quarters, where he no doubt already had a comfortable fire roaring away.

Nycos gave some real consideration to ordering the goblin to stay, purely out of vindictiveness, but decided to let it drop.

Even the trumpets seemed soured by the turn of the weather and ready to call the whole thing over and done with. They announced the challenge match between Silbeth Rasik and Sir Nycolos Anvarri with something of a wet and deflated *blat*. In the grey of the rain-smeared twilight, the two combatants saluted one another and met in the slippery, glistening grass.

Here, at least, the remaining crowds showed life still within them, shouting and cheering the advancing warriors and raised blades.

Nycos had chosen to go with the *szyandzsya* in a two-handed grip, foregoing the use of a shield—though his sabre hung at his waist, a fallback in case he should lose the spear. Silbeth bore the same longsword and buckler with which she'd fought every match, though something in the way she held them struck Nycos as ever so slightly off. He couldn't quite say what; perhaps, had he the lifelong training he was supposed to have had, he could have put a finger on it. As things stood, it was just another nagging worry.

Carefully, meticulously, he had prepared himself for this fight, mystically bolstering muscle and bone until he'd made himself as swift and as strong as he believed he could get away with, *just* below the point he would give his prowess away as obviously inhuman. Against most foes, it would have proved an overwhelming advantage.

Against this woman? He was not entirely sure he'd done more than even things up.

And still he nearly lost as soon as it began. Silbeth took one step, a second, and the buckler hurtled directly at Nycos's head, a thick steel discus that would have knocked him senseless had it connected. He barely managed to dodge aside, and in that split second of distraction she leapt upon him. Her sword, now held firmly in both hands, sprayed rainwater as it neared, and even his nearly superhuman speed only allowed him to avoid the tip by inches.

Dramatic, unexpected, but why would she risk losing her shield?

As they circled, each jabbing at the other in an exchange of blades intended to test rather than to deliver a telling blow, Nycos understood. She'd recognized an opponent both fast and strong, had decided that the extra speed and precision she'd gain wielding her hand-and-a-half sword in two fists was more valuable than the buckler's protection. She could have simply hung it from her belt or left it behind, but she'd chosen to hide her intentions, and take an unexpected shot in the process.

He couldn't help but grin, impressed. She returned the expression, teeth shining through the chilling shower.

Nycos slashed. Silbeth dodged. She stabbed; he deflected. He lunged; she sidestepped. Their weapons came together, scraping and shedding rain. Where he began to overpower her, she danced aside. Where she came in fast, blade weaving a web as it seemed to strike from a dozen directions, he relied on his heavier weapon to bat aside the first and his innate speed to avoid those that followed.

The crowd had fallen into a hush, so that only the sounds of the weather cheered them on. The wind caught her hair and Nycos watched for an opening, but she had tied enough of it back before the contest began that it never blinded her for even a moment.

Twice he wound up on his back, tripped up by a maneuver he never saw coming, and both times rolled aside just before she could land a final blow. Once he managed to deliver a fearsome punch to her gut, the sheer strength of his spinning *szandzsya* having forced a hole in her guard, but she twisted fast enough to avoid the worst of the impact and her hauberk took care of the rest.

It was all, perhaps, less showy than her earlier championship bout, less leaping and tumbling about, but it was faster, fiercer. Tomorrow, when those who had departed early heard their friends speak of this final match, many would refuse to believe it.

Understandable, that. Having watched her for days, even standing in the face of it now, Nycos himself could scarcely believe the woman's sheer skill. Even as a dragon he had heard the occasional tales of the Priory of Steel, and had always dismissed them. Humans were humans, were they not?

Now? Even in his old form, his true form, Silbeth Rasik would have been more than a nuisance; as great a threat as any lone human could possibly be, without the aid of magic such as Wyrmtaker. Trapped in his current body, Nycos knew that he would have to tap into magics beyond what he was willing to reveal, would have to become *far* faster and stronger than human to win this match.

Unless...

He'd fought her, thus far, to a standstill, and inhuman *stamina* was far less conspicuous than potence or agility. No matter her training, her experience, Silbeth couldn't possibly keep this pace indefinitely. She must tire, before long, and if he could simply keep her from victory until that point—no sure thing, but conceivable—he just might prevail.

Again they circled, and the wind briefly parted the thick rain like a curtain. In that moment, Nycos saw clearly the audience of royalty and nobility watching from within the shelter of the king's pavilion. He saw that Mariscal, seated comfortably beside her father, was among them.

Conflicting thoughts clashed against one another in Nycos's mind, louder than the steel. He'd all but forgotten his efforts to impress her, draw her nearer, repair the lingering damage to their relationship, and suddenly he found himself uncertain how best to go about it.

Her prior comment about seeing a woman as champion, how seriously had she meant it to be taken? Idle musing, or was it genuinely important to her? Would she be impressed at his ability to overcome one of the tournament's most impressive victors, or would she be angry at him? Would—?

Then the choice, if it ever had been, was no longer his to make.

*Where in Vizret's hell did that kick even come from?* He never took his eyes off the woman, could not have been distracted by those whirling thoughts and questions for more than a fraction of a second—and nothing in his stance or his expression should have given away that he was distracted at all! Nevertheless, Silbeth's sword had come swinging down at him, he'd raised the *szandzsya* to parry, and then his knee had simply given way, caught and hooked by a boot he'd never seen coming.

He staggered, his unnatural resilience preventing him from toppling outright, but it was enough. Off-balance, he could do nothing to prevent Silbeth twisting inside his reach, knocking his weapon aside with an elbow, and jabbing the tip of her sword into his hauberk.

The scar-tissue around the sliver of Wyrmtaker flared with remembered pain.

It was a killing stroke, or would have been had she pressed it. As much as his pride stung, Nycos nodded, stepped back, and announced, "I yield."

He remembered little of the next few moments. The roaring throng, pressing around him. The support of his friends—condolences for his defeat or congratulations for coming so near to defeating so worthy an adversary, depending on who was speaking. Mariscal's presence by his side, the occasional touch of her hand where propriety or the press of the crowd permitted. The roar of the trumpets, bringing the tournament's final afternoon to a close. The cold embrace of the rain.

But all he could see was Silbeth Rasik, and all he could think of were the many unanswered questions about her.

———

His Majesty made a brief announcement, formally declaring this year's winners—not just in the one-on-one duels, where Silbeth had proven victorious, but in contests of grand melee, archery, and the joust. Traditionally, a procession would have followed, in which the champions were displayed before the crowd, offered tokens of victory and other rewards; musicians and performers would have put on their final shows, and the tourney would officially draw to a close. In light of the inclement weather, however, tonight the king would be inviting the champions to a brief and private ceremony within the court, and the bulk of the festivities would be postponed for the morrow.

As that meant an extra day of celebration—and thus an extra day of drinking and leisure—the crowd cheered the announcement as emphatically as anything else they'd heard or seen for the past fortnight. The servants and heralds were perhaps less overjoyed, but they kept their opinions to themselves.

Once inside the crowded throne room, Silbeth and the others were named champions with abbreviated pomp and circumstance, including a lone trumpeter, and invited to attend the king's supper in a couple of hours. Marshal Laszlan asked if Silbeth would take a few moments to speak to his Majesty regarding a possible contract for the Priory, and just that easily they'd established a believable excuse as to why the king might spend some time in private conversation with a woman who, for all her skill, was just another mercenary.

It was all more or less what Nycos had expected since he'd first delivered her message, and he spent most of the shortened ceremony statue-still, fighting the unfamiliar and all too human urge to fidget, while he waited for the nonsense to be over and for the answers to finally come.

All of which made him want to scream in frustration when the king asked only his most immediate advisors—the Crown Marshal, Denuel Jarta, their Highnesses the prince and princess, and a handful of the others—to accompany him and their guest to the smaller council chamber.

Well, fine. If they weren't going to invite him to participate, he'd learn what he needed via other means. Time to take a page from Smim's book.

Nycos tagged along part of the way, concocting excuses to speak with Marshal Laszlan: something about possibly hiring foreign competitors who did well in the tournament to train Kirresci knights in some of their martial arts and fighting techniques. It was, no doubt, an idea that others had already considered, and perhaps it had even been tried, but Orban listened politely and asked Nycos to write up a formal proposal.

That done, Nycos peeled off as the group approached their destination. He'd established a reason to be *near* the council chamber, and that was all he'd required. Once on his own, he jogged through a few winding halls until he finally found a small room—really little more than a closet—close enough to suffice.

Nobody considered it a threat, in terms of eavesdropping or espionage. No human being could have heard a peep through the thick stone wall.

Nycos concentrated, transforming the pieces and contours of his inner ear until he could have heard a worm's after-dinner belch, and pressed the side of his head against the stone.

"…heard me make mention of an intelligence source I had within Ktho Delios," King Hasyan was saying, his voice made gruff and vaguely tinny by the intervening wall. "Lady Raczia was that agent."

"I only ever knew her as Ulia Povyar," Silbeth said, sounding distant, even saddened. "She didn't even tell me her real name until a few weeks before…" She trailed off.

The next to speak was Orban. Nycos could all but picture the marshal standing beside the king, a hand on his shoulder. "How did she die?"

"Ah, begging your pardon and with your permission, Marshal Laszlan," the mercenary replied, "and with yours, Your Majesty, I'd prefer to tell the tale as it happened. I expect you'll all have a great many questions, and it'll be easier to keep it all straight if we're not hopping around."

"I've no objection," Hasyan told her. "Has anyone else?" Then, after a response empty of anything but silence, he said, "Please proceed, Mistress Rasik."

So she did, regaling her audience (plus one curious knight) with the tale of her assignment, her mission to infiltrate Tohl Delian and extricate Ulia—that was, Lady Raczia, King Hasyan's spy—from the heart of Ktho Delios. She left out nothing of importance, from her difficulties in meeting up with the criminals they'd arranged to work through, the necessary bloodshed, and their near escape with Deliant pursuers, including one of the fearsome inquisitors, hot on their heels.

And here Nycos had thought he couldn't grow any more impressed with this woman!

"Koldan's smugglers got us outside the city walls," she said, "but not much further. The Deliant soldiers were not only behind us, but ahead. They'd gotten word to their patrols on the roads, since they didn't have to take the time to sneak around as we had. Ulia and I wound up fleeing overland, through the forests and eventually up into the Aerugo Mountains.

"I don't know if that inquisitor, Ilx, was still in command of the pursuit or if someone else was in charge, as we never saw him again. But they *would not* let up! Either they were truly enraged at the death of a few Ninth Citadel agents, or they'd figured out what it was Ulia had discovered."

From the sound of things through the wall, several people began to speak at once, then, but something—a gesture of some sort, perhaps—stopped them before they'd formed a coherent word. "Please," she reminded them, "I'll get there. You've no reason to trust me, not without U—Raczia to bear witness. I want you to understand why she trusted me with this intelligence, because it's *vital* that you believe!"

A moment, in which Nycos heard what he imagined was a long swallow of something liquid, and she continued. "It wasn't terribly difficult to hide from them in the mountains, but hiding was all we could do. They left us no escape routes. They watched the roads like hawks, were crawling all over the scalable slopes, had soldiers spread throughout the forests. Not that they really *had* to stand guard for long. Once the snows fell, we weren't going anywhere. We were trapped up there for *months*, and during the worst of winter it was all we could do to survive. Escape wasn't even a consideration, then. Moving between shelters so we'd not be caught, trying not to freeze, to scavenge sufficient food. We had to fight for our lives, more than once. Deliant searchers found us a couple of times, but there were also bears, something I think might have been a yeti, creatures of the ice that may have been fey… It was unpleasant."

That understatement inspired a few chuckles.

"In the mountains, of course, winter lingers. Things did grow easier, once the thaws began, but even then we couldn't get out! The soldiers figured we'd make a break for it as soon as we were able, so the coming of spring saw a redoubling of searchers. I've never heard of such a monumental effort to track down a pair of fugitives!

"Still, their numbers dwindled eventually. Either they assumed we were dead, or they simply couldn't spare the manpower from other duties. It still required a great deal of running and hiding, but we were *finally* able to make our way beyond the Aerugo range and run for the border."

Apparently it was a question Hasyan couldn't hold back any longer. "So Raczia was still alive, then? She didn't perish during the winter?"

"No, Your Majesty, she was still... still with me, then." She paused, swallowed. "Ulia and I became quite close during those months. We *had* to, to survive. Trust was more vital than warmth, you understand?"

Nycos sensed the nods he couldn't hear.

"It was during this portion of our travels, as we carefully made our way south, that she told me her real name—though we scarcely used it, as we were both accustomed to 'Ulia' by then. It was also at this time that she revealed to me what it was she'd learned. And it was in honor of that trust, and our friendship, that I chose to bring it to you, Your Majesty, once she was gone. Even though my assignment had only been to try to rescue her..."

More silence, long and dragging.

Until, "We still had to move slowly, carefully. We made our way to Lake Orist, skirted around the shore. We actually passed through the edges of Gronch, in order to avoid the Deliant patrols. Perhaps we were fortunate, but we encountered nothing within worse than a few wild animals. If the legends of monsters in that forest are true, they must have been elsewhere."

It wasn't hard for Nycos to imagine the looks that must have passed around the table at that declaration.

"We took a bit of time in a small town in Suunim, recovering, regaining our strength. Ulia was in a hurry to return, Your Majesty, but we both knew we needed the rest.

"Our journey through Suunim and Wenslir was long but largely free of excitement, and thank the gods for that! I think we were both feeling almost human again as we approached the Kirresci border. We were intercepted, then, by a Wenslirran patrol."

Her voice dropped to a near whisper, so that Nycos had to strain mightily to hear. "I should have been more watchful. More alert. We just… we had no warning, no reason to suspect they were anything other than what they seemed…"

Given there were fewer than a dozen people in the room, the uproar was intense. Nycos pulled back from the wall, and from the volume, until his Majesty had calmed everyone down.

Not that the king himself was precisely calm. "Are you suggesting," he asked, every word quivering with anger at the possibility of such betrayal, "that soldiers of Wenslir killed Raczia?"

"She died in the attack," Silbeth answered. "I barely escaped—and make no mistake, I would have fought for her to the death, but she was already gone before I knew what was happening.

"They were *dressed* as Wenslirran soldiers. I don't think they actually *were*. I think the Deliant spread word to watch for us—for Ulia specifically, since they had a better description of her."

"That would mean the Deliant have agents in Wenslir," Princess Firillia mused. "That's disturbing to say the least."

"There could be spies anywhere," Silbeth said. "Though not necessarily Deliant." Before anyone could ask what she meant by that, however, she continued. "That's why I approached you as I did, Your Majesty. I'd finally made it to Kirresc, and then to Talocsa, but I didn't know what to do. I couldn't just walk up and see you, not without Lady Raczia's rank to gain us an audience. Some random mercenary asking to see the king? It would have taken weeks, if it happened at all, and gods know who would have learned of my presence during that wait? They'd have taken steps."

"The code phrase you used to identify yourself to Raczia would have gotten my attention," Hasyan reminded her.

"Eventually. If the guards recognized it as a code phrase and not nonsense, and bothered to repeat it to anyone who could bring it to your attention. But again, how long would it take? How many people would the request have to pass through, how far would word spread that some no-name warrior had arrived to see you? How could I be sure none of the messengers were themselves enemy agents? I had to find a way to speak to you that wouldn't attract the wrong sort of attention. But a meeting with a tournament champion? Nothing about that says 'espionage' or identifies me as the woman who'd traveled with Ulia."

"And if you'd been slain in the process?" None of the Kirresci tournaments were *deliberately* waged to the death, but they were hardly a safe pastime. Severe injuries and fatalities were far from unheard of. "Who would have delivered your report then?"

"I thought it worth the risk, Your Majesty. And I thought it... unlikely I'd be killed."

"Fair enough," he conceded. "Still, such dramatic precautions really only seem necessary if Oztyerva were crawling with Deliant spies. While I am forced to admit that we may have one or two, they're hardly present in the sorts of numbers you seem to fear."

"That would be so, Your Majesty, if it were only the agents of Ktho Delios I was concerned about."

Nycos heard her take another drink, then another breath. "This, you see, is what Ulia discovered, what you *must* know. She had developed a friendship with a young Deliant officer, a man who served under one Colonel Vesmine Droste—one of the new favored protégés of Governor-General Achlaine himself."

The whole room had hushed, and even Nycos had to remind himself to breathe. She had told her entire story, explained her motivations, and now listed the provenance of the intelligence she carried, all before delivering that information for which the king's agent had died. What was *so* awful, so earth-shaking, that she felt they would struggle to accept it, might look for reason to disbelieve?

"The spies and assassins I've been hiding from, Your Majesty, are not just those of your enemy, but of one of your nearest friends. Ktho Delios has been holding secret talks with the royal house of Quindacra. Talks that, if they succeed, will result in Quindacra withdrawing from the southern nations' mutual defense pact."

# CHAPTER TWENTY-ONE

Once, so very long ago, it had been called Castle Tzirkrav, named for the powerful but decadent royal lineage that ruled from within its monolithic walls. When the last Tzirkrav king had finally been overthrown and executed, the nation and its government placed under pure martial law, it had been rechristened with the unimaginative but oh, so military designation of the First Citadel.

It was properly called that still, but in this day and age, most who spoke of it referred to it simply as the Fortress. It was title enough for the unbeating stone heart of the Deliant.

Colonel Vesmine Droste, proud and ambitious officer of that military parliament, stalked the corridors of the Fortress, her impassive features masking a whirling maelstrom of worry and profanity. She was slender, fit, her striking blonde hair pulled back so tightly that one might trace the contours of her skull beneath her skin. Nothing save the officer's red trim on her black tabard made her stand out from hundreds of other Ktho Delian soldiers, but she was so much more. One of the youngest ever to attain so high a rank within the Deliant, she fully intended to be the youngest to attain ranks higher still.

Assuming nothing had gone disastrously wrong with her plan. It was fear over just that possibility, sparked by the Governor-General's unexpected summons, that had her thoughts in such an uproar. The only thing worse...

Would be if they'd somehow, though she couldn't begin to imagine how, learned with whose help she'd concocted that plan.

Soldiers and couriers wisely stepped from her path. All the soldiers, that was, until she finally reached her destination.

A long hallway—narrow and easily defended—opened up its end, forming a broad antechamber before a massive, iron-bound door. Posted within that wider space stood four of the nation's true elite, Deliant Fortress guards who could not be bribed, could not be intimidated. All wore gloss-blackened mail with plate reinforcement, all were armed with arbalest, halberd, and broadsword. Three wore the standard black tabard; the fourth bore the dark blue of an inquisitor.

All of them moved to intercept, their leader demanding her identity and a sequence of code words while the inquisitor invoked his witchcraft to ensure she was cloaked by no illusion or other magic. Only when they were fully convinced of her identity—no matter that each knew her by sight—did they stand aside for her to pass.

None opened the doors for her. That would have been a distraction from their duties. She grunted sourly, despite approving of the practice, and hauled the massive portal ajar. It swung with relative ease despite its weight, thanks to a system of counterweights that could be disengaged from the room beyond.

She first noticed, as she always did, the change in scent, the fading of the sting in her eyes. The corridors of the Fortress were well lit, but the lanterns within the parliamentary chamber burned a cleaner, higher quality oil. The leaders of the Deliant often spent hours or even days within, after all.

The second thing she noticed was how that light was directed.

A horseshoe-curve of seats and podiums wrapped the room on all sides except the entrance, raised so that the Deliant officers could look down upon whomever addressed them. Directly opposite that entrance was the highest seat, that of the Governor-General himself. The remainder gradually grew lower around the curve, until those nearest the door were raised only by a few steps. Had this been a standard meeting of the parliament, the lights would have shone evenly throughout the chamber, and she would have taken her seat roughly halfway around and up the room's right side.

Today, only the floor itself was illuminated, suggesting she was to take a position there, gazing up at the others. Today, she was not an equal, but a petitioner.

*So be it.* It wouldn't be her first time.

Concealing her irritation as thoroughly as she had her earlier worry, she stepped into the light and slammed a fist to her chest in salute. "You sent for me, Governor?"

Vesmine couldn't see Demyand Achlaine with the lanterns focused as they were, but he was hardly a stranger. It required no effort at all to picture the hawkish features; the head bald as an egg save for the fringe of white; the body grown gaunt with age, yet still possessed of strength and cunning enough to defeat challengers half as old.

"King Hasyan," he announced without preamble, his sharp tones even more clipped than usual, "has sent couriers to every corner of Kirresc. He is calling his *entire* court to assembly, all his nation's dukes and high nobles."

The colonel nodded, her mind racing. Hasyan wouldn't take such steps lightly, and certainly not this late in the year, with winter snows threatening.

No, not much would inspire the man to go to such lengths, and only one thing that would result in Vesmine Droste being called before the rest of the parliament like an errant student.

"You suspect he knows of the Quindacra negotiations?"

"This summons to court," Achlaine continued without answering the question, "occurred not long after Hasyan took a private meeting. None of our people are in a position to learn precisely who attended, let alone what was discussed. But we do know that many of his closest advisors were present, as was a woman by the name of Silbeth Rasik."

"I'm not familiar with the name, Governor."

"Nor should you be. She was among the champions of the Kirresci tournament, and—it turns out—a member of the Priory of Steel."

Still she failed to see where this was going, how any of it was relevant.

"Having backtracked her movements as best we can, we now believe that she entered the tournament solely as a means of meeting with his Majesty in a way that wouldn't appear suspicious to… anyone who might be watching."

Vesmine caught the curse on her lips before it escaped, but it was a near thing. "The woman who aided in Povyar's escape?"

"So it appears."

More internal cursing. She'd already tracked down the officer under her command who'd let information slip to Povyar, and had him executed, but the damage was done—and, ultimately, her responsibility. It had slowed her meteoric rise through the ranks to a glacial pace. Only the fact that the ongoing plan was hers had mitigated some of the damage to her career, and it would take the success of that plan to set things back on course. After the two fugitives had somehow survived the mountains and eluded her soldiers, she'd all but given thanks on her knees at the report of Ulia's death from Quindacran spies in Wenslir. She'd known then that the traitor's accomplice was a loose end, but she'd hoped—

"The Quindacran operation is yours, Colonel Droste," Achlaine said, as though listening in on her thoughts. "The failure in our security was yours. Which means the responsibility for fixing this is yours. Kirresc and her allies cannot be allowed to confirm their suspicions, and they *certainly* cannot be allowed to pressure the Quindacrans into changing their minds."

"King Boruden is a coward at heart," Vesmine declared adamantly. "He's more frightened of us than he is of Kirresc or their allies!"

"Don't be so certain, Colonel. Yes, Boruden is a coward, but he's also a cunning little weasel. At the moment, he wants what we can offer, but he shares a border with King Hasyan, not with us. Should Kirresc bring enough pressure to bear, particularly if they recruit Wenslir to the cause as well…"

"You're correct, of course. We can't chance it."

"So what do you propose to do about it, Colonel?"

She wanted to lick her lips, gone suddenly dry. A small amount of magic—such as the agitation of a few of Gronch's monstrous inhabitants, to draw attention from Ktho Delios's activities—she could readily justify; she'd had several inquisitors assigned to her for the duration of the operation. What she and her partner planned for later could be explained away as a result of that initial agitation, a natural spread of activity throughout that haunted forest. Could they move up the timetable, though? Would she still be able to hide her outside assistance—sorcerous assistance—from her peers?

"Let me speak with my inquisitors, Governor," she hedged. "I think we can put something together fairly quickly."

"More of your 'monstrous distractions'?" asked another of the shadowed Deliant officers, clearly unimpressed. Many of her fellow officers had been less than taken with that aspect of her plans—particularly since one of Hasyan's knights, according to their spies, had already guessed at a Ktho Delian hand in the ogres' recent activities.

The same man, in fact, who had killed one of their most useful contacts among the Mahdreshan banditry: a troublemaker who kept cropping up, seemingly by accident, around the edges of her operation. *Sir Nycolos Anvarri.* With any luck, she'd find a way to work his unpleasant demise into the next phase of her operation.

"If we can make it work," she said, responding to the snide inquiry. "Kirresc may *suspect* our interference with Gronch, but they cannot prove it, nor can they ignore the danger the ogres pose. And if we can't, well, I'm sure a cadre of inquisitors and mercenaries can provide a modicum of distraction for King Hasyan. Either way, they'll have too much to worry about, too many problems, to devote their full efforts to investigating or pressuring Quindacra."

The darkened shape of the Governor-General nodded slowly. "Go, then. Make your plans. But Colonel? While I still have faith in this operation of yours, that faith is not without its limits."

Vesmine could do nothing in response to that save salute, pivot on her heel, and hope, as she marched from the chamber, that it wouldn't take her partner long to respond to her summons.

———

Here, deep in the darkest heart of Gronch, the sun never shone, the rain never fell, the wind never blew. Weather was a myth; the seasons were marked by a faint warming or cooling, by a change in color in the trees, and nothing more. The leaves overhead were packed too thick, forming a cavern's ceiling. From above hung stalactites of moss, while branches clutched or hung limp like the fingers of countless dead men.

Nothing smelled dead, though. Rather the air was redolent with the scent of growing things, moist and thriving things that should have been wholesome, yet felt vaguely unclean. The soil was thick, black, like a residue of the invisible night sky. Roots snaked just beneath the surface, angry serpents lurking to strike. The brush and fungus-covered fallen logs were as thick as the canopy above. Trunks and branches pressed together to form a maze of walls, and every curve, every arch, might have been the lair of some beast, or the doorway to another world.

It waited, did Gronch, here in its core. Patient. Hungry. Even the boles appeared hostile, leaning in, looming, claustrophobic. Eyes watched. Limbs shuffled. The things that dwelt here were no mere wolves or snakes, crows or bears. Such creatures avoided this part of the forest, for they preferred realms where the natural order held sway. Where they were the predators, not the prey.

Here, not far from the swampy shore of Lake Orist, that soil had piled up, those fallen boles formed natural archways, creating a twisted, sickly entryway into the depths of an earthen hill. Centipedes, beetles, worms, and things far less natural writhed and wiggled from the mud around that entrance. They wound around blades of grass, across protruding sticks and over lichen-covered rocks, but never did they pass more than a few yards deep into the crooked, gaping tunnel. Even they, driven by some mindless instinct, knew better than to approach what slumbered within.

It was into this twilit nightmare the stranger came. Where few humans dared, where even the wolves and the poisonous things that crawled in the earth did not dare, he did. And not for the first time.

No natural traveler, he hadn't walked through the bulk of the Ogre-Weald to arrive in its heart. One moment, the shadows beneath a pair of intertwined arboreal giants had been empty, the next he had stepped from between them as though they were, indeed, a long-hidden door. Had he wished, he could have appeared inside the hill itself, in the winding bowels of that awful tunnel, but penetrating the wards—primitive though they were—would have taken effort.

Also, it would have been rude. And even one such as he found it wise to be courteous when dealing with the uncrowned sovereign of Gronch.

Beneath his torn and ratty cloak, with its equally ragged hood, he didn't look fearsome. In fact, he appeared to have no business remotely near the Ogre-Weald, nor anywhere more dangerous than a pigpen, or perhaps a pastoral hillside overseeing a particularly docile herd of sheep. A disheveled mop of straw-colored hair topped a face equal parts boyish and mannish. Any halfway intelligent guess would have put him only a year or two past the changing of his voice, and though he hadn't bothered to shave in months, the result was little more than a downy layer of fuzz that pooled haphazardly across cheeks and chin. He was tall, but not strong; lanky and rangy, not muscular or graceful.

He was, in short, soft. Lost and weak, a lamb or fawn abandoned in the darkness.

Or so, at least, did the denizens of Gronch see him.

They appeared from the shadows, much as he had, a trio of monstrous forms, roughly human in shape but none remotely human. The shortest and squattest still topped eight feet, and that was without counting the spidery limbs protruding in all directions, including upward, from the lumps of gristle that were its shoulders. Of the other two, one was an asymmetrical thing of two legs but only a single muscular arm, clutching a rusted iron axe; a voracious, canine snout sprouted from beneath a single bloodshot eye, drooling a pus-like ichor that spattered and matted filth-encrusted fur. The last was easily the least alien—discounting the ten-foot height and the array of horns and spines protruding at random from its flesh and bones and even one of its eyes, which constantly wept a clear, glistening stream.

He watched them, the stranger did, unblinking and unflinching, with the cold analysis of one who had seen more than should ever have been possible at his apparent age.

"I have an errand here," he told them, steady and calm. "You do not want to interfere."

Two of them advanced on him, slathering and gibbering, deaf to his words or at least to their meaning. The other, the canine being with the axe, hesitated half a breath before joining its companions.

"Ogres," the hooded stranger sighed.

When he spoke again, it was to produce sounds that bore precious little resemblance to any human—any *sane*—language. The syllables were harsh, rough-edged, somehow hollow. That any human-shaped throat or lips or tongue could form them was very nearly an eldritch mystery in itself.

Branches creaked, bending, stretching, shedding leaves and oozing thick sap where bark splintered. Roots coiled and bulged, raising serpentine heaps of soil before bursting into open air. The surrounding trees groaned in hateful protest.

The one-armed marauder barked and spat as it was dragged from its feet by the winding tree limbs, lifted and bound so that it hung, motionless and quivering, high above the forest soil.

"You, at least, seem to have a sliver of a brain," the stranger said. Then, to the other two ogres, who had frozen in puzzlement for an instant at their companion's predicament but swiftly resumed their advance, "I fear the rest of you are hopeless."

From a single pace away, a spiny hand the size of a pony's head reached for the cloaked figure. He extended a hand of his own, as though preparing to grasp the other halfway.

Instead, he spat another throat-rending phrase. From his fingers poured a gout of white liquid fire. On it came, and on, lighting the surrounding forest in its unnatural glare. It not only coated but penetrated the skin of the massive ogre, boiling flesh and fluids, igniting organ and bone. The creature spun away at the impact, dancing like a puppet on a string of flame, twitching, flailing, rotating as it burned. Directed by the hellish stream and the will of the impossibly young wizard, the dying thing slammed into its spider-limbed companion. Licks of flame leapt joyfully from one to the other, cavorting between them, while lengths of half-melted bone gouged deep rifts in unburnt flesh. Long after it was dead, until it was nothing but smoldering ash and charred fragments, it flailed and stabbed, so that the other perished soon after.

A few final embers flickered, then the heart of Gronch once more subsided into shadow.

"Stay," the stranger ordered the surviving ogre, though it remained tightly bound by the animated boles and branches. Then, with no sign that the brutal magics had caused him the slightest strain, he resumed his trek, passing into the depths of the wooded hillside.

His careful trek through the winding tunnels was long and slow, for though he knew well how to avoid the hidden deadfalls and savage wards, bypassing them required no small amount of care. Finally, he emerged into the hill's central cavern: a massive earth-walled cave, half-swamp thanks to leaks from Lake Orist just beyond the northern wall. He cautiously picked his way around the stalactites and stalagmites of numerous roots, and gazed intently at the slumbering visage of the entity for which he had come.

Both hands raised, he spoke in a voice augmented by sorcery, so that it resounded not merely in the air but in the dreams of the thing before him.

*"Awaken, exalted Vircingotirilux! I call to you, dread wyrm of the ancient wood! Awaken!"*

Multiple piercing howls, carrying the strength of the quaking earth and the fury of the unjustly damned, blasted through the cave until the hillside shook and the trees beyond trembled. Against that scream even the sorcerer could not entirely stand, staggering back two steps, though he neither cringed nor raised his arms in futile defense.

On they went, and on. All he could do was wait, and endure.

One of those voices fell silent as three pairs of hellish, gleaming eyes blinked open in the dark. The other two transformed into bestial roars of rage, mindless and murderous.

"BACK! CYOLOS! DZIRLAS! I SAID BACK! SILENCE! *SILENCE!*"

The roars subsided into resentful growls at the command. The speaker was less animalistic but no less savage, a monstrous voice that somehow intertwined a guttural thunder and a shrill shriek together as one. As four of the unblinking eyes retracted into the shadowy cave, the third pair turned to look down, down, down upon the newcomer.

"WHY HAVE YOU WOKEN US, LITTLE MAGUS? WE STILL TASTE THE HARVEST ON THE DISTANT AIR. IT CANNOT BE TIME YET."

"Indeed it is not, dread Vircingotirilux. With apologies, circumstances required that I rouse you ahead of schedule."

"CIRCUMSTANCES?"

"My ally in the nation of Ktho Delios has learned—"

"HUMAN CONCERNS! PRIMITIVE LANDS! SCURRYING INSECTS AND JABBERING PRIMATES! SUCH WORRIES ARE NOT OURS! HOW DARE YOU—!"

"I dare because, in the process of studying my ally's foes among the 'scurrying insects and jabbering primates,' I have found one that intrigued me. And in further study of *him*…"

The young man, whose behavior and demeanor now were anything but youthful, craned his head upward as he leaned in, meeting the inhuman gaze with his own. "I think I have located an enemy you and I share. A rival of yours who may not be as dead as we believed."

Something lashed angrily at the cave wall, sending a cascade of earth and soil tumbling to the floor. Fearsome growls again echoed throughout the chamber. Clearly, Vircingotirilux, whatever it was, understood exactly of whom he spoke.

"THIS NOTION DOES NOT MAKE US HAPPY, MAGUS!"

"I'm not precisely celebrating, either. After all the effort I went to…"

"TELL US WHERE! WE WILL LAY WASTE TO THEIR MONUMENTS, THROW DOWN THEIR RULERS, WIPE THEIR CIVILIZATION FROM—"

"I was considering something perhaps a *little* more subtle, great wyrm."

Another twitch, another—albeit smaller—avalanche of earth. "WHAT DO YOU PROPOSE?"

"Well." The wizard leaned against a protruding root, half sitting in the wooden loop. "To begin with, I might like to borrow one of your pets."

# CHAPTER TWENTY-TWO

The throne room, deep and broad as it was, and despite the fact that many of Kirresc's lesser gentry had been barred from this particular gathering, was tightly, even stiflingly, packed.

Almost decadently comfortable, richly upholstered chairs had been placed to either side of the dais, forming thin wings that curved around the hall's farthest edge. In them were seated the highest nobles of Kirresc, many of whom had traveled weeks to be here. Over two dozen other chairs, smaller and less ornate, sat in the empty center, facing the throne, in which sat those of lower rank. Both walls were packed with those less important still, yet powerful or knowledgeable enough that their presence was deemed necessary. The assembled riches and finery could have purchased a small town in its entirety, and if anything catastrophic were to occur, the leadership and potential leadership of the whole kingdom would have been obliterated to the third or fourth generation.

The veritable army currently occupying the grounds of Oztyerva—not merely the king's soldiers, but those of every duchy, countship, and barony represented—stood steadfast to ensure that no such catastrophe occurred.

Nycos—who, as one Kirresc's knights and possible successors to Marshal Laszlan, was considered important enough to attend but didn't rate a chair—stood against the leftmost wall and idly counted the many colorful banners, representing all those Kirresci territories, currently waving from the arched ceilings. Since he was required to take no particular position in the hall, and since Kortlaus's rank entitled *him* to a seat, and thus wasn't available to talk to, Nycos had chosen to station himself as near as he could to

351

Silbeth Rasik. She, as a potential speaker at this gathering, stood near the dais but not upon it, and grumbled to herself at a volume only Nycos could hear. She was, he gathered, uncomfortable with the amount of attention she expected to receive, and that so many people would learn of her involvement in recent events.

For all that, she'd never, in the weeks it had taken to orchestrate this extended court, made any effort to depart. Given that she owed no loyalty to Kirresc or King Hasyan, and her assignment had ended with the delivery of her intelligence—if not earlier, with the death of Lady Raczia—she'd have been within her rights to insist on leaving.

A single horn sounded and those who were seated instantly rose. A curtain parted, revealing a smaller entrance near the dais, and through it entered his Majesty and the great leaders of the nation.

Nycos knew most of them personally, of course, particularly those who dwelt here in the palace: the prince and princess; Orban Laszlan; Denuel Jarta; Amisco Valacos, Judge Royal; Prelate Domatir Matyas; Balmorra Zas, his Majesty's astrologer. He knew, as well, Duke Ishmar of Hesztilna, Mariscal's father, who hadn't bothered to return home once he'd learned this assembly was coming.

The others, he had never met, but recognized by description. Gostav, Duke of Janu-Vala; Matilya, Duchess of Dalgran; a small array of counts and countesses.

And seated directly beside the king, in a position of power scarcely less than his own, an older woman, sharp of visage, black of hair, and so piercing of gaze that Nycos would have been only mildly surprised had she pointed his way and announced his true nature. She, he knew, could only be Pirosa, Archduchess of Vidirrad, Kirrsc's most powerful ruler save Hasyan himself, and not incidentally the mother of Andarjin, Nycos's most very favorite margrave.

One other entered with them, though unlike the rest, she took her seat in the front row of the chairs facing the dais, rather than those set up alongside it. That Ambassador Leomyn Guldoell of Quindacra was the only foreign representative present amidst what was otherwise a purely Kirresci assembly did not escape attention. Many gazed her way, manners warring with intense curiosity, and Guldoell herself, though a consummate diplomat, couldn't quite keep a worried moue from darting across her face.

"Thank you," Hasyan said simply. "We know many of you have traveled far in what is not a good season for travel, leaving your own affairs untended, at our call. We are grateful."

Jarta rose and gave a much more flowery speech of welcome on his Majesty's behalf. More flowery and yet, for a gathering of this magnitude, still remarkably brief. Either the palatine had been ordered to keep it short, or he was as eager as anyone to get to the meat of things. Then it was Domatir Matyas's turn. He offered up his usual prayer that the gods (and God, and the Vinnkasti) bless this gathering and their endeavors.

"We are certain," Hasyan resumed after the prelate, too, returned to his seat, "that some of you have already guessed, in part, at the reason for this assembly. You have heard some of the rumors, received some reports, of Ktho Delian troop movements near our borders, and those of our neighbors."

Rumbles of assent, anger, worry, in reply.

"Many of you have also been informed that we recently rooted out a spy in our own midst, one we believe but cannot prove to have been Ktho Delian. And that his escape was aided by an operative they had placed within a Mahdreshan bandit gang.

"In addition to *that*, our friends in Wenslir have been fretting over increased activity along the Ogre-Weald. We've had no confirmed reports, but even rumors of such horrors can prove damaging if they force the southern nations to split our attentions. It has been suggested," and here his eyes flickered briefly toward Nycos, "that we consider the possibility of a Ktho Delian hand even in this. That they might deliberately stir up the beasts of Gronch—or spread tales of their activities, if you choose not to believe in things such as ogres—as a diversion."

Once more he waited for his audience's questions, exclamations, and protests to die down. "Again, we've no proof of this. It's but a hypothesis. Considering the timing, however, it's one I believe worth considering."

"Your Majesty, if I may?" Archduchess Pirosa's tone was crisp, cultured, razor-sharp—precisely what Nycos would have expected. "I agree with you completely that we ought to be concerned about the possibility of Ktho Delian activity. If the amount of movement we've heard about is accurate, and especially if they're orchestrating other diversions or unrest, it would certainly appear to be more than their usual exercises or sabre-rattling. If you'll forgive my bluntness, however, all this could have been conveyed via courier, or perhaps messenger pigeon."

The archduchess, Nycos saw, was a born politician. She *must* know Hasyan had more than this, that he would not have called for the nobles to travel across the kingdom to discuss mere rumors. He was leading up to something, and anyone with half a brain would recognize that fact. By demanding an explanation—and no matter how politely she'd couched it, that was precisely what she'd done—she'd flexed her authority before the assembled court, suggesting however subtly or slightly that even the king must answer to her. He wondered if she was even conscious she'd done it, and if that was how she approached all her interactions.

No wonder Andarjin was so wrapped up in his own constant scheming, if that was what he'd been raised with, had to live up to. Nycos wished briefly that Smim was at his side. The goblin was more up to date on palace politics and personal gossip than he, could probably have answered whispered questions or pointed out other such maneuvers Nycos might have missed. Like many other trusted servants, however, Smim currently waited in the hall beyond the throne room doors, ready to respond if called but not permitted to attend the assembly itself.

"Almost a year ago," his Majesty continued, "we received a signal from a spy who had managed to attain a position in the ranks of high society within the walls of Tohl Delian itself." His volume rose as he spoke over the next round of astonished comments and whispers throughout the court. "She'd discovered something of vital import and required aid in escaping without being discovered by the Deliant."

Pirosa was hardly the only accomplished political dancer present. By continuing without acknowledging the archduchess's comment, Hasyan made it clear he would not be ordered about—while answering her query, thus giving her no room to claim any slight had been done her.

"This," the king said, gesturing for the waiting mercenary to step forward, "is Silbeth Rasik, of the Priory of Steel. It was to her we assigned the task of extricating our operative."

"Your Majesty!" One of the counts whose territory fell within the duchy of Janu-Vala, a slender and dusky fellow whose name Nycos hadn't caught, raised his voice in protest. "How could you trust something so vital and so secretive to a—a *sellsword*? I understand the need to avoid implicating Kirresc in any official activity within the Ktho Delian interior, but—"

"We said she was of the Priory, Count Lajos," Hasyan interrupted, as though that ought to explain everything.

"You did, Your Majesty. And..." Lajos took in the faces of those around him. "It's clear that means something to most everyone that I'm apparently missing. I apologize for my outburst, but if I might request an explanation?"

He was the only one to have spoken, but a smattering of others appeared equally confused, as well as relieved that someone had asked the question so they didn't have to. Indeed, Nycos himself would have been equally bewildered, had he not read up on the organization in the weeks since he'd overheard Silbeth's story.

"We see. Mistress Rasik, would you care to edify the good count?"

"Of course, Your Majesty. I…" She began, halted. "Actually, Your Majesty, this might sound self-serving and unconvincing coming from me. Perhaps Prelate Domatir? I'm sure he's aware of the nature of the Priory, whether or not he takes us particularly seriously."

A brief exchange of expressions, then Domatir Matyas repressed a sigh and stood. "The Priory of Steel," he intoned as though reciting from a text—whence, indeed, he'd most probably learned all of this, "isn't a mercenary guild in the traditional sense, Count Lajos. As the name implies, it is a religious organization. Its members pay particular homage to the more martial gods of the Empyrean Choir. Inoleare, Alazir, Louros, Teslak, and so forth."

"Many of us," Silbeth corrected politely. "Myself included. But some of our number revere Deiumulos, the One God."

"Yes, quite. Well, regardless, the point is that they consider their expertise and practice of martial prowess to be a religious observance. Prayer, essentially, a means of honoring the gods. Or God. Which, yes, makes them among the greatest warriors known to Galadras, but of equal import is the belief that those skills must be exercised only in causes that honor their faith. That may vary from member to member, depending on their own ethics, but the result is that their contracts take on the import of religious doctrine. A member of the Priory of Steel is as religiously faithful to an assignment as any true believer to scripture, or the most zealous patriots to their nation.

"I take... some issue with the Priory's notions of what a proper religious observance or organization ought to be," the prelate admitted, "but I know from experience that they are true to their beliefs. For a mission such as this one, vital to Kirresc and yet one to which Kirresc must not be connected, his Majesty could not have made a wiser selection." Then, with a bow to Hasyan and a brief bob of the head toward Silbeth, he sat.

"Does that satisfy you, Count Lajos?" Hasyan asked.

"I... Yes, Your Majesty." He didn't look entirely certain, but if nothing else the count recognized that further questioning, let alone protest, would accomplish little but to irritate some very powerful people.

"Good. Then, Mistress Rasik, we invite you to tell your tale, precisely as you told it to us."

And so she did, repeating almost verbatim, albeit with less obvious emotion, what she had told the king's council weeks before. Since he'd already heard it, Nycos allowed himself to focus on how the rest of the court reacted.

He saw various degrees of shock, sympathy, doubt, even a bit of vague indifference, all as he'd have expected. That last, of course, would vanish once she revealed the intelligence for which she and Lady Raczia had struggled so hard, but as she'd done before, she was saving that particular revelation for the conclusion.

It was an omission that many of the gathered nobles swiftly picked up on. Nycos watched as numerous lips frowned and brows furrowed, as several of them drew breath to interrupt and then decided against it. He saw the dukes and duchesses intently focused, waiting for the thunderbolt they knew must be coming. Archduchess Pirosa ran a fingernail across her lip in thought, theories and calculations whirling almost visibly behind her pupils. The chamber all but reeked with anticipation.

As for Hasyan... Throughout Silbeth's story, the king himself kept his gaze, subtly but squarely, upon Ambassador Guldoell.

And that, Nycos realized, was precisely *why* his Majesty had instructed Silbeth to again save what she'd learned for the end, why Guldoell was the only foreign emissary present in this small sea of Kirresci nobility. He wanted to see her reaction, unplanned and unprepared, firsthand.

As the recitation wound toward its inevitable end, Nycos chose to follow his king's lead. When Silbeth reached her revelation, the knight's attention was fixed on the Quindacran's face.

Silbeth leveled her accusation. The chamber erupted, with many present demanding answers, demanding proof, demanding Guldoell be clapped in chains, all depending on how readily inclined they were to believe. A few even moved as though to restrain her physically—or worse—but Hasyan's bodyguards stepped forward to restore order, and to ensure no blood was shed, no international crime committed.

Through it all, Guldoell sat, eyes closed in sorrow and a mounting despair, cheeks grown paler than the whitest of the moons.

"Was it truly necessary, Your Majesty," she asked with shaking breath when the furor had subsided, "to spring this on me? In public, no less?"

"Our apologies, Ambassador," Hasyan replied, every word firm but not unkind. "We couldn't allow even the appearance of secrecy in this matter, and we had to—"

"Had to see my reaction. Yes, I understand. I suppose I might have done the same."

If she'd been at her best, or anywhere near it, she'd never have interrupted the king, but he chose to let it pass. "As it was, it took the whole weight of the crown for me to forbid any of the other ambassadors from attending. They know something's amiss. But I wanted to have a better understanding before I bring this to them."

Nycos noted Pirosa nodding to herself, as were the other dukes, presumably in approval of Hasyan's decisions.

"We've known you for many years, Ambassador Guldoell," he continued, "and we've worked well together. Your expression at Mistress Rasik's news, as well as the fact that you didn't immediately leap to your feet to accuse her of lying, tells me you are as surprised to hear this as we were."

"I am. For the most part. Your Majesty…" Guldoell started to rise and all but collapsed back into the seat, her whole body visibly trembling. "We have, as you say, worked side by side for a long time. You have been a friend, to Quindacra and to me, most of that time, and where we clashed, you have always been reasonable and honorable in your dealings. I couldn't live with myself if I did any less now."

Again she stood to address the dais and the assembled nobles, this time forcing herself to remain upright, though it required she turn the chair about and maintain a tight grip on it.

"I know nothing of any such communications, any such schemes, on the part of King Boruden or any other party of influence in Quindacra. But in complete candor Your Majesty, my Lords and Ladies, I would be among the last to hear of it were it true. The mere fact of my position here, my close ties to and respect for the Kirresci court, would make me… a risk to any such conspiracy, and everyone back home knows that. Some already worry if my loyalties are too deeply split.

"They are not. I am loyal to my country. But that loyalty includes speaking out if I feel Quindacra is making a mistake."

"A pretty speech," one of the lesser nobles sneered. Harsh whispers from those around him and a murderous glance from Marshal Laszlan silenced him. Other than the breathing of the throng, only the faint grind of the ambassador's chair on the stone broke the stillness.

"I don't believe it's any great secret that certain segments of Quindacran society are…" Her lips twisted dramatically, as though trying to change places. "…envious of Kirresc. Your wealth, your farmland, your timber, your highways are all superior to ours. You know it, we know it. Normally those factions, those voices, are hushed, their bitterness overshadowed by all we have to gain from our relations with you, but…" She started to shrug, stumbled, and recovered her handhold on the chair. "I fear I cannot say I would be *entirely* shocked if what your agent discovered is true.

"I can make you no promises, Your Majesty. I won't disobey any of my king's royal commands, or return here if I'm ordered not to. But I will travel to Vidiir, and if possible I will let you know what I can learn about this."

Again a number of voices sounded in protest, objecting to letting her return to Quindacra, doubting the veracity of anything she'd said—not many voices, no, but more than a few. Hasyan raised a hand for calm, and when that didn't work, he whispered a command to Orban. The marshal reached out, took the horn from the herald who'd signaled their entry earlier, and sounded a blast like the ones used to signal his troops clear across a battlefield. The chamber fell into a shocked silence.

Several guards peeked in from the hall outside, ensuring everything was all right, before once more closing the doors.

"Thank you," Hasyan said fondly. Then, to the gathering at large, "We understand your fears, your frustrations, your suspicions. Even if we shared them, however, what would you have us do? Ambassador Guldoell has not acted against us. She has committed no crime. We have no hard proof of Quindacra's communication with the enemy, nor are we at war with them. On what grounds would you have us detain the ambassador? With what justification would you have us commit such an offense, even potentially an act of war?"

A few angry mutters rose in reply, but no clear answers or useful suggestions.

"Right. Ambassador, we *do* have to assign guards to watch over you until you have gathered your belongings and departed. They'll travel with you as far as the border. We hope you understand, and we assure you this is to protect you from any, ah, over-enthusiastic citizens as much as to protect any of Kirresc's secrets from you."

"I understand, Your Majesty," she replied, albeit stiffly.

Nycos thought Hasyan looked very much as though he wanted to further explain, or perhaps just to sigh. Instead, he nodded. Again the doors opened and Leomyn Guldoell departed, a quartet of Kirresci soldiers marching in step around her.

"We believe," Hasyan declared, "that this is sufficient food for thought for now. Please feel free to return to your quarters, or enjoy whatever hospitality Oztyerva has to offer, though I suggest you ruminate on what we've been told here today. Servants will find you when it is time for supper. Your Graces," he said, gesturing to the dukes on either side, "and Mistress Rasik, if you would remain here with us and our advisors, we'd like to spend a bit longer discussing possible strategies…"

Nycos, whose senses were currently only a bit better than those of normal humans, lost the thread of the king's declaration amidst the multitude of other conversations and other sounds filling the hall. Lower-ranked nobles moved toward the open doors or milled about beside the rows of chairs, discussing or arguing over everything they'd learned. From beyond, more voices still, as servants and gentry called to their betters, or guessed and gossiped about the meeting from which they'd just been excluded. The movement of so many bodies, and the drafts through the open door, set the banners above to a lazy, languorous flapping.

Unsure as to whether Mariscal would expect him to meet up with her, or whether she would make her way toward the exit with the rest of the crowd, and made vaguely uneasy by the thought that Silbeth Rasik might soon depart, now that her role in this international drama seemed near its end, Nycos stood where he was. If nothing else, he would give the meandering throng time to clear out, so that his bad mood and nagging worries wouldn't compel him to elbow a few lingering aristocrats from his path.

He stretched a bit, casting about over everyone's heads— scowling briefly as Margrave Andarjin, currently pontificating to his cronies and hangers-on, passed through his view—trying to locate Smim amidst the horde of waiting servants. He knew the goblin must be there, but the creature's short stature made him difficult to pinpoint among—

Hmm.

At the side of the broad doorway, one of the guards politely but firmly directed the edge of the human current aside so that a man clad in the tabard of a Kirresci royal courier could squeeze his way in. Clearly the messenger must carry some word of great import to demand entry now, rather than waiting for a less busy, less chaotic time. Nycos almost shrugged it off, assuming he would learn of the matter later if it involved him or his interests, almost turned away.

Almost. Something about that courier nagged at him, something in the way the fellow moved. He couldn't identify it, and clearly nobody else saw it. Because of his enhanced vision, or because he was paranoid and imagining things? Just in case, Nycos began to push his way through the thinning mass of humanity.

"My king! Beware!" Balmorra, the old astrologer and seer, pointed a gnarled and shaking finger at the oncoming courier. "*Beware!*"

Hasyan and the nobles twisted about, seeking to understand the danger she'd seen. The royal bodyguards rushed forward, as did Nycos and the other knights still in attendance; he found himself several paces ahead of Zirresca, though both drew their sabres in near perfect unison. The nobles who had lingered in the throne room scattered, many dropping half-empty goblets and glasses as they fled.

Chanting under her breath, Balmorra dipped two fingers into the cup of wine from which Duke Ishmar had been sipping and then daubed her eyelids with the rich crimson liquid. An invocation, no doubt, meant to show her clearly whatever it was she'd sensed in the messenger, to pierce any magic or illusion that might hide—

Every muscle in Nycos's body clenched so tightly it was all he could do not to topple over, rigid as any statue. *What would she see when she looked at him?*

Her attention, for the moment at least, remained focused on the danger at hand. And the cry that followed a heartbeat later had nothing whatsoever to do with dragons.

"*Psoglavac!*"

They knew the word, all of them—the Kirresci from their myths and fairy tales, Nycos from the experience of centuries. A living nightmare, a voracious eater of flesh both living and dead, a ravenous ogre with a lust to kill and consume.

But *not* a creature, to Nycos's knowledge, able to alter its shape. So how—?

He—*it*—looked at them all and grinned, drool running unchecked over its lips to dangle from its chin. It swept the assembled warriors and nobles with unblinking eyes as they closed ranks to protect their king, and yet Hasyan was *not* its prey.

It snarled, screamed in furious triumph, charged the line of sword and spear without hesitation. And Nycos wondered, his heart pounding and his head abruptly full of questions, if the others had even noticed that the attack had come not when its gaze had landed upon King Hasyan, but upon *him*.

The first of the king's bodyguards, a tall and powerfully built soldier, drove the tip of his spear directly into the "messenger's" chest. Steel tore through fabric and seemingly through skin before deflecting from something unseen beneath. From nowhere, the attacker produced a massive axe—the haft uneven, twisted, knotted, more branch than handle, the blade bedecked with blooming flowers of rust. The whole thing was impossibly huge, taller than its wielder, and yet he swung it as the lightest sabre. Mail, flesh, and bone crunched beneath its bite, and the mangled lump that had been a brave warrior flew through the air to sprawl across the lower step of the dais.

Nycos leapt, channeling his will and his magics through his body, stronger than any three soldiers by the time he landed. He struck the human-shaped ogre a vicious blow, yet even his supernatural might fell short. His sabre shivered, ringing like a wind chime as it rebounded from whatever lurked beneath mundane flesh.

The false messenger staggered, knocked off balance by sheer force of impact, but lashed out with a backhanded fist. Nycos dodged beneath, if only just, but the knight who'd charged in behind him was less fortunate. Bone audibly shattered, piercing muscle in a dozen fragments, and the woman fell screaming to the floor, her left arm limp as rope from the bicep down.

More soldiers struck, more blades landed without visible effect, more people died beneath murderous axe and devastating fist. Silbeth Rasik lifted one of the fallen swords and joined the struggle, landing countless blows and easily dodging every riposte, yet she, too, seemed unable to deal this foe any real harm.

Although he fretted at the risk, fearing his own exposure, Nycos caused his limbs to grow stronger still. He lunged, grasping the haft of the monstrous axe, and for a long moment they struggled, shifting to and fro, a step forward, another back, twisting and turning.

As he stepped to his right and the dais came into view, Nycos spotted Balmorra standing beside the throne, Duke

Ishmar's wineglass still clasped in her hand. Again she'd dipped her fingers into it, and he recognized the tension in her old and hunched shoulders. She was prepared to act, to do *something*, yet she hesitated. Something stayed her hand.

His opponent snarled and Nycos leaned back, launching a kick at the thing's knee, but it proved faster. In that moment when the knight was off-balance it twisted, yanking the axe from Nycos's grip and sending him flying across the chamber. He crashed through multiple rows of seats to land in a heap upon the stone, and he knew that any other man would have been as broken as the chairs.

As if that was precisely what Balmorra had waited for, she flung out her hand, sending drops of wine spraying across the dais, and then she lifted her palm to her lips and blew. A tiny stream of droplets flew over the heads of the guards and the knights, much further than they should have gone, becoming a faintly violet mist that settled over the false courier.

Instantly the figure grew, doubling in height, splitting the human skin it wore and leaving it in tatters upon the floor. The thing thus exposed reeked nauseatingly of rotten meat and plague-ridden dog. Its hide was thick, mottled, hairy; its features canine, with one central, bloodshot eye. It boasted only a single muscle-bound arm in which it clutched its axe, leaving Nycos to wonder if the fist with which it had lashed out had been purely a function of its human guise, or perhaps the horrid thing's tail.

*Psoglavac.* The tales did the foul thing no justice.

It screamed in agony and fury, a grating, piercing cry like a wolf howling around a mouthful of broken glass, and redoubled its attack.

Even in the face of that monstrosity, though, Nycos couldn't help but shudder at the thought of what had *almost* occurred. For whatever magics the diviner had thrown, whatever spell had revealed the ogre, it was only because she'd hesitated that Nycos hadn't been caught in it, too.

By now, more soldiers had flooded into the hall, drawn by the commotion; guards not only in royal service, but loyal to the other attending nobles as well. Crossbows fired from the entryway, embedding themselves shallowly into the *psoglavac's* skin. Spears and swords stabbed, aiming at the eye, the ears, the throat, the groin, anything that might yield to blade more readily than its hide.

None of it helped. With no more reaction than the occasional wince or grunt of pain, with no more difficulty than it took to press through a mild hail storm, the ogre again advanced on Nycos, swatting and slashing at anything standing in its way.

And Nycos grew afraid.

Not for his survival, no. He'd no doubt he could destroy this thing, and probably without too much difficulty, once he put his mind and his full efforts into it.

What he could *not* do, he realized with a mounting sense of dread, was to defeat this opponent without giving away his own nature. The strength and speed required to kill it, to say nothing of the other powers on which he might have to draw, were all too obviously inhuman.

Unless he found some means of concealing them.

He cast about even as he scrambled to his feet, examining the crowd of servants and guards who were gathered in the entry hall, unable to help yet too fascinated to flee. And there, in the forefront…

"Smim!" Nycos lurched to his feet—snatching up one of the unbroken abandoned wine glasses in the process—and sprinted toward the door. "Smim, come here!"

The goblin's whole face bulged in horror, until he very much resembled an apoplectic frog, but he obeyed. A few shaking, staggering steps, and he met his master at the very end of the throne room.

"I—I don't really believe there's very much I can—"

Nycos had no time to explain, not with the *psoglavac* closing from behind, the tumult of the fierce but futile struggle advancing audibly through the chamber. Instead, with a strident shout of "Have you got it?" he thrust a hand inside the goblin's coat.

"Master?" Smim whispered, utterly bewildered.

"Later. You'll understand." Nycos pulled back, one fist closed tight about the glass goblet he'd palmed earlier so that it would appear he'd taken something from Smim's pocket. His other hand shot out to the side, yanking a small burning lamp from its sconce by the door. Immediately he raced back toward the rampaging ogre, leaving a flaming trail of splashing oil to flare and gutter in his wake. With every step he concentrated, felt the uncomfortable and unnatural shift inside his jaws as glands changed shape, producing a substance that most definitely was not saliva.

Silbeth saw him coming, saw that he had something in mind, and called out. The others surrounding and hacking at the *psoglavac* drew back, clearing a path—which suited not only Nycos but the beast itself. Again it howled as it hurled itself at its target, axe rising high.

Nycos jumped, hard, off his running start, twisting in midair to avoid the arc of the rusted blade. For the barest moment he wrapped himself about the head and chest of the ogre.

His first blow shattered the wine glass atop the dog-like head, even as he spat his newly formed mouthful into the matted fur. In the speed and chaos, and with a modicum of luck, it should look like he'd broken a container of some mysterious fluid on its skull.

His second, delivered just as the beast's writhing shook him loose to go tumbling back to the floor, smashed the burning lantern with its open flame on the same spot.

The sudden gout of fire was blinding in its intensity, hellish in its heat. The *psoglavac*'s scream was impossibly high and grotesquely wet. It staggered amongst the knights and soldiers, many of whom were forced to look away from the blaze. Maddened by the pain, the creature dropped its axe to beat mindlessly at its own scalp, desperate to extinguish the searing flame.

A hopeless task, that. Little in this world could extinguish dragonfire before it burned itself out. Given the tiny quantity of saliva Nycos had managed to work up, however, it was only a handful of seconds before it did just that, dying, sparking one final time, and finally fading to nothing.

The *psoglavac* still stood, but it was not what it had been. It teetered drunkenly, its single eye bulging and quivering. The hair was gone from its head, and much of the hide on its scalp had melted and burned away, revealing cracked and blackened bone. Various fluids bubbling through those imperfections to run along the exposed skull, often steaming where they met the open air.

It would probably have died in moments, but the defenders of Kirresc were unwilling to wait. It was Dame Zirresca who stepped forward, sabre raised high, to bring her sword down upon charred and weakened bone. Skull split with a sickening crack, as did the organ beneath. The ogre shuddered a final time, its maw gaping to drool a mouthful of blood, and collapsed.

The throne room was a frozen tableau. Soldiers stood throughout, exhausted, horrified, surrounded by the blood and bodies of fallen comrades. Near the rear door huddled a pack of those guards, along with his Majesty's advisors and the king himself. Doubtless his bodyguard and Marshal Laszlan had attempted to drag Hasyan to safety, and just as certainly he had resisted, refusing to leave those who fought in his defense.

Silbeth, not legally permitted to carry steel in the throne room—only the nobles and their guards had that right, no matter that she was his Majesty's guest—immediately dropped the sabre she'd scavenged. Nobody would speak ill of her efforts to protect herself or others, but now that the crisis was passed, propriety must again be obeyed.

Zirresca and the young Sir Tivador moved to Nycos's side and helped him to his feet. He cast about in sudden fear, worried for his friends, but Mariscal had already run to her father's side, ensuring the old duke was unharmed, and Kortlaus... Nycos only now remembered that the baron had been among the nobles to leave the throne room as soon as the court was dismissed, on his way to attend other duties. He hadn't been present when the monstrous assassin struck.

The assassin who, no matter what everyone else assumed, had not been here for his Majesty Hasyan III.

Or *was* it everyone? As the king and his inner circle returned to the dais to oversee the cleanup, to ensure the living were properly treated and to honor and commend the fallen, Nycos strove to figure out what Balmorra knew, what she had seen beyond the *psoglavac* itself. Her features remained impassive, however, save for her sorrow over the loss of life, and she avoided meeting his gaze.

"I think I can safely say that we're all grateful for your brave efforts in protecting his Majesty and the rest of us." Margrave Andarjin spoke from the doorway, surrounded by his own bodyguards as well as his usual flunkies and hangers-on. Although he remained pale to the lips, any lingering fear was absent from either his words or his posture. "You are all brave men and women, and you should be proud. You've done yourself and the court honor today."

*But?* Nycos asked silently, waiting for it.

"But I think we'd all very much like to know, Sir Nycolos, what that flammable substance was that you used to assist Dame Zirresca in making her kill…"

Her *kill. Nice.*

"…and what could *possibly* have possessed you to give such a potent weapon into the care of a *goblin* for safekeeping? I understand that you trust the creature, for whatever reason, but that still strikes me as unconscionable."

If the margrave had hoped to attack at a weak point, to lessen Nycos's standing in the wake of this catastrophe, it appeared a tactical failure. While his close allies and friends voiced instant approval, adding their own demands for an explanation, the others throughout the throne room seemed at best taken aback, and some actively angered, by his efforts to politicize what had just occurred. Neither Zirresca nor the Archduchess Pirosa looked remotely impressed with his actions.

When Nycos answered, he squeezed as much contempt into his tone as possible without making his words overtly offensive to Pirosa, as Andarjin's mother. "My Lord, Smim has been my loyal vassal for some time, and more to the point, he has served here in the palace for nigh unto a year now. I believe he has more than proved himself a faithful and zealous worker." He turned, briefly, to a group of servants huddled in the throne room doorway. "You have all worked alongside him. Has he, despite his lineage, given any of you reason to mistrust or mislike him?"

More than a few seemed nervous about answering, either because they still held an intrinsic antipathy toward the goblin or for fear of angering the margrave, but enough of them responded to make the knight's point.

"As for the oil," he continued, now spinning a tale from pure moonbeams, "I 'allowed' Smim to hang onto it because it is *his*. It's an alchemical mixture taught to him by his former master.

Rather than questioning his loyalty, you ought to be grateful he had the foresight to think such an important assembly might draw danger. He's been carrying it since his Majesty's guests began to arrive, against any sort of emergency."

At this, several of the attendees—not just servants, this time, but nobles as well—rumbled their assent, expressing their gratitude to the startled goblin.

Seeing the moment slipping away, Andarjin bowed, albeit shallowly, toward Smim. "All fair points. My apologies.

"However, I *do* think it would be a reasonable request that he make this, shall we say, recipe available to the Crown Marshal's soldiers. It's certainly a potent advantage."

"It is," Nycos said, flavoring the lie with a sprinkle of truth. "One that requires, among other rare ingredients, the saliva of his former master, or another dragon. That's why he only has what small quantities he escaped with. Have you a live wyrm handy, my Lord?"

Rather than let this continue, Hasyan chose that moment to call the guards and nobles to attend him, to discuss the implications of this attack and determine strategies to defend against others like it. Was this another manipulation by Ktho Delios? Did the recent activities in and around Gronch represent a greater, more wide-reaching threat? What sort of sorceries were involved? And so forth.

Nycos briefly hung back, ignoring Andarjin's cold regard, and gestured for Smim to join him. "King Hasyan wasn't the target," he whispered without preamble.

"Yes, I thought that might be the case, Master. Are we assuming the obvious suspect?"

"I don't know," he admitted. "Ogres do exist outside Gronch, but they're so rare... And I can't think of anyone *else* I might have angered who has any truck with the creatures."

"Yet you sound unconvinced."

"Because this doesn't *feel* like her. Sending one of her minions so far in order to murder me? Vircingotirilux isn't much of a schemer. If she wanted to strike at me here, no reason she'd not come herself. And she lacks the sorcery to perform the sort of shape-change we just saw. Besides how she could have found me out at all? She's neither clever enough nor mystically inclined enough for *that*. There's a skilled wizard mixed up in this, somewhere."

"One of Ondoniram's followers, Master?"

"I suppose it's possible, but it's been, what? At *least* four or five human generations since I slew him. Would they have passed along a grudge that long?"

The rest of the conversation would have to wait, as Nycos could no longer justify delaying his own approach to the dais. He would be some time, he knew, involved in his Majesty's discussion, then longer still explaining the repercussions of what had happened to Prince Elias. Throughout it all, however, his mind roved down the list of the many enemies he'd made in his centuries of life.

The fact that he could come up with few, if any, who were both capable of the feats he'd witnessed and were still among the living, no longer offered him the sense of victorious accomplishment, of comfort or of safety, it once might have.

# CHAPTER TWENTY-THREE

Autumn grew long in the tooth and gave way without much struggle to winter—and with the turning of the seasons came an ever-increasing torrent of rumor and reports as chilling as the mounting winds.

From Kirresc's easternmost borders, from neighboring Wenslir, even on occasion from distant Suunim, traveled tales of horror. Farms, hamlets, some entire villages wiped from the soil by forces unseen; reduced to empty husks or smoldering ruins between one day and the next. Details were scarce, verification difficult, but after the first handful of stories, and after hastily dispatched riders confirmed at least one Kirresci community was indeed a heap of cinder and ash, few skeptics remained within the halls of Oztyerva.

And through it all, just far enough from their own borders that it was impossible to keep track of maneuvers or troop movements, the Ktho Delian legions continued to mobilize, churning like a long-boiling pot.

Were they responsible, in some way, for what was happening in and around Gronch? Or was the combination of threats sheer coincidence, or perhaps divine whim? No evidence presented itself either way, and even if it had, the course of action was the same: All the southern nations could do was watch, wait, hunker down and try their best to prepare.

The timing was particularly poor for Kirresc (not that any time would have been *good*). Since major conflict was now a looming possibility, Orban Laszlan had chosen to begin the Marshal's Trials.

This was far from the first time in history that Kirresc's Crown Marshal was faced with multiple viable candidates to succeed him. Had one of the three been an obvious choice, the situation would have been simpler, but while Zirresca remained the odds-on favorite, her qualifications did not so obviously exceed the others' as to assure her of victory. To serve as a tie-breaker, a means of final selection, one of Laszlan's predecessors had devised a series of military tests, problems and exercises that would, over the course of several weeks, determine a front-runner. The Marshal's Trials were not based in statute, neither binding nor required—but the weight of tradition made them all but a necessity when two or more campaigns of succession had dragged on without resolution.

Normally, they would not take place so soon after Kirresc's royal tournament, nor during the icy months of winter. With war on the horizon, however, Laszlan wanted the matter decided before it was too late, before the soldiers and resources—and indeed, the candidates themselves—were needed elsewhere.

Today was day three of the first trial: a four-day test, with Nycos as one of a quartet, rather than the anticipated trio, of competing generals. As a means of enhancing his Highness's own military experience, however simulated, King Hasyan had asked Laszlan to include Prince Elias in the exercise, along with the three contenders. Each "general" was responsible for conquering as much of the others' territory as possible while defending his or her own. The battlefield, located in the wilds just outside Talocsa's walls, was hundreds of acres across, consisting of grasslands, rolling hills, and multiple copses of trees. Just like a real engagement, each of the four factions had different numbers of troops, different defensive capabilities, and differing stores of supplies, all determined randomly at the start of the trial.

Between the soldiers assigned to each faction, the judges responsible for ensuring that those soldiers "died" properly and honestly based on their melee with blunted training weapons, and the noble observers who had the right to oversee any given battle or play audience in any contestant's headquarters, it was a lively battlefield indeed.

A light snow had begun to fall, a faint dusting of white turning grey, limiting visibility and melting swiftly to trace frigid trails down the insides of even the most tightly sealed kaftans, coats, and armor. Standing inside a makeshift fort atop a tree-covered hillside, Nycos was spared the worst of the weather's discomforts, but he might as well have been out and about. His mood was a perfect, chilly match.

He peered, fists clenched, over a hastily sketched map of the region, enemy emplacements and forces marked in charcoal where his scouts had managed to locate them. At his side were two military advisors, chosen from among those gathered by Orban at the start of the exercise. Sir Jancsiv was a broad-shouldered fellow, ebon-skinned and white haired, the sort of man who maintains a dashing and rakish charm even into his middle years. Captain Natalin was a short, slender woman, pale as Jancsiv or Nycos himself were dark, who would have looked more at home attending a formal ball than on the battlefield. She'd threatened to break more than one man's bones for telling her precisely that.

Both were among the top military tacticians Nycos could have chosen, and both were as bewildered by the events of the day as he was.

"Let's go over this again," Natalin said, leaning on her knuckles until the map crinkled.

"Yes, because we might have missed something the first fifty-seven times," Jancsiv muttered.

"Sir Nycolos has been focused on Sir Kortlaus and Dame Zirresca," she bulled on. "He's only been directing attacks against his Highness's territories since yesterday evening."

Nods all around.

"His first two offenses were both direct thrusts, using overwhelming force to punch through Prince Elias's lines."

Indeed, Nycos—though more than willing to change things up when necessary—was quite fond of engaging in swift shock-assaults from a secure defensive position. (That was, after all, the primary attack pattern of *most* dragons: soar out from the lair and obliterate whatever or whoever needed to not exist any longer.)

So, another pair of nods.

"Then how in God's name did Elias, of all people—no offense to his Highness," she added, belatedly and somewhat unconvincingly, "—figure out this afternoon's offensive was a feint?!"

"My goodness!" Sir Jancsiv remarked. "You're absolutely right! If only we'd thought to ask that question the first fifty-seven times we—"

"Bicker later," Nycos snapped. "I lost a skilled unit in this fiasco. I want to know why."

"I might be able to shed some light on that, Master."

Smim, wrapped tightly in a fur-lined coat that was far too large and dragged in the dirt and snow behind him like a bridal train, shuffled in through the door, accompanied by a gust of frigid air. Just behind him came Mariscal, clad far more elegantly in multiple layers of stoles and fine cloaks. She carefully picked her way through the goblin's slushy trail to stand beside Nycos. He offered her a brief smile—it wasn't the first time she'd taken advantage of her status as a "noble observer" to visit and offer her support during this first of the Marshal's Trials—but his attention remained focused on his servant.

Servant and, for the duration, spymaster. It was Smim's responsibility to consolidate and deliver all the information reported by his master's scouts.

"Tell me," Nycos commanded.

"We've learned who Prince Elias chose as his two military advisors, Master."

"They'd have to be pretty damn good," Natalin grumbled.

Smim half-shrugged, a gesture that set the overlong sleeve flopping well beyond the reach of his hand. He glared at the garment, sighed, and then said, "Would Silbeth Rasik and Marshal Laszlan qualify as 'pretty damn good,' Captain?"

Natalin and Jancsiv both subsided into slack-jawed silence, and Nycos teetered on the edge of literally sputtering in outrage. "That—that is unacceptable! His Highness's rank and titles don't entitle him to cheat in an exercise of this sort! We were clearly told... Clearly..."

He trailed off, thinking back. *Had* they been told? Marshal Laszlan had assembled a group of knights and officers to stand at his side when explaining to Nycos, Zirresca, Kortlaus, and Prince Elias the rules of this first trial; had specifically pointed all of them out as viable choices when instructing the competitors to consider who they would choose to advise them.

But had he actually said, in so many words, that the choices were limited *only* to those specific men and women standing there? Now that he pondered it, Nycos didn't recall him ever having done so. He and the others had simply assumed, taking it as a given.

"Well, I'll be damned." Even as he shook his head, chewing on the bitter taste of having been outsmarted, he couldn't help but chuckle. Had Elias made an abnormally clever choice? Or had his simplemindedness actually worked for him, saving him from the "obvious" conclusion everyone else had drawn?

Either way, there was a lesson to be learned from this.

"All right then," Nycos said, shaking himself and the others from their amazement. "So we're up against the most senior and most experienced officer in Kirresc and one of the most skilled combatants I've ever seen." His smile was grim. "It just means this'll be a little harder. It's still Prince Elias making the decisions, and they still don't know the full extent of our resources. We've got to be clever, is all."

The knight and the captain both looked more than a bit skeptical, but obediently turned back to the map. Mariscal tried her best to appear reassuring, but he could see the doubt in her expression as well.

So be it. Let them doubt. Orban, above all others, would take this test seriously. He wouldn't permit his Highness to turn command over to him, or to Silbeth. They really were still dealing with Prince Elias, first and foremost—*and* it remained possible that Zirresca and Kortlaus were yet ignorant of Elias's choice of advisors. With a bit of thought, Nycos might even be able to turn this to his advantage.

*If* he could focus on the matter at hand.

Nycos had never entirely shaken his fascination with the Priory of Steel swordswoman; her skill, her demeanor, her sheer predatory grace. He had assumed, with no small measure of disappointment, that she'd departed weeks ago, her task completed, and had bemoaned to Smim on more than one occasion his failure to find any excuse to speak with her in depth before she'd gone. To learn, now, that she remained at Oztyerva was welcome news—but also a distraction, and one that bore with it a number of new questions.

Why had she stayed? What was she doing here? How might he contrive to get to know her, learn how she had become what she was, study her techniques and her beliefs? And above all else, how had he not known she was still here? Had she deliberately avoided him? The notion disturbed him intensely, for reasons he didn't entirely understand. What sort of offense might he have—?

Smim peered at him between narrowed lids, as though sensing his dismay, and Nycos gave himself a sharp mental slap. What was he *thinking*? Silbeth would have had no reason to avoid him, but above and beyond that, what reason would she have had for seeking him out? It was *entirely* possible, given the parameters of his own duties and responsibilities, that they'd just never crossed paths, and the woman certainly had no cause to come looking for him. Attributing deliberate intent was just... silly.

It never once occurred to Nycos, as he moved to join the others at the map, to question why he was so fascinated, so captivated, by Silbeth in the first place.

Whether the four of them—Nycos, Sir Jancsiv, Captain Natalin, and Smim—could have altered their plans and tactics well enough to account for the prince's unexpected advisors, they were never to know. An in-depth planning session, with Margravine Mariscal observing around the edges, came to an abrupt halt after an hour or so with the sound of horns, a series of coded blasts alerting Nycos to an attack on his territory's southern edge.

And he had only just responded to *that*, riding Avalanche to the edge of the trees to spot a large force under Zirresca's banners appearing like phantoms from the drifting snow, when the entire battle, the entire exercise, was jerked to a halt by a different sequence of calls from a separate set of trumpets. Though flattened by the slush-laden air, the signal carried, snagging the full attention of soldiers and commanders on every side—for this was no factional code, but one restricted to royal heralds.

*Return at once to Oztyerva. His Majesty requires your attendance.*

During the trudge back to Talocsa—a journey of only a few miles, but rendered slow and unpleasant by the weather and the sheer number of travelers—Nycos reined Avalanche back, eventually clopping along beside the silver-trimmed carriage in which Mariscal rode. The two gold-bedecked palfreys pulling the vehicle groused and snorted at the snow, tails and heads flickering with equal discomfort. Avalanche, as proud a veteran as any senior officer, gave no indication of unhappiness at all, save for occasionally chafing at the slow pace. The whinny he directed at the smaller, more sensitive horses sounded for all the world like contemptuous snickers.

"I'm sorry things were going poorly back there," Mariscal said through a half-opened window, voice raised over the clacking of the wheels. Her smile, an obvious effort to be supportive, rang hollow.

Nycos, holding himself rigid to avoid shivering and inwardly cursing the idiotic rules of propriety that kept the margravine from offering him a seat in the carriage, took a moment to thaw out his response. "His Highness caught me by surprise, but we could have dealt with that, given the opportunity."

"Oh, I've no doubt. I… wasn't speaking of his Highness."

For that, the knight had no reply. The margravine had gotten a good look at his map, and it didn't require a military scholar to recognize that the faction to have taken the most ground, by far, was Zirresca's.

It was difficult to admit to himself, let alone to others, but Nycos knew Mariscal had good reason for worry. Given how swiftly he learned, and his ability to contextualize new information with the knowledge of centuries, he could become both Zirresca's and Kortlaus's superiors in every way that mattered within another year or two. Unfortunately, with the Marshal's Trials now underway, he clearly wouldn't have those years—and at the moment, Zirresca's strategic and tactical acumen, where human forces were concerned, exceeded his own by every measure.

He still had a chance at becoming Orban Laszlan's successor, but the odds were not in his favor.

"Do you suppose," Mariscal asked after a few moments of relative quiet, "that the other emissaries have finally arrived?"

Nycos was absurdly grateful for the topic change. "I *hope* that's what this is. We could just as easily return to news that Ktho Delios is on the march."

"What a dreadful thought." She paused, brow furrowing. "Would they do that in the dead of winter?"

"Probably not," he admitted. "I just meant, until I hear that this news is not about some new catastrophe, I'm going to brace myself with the assumption that it is."

Nor was he alone in that attitude. In point of fact, the bulk of the Kirresci court waited in anticipation of some disaster or another. They'd received no official word from the Quindacran government since Ambassador Guldoell had returned to Vidiir. No notification of her safe arrival, no acknowledgement of King Hasyan's further missives, certainly nothing to suggest that either Guldoell, or any other emissary, would be returning to Talocsa. While a few nobles still held out hope, and the king was unwilling to take any precipitous actions, most in Oztyerva took that silence as tacit admission that the accusations of collusion held some weight.

Hasyan had called for an emergency assembly of envoys from the rest of the southern nations—every signatory to the mutual defense pact, and even Ythane as well. As of yet, however, few such emissaries had arrived—unless, as Mariscal theorized, the assembly to which they'd been summoned was meant to inform them otherwise.

That particular theory was dashed when Nycos and the others finally strode between the great doors of Hasyan's throne room, after pausing only long enough to wash and change into clothes not drenched with the slurry of melted snow and caked road mud. Only two foreigners were present amidst the Kirresci knights and nobles: Ambassador Kidil, who had already been here in Talocsa; and Ambassador Razmos of Althlalen, who appeared as freshly changed out of traveling garb as the contestants themselves.

Nycos briefly caught Mariscal's eye and frowned with new worry before taking his place among the other knights of his rank.

Hasyan spoke without preamble from the throne, surrounded by the usual group of counselors and advisors. "We are grateful to all of you for coming," he said. Nycos found himself startled by how weary the king sounded. "And to those of you who were engaged in the Marshal's Trials, we apologize for the interruption. Sadly, the urgency of the situation left us no other course.

"You have all, of course, heard tales and rumors of trouble along our borders, and those of our friends in Wenslir and Suunim. Creatures out of Gronch—creatures that," he added with a faint shudder, "we now know with far too much certainty are more than mere ghost stories. Villages destroyed overnight. Travelers who failed to reach their destinations, though they walked the most well-trod and well-patrolled highways."

He waited for the various mumbles of assent to fade. "Ambassador Kidil," he said in an apparent change of direction, "do we understand correctly that you have found it difficult of late to communicate with Suunim? That many of your couriers have failed to complete the journey?"

The old man bowed his head sadly. "I fear you understand quite correctly, Your Majesty. I have begun to feel that I ought to be making the trek myself."

"It's well you did not, Aadesh." The switch to an informal, friendlier form of address was not lost on Nycos. "You would likely have accomplished nothing but to join your lost couriers. Friends, it is our sad burden to inform you that we have finally received some more detailed reports, tales carried by fortunate survivors—and the situation is far more dire than we ever feared."

"Because things were going so easily and peacefully up to now," Zirresca, standing a few places down from Nycos, muttered under her breath.

"The villages that have been razed were not destroyed by any ogre. We have heard stories of... Of a great winged shape, scarcely visible against the stars or when it passed briefly before the face of a moon. Monstrous, wreathed in flame."

He could have stopped there. The horrified silence that choked the throne room was evidence enough that everyone knew what he implied.

"After decades of freedom from their kind," he pressed on, driving the point home, "we now face the distinct possibility of a second dragon in as many years."

Vircingotirilux? Nycos had suspected her before, and it seemed near certainty now. That vile beast of a wyrm dwelt deep within Gronch, commanded the ogres of the wood as her minions, just as he himself had once ruled over the goblins, the wyverns, and other creatures of the Outermark Mountains.

And yet, as before, so much seemed... off. Random devastation and the deaths of whole communities, that indeed sounded like Vircingotirilux, but the subtleties of her earlier attack? The magics required to transform an ogre into a man? Those were beyond her. Nor could he imagine common cause between the ravening, lunatic wyrm and the highly disciplined military machine of Ktho Delios.

All signs to the contrary, could it be a different dragon entirely? Nycos could think of only a few with both the magic and cunning to orchestrate all they'd seen. None dwelt nearby, but it was conceivable that such a wyrm might turn its attentions to territories far beyond its own. And as rare as dragons were, Nycos couldn't be positive he knew of all those living in southern Galadras. A particularly secretive wyrm might have kept itself concealed.

He wished they had a more precise physical description of the dragon, but it sounded as though a "winged shape in the night" was the best available. Still, he drew breath to ask, though he would need to phrase the question carefully so as not to give away that he knew more than he was letting on.

Someone else beat him to the punch, however, and with a far more sinister question. "Are we entirely certain," Margrave Andarjin asked, as though the notion had just occurred to him, "that this *is* a 'second' dragon?"

It took a moment for the implications to sink in.

"Petty, my Lord," Nycos snapped. "Have you grown so hopeless of ever having accomplishments of your own to tout that you've decided it's easier to question everyone else's?"

"*There will be none of that!*" King Hasyan shot to his feet. "We will have no squabbling among the court, and we will have no such accusations or insults thrown about!"

Teeth grinding like a millstone, Nycos bowed his head.

Then, to the surprise of all, Balmorra stepped forward to stand beside her liege. "Let me assuage the margrave's, ah, *concerns*. And any others he might have raised. I may not see all, with my magics or in the stars, but I see enough. I can assure you, with no doubt, that whoever or whatever we face from the depths of the Ogre-Weald, it is *not* the dragon Tzavalantzaval."

That was sufficient for most of those gathered, to judge by the murmurs that followed. Andarjin bowed his head to the old astrologer, then more deeply to the king. He *should* have also extended Nycos an apology, but apparently even he couldn't take his insincerity that far.

For his own part, Nycos once again wondered and worried over just how much Balmorra knew.

Hasyan sank slowly back into the depths of his throne. "Crown Marshal?"

Orban advanced to address the court. "This dragon, and the beasts of the Ogre-Weald, are a greater threat than we had expected to face. Suunim, Wenslir, and our own eastern provinces are effectively under siege. Trade, travel, and military maneuvers are hampered. This is why, among other consequences, Ambassador Kidil has received no messages from Suunim, and why Wenslir hasn't sent an ambassador to discuss our current situation." He scowled contemptuously. "It is also why Mahdresh has failed to do so, or so they say, despite sharing no borders with Gronch. Opportunists and cowards, the lot—"

"Manners, Marshal," Hasyan interrupted, not unkindly. "And focus."

"Of course, Your Majesty." He frowned, apparently irritated at himself. "My sincere apologies. My point is that we have a great deal of potential trouble ahead, and that's just Gronch. Whether Ktho Delios is behind this or not, they'll doubtless try to take advantage, and we still don't know for certain where Quindacra stands..." He trailed off, abruptly sounding as tired as the king.

"For the foreseeable future, we're going to need all our greatest military minds developing strategies and contingencies, and all our soldiers at station and prepared to march. As such, as much as I'd hoped to complete them before war is truly upon us, I am suspending the trials to determine my successor until the situation calms."

Nycos abruptly felt as though every eye in the throne room was upon him, though he knew that Zirresca and Kortlaus feel equal scrutiny.

"I apologize to all three worthy candidates," Orban said. "But I assure you that we'll return to the matter as soon as his Majesty and I consider it viable. Who knows, perhaps the upcoming struggles will allow one of you the opportunity to perform feats so great, I won't *need* the trials to make my choice."

This was nothing but good news for Nycos. Any delay was an opportunity to improve his skills, to narrow the gap between himself and the obvious frontrunner. Others, however, were far less pleased. Zirresca's whole face had gone red with fury and frustration, and Nycos heard Margrave Andarjin swallow once, hard. No doubt choking down a protest that he must have known would go over poorly.

Kortlaus, so far as Nycos could tell, was untroubled, equally content one way or the other, but then, Kortlaus had never seemed as emotionally engaged in his campaign as either Nycos or Zirresca were in theirs.

A few more moments of general discussion, and then his Majesty dismissed the bulk of the nobles and gentry—Andarjin managed not to storm out in a huff, but an abnormal stiffness in his gait implied he wanted to—while the royal advisors and military leaders moved to the council chambers for the first of what promised to be many tense strategy sessions.

It was on their way to that smaller room, passing through winding and heavily guarded halls, that Prince Elias dropped back to fall in beside Nycos. So preoccupied was the knight with questions of dragons and other hidden foes that it took him a moment to realize the heir apparent had asked him something.

"I'm deeply sorry, your Highness. My mind was elsewhere. Might you repeat that, please?"

"Oh, I was just requesting that you stay at my side during the discussion, in case I have any questions."

"Of course, your Highness." It was an aggravation Nycos didn't need at the moment, but he'd agreed to advise the prince, and had done so on several matters of lesser import. It seemed inappropriate, and potentially damaging, to refuse now.

So, trying to think as an instructor, he continued, "You have a solid grasp of the situation thus far?"

Elias smiled, though somewhat self-mockingly. "I'm not a *complete* fool, Sir Nycolos."

"I never thought you were," Nycos lied. Then, just as the prince's smile began to brighten, "So run through it for me, your Highness. I need to know what you know if I'm to advise you properly."

In a tone not unlike a schoolboy reciting a lesson, the prince explained Quindacra's importance to the treaty. Although that nation shared no border with Ktho Delios, it controlled a vast stretch of coastline. Should Quindacra grant them access to said beaches, the Deliant navy could easily sail about the cape of the continent and disgorge an army to come at Wenslir from the south and Kirresc from the southwest. Both nations would be required to split their forces, with potentially catastrophic results, and that assumed Quindacra merely allowed the enemy safe passage. If they were to actually *join* with the invaders…

"And of course," Elias concluded, "the loss of their soldiers on the front lines would be a massive blow to our defenses, before even taking the rest into account. So, teacher, did I pass your test?"

"Yes, your Highness. But not well."

The prince blinked his royal eyelids. "What did I miss?"

*Give the young man credit. He sounded more curious than offended.*

"Two points." Nycos raised a hand, counting off fingers. "First, neither we nor Wenslir have any major cities near our shared border. It wouldn't be difficult for Quindacra—or Ktho Delian forces moving through their territory—to cut off communication between Kirresc and Wenslir. Or, by extension, between us and Suunim."

"Oof. You're right."

"Second, any Kirresci war effort against Ktho Delios might be crippled without Quindacran goods. Tools, weapons, raw materials."

"But Quindacra doesn't craft anything we can't make for ourselves! And most of their materials aren't as good!"

"True. But if Ktho Delios invades Kirresc, the first thing they're going to do is try to take or destroy our resources. Lumber. Crops. Mines. Smiths and carpenters, if they reach any of our cities. Quindacra's farther from Ktho Delios than we are, so they'd be able to maintain those industries longer than we might."

Elias nodded slowly. "I hadn't thought of any of that."

"Think beyond the moment," Nycos advised, though he wondered if there were any real point, if the prince *could* alter his thinking. "Don't just envision the immediate threats. Try to think about where you might be a week, a month, a year from now."

"I'll try, Sir Nycolos. Thank you."

At which point the conversation, and indeed the walk, ended at the door to the council chambers. While everyone else gathered, Nycos found himself once again chasing his own thoughts, and every single one of them eventually came back to the same roost.

*Vircingotirilux.*

Nothing he could come up with, no angle of approach, forced any of this to make sense. She *had* to be involved, and yet so much of what had happened was beyond her abilities, her maddened mind, or both. Did she know who he was? How? What was she planning? Who or what was she working with?

He *had* to know—for the sake of everyone around him, yes, but particularly for his own. And unfortunately, though he passed the hours of the council meeting in trying to envision another option, in the end he could come up with only one way to find out.

———

"He barely let me finish speaking before he told me it was insane and he wouldn't even consider allowing it."

"Good!" Mariscal poked Nycos in the arm, hard. "Because it *is* insane, and he *shouldn't* even consider it!"

The two of them walked, side by side but not quite arm in arm, through what Nycos had come to think of "Mariscal's garden." The flowers he'd long ago arranged to bloom for her were dormant, slumbering beneath a confectioner's dusting of sugary snow. The garden smelled only of winter, without a trace of the floral aromas of the past. Still, it held great meaning for the pair—although Nycos was sure that meaning was very different in her mind than it was in his—and they came here often to talk. Other than a handful of Mariscal's ladies-in-waiting, who hung back far enough to grant the knight and the margravine a modicum of privacy, they were the only souls present.

"He then went on to call *me* insane," Nycos complained.

Again she poked him, hard enough to suggest some genuine anger. "I'm not sure he's wrong there, either."

"You don't believe I can do it, either, my Lady?"

Mariscal stopped, then dragged him to a halt and turned him to face her. "Nycos, you had an enchanted blade last time. One specifically crafted to slay dragons! And you *still* survived only through sheer luck! Donaris doesn't smile so broadly twice on *anyone!*"

"It's true, I no longer have Wyrmtaker." *Well, most of it*, he added mentally as the old wound twinged. "But I learned much about dragons during that hunt, and Smim knows much as well. Between the two of us, we could come up with another means of hurting Vi—the beast."

"Besides," he continued quickly, both to cover his slip of the tongue and forestall the argument he knew was coming, "the plan would be to try to kill the dragon only if a near-perfect opportunity presents itself. Otherwise, this is intelligence-gathering. Where does the dragon lair? Is Ktho Delios somehow in contact with it?" *Who is she working with? Does she know who I am? How?!*

"It's madness," Mariscal insisted. "Marshal Laszlan was right to refuse to hear anything more of it!"

Of course it was madness! For all his power, everything he could do to grant himself might and abilities far beyond human, Nycos was only a fraction of what he once had been. The thought of facing Vircingotirilux in his current state was utterly terrifying.

But what choice had he?

"Don't you *dare*! Don't you even *think* it, Nycolos!"

"What? What are you talking about?"

"I can see it in your face. You're thinking of going anyway!"

*Damn it, I'm not even the Nycos she knew. How can she read me this way?!*

"Mariscal..."

"No!" Snow puffed up in a small cloud where she actually stomped an angry foot. "Putting aside the danger, if you abandon your duties, leave against orders a second time? You'll *never* be Crown Marshal. We won't be... It won't be good for any of us."

"Even if I can learn something, or accomplish something, that would save the lives of Kirresci soldiers?" he demanded. "That would save us from having to divide our forces? Would that not make it worthwhile?"

Mariscal, shivering with more than the cold, began to turn away.

"What if," Nycos asked softly, "I could solve the Quindacra problem while I was at it?"

The margravine stiffened. "How in the name of the gods," she hissed between clenched teeth, "would you even imagine you could do that?"

"I'm... just considering a few wild ideas," he hedged, mentally lashing himself for bringing it up. It's not as though he could explain even if he wanted to!

"You seem to have a lot of those. When you want to go into detail, we'll talk. Until then, don't do anything foolish. Consider that a command from a margravine as much as a personal plea, *Baronet* Nycolos."

She swept from the garden, her servants rushing to follow, and Nycos let her go. He knew her anger was a mask for her fear—for him, for *them*. It was a fear he shared, at least in part. And perhaps she was right. He didn't want to go, didn't want to take the risk, didn't want to face the consequences.

But neither did he wish to face the consequences of his ignorance.

Ignoring the cold, ignoring the layer of frigid slush, Nycos found the nearest of the garden's marble benches and sat, staring at the stone walls and feeling nearly as lost now as when he'd first awakened, his body a strange and foreign land, in the slavers' wooden cage.

———

"I am a great believer in seeking knowledge wherever one may find it, Sir Nycolos. But I rather doubt that these particular walls have anything more to tell you."

Nycos blinked and looked around for what felt like the first time in hours. The sky had gone dark, with only a few brighter patches in the clouds suggesting the presence of the moons. The snow fell more thickly, in spinning flurries. He discovered that his boots, his knees, and his shoulders were well coated.

And standing before him, tightly wrapped in several layers of cloaks and shawls, was the old astrologer.

"Time appears to have gotten away from me," Nycos admitted, rising politely.

"It's slippery that way, yes."

"I, um. I didn't realize you enjoyed the garden."

Balmorra gave him a flat and vaguely pitying look.

"Or," he amended, face flushing, "you might have been searching for me."

"Considering the weather, and the absolute lack of visible plant life, that *does* seem a rather more probable motive for me being here, doesn't it?"

"So what can I do for you, Mistress Balmorra?"

Despite her earlier comment, it was her turn, now, to stare blankly at the far wall. "The stars and the signs," she said slowly, "tell me that you have a momentous choice before you."

"Do they?" he asked in a dull monotone.

"I've seen few specifics—and they aren't necessarily mine to know, anyway—but I see bits. Pieces. And more importantly, I see the ripples made by your choice, spreading out to mar the image of Kirresc itself, and perhaps even beyond."

Nycos's throat closed tight. "What..." He tried again, each word an act of will. "What should I do?"

"If you choose the path of greater danger, you will lose much. We all may."

"Oh." Nycos felt a weight, a tension in his shoulders, begin to fade. "Well, that seems—"

"Choose the easier, safer path, and we stand to lose far more. *Everyone* will suffer for it."

Nycos cursed, long and loudly, at one point pounding a fist into the statue of an old knight that topped a tiny fountain. As though responding to his frustration, the snow fell more thickly still, so that the far side of the garden became invisible.

"That," he spat, his brief fit of temper spent, "is not much of a choice, Balmorra."

"No, it isn't." She had all but disappeared behind the curtain of white, and her voice sounded somehow more distant as well. "It's an awful, discouraging choice, and that it lies on you to make is unfair in the extreme.

"But that's all a part of being human, is it not, Sir Nycolos?"

She was gone before the question could penetrate the veil of his anger, before he thought to wonder at the implication of her words. Again Nycos stood alone in the white-cloaked garden, unanswered questions and impossible decisions weighing on him far more heavily than the snow.

# CHAPTER TWENTY-FOUR

He'd taken a day to ruminate, or perhaps to hunt for some excuse. It had changed nothing, as he'd expected. He'd known what he would do since Balmorra's warnings had passed her lips.

"I intend no offense by this, Master," Smim whispered as they slunk through the largely empty and, at this hour, poorly lit halls of Oztyerva's outer wing. Each carried a small sack of supplies, the last of several batches they'd been hiding beneath the straw of the stables throughout the night. "But you're insane."

"For future reference, Smim, I'd be more inclined to *believe* you meant no offense if this weren't the ninth time you'd said that to me."

"Forgive me, Master. One must sometimes belabor the point when speaking to lunatics."

Nycos snorted and continued on his way.

Stone halls led to a hefty wooden door with—thanks to the goblin's earlier efforts—newly oiled hinges. Only a few guards patrolled near the stables, and it was simple enough for Nycos to listen at the portal until the sound of footsteps crunching on the thin carpet of snow passed out of range. He and Smim slipped swiftly through the door, keeping to the darkest shadows of the curtain wall, and scurried across a few dozen yards of the bailey.

"Ready, Smim?" They would have to work quickly and quietly to saddle Avalanche and Smim's chosen mount, and load their supplies in the saddlebags, without being caught. Not that Nycos was by any means forbidden from taking his own steed out on a late-night ride, but it would certainly raise questions—questions that couldn't be avoided, but might at least be delayed.

"It's not too late for us to return to our nice warm beds and forget about this," Smim replied.

Nycos chose to take that as a *yes*, unbolted the outer door of the stable, and darted inside. The goblin followed a half-step behind.

"I thought you gentlemen were *never* going to arrive. What did you do, stop for drinks?"

Nycos's sabre leapt to hand in a flash of steel lightning. Smim uttered a high-pitched wheeze and dropped into a crouch equally suited to springing toward or away from whatever appeared.

A soft chuckle ended in the scrape and spark of flint on steel. A small candle caught, the wick dancing as though it, too, shivered in the cold. It wasn't much light, but enough to make out a fully saddled Avalanche, alongside not one but two other mounts, equally equipped and ready for travel.

Leaning against the extra, a dappled grey not much smaller than Avalanche himself, was Silbeth Rasik. She wore a fur-lined coat, Wenslirran or Ktho Delian in style, and belted slightly open to allow her easy access to her sword.

"Um," Nycos commented.

"Astute, Master."

For all that he'd longed for the opportunity to speak with her, this wasn't precisely how Nycos had envisioned the conversation taking place. "I'm, uh… Mistress Rasik…"

"Silbeth, please, Sir Nycolos. We are going to be working together, after all."

"Um," Nycos said again, possibly unsure she'd properly understood him the first time.

"She's saddled herself a horse, Master. I think she's planning to come with us."

Silbeth grinned. "Astute, goblin."

Nycos finally got a hold of himself, forcing his startled bewilderment aside for later examination. "Silbeth, I don't know how you found out I was planning on a journey—"

"Margravine Mariscal. She hired me. Didn't even balk at the price."

Things fell into place with a series of clunks so loud Nycos was surprised they didn't spook the horses.

"And you're here to…?" He let the question linger.

"Accompany you. Assist you. Make certain you return in, if not one piece, then at least usable condition."

Nycos breathed a bit more easily and sheathed his blade. "I'm a bit surprised," he admitted, "that your orders weren't to knock me senseless and drag me back inside."

"Oh, we discussed that." It was the casual, even offhand way she said it that convinced Nycos she wasn't remotely jesting. "She came quite close to it a time or two. Ultimately, though, she recognized that wouldn't have been a good idea. You'd just try again later." She shrugged. "She knows that once you've decided that something needs doing, you're going to do it. She'd rather you not get horribly killed in the process."

"We've been around the humans too long," Smim grumbled at a volume only Nycos's hearing could possibly have picked up, "if you're getting this predictable."

For a long moment, Nycos said nothing, stroking Avalanche's nose as he pondered. He found himself moved by Mariscal's actions. Nor was he remotely displeased with the thought of spending some time in the mercenary's company, getting to know her, possibly watching her skills in genuine battle.

However…

"I'm grateful," he said at last. "To both of you. But what Smim and I have planned is not only dangerous, but private." Indeed, her presence would make it exceedingly troublesome for Nycos and the goblin to converse freely, to ask the necessary questions, or for him to draw upon many of the abilities he might require. "So I'm afraid I must decline your company."

"I'm afraid you misunderstand, Sir Nycolos. This wasn't an offer. I was hired to do a job. I will do it."

"I can't permit you to come with us," he insisted.

"You can't stop me."

"Are you so sure?"

"You would have to physically force me to stay. Kill me, or injure me so badly I can't follow. I don't think you're prepared to do that."

"I—"

"After our match at the tournament, I don't think you're *capable* of doing that. But even if you are, do you believe you can outfight me without your efforts drawing the attention of every guard walking patrol?"

Nycos growled something that would have been unintelligible no matter *what* body he wore.

"Wonderful!" Silbeth swung into her saddle in one smooth motion. "Shall we be off, then? I think I packed everything you had hidden in here, but you might want to take a quick pass just to be sure. And," she added, gesturing at the long, leather-wrapped bundle she'd tied across the back of Avalanche's saddle, "you're going to have to explain to me at some point what those are for."

In no mood to explain much of anything, Nycos hauled himself into Avalanche's saddle and rode toward the stable doors.

Departing in *complete* secrecy, as Nycos was well aware, had never been an option. In these pre-dawn hours, the gates of Oztyerva were firmly shut, and only his rank as a knight of the realm granted him the authority to order that one be opened long enough for the trio of riders to make their exit. Doubtless the sentinels had many questions—why he and his companions had to leave at such an indecent hour, why they were so heavily laden with supplies—but none had the right to question his order. The tale of his departure would spread, particularly once these soldiers' shift had ended, but by then he ought to be far enough away that it wouldn't matter.

Between the white flurries and the black of the night sky, the streets of Talocsa were all but deserted. A very few passersby, wrapped in kaftans and coats, studied the trio with curiosity before going on about their business, but none chose to pause in the bone-deep cold to exchange polite greetings. A barking dog ran and pranced alongside the horses for a few blocks before returning, shivering, to the warmth of his den.

Even Nycos lacked the authority to order the city gates opened once they'd been shut for the night, but he had accounted for that, too. By the time they'd crossed the length of Talocsa, less than an hour remained before dawn. The three riders huddled together in a small side street, hunched against the cold, until fingers of shadow crept from the east, pursued by the diffuse light of an overcast sunrise. The gates clanked and clattered open for the new day's business, light as it might be this time of year, allowing Nycos, Silbeth, and Smim to depart as the vanguard of the morning's traffic.

The highway itself yet saw sufficient use, and the early winter precipitation had so far been light enough, that little snow marred their path. Splotches lingered here and there, like a mildewy growth, and heaps of murky sludge lined the roadway, churned up and kicked aside by hooves and grinding wheels. So long as the weather held, they ought to make good time.

Smim had retreated into a shallow sulk, and Silbeth seemed content, for the moment, to ride in silence. Since the horses needed little guidance to follow the highway as it meandered its way between east and south and back again, Nycos found himself with plenty of time to think.

He remained torn by Silbeth's presence, a gnawing hesitation and dissatisfaction. He wanted to speak to her, yet he hadn't the

ARI MARMELL

first notion of what to say. He knew she could be of great help,
yet his need for secrecy and privacy was intense.

More than once, in those early days, he gave genuine
consideration to leaving her behind. He couldn't just sneak
away in the night. He suspected she was far too alert, too light a
sleeper, for him to get far. Traveling alone, and boosted beyond
human, he had the speed to match the horses and the endurance
to outlast them, but that would mean leaving Avalanche behind,
along with a sizable portion of his supplies. It meant leaving the
goblin behind as well, and Nycos wasn't yet prepared to make
this journey, take these risks, entirely on his own.

And, well, he *did* want to get to know this woman, this
predator in human form, almost—to some extent, anyway—
dragon-like in her own right.

To Vizret's hell with it. Let her come along. He could always
try to lose her later, if the situation required it.

Their pace remained brisk, swift enough to chew away the
miles, not so fast as to endanger the horses. Still they spoke
little, save to discuss matters of immediate import: where to
camp, who had what duties, and so forth.

On the third day, however, Nycos tugged on the bridle,
steering Avalanche off to the left. "I'm taking us cross-country
for a bit," he explained. "We'll return to the highway up ahead."

"That's going to slow us down, Master," Smim pointed out.

"Aldsolca," Silbeth said.

"What?" The goblin sounded confused and vaguely irritated,
but Nycos was nodding.

"The highway takes us directly past the city of Aldsolca,"
she explained. "On the off chance King Hasyan or Mashal
Laszlan have anyone out looking for him, they could have sent
a messenger pigeon or other word out to the major cities."

"And even if not," Nycos added, "I might be recognized here,
and I'd rather not have to explain my presence, or deal with

any formalities. It's probably an unnecessary precaution," he admitted, spurring Avalanche off into the slush-covered grass and frigid mud, "but it's worth a few hours and a little discomfort."

"You know," Silbeth said after a few moments of squelching hooves and shivering splashes of muck, though at least they'd gotten no new snow that day, "this reminds me a little of one of my earliest hired missions for the Priory. We had to get into Mahdresh—I mean the city-state proper, not just their territories—but the criminal guild we were supposed to strike at knew we were coming, and they had a *lot* of the city guards on their payroll..."

It was as if the brief conversation about Aldsolca had jarred something loose, though Nycos suspected her sudden loquaciousness was more about distracting them from the unpleasantness of off-road travel. And indeed, he found himself captivated by her tale, even though there wasn't really much to it. The miles of uneven terrain, unsure steeds, and chilly muck seemed to pass far more swiftly than had the far easier miles of the road behind.

For him, at least. Smim just hunched deeper into his coats and glowered as though all the world had offended him.

The tales continued, now that the dam had been breached, even after they rejoined the main road beyond Aldsolca. With seemingly endless breath and enthusiasm, Silbeth segued from the infiltration of Mahdresh to bodyguard duty for a low-ranking but highborn priestess of Uldamboros, god of the mountains—and thus of gems, metals, and wealth in general—on a pilgrimage from Wenslir. "And make no mistake," she insisted, "a *lot* of people have a bone to pick with the clergy of a god they feel should have made them rich, and didn't."

"I can imagine..."

And from *that* story, she'd gone on to describe a fierce four-way battle at the border of Quindacra, between two different robber-barons, the soldiers of the king, and an uninvolved mercenary company whose ill-luck had them passing through at just the wrong time, and whom each side assumed was working for one of the others.

By that point the sun was threatening to dive off to sleep and the snow was falling once again, though in flurries and spurts as light as dandelion fuzz. The trio made camp in the shelter of some trees, and Nycos, in thanks for Silbeth's storytelling, offered both to cook and take the first shift at watch.

For a time he sat, back up against a heavy bole, the fire crackling softly off to his right, and gazed into the empty dark. Something about this night, in particular, made him miss the open sky, the rush of air over his wings, the earth scrolling beneath him like an endless tapestry. He wished, if nothing more, that the overcast would part enough for him to see the moon and stars.

He didn't turn or even glance aside as Smim carefully picked his way through the camp to come crouch at his side. He knew well the sound of the goblin's movement.

"Something on your mind, Smim?"

"Master…" The pause that followed was startling. Usually Smim was quick with his thoughts, and not remotely shy about sharing them. "How much longer are you going to humor this woman?"

*Ah.* He'd been expecting this, sooner or later. "And what would you have me do?"

"You know me, Master, and what I can do. Nobody sleeps *that* lightly. I could—"

The conversation, Nycos might have anticipated. The surge of fury at the goblin's implication, however, caught him by surprise. "Don't you dare so much as *think* it!" That he kept his voice to a whisper—or perhaps it was a low growl—was nigh miraculous.

"I needn't kill her!" Smim insisted, backpedaling. "Just a... a mild injury, enough to hobble her for a few days! We would be long gone by—"

"No."

"Master—"

"I've decided I prefer to have her along, at least for now."

The goblin appeared almost physically ill as he rose. "If you say so, Master."

He'd started away, a single footstep crunching in the snow and dead leaves, when, "Smim?"

"Yes, Master?"

"On occasion, you have taken it upon yourself to act, to 'help' me, if you feel I'm not able to manage something, or that I'm making a grave mistake. We've talked about this a few times."

Nothing. Only the faint whisper of the wind.

"There have been times, I admit, when I've been grateful for that propensity. I'm sure I will be so again. But on this matter? You have been an excellent servant, and a good friend to me, but if you try to harm or otherwise get rid of Mistress Rasik behind my back, I will roast one of your legs for supper and leave the rest of you to the wolves."

"I obey, Master, as always." The words came colder than the snow. Nycos swore even the fire dimmed.

Well, he might have taken that a step too far. He'd decide if it warranted an apology in the morning. Not an *overt* one, of course, but perhaps an unexpected compliment or reward. Smim would know what it meant.

Why *had* he reacted so fiercely? Yes, Silbeth was a useful ally, as well as fascinating company. He wanted to build trust with the woman, and he had to know for certain that Smim wouldn't sabotage that. Still, that didn't explain the strength of his outrage. Perhaps—

"Your manservant—ah, 'goblinservant,' I suppose—doesn't seem particularly happy to have me along."

Nycos tried not to jump. Had he allowed himself to grow *that* distracted? He glanced up at Silbeth, nearly panicked. She was speaking of his general attitude since Oztyerva, not tonight's conversation, wasn't she? How much had she overheard? They'd spoken in low tones and she'd been in her bedroll across the camp until a moment or two ago.

Hadn't she?

"Smim is… protective," he said at last, gesturing for her to sit on the large tree root beside him. It wasn't much of a stool, but it kept them off the frigid soil. "And he doesn't readily trust."

"I imagine he's not the only one," she said, lowering herself to the root. Then, before he could ask what she meant, "How did you two become friends?"

So he told her the same tale he'd offered Hasyan's court, that the goblin had been a servant of Tzavalantzaval, that he'd chosen to accompany Nycos after the dragon's defeat, and that they'd saved one another's life multiple times on their harsh journey across the Outermark.

"I'd enjoy hearing that entire story, Sir Nycolos. I've seen much and heard more in my time, but never the slaying of an actual dragon!" She sounded almost childishly excited by the prospect.

Nycos was less enthused at the notion of recounting those particular events—either version of them. "Perhaps you will someday," he said, staunchly noncommittal. Then, "And it's Nycos. 'Sir Nycolos' may grow cumbersome if we're to be traveling together."

"Oh, no need to worry about that." She grinned. "I assure you, it already had."

He smiled in return, reflexively and genuinely, but then subsided once more into silence. *Why was it so hard to think up anything to say to this woman?*

Silbeth gazed briefly into the same darkness he had, then dug into her pack for oil and a whetstone. She'd unwrapped the both, and gotten as far as laying her sword over her knees, when she paused to glance back, frowning, at the now-slumbering goblin.

"It's fine," Nycos told her. "He's slept through a lot worse."

"No," she said, repacking her supplies with a soft sigh. "It doesn't actually need it yet, anyway. Just habit."

The various metals, and some of the leather, glinted in the dull firelight. "May I?" Nycos asked, startling himself.

She paused, considering, then slowly slid the sword—belt, scabbard, and all—over to him.

Carefully, almost reverentially, he drew the long, narrow blade, holding it before him and admiring the feel in his grip. He'd rarely paid much attention to weapons beyond the basic "How long and sharp are they?" for the bulk of his existence. Since sliding into the life of Nycolos Anvarri, he'd observed any number of cultures' armaments—during practice, during his patrols, and particularly during the tournament. And yet...

"I don't believe I recognize the style," he admitted.

"I'm not surprised," Silbeth said, a response he found faintly relieving. "It's actually of Ktho Delian make."

Nycos frowned. The shape of the blade and the feeble illumination turned it into a monstrous, twisted scowl in his reflection. All the Ktho Delian swords *he'd* seen had been heavier, thicker weapons, and most had been notably shorter.

Either she saw his confusion, or she'd anticipated it. "It's an older style. You only really see it today among some of their aristocracy. Modern Ktho Delian swordsmanship developed to favor shields, so they prefer shorter arming swords or the like. Me?" She shrugged. "I prefer the buckler, or else to fight with a two-handed grip, so the older, narrower hand-and-a-half suits me well enough. It loses some striking power," she confessed, "compared to the heavier longswords a few of them still use instead of carrying shields, but it's quicker. Better control."

"So I recall," he said, grinning and passing the weapon back her way.

"And you? Are you required to wield the traditional Kirresci arms as a loyal and faithful knight of the realm?" she asked jokingly.

"It's not a requirement, but we do get the dregs of wine and the most gristly cuts of meat at supper if we don't."

He was absurdly pleased when that response drew a laugh from her. "You seemed to favor the *szandzsya* in the tournament."

"I do. The sabre's well and good, and the shield has its place, but I prefer hitting hard and fast as possible. Dead enemies don't require much defending against, by and large."

"You know, I think I remember the Priory teaching us something to that effect."

That led neatly enough to the question he'd been sitting on for a while, but he decided, even with his still imperfect grasp of interpersonal etiquette, that he hadn't yet earned the right to ask. They subsided again into silence, but at least it felt more companionable this time, less awkward.

A small log in the fire split, sending up a shower of sparks. "Nycos," Silbeth said, as though that crack had been a signal, "shouldn't we have left the road and moved into the Brackenwood by now?"

"That... would be a more direct route to Gronch," he hedged, not yet prepared to explain that Gronch *wasn't* their first destination. "But I'd rather cleave to the highway a bit longer. It may add some distance, but I think we'll more than make up for it in speed."

"Your decision," she said, rising lithely from the tree root. "There's a price attached, though."

He blinked, startled. "How do you mean?"

"If we're going out of our way," she told him as she headed back toward her bedroll, "you're *definitely* going to have to take on some of the storytelling duties. Starting tomorrow. Wake me when it's my turn on watch."

It was just as well that she'd walked away, as he hadn't the first notion of what to say to that.

———

Snow would have been preferable to the next day's sleet and freezing rain. Although light, sporadic, it soaked into everything, slipping through even the tightest folds in cloak and kaftan. The horses trudged miserably along the roadway, heads bowed, while those who sat atop them shivered despite every effort to keep warm.

Warm, or at least distracted.

Endeavoring to make the telling of it as exciting and suspenseful as he could, Nycos spoke of his patrols along the border with Mahdresh, the pursuit and ambush, the discovery of the Ktho Delian agitator amidst the bandits. As best he could recall, he detailed every question, every cry, every blow and every parry.

Although he did, of course, alter or omit a few details— specifically those pertaining to his more-than-human abilities and techniques. He wasn't entirely certain how well he succeeded in making the tale remotely entertaining, but at least several miles of sodden roadway and bare, depressed forestry had passed them by when he was done, and if Silbeth found the recitation lacking or dull, she was polite enough to hide it.

"All right," he announced around a quivering mouthful of sleet. "Your turn."

"My… I seem to remember telling a good five stories in a row yesterday!"

"Um." Nycos thought back, then actually held up a gauntlet-wrapped hand to count off fingers. "It was three, in fact."

"We'll compromise. Call it four."

"But it *wasn't* four, it was—"

"My point, though, is that you can cough up a few more tales before it's back to me."

He was grinning again, despite the ache of the cold against his teeth. "No, you see, I let you go on yesterday for *your* sake."

"My—?!"

"It would have been rude to interrupt you, would it not? I was being chivalrous. That's what we're supposed to do, with people of lesser station."

"Let me guess. And if you don't, you get dregs and gristle at supper?"

"Precisely. You wouldn't want to *punish* me for being chivalrous, would you?"

"I think," Smim declared disgustedly from behind the both of them, plodding along on the smallest of the horses, "that I would very much like to freeze to death now."

In the end, Silbeth talked him into telling one more before she took over, and they alternated turns after that. Nycos didn't have terribly many experiences to relate, of course, but he'd learned enough about the life of the other Nycolos that he was able to come up with several mixtures of fact and fiction that *sounded* believable.

Which did, in turn, make him wonder for a moment how many of Silbeth's own stories were entirely truthful. Ultimately, though, he decided it didn't matter. They were interesting enough to listen to, helped pass the time, and—her jesting protestations to the contrary—she clearly enjoyed telling them.

No story, however, was *so* all-consuming as to make the damp and frigid journey at all pleasant. After another day and a half, when the highway had begun to lead them ever-further south, no amount of diversion could keep the inevitable questions at bay any longer.

"We're not going to Gronch," Nycos finally confessed, when Silbeth pressed him yet again about his choice of routes, about electing the highway over the Brackenwood. "I mean, yes, we are, but not yet."

"I'd more or less picked up on that," the mercenary said around a shallow scowl. "So where *are* we going?"

"Just a slight detour."

"Nycos, *where?*"

Well, he was going to have to tell her sooner or later. "Vidiir."

"*What?* That's… You're adding over four-hundred miles to our journey! In the dead of winter!"

He yanked open a saddlebag and began hauling out lengths of canvas to set up a tent for the night. "I hadn't actually done the measuring on a map, but that sounds about right, yes."

"For the gods' sake, why?"

"Because that's where Vidiir is?"

One look at Silbeth's face and the grin slipped from his own. Apparently, this was *not* the proper time for the sort of jesting that had become a habit between them over the past few days. *Damn fickle humans.*

"Because," he said far more seriously, "I figured as long as I was setting out to try and neutralize the threat posed by a mad dragon, I might as well also swing by the Quindacran court and make them change their minds about withdrawing from the treaty."

He smiled tightly over the wrinkled canvas, mildly amused that, for once, Silbeth appeared honestly speechless. "I mean, once you're already performing the impossible, it's not as though things can get any *more* difficult, right?"

Oddly, though she continued to say nothing at all, Nycos couldn't shake the vague sense that she didn't entirely agree with his logic.

# CHAPTER TWENTY-FIVE

"What the hell sort of name is 'Wayloq,' anyway?" Silbeth groused. "It doesn't really sound Kirresci." She seemed as though she were trying to maintain the irritation she'd felt—and shared—since Nycos had announced their detour. Trying, and failing, thwarted by the warmth of the crackling fire in the hearth and the other gathered patrons, to say nothing of their recent hot meal, now reduced to steaming leftover scraps of mutton and fish spread about various plates. Truly comfortable and well-fed for the first time since leaving Talocsa, neither of them were able to keep their mood from partially thawing.

Smim doubtless felt otherwise, but since he was confined to the rooms they'd let for the night—they'd all decided, some more grudgingly than others, that they couldn't afford the attention a goblin would draw in the common room—he was in no position to complain. He'd feel better once Nycos brought him up some food.

Nycos leaned back, a pewter tankard held at his lips, and glanced around. Walls of carefully fitted logs, tables bustling with clients and servers, a long bar along one end of the room, and the thick scents of heavy brews and roasting meats… It was the very spiritual ideal of a traveler's tavern. It was less the ambience, here at the Inn of the Hungry Dog, that concerned Nycos, however, but the patrons. Most, to judge by the rougher cut of their furs or the oiled sheen to their kaftans, were probably locals; trappers, sailors, or craftsmen, making their lives here at the very edges of Kirresc. The gazes they cast at Nycos and Silbeth in turn were inquisitive, but not hostile. They might wonder what these strangers were doing, traveling in such an unfriendly season, but it was an idle curiosity at worst.

"It's not," Nycos finally answered, having reassured himself—for the umpteenth time—that the inn concealed no hidden enemies or looming threats. "Wayloq's been here since before Kirre the First claimed Talocsa as the capital of his kingdom-to-come. I understand it hasn't changed much in all those generations, either. Grew all the way," he explained sarcastically, "from a large fishing town to a small port town.

"It's moderately important to Kirresci trade, but not big enough or close enough to the rest of civilization to be worth more than a modicum of royal attention, so..." He shrugged, then drained his flagon. "It sits out here and does what it does, without much concern for what anyone else thinks."

"Oh, you mean like some people I know," she retorted. "No wonder you wanted to come here."

"I wanted to come here so we'd have the chance to warm up and fill our bellies with something other than camp fare before approaching the border. I didn't hear you complaining about the fire or the food."

"I didn't say it was a *bad* idea," Silbeth grumbled.

Nycos, who had rarely felt the urge to sigh until he'd become human, swallowed one now. He couldn't really hold her resentment against her. It wasn't the change in plan, or even the perceived insanity of his intentions, he knew, that bothered her. It was the fact that he'd steadfastly refused to tell her what he meant to do in Vidiir, *how* he could possibly go about altering the course of an entire nation.

After several days of building comradery, she'd taken his abrupt reticence on this one vital topic as a lack of trust. And to be fair, it was; she just couldn't possibly comprehend the magnitude of the secret he felt obliged to keep.

He *did* have to keep his true nature secret from her. Didn't he?

Around them, conversation hummed, punctuated by raucous laughter and the clatter of dishes. Beyond, the peculiar melding of sleet and the lapping tide of the Cerenean Sea melded into a low, whispering song. An urge overtook him, to invite Silbeth to join him for a walk along the shoreline, along Wayloq's piers and the nearby inlets. It was only the sudden memory that the cold would bother not just her but—in this form—Nycos himself that stayed his tongue.

"Well," Silbeth said, pushing back from the table. "If we've only got genuine beds to sleep in for one night, I don't intend to miss the opportunity. Good n—"

"How did you wind up joining the Priory of Steel?" He'd been sitting on the question since they'd begun this trek, if not longer, and he hadn't meant for it to slip out here. Now that it was out, however, he found himself relieved, though that would doubtless change should she refuse to answer. It wasn't merely a matter of learning more about her, either, although that was certainly part of it. He couldn't yet have described why if he'd been asked, but he felt that this was the first step toward making a much bigger decision regarding how much of himself it would be safe to share.

Silbeth had stopped, half-standing, so that she now hunched over the table. Her arms and her expression were equally stiff, while a dozen different emotions danced with the firelight reflected in her eyes. She spoke not a word, but Nycos could hear the questions and challenges all the same.

Most of them amounted to, *Why should I tell you something so personal when you so clearly don't trust me?* And in all honesty, had she actually come out and asked him that, he would have been hard pressed to offer up an acceptable answer.

For whatever reason, though, she didn't ask. In fact, she seemed ever so slightly to relax as she sat back down. She tried to take a sip of her drink, discovered the flagon empty, and waved vaguely at the nearest server for another.

"My family is from Wenslir," she began, her words taking on a very different cadence than when she'd told so many of her other stories over the past few days. "I was born in Imirrin.

"I know what you're thinking," she told him, even as he'd begun to nod in understanding. "It's what everybody thinks. That everyone from Wenslir is a religious zealot. That's not so, of course—but then again, there are a lot of reasons people believe it. My family is one of those reasons. I was seven years of age before I knew the difference between conversation and prayer."

Her smile in response to his chuckle was faint but genuine, the first in two days. "Close to half of my family were clergy of the Empyrean Choir. If you hadn't shown a penchant for some other craft or profession by adolescence, then it was just a matter of figuring out *which* god of the Choir you were best suited to serving."

"And did you? Show a penchant for something else?"

"That… depends on your definition." Her new drink arrived, dropped off by a massive, broad-shouldered man of dark skin and even darker hair. He'd been working in and around the bar since the two of them had arrived, and gave every impression of owning or at least running the place. Silbeth seemed not to notice him, and had apparently forgotten that she was thirsty.

"Children fight," she said. "It happens. Someone goes home with a split lip, maybe a broken nose, and quite possibly gets worse from their parents.

"*Most* children don't dig kitchenware into their opponents, or look for blunt objects as a reaction to perceived insults. I don't know how many people's bones I'd broken by the time I was eleven, but there's a fairly good chance that was when I first killed somebody."

Nycos couldn't move, could scarcely breathe. To say that this was not the story he'd anticipated was a colossal understatement. To say he couldn't entirely comprehend why she would confide this in him, especially under their current circumstances, even more so.

"I don't know for certain that the boy died." She spoke almost by rote, as if reciting off a written page. "People pulled me off him, hustled me away, and my family moved soon after. But I'd hit him in the head with a loose paving stone from the street. If I *didn't* kill him, I can't imagine he hasn't wished every day since that I had."

She finally reached out to take a drink. Despite the apparent lack of emotion in her face, her voice, her posture, Nycos could hear the beer sloshing violently in the mug.

"Silbeth—"

"No." She wiped her lips, lowered the flagon. "I had a knack for the fighting, skills I'd picked up from watching others or practicing behind my parents' backs. It wasn't just wild blows and fury. In fact, I really don't remember ever feeling all that angry. I know I must have been, on some level, to react with such violence, but I didn't *feel* it.

"If my family didn't do *something*, I was going to wind up dead, either in a fight or on the gibbet. So of course, they turned to the gods. And it was through some of our friends in the priesthoods that I was eventually passed into the custody of various temples. Temples of war gods, of course. And from them, the Priory.

"Whatever was broken inside me, they fixed, though it took years. And I don't just mean they taught me to control whatever it was, though they did. Through various martial practices, meditations, all of that. There was magic involved, Nycos. No overt sorcery, but more subtle mysticism, through ritual and prayer."

What was he to say to that? "I can only imagine how grateful you must feel to them."

"Grateful, absolutely. But of far greater importance, I *believe*. I've seen, *felt*, what the forms and focus of battle can do for me. I know there's genuine power there. And I know that I've a knack for these skills, that the gods must have made me a warrior—even before I knew what to do with that—for a reason. That's why, of all the martial gods of the Choir, all those to whom the Priory offers its veneration, I've chosen Louros as my primary patron."

"The Lady of the Moons? Why?" he asked, startled.

"Because she watches over those who travel by night. Those who are lost in darkness. As I was, in my own way." For the first time she looked away, gazing into her flagon or perhaps at the whorls in the wood of the table. "A lot of people scoff at the Priory of Steel even as they respect our skills. They don't understand how we can consider what we do to be a religious practice, but—"

"I understand. Or I think I do, anyway." He felt dizzy, his entire view—of the world? Or just of Silbeth Rasik?—shaken slightly from its axis.

"Maybe you do at that." Again her chair scraped as she rose. "Good night, Nycos. I hope you heard whatever answer it was you were seeking."

He watched her go, winding between various tables on her way to the stairs. He had no idea what answers he *had* sought, or whether he'd heard them—but he knew, now, that he had more than a few new questions. That he might just be insane for even considering them.

And that he probably ought not tell Smim he was thinking of asking them.

---

The morning was crisp, cold, windy but surprisingly clear as they left Wayloq, the Hungry Dog Inn, and the coast of the Cerenean Sea behind. And fortunate for them that the weather held, that—though uncomfortable—it never approached the levels of misery it had reached during their earlier travels. For they rode in silence the bulk of that day, and a portion of the next, each far too deeply lost in his or her own thoughts and emotions for the telling of tales or the trading of jibes.

It was just past noon, on the second day since they'd departed the port-and-fishing town, when they approached the border between Kirresc and Quindacra.

The border, and one particularly devastating error in judgment.

While thick woodland lay not far to the north, an extension of the same sprawling forest of which the Brackenwood was part, vast stretches of the border were grassland with sporadic copses. Between that, and two days without much precipitation, going off road would scarcely have slowed or inconvenienced them. Sneaking into a sovereign nation carried with it some risk, certainly, but the odds of discovery in the vast expanse were negligible. It would have been simplicity itself to avoid the official crossing, and the tariff-collecting border station that sat alongside the highway.

In fact, the trio *had* gone off the road to avoid the Kirresci station. Nycos hadn't wanted to risk being recognized, however remote the chance. It would have been simple to stay off the highway, to enter Quindacra with the same stealth they'd exited Kirresc. Both nations kept such outposts a couple of miles back from the actual line on the map, to avoid stepping on one another's toes; a league-and-change across the grasses would have proved easy enough.

But Nycos had fretted over the various ways his plan could go awry, and he'd decided that being caught trying to sneak into Quindacra—however improbable—was a gamble not worth taking. He'd chosen to approach the crossing openly.

It was a simple hut, manned by roughly half a dozen soldiers, with little to differentiate it—or them—from their

Kirresci counterparts, save colors and emblems on tabards. Perhaps their arms and armor were of slightly lower quality, their discipline suggestive of training not *quite* up to Kirresci standards, but not by any great degree.

The guards emerged from shelter as the trio approached, their faces chapped red and their breath steaming in the chill. Smim put his arms around himself and shivered heavily to explain why he kept his face wrapped, while Nycos and Silbeth stepped forward to speak. They answered a few perfunctory questions with a tale of an emergency in a cousin's business affairs, one that required winter travel. They were headed to Vidiir, the capital. Yes, they'd been here before and knew which highways to take. And yes, of course they were happy to pay an entry tariff, though Nycos made sure not to sound *too* content with the prospect.

A smattering of silver Kirresci *zlatka* changed heavily gloved hands, the three of them began to ride on, and it was just as Nycos prepared to pull his scarf back over his face that the whole thing went to hell.

"Sir Nycolos?" The death knell of a question came from a soldier at the back of the squad, a middle-aged man with the bearing of low gentry. "Captain Arvisk! Remember? We met when you escorted Leomyn Guldoell home for Duke Hemmet's funeral."

*Oh, damn. Damn, damn, damn,* damn*!*

Nycos had no memory of any such thing, of course, but he couldn't exactly explain why to the excited soldier. And it wouldn't have mattered even if he could.

"Why in Alazir's name are you traveling without a retinue, and in this weather no less? You could—"

He died instantly, his skull neatly cloven with a single arc of Nycos's *szandzsya*. He would go to Vizret's realm, or wherever else, never knowing what had killed him, and for that, Nycos found himself oddly grateful. It would occur to him only later that what he felt in that moment was a pang, however faint, of guilt. That, though once he would have given it nary a second thought, today he actively wished he need not do what he was about to do.

He wished, but it wouldn't stop him.

Avalanche spun at the merest pressure of his rider's knees, the scent of blood driving the warhorse into a screaming exultation. The sabre-spear whistled, slicing cold air and hot flesh, and a second soldier fell, features locked in a mask of permanent bewilderment.

By now the rest of the border guards had overcome their shock, crying out in alarm, hefting spears and yanking swords from scabbards. Nycos lunged into their midst, his mount surging beneath him, a living siege engine. Two more Quindacrans died, one by *szandzsya*, the other beneath the winter-wrapped but still iron-shod hooves of Avalanche.

That left only two of the original six, but their shouted warnings had quickly drawn—perhaps awakened—others. Although unarmored, a few still blinking the sleep from their eyes, the second shift poured from the hut, and if any remained drowsy, the twin slaps of the cold and the sight of comrades sprawled across hard earth woke them well enough.

Of greater concern to Nycos, three of them held not sword or spear, but recurved bows crafted in the Kirresci style. That last was an irony the knight felt unable to appreciate.

Only two arrows flew, however—both of which Nycos evaded, though he nearly hurled himself from Avalanche's back—before the newly arrived soldiers found themselves threatened up close. Silbeth was among them now, sword and buckler flashing, forcing the archers to drop their bows in favor of blades. Blood flew, the horse reared, and steel shrieked against steel.

Smim appeared behind the pair still facing Nycos. He clutched a short chopping blade he'd acquired somewhere in Oztyerva, more cleaver than sword or sabre. One soldier fell, screaming, having never seen the goblin coming. The other perished an instant later beneath Nycos's larger weapon.

Nycos paused only an instant, troubled by Smim's peculiar expression, then once again prodded Avalanche into a sprint. Skilled as Silbeth was, Nycos wasn't prepared to leave her facing six-to-one odds on her own.

Or even four-to-one, which is how the confrontation stood by the time he reached her side. Between the pair of them, those remaining four dwindled to zero in moments.

Blood and other fluids steamed heavily in the winter air, while the miasma of offal and human pieces never intended for the light of day scratched at their nostrils, their throats, their lungs with ragged nails of fume. The horses shifted, whickering uneasily, their pulses still racing but no threats left to face. Silbeth reached two fingers to her forehead, wiping away a sheen of perspiration that was already freezing into a thin glaze.

"Explain to me," she said in low tone, "why we just slaughtered twelve people who were not our enemies?"

He cast about him, his attention tugged in morbid fascination to the swiftly cooling pools of crimson, rippling glutinously in the breeze. When he did reply, his words were softer even than hers. "I… It never even crossed my mind that someone here might recognize me! Some random soldier, not even Kirresci? It… The odds…!"

"Yeah. I've been on the boot-end of Donaris's fickle moods more than a time or two, myself." She, too, turned about as though burning the sight of the bodies into her memory. "You—we killed them to keep a secret?"

"We killed them to prevent a war." Nycos straightened in his saddle. "If anyone—*anyone*—learns that Nycolos Anvarri was here in Quindacra, what I'm planning won't work."

"I suppose I'd have known that, if I had any idea what you were planning." She no longer sounded accusatory or even especially irate over his reticence, just mildly discontent. "What are we doing with these poor idiots? The highways may not see a lot of travel at this time of year, but someone's still going to find this mess well before we've reached Vidiir."

"We need to make this look like bandits," he decided after a bit of thought. Then, "Yes, I know, it's peculiar for bandits to attack an armed border station. Maybe they were desperate over the lack of winter traffic. I don't know. It just has to look right. Smim?"

"On it, Master." The goblin dropped from his horse and set about rifling the bodies for valuables. Silbeth, vaguely disgusted, gathered the better of the fallen weapons, while Nycos went inside to find the strongbox, or wherever they kept the tariffs they collected.

They even went so far as to leave some extra drag marks where the earth wasn't too rock-hard to accept them, used a few of the dead—after careful maneuvering—to scatter extra bloodstains about the battlefield. It wouldn't look right without some evidence of wounded raiders.

And then there was nothing else for it but to move on.

Nycos dropped back as they rode, letting Silbeth take the lead. "It's not like you to keep your opinions to yourself, Smim," he said to his old companion. "But you've clearly had something to say for a while now."

"Nothing important, Master. I'm just fine."

"Ah. Just being sullen and resentful for the warmth, then?"

Beady eyes glared from a woven bird's nest of scarves.

"Come on, Smim. What's bothering you?"

"What's bothering me, Master, is that *you're* bothered!"

It took Nycos a moment to work through that and figure out what the goblin referred to. "You mean the fight back there."

"Not a fight, Master. A massacre. The soldiers never had a chance, and you know it."

"Are you trying to make me feel worse about it?"

The goblin's fists clenched so tightly on the reins that his horse stumbled, twisting his head in confusion. "No, damn it, but that's precisely my point!" He calmed himself, quieting his voice with a suspicious sneer at the woman riding ahead. "You shouldn't feel *anything* about it!"

Nycos shrugged. It wasn't a *huge* weight, but... "Those people shouldn't have had to die, Smim."

"And they didn't especially have to live, either. Why does it *matter*, Master? Why are you giving it a second thought? They're just *humans!*"

"I... Yes, they are. And I did what I had to do."

"Yet you're still fretting over it. Tzavalantzaval wouldn't mope about it."

The many layers Smim wore to protect himself from the cold guarded him against the worst of the blow as well. Still, it was more than sufficient to bruise, and to send him hurtling from the saddle to the cold, packed earth.

"I *am* Tzavalantzaval!" Nycos hissed at him, near shaking with rage. He couldn't remember ever raising a hand or a claw to the goblin, but the implication behind Smim's words gouged his soul. He only just kept his voice low enough that Silbeth, now riding madly back their way, would not hear the declaration. "Do not *ever* forget it!"

"I'm not the one, Master," Smim said, hauling himself upright with a hand on the stirrup and no doubt already coming up with some lie to tell Silbeth about what had happened, "who seems to be in danger of forgetting."

# CHAPTER TWENTY-SIX

More people would die tonight. He would take pains to avoid it where he could, and if fortune were with him they would be few, but Nycos had no illusions. Under no circumstances would he greet the dawn with clean hands.

He wondered idly, as he peered at the flickering lights of Vidiir through a veil of sleet, why that thought disturbed him less than the murder of the border guards, now almost a week gone by. Did their proximity to the king, these soldiers of the capital and of Castle Auric, bestow upon them, in Nycos's sight, some of the guilt and treachery of their sovereign? So that he felt they deserved an unkind fate more than their distant brethren?

Or had the fact that this was always an element of his plan, that he'd had longer to adjust to the idea, simply rendered their possible deaths less impactful?

Nycos shook himself, and not just to rid himself of the chilling snow accumulating on his shoulders and hood. It didn't matter. He was here, and he knew what he had to do. The night was already half over, and he must be done and away by dawn.

They had camped, the three travelers, in the wilds just outside Vidiir, hidden behind a small rise and within a copse of bare boles. Nycos had departed the moment Silbeth was asleep, leaving Smim with a variety of instructions—and a warning, in no uncertain terms, of what would happen to the goblin if the woman was to suffer any sort of "accident" in his master's absence. He'd also left behind his weapons, which were too obviously of Kirresci make, and his armor, which would have rendered stealth nigh impossible.

Anyone but Smim would have thought him a fool, that he'd rendered himself helpless.

From there, Nycos chose a roundabout way to the city proper. The ice and snow fell heavily enough, but the weather was fickle, and the drifts that had already accumulated lay thick. He had no wish to risk leaving a trail, however unlikely, to his companions' camp. Thus, Nycos had instead made his way to the shore, and through the lapping tides that would hide any tracks.

He crouched now in those same frigid waters, soaked to the knees, leaning against the slimy pylon of a pier and studying, as best he could, the great port that was Quindacra's seat of power. It scarcely bothered him, that cold. Little in the way of discomfort would bother him now.

Beneath his heavy cloak and thick winter garb, Nycos had become something that nobody he would meet tonight had ever seen. Something with little concern for trivialities such as weather.

Finally certain no passersby lurked between the docks and the streets beyond, Nycos broke into a run. The sound of his steps was lost in the pounding surf behind, the wind and frozen rain all about. In seconds he crossed the gap, a slightly darker blur against the icy night. None saw him, and even if they had, they would have dismissed him as a trick of shadow, for nothing human could move so fast.

In that sprint, with the wind in his face, he exulted. Never since he had become Nycolos Anvarri had he willed such strength into his limbs, such power into his body. He could not be a dragon, not now, perhaps never again, but tonight he came as near to it as he could without the sliver of Wyrmtaker piercing his heart.

Tonight, he need not pass as human.

He reached the edge of the street and sprang for the rooftops. His talons stretched out, ready to pierce the walls be they wood or stone, but they proved unnecessary. His jump carried him more than high enough, and he alighted firmly on the eaves of a fishmonger's storehouse. Again he ran, until the edge of the rooftop loomed, and another leap easily cleared the narrow avenue with room to spare.

Thus did he cross the breadth of Vidiir, yards above the streets, above the view of any duty-bound guards or unfortunate pedestrians forced outside this miserable night.

It wasn't too unlike Talocsa, this city. The buildings trended slightly narrower, the whitewashing and paint less colorful. Fewer streets were paved or lit with any regularity, and to judge by those few souls he observed, simple cloaks were favored over coat or kaftan. All he had heard over the past year proclaimed the wood and stone here were of poorer quality than in Kirresc, but between the haze of the storm and his own lack of expertise, Nycos saw no difference.

It didn't *smell* at all the same, though. All those ambient scents he'd grown accustomed to—the vegetation (however muted by the season), the lingering cookfires, the nearby woods, they were all different. Even the people had dissimilar odors, doubtless due to their diet. The aroma of fish, and the tang of the Cerenean Sea, infused it all.

Building by building, street by street, he neared his goal. Most of the rooftops he could reach with an inhuman bound, sometimes covering several dozen feet with each. Occasionally, as he passed through wealthier parts of town, he had to climb to the top of a particularly high structure, and that was when his claws proved their worth. While most Vidiirians were surely asleep, or attributed his sounds to the frozen rain, he doubtless drew *some* attention with his footsteps, or the crunch of talons on stone. If anyone came out to investigate, however, he was gone long before they appeared, the evidence of his passing already hidden by his co-conspirators, the wind and snow.

Only twice did he come across a gap too wide to traverse, where open courtyard and grand avenue combined into a veritable chasm between the buildings. There he clambered down and dashed across the roadways, and just as before, he moved unseen.

Until, finally, he stared at the moat and the outer walls of his destination.

*Castle Auric. What sort of insecure, puffed-up jackass names his fortress "Castle Auric"?*

Despite the grandiose epithet, the keep boasted no actual gold, or even gold coloration, that Nycos saw—though that could, he acknowledged, have been a trick of the light and the weather. Still, all he observed was stone, from the curtain wall to the looming silhouettes of towers rather more slender and more square of roof than those to which he was accustomed. At the base of that wall flowed a narrow moat, sluggish and half-gelid, splotched with leprous scabs of dirty ice.

All protected, but the sentries at the gate huddled in the mean shelter of the guardhouse, while those who patrolled the walls hurried through sporadic rounds and otherwise took refuge within the watchtowers. Any given length of parapet remained absent of witnesses for minutes at a time.

Sloppy, perhaps, but understandable. No invading army besieged those walls, and even if an assassin were somehow skilled enough to anchor a hook and climb the stone unheard, none in his right mind would try on a night such as this. What did they have, really, to stand guard against?

Nycos retreated far enough for a running start, waited for the gusts and the crunch of sleet to pick up, and then hurtled the moat. He soared briefly through the frigid air, then thrust out his hands as the wall loomed to meet him.

Talons crunched into stone, catching fast against the pull of gravity and the push of wind. They didn't sink in too deeply.

With the might of his true body he could have dug whole craters from the rock, but he lacked much of that strength now, however he enhanced his human form. Those claws though, remained as sharp and as hard as always, and that was enough to hold.

It was also why, at some point between here and Gronch, he would have to…

Nycos shuddered and cringed from that unpleasant thought. It was a travail for another day, and he had enough to worry about right now.

Hand over hand, he hauled himself upward, the tips of his talons digging the tiniest furrows. Once or twice he regretted not having shed his boots, wishing he could have used his feet to cling against sudden blasts of wind, but the strength of his arms proved sufficient. He peered over the parapet, ensuring that none of the soldiers lurked nearby. Then, satisfied everything was clear, he scrambled over and across, took another quick look to ensure the inner bailey beyond was equally deserted, and dropped.

A vicious chorus of barks and snarls burst from what must have been the kennel as the royal hunting hounds caught his scent, but either the to-do went unheard amidst the freezing storm, or the beasts' keepers assumed they were reacting to the weather.

Shadow to shadow he flitted, ducking behind various outbuildings where he could, no matter that the entire courtyard was a sea of gloom. Several flickering lanterns warred against the night as he drew nearer the main keep, and it wouldn't do to let some eagle-eyed sentry spot him now. This close, he saw that many of Castle Auric's windows and doorways, as well as some of the bas-relief adornment on waterspouts and supporting columns, were indeed trimmed in gold—or at least something gilded. Given the place's smaller, more utilitarian construction as compared to the likes of Oztyerva, it felt rather akin to putting a goblin in a wedding gown.

He decided against sharing that particular observation with Smim when he told his companions of this night.

Penetrating the inner keep proved bloodier work. None of the doors were barred; since the inhabitants weren't currently besieged, they saw no need to make the jobs of the soldiers and servants any more difficult. Even the smallest and most insignificant of those entryways, however, boasted a few guards within.

Those same claws that had punctured stone felt little resistance in chainmail and flesh. Nycos dragged the trio of bodies into the first side chamber he could find, and quickened his pace.

Most of the castle slumbered, so he was forced to kill on only two further occasions before finally reaching the uppermost floor of the keep. It took almost another hour, hall by hall, door by door, to figure out whose chambers were whose, and then to sneak into one without waking the inhabitants.

He didn't *quite* succeed. As he slipped inside, a young servant on a bed near the door sat upright, blinking in drowsy confusion. A few candles on a side table cast a bit of light throughout the room, enough for her to instantly recognize that he didn't belong. She drew breath to scream, hands clutched to her chest, and Nycos had no choice. A brief lunge, and the only sound to emerge was the harsh snap of her neck.

Long he stood over the body, in part listening to make sure the sleepers across the suite hadn't awoken, but mostly staring unhappily at the limp form. He'd killed many since becoming Nycolos, quite a few on this journey, and several this very night. But the others, to the last, had been some manner of threat. Soldiers. Bandits. The woman who'd purchased him, held him, as a slave. Even if not an enemy in the moment, they'd been people of violence in one form or another, people who, while maybe not deserving of death, had chosen a life where they must regularly face it.

Not this one. She'd been a maidservant, nothing more, had probably counted herself intensely lucky to work for the royal family. Guilty of nothing, not a woman of violence who'd known death potentially lurked around the next corner.

Smim had been right. This sort of thing shouldn't disturb him. He did what he must—and not merely for himself, as had long been his wont, but for the greater good of others. He shouldn't feel remorse, shouldn't give it a second thought, shouldn't *care*.

So why did he?

Despondent, he cast about the room until he found what he needed. Carefully, quietly, he took it from the floor beside the other bed, where a pair of small figures still slept, blissfully unaware. Slipping his prize into a pouch at his belt, he crept back toward the hall, pausing only to lay a heavy quilt over the body. He didn't want anyone awakening to that sight, if it could be helped.

Then, softly shutting the door behind him, he moved toward his final destination of the night.

The doors to the royal couple's bedchamber were larger, the lintel trimmed in gold. It was also guarded, though not from without. Careful listening with inhuman ears revealed a pair of individuals standing on either side of the door within the room beyond. Doubtless the king and queen had a full suite, so the presence of the guards inside was no invasion of their privacy.

Tricky to deal with, but not impossible.

Nycos scraped a claw across the wall not far from the door, just loud enough to be heard. The guards would ignore it, doubtless taking it for some servant delivering a late-night message or snack to someone.

So he waited a moment and repeated it.

And then again. And again.

Enough to draw attention, not enough to raise genuine suspicion. If he'd read the atmosphere in Castle Auric right, the soldiers—expecting no danger, fully secure in their fortress—should grow curiously irritated long before the idea of a genuine threat even crossed their minds.

It was after the fourth scrape that the lock opened with a heavy thunk and the door swung gently inward. "What's the ruckus out here?" one of the soldiers demanded, poking his head out into the hall. "Their Majesties are trying to sl—"

Nycos grabbed the man's skull, talons punching through bone. The second guard hadn't yet brought her halberd around, nor drawn breath to shout a warning, before he was inside. He wrapped a fist around the haft of the weapon, yanked it and her forward, and opened the front of her throat, only just pivoting away from the crimson jet that followed. Catching the body before it could clatter too loudly to the floor, he lowered her, pulled the other corpse inside, and then carefully shut the door.

A quick glance around the suite showed a number of rooms for this purpose or that, all larger and rather more ornate than necessary, but only a single shut door. He'd have known that for the bedchamber even without the faint snoring he heard from beyond.

Nycos hit that door, a living battering ram, crossed the room and was crouched atop the mattress, claws to the king's throat, before either he or the queen knew what was happening. A heavy rope hung beside the bed, doubtless to summon servants or aid. Nycos turned his head far enough that it was clear, even under the hood he'd worn against the weather, where he was looking.

"Listen to what I've come to say, your Majesties," he told them, his voice made rough and raspy by his partial transformation, "and you will both see the dawn. Try to escape, try to raise an alarm—*any* sort of alarm—and if you're fortunate, I'll kill you *both* before I leave. Do you understand?"

"How dare—?!" the king started to squeak, while her Majesty drew breath to scream.

Nycos lifted his other hand, the talons still wet with the blood of the guards, and allowed the viscous mess to drip across the velvet quilt. The other tightened, just enough to press against skin without *quite* puncturing it.

"Do you. Understand?"

Both nodded, although the king moved rather more timidly of the two.

Nycos drew back to stand beside the bed rather than atop it. He moved through the gossamer canopy then ripped it off the frame, tossing it behind him, so nothing stood, even symbolically, between him and the royal couple. Then he reached up, grasping the rope with one hand and severing it flush against the ceiling with the talons of the other.

Up close and without his regalia, King Boruden was a nondescript man: slim, of average complexion and brownish hair, a faint beard not much thicker than an adolescent's. His wife, Queen Emdara, was taller, more attractive; her pale skin and blonde hair implied an almost pure Elgarrad ancestry. She also had the vacant (if currently fearful) features to suggest that Boruden had married for appearance over ability.

*How like the man.*

"People have died here tonight, your Majesties," Nycos said, "and you brought that on them. Though I'd have wished otherwise, I will kill to achieve my purpose. Said purpose would be *better* served with the two of you alive, but I can work with your successors if need be."

"How do you propose to get away with this?" Boruden demanded, though he kept his tone low. "When I learn who sent you—"

Nycos finally drew back his hood. And had someone compelled him to be honest in that moment, he would have admitted that he missed, desperately, eliciting the sort of reaction, the sort of *terror*, his appearance wrought; the fear and obedience that were his by right...

Beneath his cloak was a visage scarcely human. Lizard-like scales the hue of rich wine covered every inch of flesh, down to lips and eyelids. His face was distended by unhinged jaws and predator's fangs, and his eyes were a gleaming, slitted gold. Nobody, not even Mariscal or Kortlaus, would have recognized Nycolos Anvarri in that image.

He didn't know if Borduen was aware that Ktho Delios was somehow working with Vircingotirilux, but he'd doubtless heard the tales of the dragon's rampages. Let the wyrm of Gronch serve *Nycos's* purposes for once. "*Look* at me, Your Majesty. Who do you *think* sent me?"

The rulers of Quindacra nearly choked on their screams.

"What do you want?" Boruden finally forced through clenched throat.

"Open warfare doesn't suit our needs at this time. We can't have Ktho Delios trying to expand its borders. So Quindacra is going to remain a faithful signatory to the southern nations' treaty."

"How... How could you possibly—?"

"You are going to send couriers to the court of every other pact nation, with a sealed message. In it, you are going to declare that you pretended to go along with Ktho Delios's scheme to learn more about it, but that now you are prepared to share that information with your allies. You will, then, proceed to detail everything—dates, names, methods of contact, *everything*. They won't believe you, but they'll accept the explanation if it means keeping you as an ally, and it will allow you to save face."

"You can't—"

"Don't send only one messenger to each nation. Send five or six, to make *certain* the message arrives. You will follow that up by sending ambassadors back to all the other courts. You will also make a public proclamation to your citizens, explaining how Ktho Delios approached you to be part of their dishonest, unworthy scheme, and how you are assisting your neighbors in standing up to them. Use words such as 'honor' and 'loyalty' and 'as the gods would expect of you.' Humans seem to respond well to that sort of thing."

The queen spoke for the first time, through trembling lips. "Won't... won't that let Ktho Delios know that we've turned on them? They're... They've almost certainly got people in Vidiir, watching."

"Yes, it will. You won't have the option of changing sides yet again."

"You don't understand!" Boruden was practically begging, woefully unkingly behavior. "Quindacra could gain so much from—"

Nycos hissed, a hideous reptilian sound. "This is not about your nation! This is about you, your delusions of persecution and poverty! You will gain nothing! But let me explain what you have to *lose*.

"If you turn on Ktho Delios, you will anger them, but they cannot attack you, not without facing every other nation of the south. But if you do *not* do as I say, your Majesties, you die. Pure and simple. You have no comprehension of what I am, what I can do. You cannot keep me out. You cannot hide from me. And even if you could, you have *no* defenses against the one I serve. We have spared your nation from our ravages thus far." *Because the Ktho Delians think you an ally, but you needn't know that.* "That can change."

Nycos moved around the bed, so he now stood at the foot of the mattress. "While I think it unlikely, it's possible I've misjudged you. It is possible that fear for your own lives isn't the motivator I think it to be. So I leave you with this."

He reached into his pouch and tossed onto the bed the item he'd taken from the adjoining room, where he'd killed the unfortunate servant. It was a toy animal, a knitted and stuffed unicorn, taken from where the royal couple's youngest child had dropped it sometime during the day.

"Your lives are not the only ones forfeit if you disobey." He stepped back, knowing that, to their limited vision, he had faded into the shadows. He would, he decided, break the latch on the door as he departed. Without the rope to summon aid, it would take the king and queen some time to get out or attract attention, giving him plenty of opportunity to vacate the castle. "I am going to intercept several of your couriers, chosen at random. If the messages do not read as I have instructed, if their orders are anything other than I've instructed, if you haven't delivered your address to your people *before the sun sets tomorrow*... Then I will be having this conversation with your successors the day after.

"And those successors will *not* be your children. Have a lovely night, your Majesties, and try to get some sleep. You've a busy day ahead of you."

# CHAPTER TWENTY-SEVEN

Baron Kortlaus and Crown Marshal Laszlan proceeded up the gently winding stairs with the too-steady and overly precise steps of men fully aware they've imbibed just a little bit more than they ought.

The bulk of the evening, over which much wine was consumed, had been spent in discussions of a martial nature. Orban held many such meetings with a variety of nobles and officers, putting together countless possible plans and counter-plans for the moment Ktho Delios finally made their move. Kortlaus was present for of those sessions, as one of Orban's three—or two, to hear him speak of it now—possible successors. Tonight, however, he'd attended not as a potential Crown Marshal, but as Baron of Urwath, since the territories and strategies under consideration involved his own lands and soldiers.

Once the borders on the map had begun to move under their own power—an effect, to be fair, caused as much by exhaustion as by drink—they'd elected to wrap up the conversation. The talk, then, had turned to more personal matters, a discussion that continued as the baron politely walked the old marshal back to his quarters.

"...doesn't matter," Orban explained as the steps gave way to carpeted, lantern-lit hallway, "how sure you are that you won't let your affections influence how you command him in battle. It *will* interfere. You'll find yourself wondering, 'Does his station really need to be over *there*, where it's so dangerous? Surely he could do just as much good over *here*.'"

"I don't know, Orban, I really feel I could separate—"

"We all do, initially. But you can't. And even if you could? He won't believe it. He'll wonder if he's earned every opportunity you give, every choice assignment, or if you're doing him personal favors. He'll wonder if every shit duty you give him is you *compensating* for any potential influence. And what about the other men and women under you? They'll wonder the same. It breeds resentment, and resentment between a commander and his soldiers is lethal. To people and possibly to nations."

They turned a corner, the shadows around them seeming to dance in time with their footsteps. "You make it sound as though a bit of dallying is going to bring all of Kirresc crashing down."

"It probably won't. But it's not impossible. There's a reason we have rules about officers fraternizing with soldiers under their command. And while those don't necessarily bind you, as baron and lord of your own vassals, let us just say that it remains a *strong* suggestion."

"How strong?"

"'Keep it behind your codpiece where your subordinates are concerned if you ever want to be Crown Marshal, or to prevent your troops from being co-opted by royal decree' strong."

"Ah. That *is* strong."

"Isn't it, though?" Orban suddenly laughed. "I promise you, you're not the first officer *or* nobleman I've had this talk with, Kortlaus. You'll get over it."

"Oh, I've no doubt. When did you and his Majesty have it?"

The Crown Marshal froze, and Kortlaus—feeling suddenly a lot more sober—wondered if he'd just stepped in something too deep to easily yank himself out. But while Orban's smile turned sheepish, it didn't fade. "Would you prefer the official response to that, or the unofficial one?"

"How about both?"

"The truth is, King Hasyan and I *did* give this a lot of thought, before we... became too deeply involved. I've a signed and sealed royal proclamation, granting me permission to ignore even the king's own commands if I ever feel they're intended to protect me at the cost of a military objective or any of my people."

Kortlaus boggled.

"That's the official response," the marshal continued. "Unofficially? Um, I'm an old hypocrite, and you should do as I say, not as I do."

Between the wine and his relief at not having offended the man who held his future in his hands, Kortlaus's laughter was more uproarious than the comment warranted. Either way, however, both men were in high spirits when they finally reached the door to the marshal's quarters.

"Remember," Orban said. "We've an early morning briefing with Sir Jancsiv and Dame Zirresca on saddlery and barding stockpiles."

Kortlaus groaned aloud and staggered theatrically against a buttress in the stone. "Surely we can put that off for later in the day!"

"Not a chance. My schedule's too full, and if *I'm* rising early after tonight, *you're* rising early."

The baron sighed loudly. "Taskmaster."

"And don't you forget it."

The younger man began to walk away, and then, unable to help himself, "Orban, have you heard any news of—?"

"The idiot? No." As always when the subject of Nycolos Anvarri came up, the Crown Marshal sounded equal parts furious and afraid. "No, I have not."

He'd known better, but it had been over a week since he'd last asked. Worry had gotten the better of him. He *definitely* knew better than to press the topic. "Understood. Sleep well, Marshal."

Orban grunted something vaguely polite. Kortlaus left him fumbling at his door, retracing his steps down the hall and wishing his own quarters were nearer.

What the hell was Nycos thinking?! Did he understand what he'd done, how much trouble he was in, the opportunity he'd assuredly torched without hope of repair? Kortlaus had no doubt his old friend believed he was doing something important, something right, but he still wanted to strangle the man with his bare hands. He'd only barely climbed back into everyone's good graces from the *first* time he'd pulled something like this. He couldn't possibly have thought he'd be allowed to do so twice!

As he'd done so many times, Kortlaus silently begged the gods and the heavens for some kind of answer, some flash of insight that would make Nycos's actions make sense. And as every time before, they failed to answer.

This time, though, Kortlaus heard *something*. The clatter of toppling furniture, the familiar limp thump of a falling body...

He shouted, calling for help from whomever might hear him, even as he pounded back toward the marshal's chamber. He hit the door hard, shoulder first, unconcerned now with courtesy or propriety.

The room beyond was unlit, a murky swirl of shadows as unsteady as a wind-swept pool. Still, the illumination from the hallway peeked furtively around the corner, enabling him to make out a pair of figures—one sprawled awkwardly beside the table, the other standing, one hand raised high and clutching a blade that reflected the feeble gleam.

Again Kortlaus cried out, tensing to spring at the mysterious figure, enraged beyond measure that anyone would dare attack the old Crown Marshal here in his own home, in the safety of Oztyerva Palace. And then he too collapsed, a flash of agony swiftly fading into soothing unconsciousness, felled from behind by a second assailant he'd never seen.

———

The commotion spread through an entire wing of the palace. Servants and soldiers raced through the halls, drawn first by alarmed shouts and then by frantic commands as word of what had happened spread through Oztyerva. Nobles awakened to the furor and either opened their doors to learn more or barricaded them for extra safety against the unknown tumult, depending upon their individual natures.

All save one particular nobleman, who did neither.

He'd known this was coming, if not tonight then soon enough. He'd arranged it, provided servants' garb, patrol schedules, the layout of Oztyerva, everything necessary to make it possible. Still it came as a shock to hear it actually happening. Only now was it real, and he felt as though the blood had drained not merely from his face but his entire body. He grew weak, dizzy, and found himself kneeling beside his great, almost decadently lush bed.

He'd done what he must. With so much at stake, he'd *had* to take such drastic steps! Not just for his own ambitions, but for the greater good!

They'd *made* him do this!

Margrave Andarjin tried so very hard to pray, but even the gods could hardly have understood him through the tears he would never have shed before another living soul.

———

Saying only that he needed to be sure his plan had worked, Nycos had insisted on remaining in the vicinity of Vidiir for another couple of days. In that time, he'd snuck back into the city to ensure King Boruden carried through with his proclamation, and that the messengers were dispatched as ordered. Nycos was fully prepared to pay the royal couple another visit if necessary, despite the fact that Castle Auric was now swarming with additional soldiers. Fortunately, it *hadn't* proved necessary. Whether fearful for their own lives (a threat on which Nycos would have followed through without a second thought) or for their children (a threat Nycos honestly didn't know if he'd have carried out), the king and queen obeyed. They addressed the populace from the walls of Castle Auric, and indeed dispatched several dozen couriers—couriers who, to judge by the one Nycos intercepted on the snowy highway, carried precisely the message he'd demanded.

It had been, all told, a brute force effort, but Nycos was convinced that was why it had worked. Facing a known opponent or diplomatic pressures, Boruden would have been in his element. This? A monster in his own bedchamber? He'd been helpless. Perhaps he might eventually have devised some scheme or deception to get around the problem, but that was why Nycos had given him no time to think.

Unfortunately, Nycos had decided, he himself was also out of time. He'd something he needed to do, and he'd already put it off as long as possible.

After scouring the grasslands around Vidiir for a while, he finally found a rock large and flat enough to serve his purposes. Hauling it from the earth, he'd then carried it to the nearest copse of trees and settled within.

Wincing in anticipation, he laid his left hand on the rock. An instant's focus, and the fingertips of both hands again transformed into those fearsome, piercing talons.

With utmost care, he placed the tips of his right-hand claws against the first knuckles of his left hand; any higher and he wouldn't get the roots. A deep shout in defiance of the pain to come, to summon the fortitude he needed, and he pressed his right hand down, hard, until talons met rock.

A few moments drifted by as he caught his breath, allowed the first wave of shock and pain to subside. With his undamaged hand, he carefully collected the claws he'd severed from the other, wrapped them and slid them into his pack.

Silbeth's frustration and irritation shifted to concern when he'd wandered back to camp, his left hand swathed in bloody bandages. "What happened?!"

"Tree branch broke when I was trying to climb, get a better view of the surroundings."

And just like that, her concern faded. "In this weather? Ten feet up or a hundred, you couldn't see a dancing manticore more than a few yards out. If you're going to lie to me, Nycos, at least pretend you don't think I'm an idiot."

Smim snickered. Nycos cast a sidelong glare, and the snickering abruptly stopped. Without another word, he'd begun to strike camp.

Thanks to winter's various moods and leavings, to say nothing of the lack of convenient highways, it took them almost a week to reach Quindacra's border and pass into neighboring Wenslir—deliberately far from any official crossings. The countryside didn't change much, nor were there any obvious markers out here in the wild, so the precise moment of transition was something of a guess. It hadn't been long, however, before they'd stumbled upon what had once been a Wenslirran village, now a charred skeleton half-buried by snow. Not merely the buildings, but the surrounding trees, had been razed by a flame so brutally intense that, in its hottest spots, even ash hadn't survived.

"I've never seen a fire that could do this," Silbeth whispered as they picked their way past the lonely ruin.

"I have," was the only reply Nycos could make.

Later that afternoon, he'd steered Avalanche over to pace beside her—a simple act made frustrating by his still-healing hand. "Silbeth, how does your religious devotion to an assignment impact your behavior after the assignment's complete?"

Rather understandably, she blinked at him. "You're going to need to clarify that a bit."

"I mean…" His grip on the reins saved him from waving his hands about and making himself look even more foolish. "You're here to keep me safe."

"Ostensibly. Something I'd feel a lot more confident about if you weren't constantly running off and keeping things from me."

"No doubt. But, suppose you were to... learn something about my past." He kept his gaze firmly, stiffly forward. "A secret that, were it to come out, would cause me great harm."

"Then," she said thoughtfully, "as long as this secret in no way meant that I'd been misled as to the nature of the job I'd undertaken, I'd be obliged to keep it."

"But only so long as the assignment lasted?"

It was an odd look for her, but Silbeth fidgeted in her saddle. "It's a murky area," she admitted finally. "I would... probably keep it to myself anyway. Unless I felt doing so was going to severely harm others, or a future contract somehow required me to reveal it."

Nycos slumped. "So you couldn't *guarantee* you'd never speak of it."

"No. No, I couldn't make that promise." Then, clearly sensing the unspoken importance, she added, "I'm sorry."

*So am I.* It startled him how much so, and he realized— much to his own chagrin—how deeply he wanted to be able to trust her, to stop keeping her in the dark as he had been.

It made sense, though. No matter how strongly the Priory of Steel considered its members' assignments to carry the weight of religious writ, that devotion had to end when the job did. Otherwise, they couldn't commit equally to the next one, or the next.

Except... Silbeth's faith shone through the lens of the Priory, but it wasn't *to* the Priory, was it?

"What if you swore an oath?" he asked. "In Louros's name, separate from any ties Mariscal's contract might establish between you and me?"

"If I swore such an oath, of course I would keep it. Which is why I won't do it. Put plainly, Nycos, I don't trust you that much. I'm not going to let you bind me without knowing to what end."

For a time they rode without speaking, each listening to the patter of light hail bouncing from their cloaks and from the frozen soil around them.

"I don't want to put you in this position," Nycos began sincerely.

"Then don't."

He had to force his hands not to drop the reins, to reach out, beseeching. "But we've *both* got our backs up against a wall. You can't complete your task if I run off without you—and before you say anything, we both know I can lose you if I truly wish it. And I can't do what I have to do with you around, if I can't be absolutely positive of your discretion."

Nycos swore, despite the climate, that he was about to sweat beneath the heat of her glower. "If your intent here is to *increase* my willingness to trust you, Sir Nycolos, you have *impressively* missed your mark."

"I know."

It was clearly not the response she'd anticipated.

"I could—some would say *should*—have just vanished one night," he continued, "without bringing this up at all. But the truth is, I don't *want* to continue this journey without you. I'd rather have you fighting at my side. I'm not trying to extort you into giving me your oath where you'd rather not, Silbeth. I'm trying to find an excuse not to leave you behind."

"I see. I'll… think about it."

"That's all I can ask."

"So go away and let me think."

Nycos fell back, allowing her to ride alone, a short distance ahead. He felt absolutely zero surprise when Smim's own steed swiftly sauntered up beside him.

"Master, this has gone far enough."

"Has it?"

"You cannot truly mean to trust her, or *any* human, with the truth!"

"Smim, I live among them, *as* one of them, and yet I'm unable to talk about, or act on, the central facet of my being. It's maddening!"

The goblin shook his head hard enough to set tiny hailstones flying. "I don't understand. You spent centuries at a time alone, save for your servants! Sharing with others wasn't precisely on your list of priorities."

"I'm... I know. But you were the one who pointed out, months ago, that my human body, human blood, was affecting me. I can't pretend you were wrong any longer."

"And what of me, Master? You've always been able to speak freely with me."

"Smim, you've been a loyal servant, and even a friend, since my transformation. But you're still a part of my old life, and an outsider to human culture. I need... It's not enough."

"Master, you *cannot* trust her with this! Not her, not anyone! You're going to get yourself killed, and quite possibly me along with you."

"You worry too much, Smim. I know what I'm doing."

Oh, how he wished *that* were true! All he could do, for now, was hope that Smim wouldn't do anything stupid "for his master's sake" until Nycos *had* figured out just what the hell he was doing.

———

Another few days nearer to Gronch, and Nycos decided it was time they properly arm themselves.

They'd stopped for a midday meal, sitting in the lee of a tiny rise that barely qualified as a hill, and he'd announced that they should set up their tents against the cold, start a fire—essentially make camp.

"We've still got a good few hours before it gets dark," Silbeth protested. "Why waste the travel time?"

"Because," Nycos said, carefully unwrapping that long, narrow bundle on which the mercenary had remarked back when they'd first snuck from the Oztyerva stables, "we've some preparations to make before we reach the Ogre-Weald."

Laid out upon the snow, the leather parcel revealed a couple of long prybars, a slightly shorter hook-beaked crowbar, and two bars of iron fencing. Beside them, tied together in a smaller bundle, were a blacksmith's hammer and tongs.

"Um?" Silbeth asked after taking it all in.

"Wooden hafts," Nycos explained, hefting his own *szanzsya* for emphasis, "would be too weak for what we need. Everything here is iron or steel. They'll be heavy, but I think you're strong enough to wield them. I know I am."

"We're making dragon-slaying weapons," she summarized flatly.

"Yes."

"And wood isn't strong enough."

"Correct."

"And the fact that we've both got perfectly good swords isn't relevant because…?"

"Why do you suppose it normally takes an army, or an enchanted blade, for humans to kill a dragon, Silbeth? For all the strength, the speed, the breath of flame, it's the dragon's hide that makes them nigh invulnerable."

Smim made soft choking sounds. The knight ignored him—just as he ignored his own twisting, conflicting emotions at exposing the weaknesses of his kind.

"Our swords wouldn't penetrate the scales," he continued. "We need weapons that will, or we've no chance at all."

Silbeth grunted, reached down and lifted one of the prybars. For a few moments she spun it around her body, thrust with both hands, running through an array of lunges and parries. When she was done, her breath had grown labored and she had to wipe away a sheen of sweat before it froze, but she nodded. "Heavy, and the balance is for shit, but manageable. I assume you've some idea for blades or tips, if you've thought it through this far?"

Nycos nodded and produced a thick pouch, from which he in turn poured the five black talons he'd sliced from his own hand days before. "Slivers of Tzavalantzaval's own claws," he said in what wasn't *entirely* a lie. "Smim and I kept them as trophies after the battle."

It had been long enough, he hoped, that Silbeth wouldn't think to associate these five talons with his injured digits. Even if she did, though, he'd spent enough mystical effort on forcing his hand back into its original human shape that not even a close examination would suggest that, mere days ago, he'd literally been missing his fingertips.

Whatever thoughts she had, however, whatever suspicions she may or may not have nursed, she said nothing of them. She only nodded once more, after a brief examination of the talons.

"I need space to work," Nycos said, "where we're not going to set fire to anything." He shortly had Silbeth and Smim excavating a circle in not just the snow but the frigid soil, building a small bank of earth, while he ostensibly went off to search for stones they might use to augment that miniature barrier.

Once out of sight, he removed a small metal flask from his belt. Concentrating on his throat and jaw, he felt the flesh warp, shift. Careful not to spill, he worked up multiple mouthfuls of draconic spittle and deposited them into the flask. It would retain its potency for only a few hours, but that ought to be enough.

He had little luck with the stones, but then, he hadn't really anticipated otherwise. The banked sides of the earthen circle would do. Returning to the camp, he laid out the wood for a small fire near the center of the cleared space, and the five iron "spear shafts" beside it. Finally—after claiming for Silbeth's benefit that the flask contained more of the goblin's alchemical mixture he had wielded against the *psoglavac*—he coated the narrower ends of the various tools with the spittle.

It all worked about as well as he'd hoped. As each tool was thrust into the small flame, igniting the dragonfire, the sudden burst of supernatural heat bent and softened the metal. From there it was a simple matter of taking a talon in the blacksmith's tongs and thrusting it base-first into the now pliable shaft, followed by a few blows of the hammer to ensure it was secure and more or less straight. It was sloppy, ugly, but "it would suffice.

Smim cooked them a hot stew that night, rich enough to warm them—though he hadn't been able to do much about the taste of the salted meats of which they were all growing heartily tired. Clustered around the campfire, they discussed tactics and techniques for battling dragons: the need to surprise the wyrm with their ability to harm it, to keep the fight in a contained space as best they could, to always have cover close at hand. Nycos even offered up some pointers and observations on Vircingotirilux herself, claiming to have heard tales of the wyrm of Gronch from Smim, who had in turn heard them from Tzavalantzaval.

Silbeth took it all in, listening intently, asking for clarification on this point or that, but otherwise offering no comment, no observation of her own. She'd still given no oath of secrecy, and Nycos went to sleep that night wondering just what the mercenary was thinking.

What she suspected.

Tomorrow morning, then. He hadn't wanted to push the issue, but he *had* to have an answer, one way or the other, tomorrow morning.

Because come tomorrow evening, they would stand within the shadow of Gronch.

———

"All right."

Hunched tight against the frigid morning, Nycos wasn't certain he'd heard correctly. He'd been reluctant, even sheepish, bringing it up, and he'd anticipated, at the very least, a bit more discussion.

"I'll swear to keep your secret," Silbeth continued, calmly dismantling her tent as she spoke. "But only so long as you're alive. Your death frees me to choose whether it warrants exposure or not."

"I…" The caveat made him nervous, but he saw no specific harm in it. "Fair enough. Thank—"

"Don't. Don't thank me, Nycos. I haven't yet shown you the other side of this particular coin you'd have me pay with."

He waited. She rolled up the canvas, stuffed it in her backpack, and then turned to face him. "If anything I learn suggests to me that I've been deceived into committing acts, supporting a cause, I find abhorrent? If I decide your secret makes you too much of a threat? I will stop at nothing to free myself from my oath."

"But you just said your oath binds you so long as I'm… Oh."

"Can you accept that?"

Smlm was all but hopping foot to foot behind him. "Master, might I have a word with you before you—"

"I can," Nycos said.

The goblin spat a variety of syllables that might just have inspired Silbeth to behead him if she'd understood what they meant.

"Then I swear by my honor as one chosen to serve the Priory of Steel, and by Louros, Lady of the Moons and protector of all who travel in darkness, to keep your secrets, Sir Nycolos Anvarri, until your death or my own."

"Oh-ho! Options!" Smim crowed.

"Hush, Smim. Silbeth, thank you."

She waited a moment, perhaps to see if he were going to reveal anything immediately, and then went about striking camp.

So, now what? Some humans would violate even the most sacred oath if circumstances warranted. He didn't believe Silbeth was among them, but could he be certain? He didn't know her nearly as well as he sometimes felt he did. And even if she'd keep his secret, if she discovered who he was—and who he wasn't—would that constitute a threat? An unforgivable deception? Would he be forced to kill her?

After all that, could he really trust her any more now than he had? He wanted to, desperately, and he hated that he did.

Maybe... Maybe luck would be with him. Maybe he could yet get through this without revealing himself more than he already had. He couldn't erase her suspicions or questions, but those would fade in time if she never saw, never learned, anything that might feed them.

His thoughts racing like maddened hounds, Nycos clambered up into Avalanche's saddle and began the first of the day's many fretful, worried miles.

# CHAPTER TWENTY-EIGHT

The trees stood packed together, branches intertwined. Untamed beards of moss hung from jowls of rough bark, and the undergrowth—as much fungi as vegetation, and far moister than it ought to be—slurped obscenely at passing shins.

Even accounting for the lack of wind and sleet, both blocked by the thick woods, it was warmer than it should have been. The air still carried winter's bite, enough to cause a shiver, yet the boles seemed to generate their own humidity, a sticky warmth that not only clung to the skin but somehow seeped inside. The result was an unpleasant, vaguely feverish blend of sensation to make the flesh crawl and the stomach roil.

After lengthy debate, they'd left Avalanche and the rest of the mounts at the edge of the great wood. Tethering them wasn't an option, in case they had to run or defend themselves from ogres or other threats, so all Nycos and the others could do was trust in the strict Kirresci warhorse training to keep them there for the duration. After hours of slow trail-breaking through this damnable forest, though, with the bundle of makeshift spears slung over his back and catching on every single obstruction and protrusion the place thrust in their path, Nycos would have gladly traded places with them.

Smim muttered constantly under his breath in the language of his people, jumping at every sound, snarling at every upthrust root. Silbeth, on the other hand, was almost hostilely silent, lips pressed together until they'd gone as pale as her skin.

Nycos found both grating, though he couldn't blame either of them. He wanted to lash out with *szandzsya* or clenched fist, not merely at any perceived danger hidden within the trees but at those trees themselves, to clear a space in the woodland that seemed to grow tighter by the step. It was crushing, suffocating, as though Gronch itself sought to swallow them whole. He realized he was breathin hard and forced himself to calm, drawing upon centuries of patience and self-control.

He shoved a branch from his path, hissing in the back of his throat at the greasy feel of whatever grew upon the bark, and slipped past. The limb bounced back into place and he heard sharp gasp.

"Watch it, you jackass!"

He spun, literally growling. Silbeth stood behind him, a dark smear streaking her cloak and mail hauberk where the branch had lashed them.

"I trust my companions to be able to watch out for themselves," he retorted in a harsh rasp. "If you can't even do that much—"

"I can watch out for myself just fine, it's the idiots around me that are posing a problem!"

Smim advanced on her, hand on the hilt of his short sword, a low rumble in his throat Nycos had heard from other goblins in his time.

"Look," Nycos said, fists shaking with the effort of swallowing his mounting fury, "let's all take a breath and—"

Fast enough to catch even him by surprise, Silbeth's blade was in her hand and she hurled herself at him. In the blind confusion of what followed, it took an instant to register that she hadn't, in fact, attacked him at all. She slammed into him with her left shoulder, knocking him away from the looming bole even as she swung at something dangling from the canopy above.

Something that shrieked in frustrated rage as it scrabbled to avoid her sword.

It hung from a thick, ropey web like some great arachnid, and indeed it had six spidery legs protruding from its midsection. Before and behind those, however, it boasted four canine limbs, and its body was roughly that of a mangy, blood-slicked wolf. Its jaws gaped open as it screamed and howled, exposing a pair of oversized mandibles within. They emerged, slow and slick, tearing at the soft flesh inside its canine maw until thin streams of saliva-diluted blood dribbled to the earth.

"What in the name of...?"

Even had Nycos known how to answer, he lacked the time. For while Silbeth was focused on the nightmare above, he spotted another threat below.

"Smim, stop!"

Too far gone to obey, perhaps even to understand, the goblin leapt for Silbeth, mouth wide in a drooling howl, cleaving sword raised high.

Nycos, uncaring now what Silbeth saw, lunged with impossible speed to meet him. Gripping the sabre-spear backward, just below the blade, Nycos swung the butt end as a club, catching Smim in the gut and knocking him back to the soil. He continued the turn, letting the momentum carry him around even as he spun the *szandzsya* and then, trusting in desperate strength to make up for the weapon's utter lack of aerodynamics, he threw.

Threw and missed. The hideous creature on its web dropped a foot or so, easily avoiding the clumsy, wobbling missile. It chittered at him, mandibles clacking and throat wobbling in a grotesque song of mockery.

Silbeth leapt, swung, and the tip of her blade sliced neatly through the distracted monstrosity's stomach.

Loops of ichor-smeared and *cobweb-coated* intestines spilled forth, coiling and bouncing. The beast plummeted with an agonized shriek to land, twitching and kicking, at Silbeth's feet. Her sword rose and fell, again and again, and Nycos turned back to the disobedient goblin, confident that his companion had the other creature in hand.

Smim lay beside a puddle of vomit, still dry-heaving from the blow to his gut. Nonetheless his fingers remained clenched around the hilt of his weapon and he struggled to roll over, to drag himself toward Silbeth.

"Smim? Smim!"

Nycos saw no recognition, only the instinctual, fearful hatred so common to Smim's people. The goblin screamed at him, and the sounds only vaguely resembled words.

Wrath flooded Nycos's heart. How *dare* he?! How dare this pathetic little creature defy him, turn on him now, of all times? He raised a hand, preparing to transform fingertips into talons and end the wretched, dishonorable beast…

*No.*

He couldn't stop himself from striking. The anger was too strong for that. But when he did, it was with a human fist, with roughly human strength. The goblin spasmed, face gone slack.

"Rope."

"What?" Silbeth finally stopped hacking at the thing, now long past dead and verging on no longer entirely solid.

"Bring me some rope."

"Get it yourself, you—!" She stopped, stared at her ichor-coated sword, and took a deep, shuddering breath. Carefully she lay the weapon down and retrieved a large coil of rope from the side of her own pack.

"Sorry," she muttered, stepping close and handing it over.

"Not your fault. Not mine. Not even his." Nycos played out a length of the hemp line and carefully tied the goblin's arms and feet. "Something about this place. It's… getting to us. On an emotional level. Maybe spiritual."

Was this part of why Vircingotirilux was mad? Had her home driven her out of what was left of her mind? Or the reverse, perhaps. Had her madness somehow spread through Gronch itself?

Then again, maybe neither. Maybe she was just drawn to the place, her broken mind having found comfort here.

"We've got to move," he said, hefting Smim over one shoulder and casting about for his missing weapon. "All that screaming's likely to have attracted attention."

Silbeth only nodded, took a moment to retrieve a rag from her backpack, and then collected her sword. She wiped the worst of the grime from it as they walked.

"I've never seen anyone move that fast," she said finally, dodging around a particularly gnarled tree. "When you stopped Smim, I mean. Thank you. But how did you do that?"

Even in her gratitude, she had to push, didn't she? To question? Why couldn't she just—?

*Calm.*

Nycos grunted, not trusting himself to answer, and Silbeth, perhaps for the sake of her own self-control, fell back into silence rather than press the issue.

Whether it was the tumult of the earlier struggle or something more subtle—their scent, perhaps, or even some primal awareness within the denizens of the Ogre-Weald—the trio indeed attracted further attention. On multiple occasions they had to dive for cover or scurry into the shelter of the underbrush, concealing themselves amidst thistles and dead leaves. Once, they hid from a creature near twelve feet in height, with the gait and build of an ape but a slick, cracked carapace that resembled nothing more than the enamel of a human tooth. Other times they never clearly saw what it was that stalked them, but one of the ogres walked with so heavy a tread, rustling the branches so high above, that Nycos thought it might have looked big to him even if he wore his true form.

Either Smim had regained some semblance of his civilized self, or else even in his maddened, monstrous state of mind, the goblin recognized the danger. Whatever his motivation, the bound figure went as silent as Nycos and Silbeth when stealth was called for.

On other occasions, hiding was no option at all.

———

The club, nearly a small tree in its own right, hurtled toward Silbeth with enough force to turn organs and bone into something akin to pudding. Nycos threw himself into the weapon's path, as near the ogre's fist as possible, in hopes of avoiding the worst of the impact. Still it sent him flying to collide hard with a heavy bole. He slumped amidst the roots, head ringing and spine screaming, watching dully as his *szandzsya* once more spun off into the shadows of Gronch.

But at least he'd gotten the thing's attention, drawn it away from his companions. *Fantastic. And the next step in my brilliant plan was...?*

Other than the massive cudgel instead of a rusty axe, the *psoglavac* looked very much like the one that had attacked King Hasyan's court. It was, if anything, a bit larger, and somehow smelled even more foul. Its single eye gleamed with the same fury, however, and its slathering jaws suggested similar vile appetites.

"Get the spears!" he called as the ogre closed on him, each footfall landing with limp, meaty thud. "They should penetrate its hide!"

So too, of course, would his own talons, but he still clung to a faint hope of keeping *some* of his secrets.

Silbeth dived for the parcel of makeshift weapons, which he'd dropped as he'd charged the *psoglavac*, fumbling at the ties. She'd have the shafts free swiftly, but he could see already it wouldn't be swift *enough*.

The club crashed down and Nycos rolled aside, ignoring the discomfort as protruding roots poked at his back and sides, bruising even through the mail. He rolled back just as swiftly, grasping the weapon under one arm and bringing the heel of his boot down upon the fingers that clutched it.

It wasn't sufficient to break bone, but he struck with far more strength, far more pain, than the ogre anticipated. It reared back with a low roar, dropping the weapon as it tried to shake the agony from its hand.

Nycos shot to his feet just as the *psoglavac* lunged down at him, determined to tear him apart. Palms met and fingers—one set far larger and more twisted than the other—curled around and between each other. Fists clenched, hoping to crush, and the two combatants strained.

The ogre had every apparent advantage. Its height, its mass, the fact that it stood tall while Nycos had only half come out of his crouch... This should not, could not, have been a contest at all.

Slowly, inexorably, impossibly, Nycos straightened. The *psoglavac* gawped in dumb incomprehension as first its arms were lifted upward, and then, even more unbelievably, its tinier, "weaker" foe began to force it back. No matter how it strained, how it shoved, it couldn't stop itself; one backward step, a second.

Again the ogre shrieked, its back arching and its whole body shuddering, as Silbeth drove a talon-tipped prybar through it from behind.

Nycos stepped aside as the *psoglavac* toppled to its knees where he'd stood. Silbeth pulled the spear free and thrust again, over and over, until the creature's back was nothing more than a cluster of weeping wounds. It whimpered a final time and collapsed, blood oozing from its injuries and its slackened jaw.

"That's a lot easier when we've got weapons that can actually hurt the damn things," Nycos noted. "Very nice job, Silbeth. I..."

She hadn't lowered the blood-coated spear, despite its weight. In fact, while it wasn't precisely aimed his way, it wasn't really aimed anywhere else, either.

"No more, Nycos. No more keeping me in the dark. I saw what happened back there. Nobody could outmuscle that thing. *Nobody.*"

"It… You must have seen us from a weird angle, is all. It—"

"No. You made me swear that damn oath. Now you're going to tell me why. Who are you? *What* are you?"

Nycos raised a hand, imploring—and froze.

He'd pushed it too far. Digging deep for the strength to battle the *psoglavac*, he'd allowed his body to reshape itself too much, asked it to provide more power than it could manage while remaining human. The hand he'd stretched out between them was thicker than it should have been, slightly misshapen, and streaked with jagged patches of deep violet scale.

"Master!" Although ragged around the edges, the voice of the tightly bound goblin was nearer that of his servant and friend than it was the ravening beast he'd become over the past few days. "No! You mustn't!"

In a way, he didn't have to. Silbeth's eyes flickered to Smim—as though this were the first time she'd truly heard, truly *understood*, the title of "master" from his lips—and then back to the splotches on Nycos's skin.

And she knew. He saw it in her face before she spoke another word.

"Oh, my gods…"

"I suppose," Nycos said with exaggerated resignation, "you're going to feel this qualifies as deceiving you?"

Silbeth stared as though she couldn't possibly have heard him correctly. Her eyes were nearly as wide as her buckler, her gaping jaw struggled to form words her brain clearly hadn't yet concocted.

And then, despite herself, she laughed. It was, bar none, the loudest he'd ever heard her, either unwilling or unable to control herself despite the risk of drawing further attention.

Body-shaking guffaws doubled her over. Tears ran down her ever ruddier face as she gasped for breath.

Nycos wasn't sure when he'd joined her, only that he found himself bracing with one arm against rough bark, counting on the nearest tree to keep him from toppling in his mirth.

"Might I impose on one of you to untie me before you go completely mad?" Smim demanded irritably, resulting in a new round of near hysterics.

When they finally regained control, Nycos and Silbeth faced one another, each half slumped against an opposing bole. Although it was most probably a temporary balm, he realized that the fit of uncontrolled laughter had washed away a goodly portion of the feverish temper that had beleaguered them since they'd entered this cursed wood.

"Why," she asked, coughing to keep from falling back into laughter, "would you *possibly* think I'd consider this a deception?"

Nycos grinned, but swiftly composed himself. "Silbeth, we've fought together. We've watched one another's backs." He didn't specifically mention throwing himself in front of the *psoglavac*'s club for her—he knew she'd take it as manipulative if he did—but he knew, as well, she hadn't forgotten. "And I've made no move to harm the people at Oztyerva, or anywhere else, save where Nycolos Anvarri would and should have done. Surely all that buys me at least the opportunity to explain."

She nodded slowly and planted the butt of the iron spear beside her—still ready at hand, but not immediately threatening. "Explain, then."

And he did. There, in the deepening gloom of Gronch, as though the constant threat of the haunting ogres and related nightmares had receded, he told his tale—his true tale—for the first time. From the arrival of the real Sir Nycolos in the Outermark Mountains up until that very night, and if he didn't tell her everything, neither did he lie or dissemble. He made no effort to paint himself as selfless, heroic, to pretend that he cared for the bulk of the Kirresci people. He had no desire to lie to Silbeth, and it wouldn't sound believable if he had. No, instead he confessed openly that his initial goal had been to build for himself the most comfortable and most powerful life he could among the humans, to live as well as he might until and unless he could resume his proper existence. And he told her that, over the year and more he'd dwelt among them, he had come to value a handful of Oztyerva's people, that he'd grown fond enough of them, beyond their practical use to him, that he'd prefer they come to no harm.

Nycos hadn't especially considered the truth to be a burden, so he didn't feel like any great weight had been lifted from him. Rather, he himself seemed lighter. Less alone.

He'd scarcely known loneliness as a dragon, for camaraderie, sharing, was not in their nature. It had taken him long to recognize the feeling as a man, and only now did he understand how strongly it had enwrapped him.

For long moments she watched him, absorbing and pondering all he'd told her. In the gloom of the Ogre-Wealde, he couldn't have been more than an inky shade, but she gazed into him as though measuring every detail, reading the secrets of his soul.

"We *have* fought together," she said finally, slowly. "And you've put yourself in danger for me, though I don't know, now, how *much* danger you were truly in. That matters.

"And I appreciate you telling me the truth, Nyc..." She broke off, a sudden flash of puzzlement on her face that nobody but he could have seen.

"I'm still Nycolos. Nycos. Any other name wouldn't... feel right, for the time being." To say nothing of possibly proving disastrous, if the wrong person were ever to overhear.

"Right, then. Nycos." Again she paused, doubtless chasing thoughts that had scattered like a flock of quail. "My truth, then, in exchange for yours. I'm with you until the dragon—um, the other dragon—is dealt with and we've returned to Talocsa."

"And then?" He hoped the question didn't sound as plaintive to her as it did in his own ears.

"I don't know," she answered plainly. "It's too much, too big, for me to figure all out at once. I need time to think."

To that, he could only nod. He found himself deeply disappointed, but she was right. It *was* a lot to ask her to take in; hardly unfair or unreasonable of her to need time. No matter how unpleasant the waiting might be for him, or how problematic her eventual decision might prove.

"Thank you," he said at last, "for being honest about it."

"I did *think* about lying," she admitted. "Telling you I was all right with it. Some would say I'm being foolish, that I've invited you to try to kill me in my sleep or something, now. But as I said, I owed you for *your* truth."

Nycos stood and moved over to the bound goblin. Carefully, and with a clear warning of what would happen if Smim were to lose control again, he began loosening the many knots. "And if I do try to kill you in your sleep?" he asked Silbeth, with what he hoped was an obviously jesting tone.

"Then one way or the other, you'll have made my decision a lot easier, won't you?" And *her* tone was such that Nycos couldn't even begin to tell whether she was jesting or not.

"Let's go find Vircingotirilux's lair," he said. It seemed, suddenly, to be the simpler, and possibly even safer, of the various challenges ahead.

———

Finding that lair proved a lengthy process, with multiple days spent searching the darkened wood and hiding from the things that dwelt within, but not a difficult one. Nycos's own past existence meant he knew what sorts of terrain and features to look for; what sort of accessibility to the sky and the surrounding territories the wyrm would most probably seek; what signs would indicate her presence.

Once they'd located the hidden caves, beneath the root-ridden hillside on the wildly overgrown shores of Lake Orist, it was again Nycos's knowledge that guided them safely inside.

For all their differences, all their varied personalities, strengths, even shapes, most dragons fell back on similar notions when protecting their homes. Vircingotirilux's minions, the ogres of Gronch, were unlikely to be found within her lair proper. Nycos knew his rival was unstable enough that nothing would survive so near her for long.

She was not sorcerously strong, her mind too twisted for the workings of great magics, but not totally lacking in eldritch skills. Guided by his own instincts and augmented by inhuman sight, he pinpointed the hidden glyphs clawed deep into earthen walls, steering his companions aside before they could trigger the mystic energies. Had he not, if he read the sigils properly, the roots would have burst through the surrounding soil, gripping and crushing like a ravenous beast of the deepest seas; or else those walls would have disgorged swarms of insects and gouts of boiling water to alternatively consume and sear the flesh of all who passed.

That left only the mechanical deadfalls for the others to watch for, while Nycos hunted for those glyphs. Between Silbeth's swift reactions and sharp sight, and Smim's own experience setting up similar (if far more intricate) devices on his master's behalf, those proved no more difficult to circumvent.

The tunnels themselves were curious, twisting, winding. In a way, they resembled the gnarled roots that dangled from the ceilings and stretched from the walls, writ large. Other than in the immediate vicinity of the glyphs, the place was completely free of crawling life, as though even the insects knew enough to keep their distance. Patches of mud formed where the water of nearby Orist leeched through the soil. A moldy, stagnant miasma coated the throat and seeped into the lungs, so that the urge to cough—not involuntary, but in a desperate effort to scratch an internal, unclean itch—grew overwhelming.

The complex really, Nycos felt, shouldn't have held its shape at all. The nearby lake ought to have rendered the earth too swampy, too shifting and unstable, for caves so large to survive. He wondered if Vircingotirilux had managed the basic sorceries required to maintain her lair, or perhaps hardened the walls with some sort of alchemical concoction or... or excretion. He shuddered at that last thought, and decided he needn't share his suspicions with the others.

And then, finally, they'd arrived in the veritable cavern that was the heart of the dragon's domain.

Mists rose from the entryways and condescension slicked the walls, for here the unnatural warmth of Gronch seemed to pool, mixing resentfully with currents of cooler air. Their footsteps squelched as the muddy floor clung hungrily at every pace. In the far corner, heaps of old branches and the stolen heirlooms of a dozen villages—candelabras, dishware, bits of furniture, jewelry, and the occasional decayed remnants of their former owners—twisted and intertwined to form a haphazard nest. Beside and beyond that was a smattering of rough shapes and vile stench: an unchecked midden, the leavings of gods alone knew how many months or years kept soggy and fresh by the chamber's humidity.

Silbeth gagged once, then cast Nycos a horrified, incredulous look.

"No. No, we do *not* all live like this. Vircingotirilux is vile. Savage. An animal."

Her grunt was noncommittal, at best, and Nycos found himself oddly embarrassed. He moved on to study the outer edges of the cavern.

High above, a crooked shaft led to the open air, though the many roots and constricting trees made it almost impossible to make out. That and the main passage through which they'd come appeared to be the only genuine entryways. Other passageways branched from the central cavern, smaller than the two major arteries but still large enough for the wyrm to slink through, yet these—to judge by scent and air current—offered no egress to the outside. If Nycos had to guess, he would have said they probably provided access to a smaller chamber or two, before winding back here.

Perhaps he'd have time to explore and make certain. For of the many sights and details the trio observed, here in the heart of Vircingotirilux's domain, the dragon herself was not among them. Without knowing where she had gone, what she was doing, when she'd departed, Nycos had no way of guessing whether she would be absent for minutes, hours, even days.

However long it might be, it was time that Nycos did not look forward to. Time in which he had little to distract himself from what he was doing, the situation into which he'd thrown himself.

He had always respected Vircingotirilux for her strength, if nothing else; known her to be a formidable enemy. He had wisely avoided conflict between them where it was unnecessary, and planned carefully when it proved unavoidable. But never, in all his centuries, could it have been said that he feared her.

Now? Trapped in this body? It had slowly begun to sink in, over the course of the journey, how great the differences between them had grown. Now that he was finally here, the doubts and worries, the sense of how much weaker he had become, wrapped him tight as a burial shroud.

Nor were his fears for himself alone. More than once he considered suggesting, demanding, even begging that Silbeth leave. What could one additional human, one *normal* human, do against the wyrm of Gronch? Less often, but still multiple times, he thought the same about Smim. Surely they would both refuse to leave him, each for his or her own reasons, but ought he not at least try? Yet he never did. Perhaps they *could* make a difference, at that, and even if not?

He didn't want to face this trial alone. He wondered if that made him a coward.

So they laid their plans, as best they could with what they knew, and risked a bit of exploration. And then there was nothing left but to settle in—spears held fast, guts clenched tight—and wait.

# CHAPTER TWENTY-NINE

When it finally happened, it happened fast.

What feeble light managed to leak in through the canopy of trees and the twists of the slanted passageway went dark. A blast of air, like the coughing of the earth itself, rushed through the passage to send the dust and the soil within the chamber swirling, followed by the deafening rumble of scales against unyielding walls.

A sudden sense of movement, a massive shape in the gloom as though a portion of the ceiling had begun to collapse—and she was there, plummeting into the cavern, a falling star made flesh.

*Vircingotirilux.*

They attacked even as she appeared, pushing through their shock at the sudden entry. As Nycos had instructed, knowing they could never land a killing blow as she moved, they stabbed at her wings, partially folded against her massive flanks. Claw-tipped iron pierced leathery membrane, and an impossible voice shrieked in startled pain. The great body twisted as it struck the floor, talons scattering new clouds of dirt to add to the ambient gloom.

Smim fell back, clutching the smallest of the spears, having only just scratched the beast. Nycos's inhuman might allowed him to maintain his grip on his own weapon as it tore at the wound, widening the ragged hole until it ripped free. Silbeth, however, lacked the strength to retain her hold. Cursing she stepped back, snatching up one of the two spare lances to replace the one still dangling from wounded wing.

They darted in again, thrusting at scale-clad flesh, but delivered only a few shallow scrapes before talons, thrashing in the dark and nigh invisible even to Nycos, drove them back.

He heard the inrush of breath, shouted a warning and dove aside, rolling across the muddy soil as a gout of hellish flame raked the chamber's floor. The fire's roar was deafening, and the trio squinted against the sudden light.

Squinted, and looked up—and up—at the great wyrm they only now clearly saw.

Those bleeding, membranous wings protruded from a gargantuan form that might have been birthed of the swamp and the forest themselves. Scales of stagnant green and mossy grey armored an awkward, twisted body. It bent and bulged where it shouldn't, not unlike a marshland tree bowed beneath the weight of ages. Vines like exposed veins ran across the brown hide between those scales, and a foul, watery fluid sluiced from beneath them with every move. Wingtips and talons appeared wooden, almost like bark.

The wyrm's body alone was forty feet long, easily twice that if one counted the writhing tail and twining…

*Necks.*

Not one but three savage heads bobbed and swayed, wrathful serpents, jaws agape and drooling a viscous, sickly spittle. The centermost twisted side to side, seeking, studying, while the right and left roared and snapped, howling their fury without intelligence or restraint. Near mindless hounds, forever bound to a master only slightly less bestial.

Vircingotirilux gazed upon the intruders, and for an instant all they could do was stare back in turn. Silbeth and Smim stood frozen, Nycos's tales having woefully failed to prepare them for horrid reality. Nycos himself had experienced the wyrm's hideous presence before, but never from such a small, limited perspective. His heart pounded, his breath caught, as terror he'd never imagined washed over him.

Silbeth broke the paralysis first, thrusting her spear at the growling snout that slid her way. The head recoiled, bloodied, snarling in fury. Vircingotirilux twisted about, bringing all three heads to bear—and taking all six eyes off Nycos long enough for him to dart forward and gouge an ugly wound into her leg just below the knee.

All three heads howled as one. The dragon reared nearly to the cavern's ceiling. Her tail whipped about, catching Smim as he attempted to run. He flew across the chamber, bouncing and rolling, and Nycos could only hope the goblin was merely bruised. He and Silbeth both leapt for safety as Vircingotirilux crashed back down upon them, claws outstretched to grind them into paste. They tumbled aside, shot back to their feet, and ran, talons slamming at their heels again and again.

One landed close enough, for all his dashing and dodging, to send Nycos sprawling. He sat up and jabbed at the massive paw, his own talons sprouting. Vircingotirilux recoiled, stunned at the blood and the pain—for all that the wound was tiny—and Nycos didn't waste the opportunity. Again he stood, scooped up the spear he'd dropped, and ran. With each step he focused on his magics, sending as much strength as he could possibly manage flowing through his body. Behind him, the wyrm inhaled like a great bellows.

Nycos reached for Silbeth, who was just about to duck into one of the cavern's many side passages. Grabbing her by collar and belt, he hurled her up and into a corridor much higher on the wall, then leapt after her. Another inferno roared beneath him and deep into the tunnel Silbeth had almost chosen, so near it burned the heel and sole from Nycos's boot, before he crashed into the tunnel wall and found himself flat on his back.

"I think this is going very well," Silbeth said, reaching out a helping hand. He paused, tearing off his ruined footwear, before accepting. She managed not to flinch as his own clawed and now clearly inhuman fist gripped hers.

"Could be worse," he agreed, pulling himself upright. They moved deeper into the tunnel, hoping to put a few twists and turns between them and any further torrents of flame.

"Please tell me you didn't look like *that*," she said a moment later, ducking beneath a protruding tree root.

"Not remotely." It was true, yet Nycos found the question oddly painful. Graceful or bestial, magnificent or fearsome, he believed wholeheartedly that all dragons were creatures of terrible beauty. He didn't expect, however, that Silbeth would understand, and now certainly was no time to explain. Instead, with a touch of bitter resentment, he went with the simpler answer. "Vircingotirilux is pretty monstrous even by our standards."

"Good to—"

Echoing from the great chamber came a monstrous grunt, followed by a grating noise that Nycos recognized as teeth on iron, and then a faint tearing.

"She's just pulled the spear out of her wing. Still, the pain should be—"

"SUCH A TEENY TINY CLAW. BUT WE KNOW THAT TASTE!"

"Oh, good," Nycos said. "She recognizes me."

"IS IT TRULY—" The monstrous voice was interrupted by a chorus of roars. "DZIRLAS! CYOLOS! DOWN! QUIET! I'M TALKING! I SAID *QUIET!*"

"Who…? Is she talking to her *other heads*?!" Silbeth demanded, voice as shrill as Nycos had ever heard. "She's insane!"

"More than a little, yes. To be fair, you'd be too if bits of you were unintelligent and only partially housebroken."

She goggled at him and said nothing more.

"IS IT YOU, TZAVALANTZAVAL?" Vircingotirilux continued. "YOU'VE LOOKED BETTER!" She cackled madly, as though her observation were the funniest thing she'd ever heard.

"We've met," Nycos told Silbeth in a whisper.

"I'd pieced that together myself, but thanks."

"YOU WERE SUPPOSED TO BE DEAD! WE WERE PROMISED YOU WERE DEAD!"

*Well, isn't* that *an interesting tidbit of—*

"DEAD AS YOUR PRECIOUS CLUTCH, SHATTERED AND SCATTERED TO THE REACHES OF YOUR ROCKY PLAYPEN!"

Deep in his throat, Nycos growled.

"It was... It was a long time ago," he reluctantly explained in response to Silbeth's unasked question, as they crept further down the narrowing corridor. "Well over a century. Vircingotirilux and I both selected the same dragon as a mate. There aren't many of us left to choose from, especially here in the south. He chose me, for reasons I think our host has made fairly clear. We thought we were being clever, hiding our eggs away from my lair, but she found it. It was the second clutch in a row I lost, and it's... one of several grudges between us."

He had never before seen the expression Silbeth now cast his way. "What?" he asked her.

"You're *female?*" she demanded.

"No, I *was* female, and will be again. But for now, the human form I've assumed is male, and the change of form is absolute." He shrugged. "Honestly, it doesn't make much difference to us. For dragons, if it's not mating season, it scarcely matters."

They reached a fork in the passage, and Nycos turned to call back toward the main chamber, where the wyrm still ranted. "Who promised you, Vircingotirilux? Who told you I was dead?"

The voice fell silent, though the two bestial heads continued to howl. "How did you find me? How did you transform your pet *psoglavac*? I know you, you poor, dumb beast! You haven't the sorcery to manage such tricks on your own!"

"Are you as mad as she is?" Silbeth demanded, as behind them, the dragon screeched indignantly.

"If I get her riled enough, she might let something slip."

The tunnel echoed with the sounds of inrushing air. Nycos shoved Silbeth down the side passage at the fork, following on her heels. Between one step and the next his body swelled, the wine-hued scales covering him head to toe, armoring him as fully as possible against what was to come...

Fire filled the passageway they'd just left, and though they'd escaped the worst of it, the heat pursued them, carried on a few rogue tongues of flame. Agony danced across Nycos's back, his thin and human-sized scales too weak to absorb the entirety of the inferno. He staggered, gasping, unable to catch his breath as the dragonfire sucked the air from the corridor.

Silbeth's hands closed on his shredded cloak, and though she Once they'd left at the heat radiating from his hauberk, she didn't flinch away. She dragged him upright and further from the fork, until the air had returned and he could once more stand on his own.

"Thanks," he panted.

"Thank *you*." Her skin shone red, like a severe sunburn, and she winced with every step. "When you said you wanted her to let something slip, I assume 'the flame of Erlivius's own forge' wasn't what you had in mind?"

"Well," he said through a forced smile that probably looked hideous on his now half-human features, "it proves I was right that she needed help with those magics. If I'd been wrong, she'd have taunted me with it, not tried to roast me out of injured pride."

"As opposed to her earlier attempts at roasting us?"

"That was anger. It's different."

"Huh."

"YOU WISH TO EXPERIENCE MY MAGICS, THEN, TZAVALANTZAVAL?" Vircingotirilux roared, her voice echoing through the complex.

"That isn't what I said," Nycos protested.

"Well, let's just go correct her. I'm sure she'll be—"

"SO BE IT, THEN!" The wyrm of Gronch bellowed a series of syllables that bore no resemblance to any language a human jaw could form, but a language Nycos recognized all the same.

In fact, he'd seen those same sounds in written form, in the glyphs that guarded the entrance to the dragon's lair.

"Down!"

Again he threw himself at Silbeth, but the magics that twined through the earthen caves were faster still. A writhing root burst through the soil overhead and wrapped tight about Nycos's waist, snatching him in mid-leap and constricting. His iron spear clattered uselessly to the floor.

He felt pressure, pain, as the animated limb attempted to squeeze the life from him, but he had a moment to act; against *this* threat, his armoring scales held. His breathing grew difficult, but not impossible. Already he plucked and poked at the root with his claws, as though it were a particularly stubborn belt. It would have been so much easier if he could flip himself over, attack the length of vegetation where it protruded from the ceiling, but he lacked the leverage to turn.

Silbeth struggled to work her way back to him, but she had problems of her own. Crouching low, she struck back at the veritable garden of roots trying to grab at her, from wall and ceiling and occasionally even the floor. For all her speed and skill, she clearly struggled. She didn't dare wind up for a full swing of her sword, lest blade or arm become entangled by swift-grasping tendrils from behind.

And in the other direction, back the way they'd come, something massive slithered through the tunnels, wings and legs tucked tight so that she might fit. Something that gibbered and chortled, barked and bayed, and rasped each breath three times over…

He couldn't risk trying to grow stronger, to strengthen his scales any further, for already the sliver of Wyrmtaker deep in his chest twinged and tickled as it threatened to move. He could spit into his palm and smear the root, but he had no means of igniting it. And picking with clawed fingertips shredded the root, but not nearly fast enough.

*So be it, then.*

Nycos pressed against the root, holding it tight between his fingertips and his belly, braced himself, and shoved.

Pain shot through him as his own talons dug into, and in a few spots through, his armored scales, but he dropped from the grip of the now severed tendril. Hot blood flowed over his hands, slick and sticky. Running at a low crouch, struggling to ignore the pain, he scooped up his spear and moved to Silbeth's side.

She asked no questions, only glanced at the blood on his hands and his stomach, and nodded. Working together, each watching the other's back, they hacked through the grasping roots, yard by gradual, precious yard.

Vircingotirilux neared. Their time was short, every instinct screamed at them to run—but if they rushed, if they allowed even one grasping root to reach them, they'd have *no* chance of escape.

Up ahead, the passage opened high on the wall of another vast chamber, nearly equal in size to the central cavern. The lair, Nycos realized, must encompass the entire hillside, transforming the rise into a hollow bubble of earth. Again he wondered whether it was magic or some more mundane reinforcement that kept the entire complex from collapsing.

Not that he had much time to ponder it.

"Get ready to jump," he shouted. Silbeth, who could see little if anything in the subterranean gloom, audibly gritted her teeth.

They heard the inhalation of three separate throats as they reached the corridor's end.

Nycos grabbed Silbeth as they plunged, twisting to take the impact on his far stronger legs. A jet of flame shot from the tunnel, passing over their heads as they plummeted, illuminating the chamber in shades of blood.

"Thanks," Silbeth muttered.

"Wouldn't be much good to me with two broken legs."

"Because I've been so helpful up to now," she groused. Then, before he could respond, "Any way we can lay an ambush for her?"

Nycos glanced around at the rock- and root-strewn cavern, then up at the tunnel from which they'd leapt, twenty feet above their heads. "I don't see how. She'll be coming out of there any moment. We need to find shelter, a place to hide before she spots us."

"Or roasts us."

"That, too."

The chamber *did* boast one unique feature: a pool of slightly muddy water tucked away at one end. Doubtless fed by Lake Orist through some underground artery, it probably served as Vircingotirilux's drinking cistern.

Unfortunately, it stood clear across the cavern, and Nycos couldn't tell from here if it was deep enough to conceal them— nor was it probable, even if it were, that they could hold their breath long enough to effectively hide within. In the end, then, they could do nothing but scamper up into another side passage, perhaps a third of the way around the chamber from where they'd entered. Silbeth, vaguely embarrassed, clung to Nycos's back as he scaled the walls.

They'd vanished into this new corridor, peeking around a convenient corner as Vircingotirilux slithered from the tunnel they'd so recently vacated, extruded obscenely into the chamber. Several dangling roots, nearly as thick as smaller trees in their own right, still flickered with lingering flames from the dragon's last burst. They cast the chamber, and the three-headed beast, in a confusing panoply of dancing shadow, and wafted the aroma of singed rot throughout the winding complex.

"WE CAN CHASE YOU ROUND AND ROUND, LITTLE HUMAN TZAVALANTZAVAL! WE KNOW EVERY TWIST AND TURN, WE DON'T TIRE." She rose up, towering, to peer into a high passage, while one of her monstrous heads sniffed and grumbled at a lower one. "YOU'VE ALREADY BLED. WE SMELLED IT. WE TASTED IT, LICKING IT FROM THE SOIL. SUCH AN ODD MIXTURE OF FLAVORS, FROM THE ODD SHAPE YOU'VE TAKEN. WE WANT MORE."

Her whole body rumbling, rustling against the dirt, she moved on to the next cluster of holes in the wall. "ARE YOU STILL HUMAN ENOUGH TO SWEAT, TINY DRAGON-MAN? IS THAT HOW WE'LL FIND YOU?"

Despite himself, Nycos raised his hand to his scale-covered brow, feeling for moisture.

Vircingotirilux ducked low, examining several of the bottommost tunnels, her central head peering into one, her left sniffing at another.

And abruptly she recoiled, screaming in three voices. Dark blood gushed from between two monstrous teeth in that leftmost head, dripping and spattering across the walls. Nycos's own heightened vision detected a quick flash of movement in the corridor she'd just been smelling, a small, furtive figure rolling to its feet and dashing back into the darkness, and he couldn't help but grin.

The dragon staggered back, pawing madly at the talon-tipped crowbar Smim had lodged deep in the soft tissue between her fangs. Her stumbling brought her near the far wall, and her rightmost head, raised high and howling in fury, nearly filled their field of vision from where they crouched.

Nycos and Silbeth looked at one another, raised their spears in unison, and charged.

They hit the edge of the passage side by side, neither hesitating. The intervening leap was nothing for Nycos; for Silbeth it might have been a challenge, but not an insurmountable one. He landed atop the monstrous skull, stumbled as he scrambled for footing, and stabbed downward, hard, with his iron spear. Silbeth struck the side of Vircingotirilux's head, digging in with her own weapon as much to catch herself as any sort of deliberate attack.

Both bit deep, driven by momentum, by main strength, and by the piercing power of Nycos's talons.

The dragon's earlier writhing was nothing compared to her violent thrashing now. Her agonized shrieks were a nightmare, tearing at the ears until they almost bled. Her entire body arched upward, the wounded head snapping like a whip as she struggled to dislodge the dreadful barbs, while the other two bit and flailed in blind rage. Gouts of flame shot into the open cavern, but none came near the desperately struggling pair.

Nycos dug in with the talons of his feet, shoving and leaning into the spear, trying to sink it securely before he was thrown free. Silbeth flopped and dangled, a living pennant in the side of Vircingotirilux's head, but through main strength and possibly a miracle she maintained her grip on the spear, and the spear remained lodged in flesh.

In its mad convulsions, the bleeding head whipped near the wall, nearly crushing the mercenary between earth and scales. Even in so precarious a position, Silbeth took full advantage, thrusting her legs back against that wall and pressing the spear ever deeper. The wyrm froze an instant, overwhelmed, and Nycos drove his own weapon down in a final, furious thrust.

Bone cracked, and the dragon's rightmost neck went limp even as the beast's body shook. Both warriors were thrown from their unstable perch, rolling across the floor and fetching up against the wall, each gathering a fresh array of bruises and abrasions. Quickly they darted into the nearest passage, this one at ground level, just to get out of sight before their foe could focus. Once there, they peeked back through the rough opening, unable to look away.

Vircingotirilux beat the floor with all four claws and the length of her tail until the entire hill shuddered. The wailing of her two remaining voices was as nothing Silbeth or even Nycos had ever heard, the last shreds of her sanity escaping into the ether on wings of suffering and despair. She clawed at the walls, bathed the ceiling in torrents of fire that spattered against the dirt to rain back down in flurries of ember.

Never taking his eyes from the dragon, Nycos unslung the last of the metal-hafted spears from his back and passed it over to Silbeth. "I have talons," he explained when she began to question. "You don't."

The wyrm of Gronch skittered backward a few steps, placing the far wall against her back and stood, gasping and mewling. Then, as her leftmost head swept slowly side to side, watching and scenting for any sudden attack, the center head slowly snaked sideways. For a long moment she sniffed at the third, the one now dangling limp and dead. A great forked tongue darted out, running one time along the length of the skull.

Then, after a last deep breath, she fastened her middle set of jaws on the base of her rightmost neck.

"She's not—!" Silbeth gasped.

Nycos, horrified, could only answer, "I think she is."

The crunch of scale, meat, and bone was horrifying, a sound to echo in dark dreams for years to come. Blood flew, fibers of muscle and great veins dangled free. The two remaining heads screamed again, one voice muffled by mangled flesh. It tugged, hard, but fearsome as the bite had been, it hadn't severed the neck cleanly. Bone and tissue still held fast.

Harder the center head pulled, and harder still. She barked an order, nigh impossible to make out, but the leftmost head obeyed, slinking over to help. It, too, clamped onto the dead neck further on, and then both, moving as one, gave one last, massive yank.

Flesh and bone ripped. For an endless moment the dead head and neck dangled from Vircingotirilux's jaws, still twitching. Blood and other fluids erupted from the stump, a fetid geyser that drenched a broad portion of the chamber. The soil of the floor, rocky and hard as it was, grew soft and boggy where it pooled.

She dropped her own dead parts before her with a loud and hollow splat. Again she reared, tail slamming and thrashing with agony. She clawed at the tunnels, as though to dig out anything that lingered within, and once more she bathed the room with flame. Whether by intent or by accident, she turned one of those gouts of fire upon herself, cauterizing the ragged stump with a fearsome sizzle.

"I need to get above her," Nycos muttered.

"Sorry, what?"

"Above her. She's treating us like human opponents. She's not looking up."

"We *are* human opponents. More or less."

"But I can climb. Can—?"

Nycos halted as Smim appeared in the entrance to one of the passageways, roughly halfway between them and Vircingotirilux. He carried one of the spears that had been dropped back in the central chamber, though he clearly struggled with its length, its weight. No way to speak loud enough for him to hear, not over the cacophony the dragon made, and even if Nycos could shout that loud, he'd just be announcing his plans. Instead, looking straight at the goblin, he gestured to his eyes and then to Silbeth. He wasn't certain Smim would get *watch her, do what she does* from that, but it was the best he could manage.

"Do you think you can keep her distracted?" he asked. "For just a moment?"

"Oh, I'm *sure* I can distract her. Whether I can *live* through it…"

"I'll be quick."

"Do that."

Moving low and keeping to the dragon's right, Silbeth darted from the cave. She ran a crooked course, ducking behind this rock, that heap of earth, once even behind Vircingotirilux's own limp and severed head. Even as she moved, Nycos leapt as high as he could and then drove his talons deep into the wall. Punching finger- and toe-holds into the packed soil, he scampered upward, swiftly rising.

Vircingotirilux began to turn his way, and Silbeth lunged. She sprinted hard, crossing the remaining yards of the chamber and drove her spear deep into the dragon's foot.

The wyrm yanked her leg up and slammed it back, trying to crush her tormentor, but Silbeth dove away. Again she lunged, tearing another small wound in the scales, and again she rolled aside. Smim darted from his own shelter and tried to deliver a stab or two of his own, but the ungainly weapon slowed him enough that he couldn't land a meaningful blow.

And through it all, Nycos climbed. *Just a bit longer, just a bit farther.*

He'd never thought she'd do it. The dragon's scales would protect her from her own fire to a point, but too much exposure, at too close a range, would burn even her. Vircingotirilux's rage, her frustration, her madness had, however, moved her past the point of caring. When her third effort to stomp on Silbeth failed, when the mercenary managed to dodge away even when the dragon tried to bite her in half or swallow her whole, Vircingotirilux reared back and inhaled, deeply.

All thoughts of stealth forgotten, Nycos cried out a warning. Silbeth didn't need it. Already she had turned, raced back across the cavern, but she had nowhere to go. The pool might provide some protection, if it didn't boil, but that would have meant getting past the dragon. And she was too far from the wall and its many passageways, could never possibly reach it before—

Flame filled the chamber, washed across Nycos's vision. He flinched from the sudden brightness.

When he looked back, the floor steamed where Vircingotirilux's blood had evaporated in the infernal heat. More steam, and a bit of smoke, rose from her severed head and neck.

Of Silbeth, there was no trace. Not so much as melted armor, charred bone, or even a heap of ash. She was simply *gone*.

Wrath the likes of which Nycos could never remember flooded through him, setting his soul alight hotter than any dragon's fire. Wrath and something far less familiar, something he'd come to know only sporadically and only as a man.

Guilt.

With an animal bellow, he hurled himself from the wall and dropped, talons outspread, toward his enemy. Vircingotirilux's center head roared back, unleashing flame, but the dragon had nearly exhausted her inner furnace. The sheet of fire that washed past him, over him, was thin and dull. He felt tattered cloak and tunic disintegrate, ringlets of mail grow searing, scales and flesh burn, but he remained intact when he landed hard upon her other, more bestial head.

Even as his talons sank home, however, she thrashed, nearly throwing him off. Back and forth the neck whipped, and it was all he could do to hang on. With hands and feet both he clung, unable to attack lest he lose his grip and go flying. He grew dizzy; his singed limbs weakened. And off to the side, Vircingotirilux raised her other head, jaws agape to pluck him off and rend him into pieces.

He caught a brief glimpse, as the chamber swirled and spun, of Smim, stabbing desperately at the dragon's tail, trying to distract her from Nycos, but the goblin's efforts were futile.

Vircingotirilux knew her enemy, knew the true threat, and nothing would divert her attention, would stop her from—

She froze, body and her central head both. Gleaming eyes grew wide—in pain, yes, but mostly in shock. A small rivulet of blood trickled from the corner of her middle jaw, and even the savage head to which Nycos clung slowed its thrashing, struggling to see and to understand what had just happened.

*She's alive!*

Silbeth stood below, the dragon's distraction having allowed her to come terrifyingly near. She had plunged her spear deep into Vircingotirilux's centermost neck, ripping at flesh and various pipes within. Not a lethal stroke in and of itself, but unexpected, devastating.

*But how had she...?*

He looked again, focusing past the dizziness of his wild ride. Silbeth was absolutely coated, slick with blood and saliva and other fluids, as though she'd rolled through an abattoir. It caked her clothes, gummed her hair into a sodden mass.

Nyos's gaze flickered to the dislocated head that lay, still steaming, on the cavern floor, and he knew where Silbeth had sheltered from the torrent of flame. His admiration for this woman who should, by all rights, have been born a dragon grew stronger still.

*Better not let her efforts go to waste, then.*

He reared up, plunged both hands deep into Vircingotirilux's flesh and began to burrow. Like a maddened badger, he scooped out clawed handfuls and tossed them behind as he dug. Again the head and neck thrashed, but Nycos had gone deep. A thick tendon provided a convenient handhold for one fist as he continued to carve with the other.

In seconds he exposed a patch of bone. Straightening his fingers, making a blade of his talons, he struck. And again. And once more.

Skull split; a tiny rift, but enough for a claw to penetrate. Head and neck froze. Nycos lay flat upon the scalp, arm fully extended and all but encased in the hole he'd excavated.

And then, as before, the neck went limp.

Nycos let go, allowing himself to be thrown aside. Silbeth, too, wisely retreated, as once again Vircingotirilux convulsed, tail and her one remaining head beating the floor of the cavern. Blood and fire spilled from her surviving set of jaws in equal measure, yet her maddened thrashing and her screams were weaker than before. Now and again she spat a few syllables, but they formed nothing resembling coherent words.

"Do we... try to question her?" Silbeth asked skeptically. "I know you wanted information..."

"I did. I do." Indeed he seethed with frustration, wondering who or what had told her where to find him, had provided the magics to cloak her ogre assassin. "But she's too far gone."

"Then we should finish this."

No argument there. "Smim!" He stretched forth a hand as the goblin came running. "Spear."

The shaft smacked into his palm. He lifted the weapon, saw Silbeth hefting her own, and nodded.

Perhaps too pained, perhaps too maddened, now, to even recognize the danger, Vircingotirilux didn't react as they drew near. Just like that, head by head, the wyrm of Gronch died.

And took her secrets with her.

# CHAPTER THIRTY

At first, perhaps driven by pounding hearts and racing thoughts, they'd chatted up a storm.

Silbeth expressed her sympathies, again, that Nycos hadn't learned what he'd hoped from their journey. He, after brushing it off as unimportant—a lie they both recognized—had set the trio to collecting as many of the iron spears as remained salvageable.

"Planning to hunt another dragon next year?" she'd taunted.

"For the ogres," Nycos had replied. "I've no idea how they're liable to react to their 'queen's' death, but I'd prefer to have weapons that can harm them. Besides," he added with a shrug, "the spears probably won't be any good in a year. Once the talons start to decay, in a few months, they'll grow brittle."

"I'll keep that in mind."

"They should still be more than strong enough if you plan to kill me now, though. I'm tired and I hurt, so this is probably your best shot."

Smim and Silbeth had exchanged shocked glances. "Why would you even *tell* me that?" Silbeth demanded.

"Because I don't think you'll do it. But also because I don't have the energy to lie around wondering if it's coming."

"I'm not going to kill you, Nycos. Not now, anyway."

"Oh, good. Then can you help me get this hauberk off? It's partly melted."

Once they were beyond Vircingotirilux's lair, however, they seemed to leave conversation behind with the dead dragon. Days of meandering back through Gronch, hiding sometimes from lone ogres, sometimes from shouting, rampaging bands…

then, once they'd recovered the horses, riding across snow-swept grasslands… and all of it in near silence. They didn't speak of their experiences, either their victories or failures. They told no tales of past adventure. Even the setting up and striking of camp, the sharing of meals, occurred with minimal speech.

Nycos welcomed the silence, the solitude. His head was awhirl with questions and worries, none of which he knew how to address. The death of a dragon, even one as horrid and savage as Vircingotirilux, was no small matter. He felt the weight of his actions. No guilt, not in this case, but a sense of magnitude, with repercussions he could not begin to anticipate. He racked his mind, trying to determine who might have aided the wyrm of Gronch, to think of anyone with both the magic and the motivation to throw in with the maddened beast. None of the answers made sense. Tzavalantzaval had many enemies, of course, but few were masters of the necessary sorceries. Few were of the sort to work through allies or pawns such as Vircingotirilux and her ogres. None he could come up with were both.

None who still lived, anyway.

His whole body ached with the wounds and burns he'd taken in the struggle, and though he'd resumed his human form and concentrated on his own shapeshifting magics as often as he could, healing his hurts, it would be many days before he felt whole.

He worried over his actions in Quindacra, wishing he had some means of knowing if his gambit had paid off, if he'd prevented dissolution of the pact, prevented war. He worried over Ktho Delios's schemes, wondering at their involvement with Vircingotirilux, if their own inquisitors had contributed their magic to her cause. But then, why would they have targeted him? How could they even have known of him? No matter how he chased it, over the days of freezing cold and frequent snows, he could never catch a solution.

Then there were the consequences of this journey to consider. For the second time—well, so far as anyone else knew, for the second time—he'd disobeyed a direct order and sneaked from Oztyerva on a mission he'd taken onto himself. That he'd successfully slew the dragon wouldn't protect him from the Crown Marshal's ire. That he'd saved the treaty might, except he couldn't take credit for what happened in Castle Auric. He'd had no choice, he'd had to deal with the threat Vircingotirilux posed, but he might have destroyed his life back home, or at least many of his ambitions, in the process.

And above all else, he fretted about the woman riding beside him, about whether they would remain allies—even friends— or whether she was about to turn her blade upon him, to strike down what she must surely consider a potential threat to the people of Kirresc.

More than once, during what few whispered conversations they had, Smim tried to convince him to kill Silbeth in her sleep. He never did, of course, and he forbade the goblin from moving against her, but he couldn't deny that he might well suffer for his mercy.

No, not mercy. Affection.

As for Silbeth herself, her thoughts on that long, silent trek remained her own.

The day was cold, the air smeared with gently drifting flurries, when the walls and the banners of Talocsa hove into view. The steeds, cold and tired, picked up their pace, sensing the end of their journey and the promise of shelter. Thus, it took only a few minutes for the trio to draw near enough to make out the narrow black pennants hanging beneath the traditional ensigns.

Nycos and Silbeth both went stiff. "War?" she suggested grimly.

For an instant, Nycos battled the urge to turn Avalanche around, to ride hard for Vidiir where he would peel the king and queen of Quindacra like tubers. After a few breaths to calm himself, however, and to review what he'd learned of Kirresci pageantry, he shook his head.

"Those are symbols of mourning, not conflict. Besides, look. The gates are open. They'd be sealed in a time of war."

They rode ahead at a swift trot, determined to learn what had befallen the kingdom in their absence. Several bows and spears bristled as they neared, but Nycos called out, identifying himself before the soldiers could even issue challenge.

"Sir Nycolos! Welcome home!" The guard commander scrambled down from her post atop the wall. It was, as fortune would have it, the same captain who had been on duty that day—so long ago, now—when he'd first arrived after stumbling his way through the Outermark. "We're so glad to see you well, particularly—"

"Captain." He raised a gloved hand. "I apologize for my rudeness, but please. What's happened?"

"I…" The officer stopped, exchanged a look with her soldiers, cleared her throat. "I'm truly sorry to be the bearer of this sort of news, Sir Nycolos. Crown Marshal Laszlan was… He's dead. Murdered."

Nycos felt as though he'd once again been burned by Vircingotirilux's breath. He literally rocked in his saddle. "What… I don't… How?"

"I've only heard rumors and thirdhand reports, sir. Apparently enemy operatives or assassins somehow gained access to Oztyerva. They… Sir, there's more. Baron Kortlaus apparently interrupted the struggle."

Now he had to dismount, to lean on Avalanche for support lest he topple. "Dead?" He'd barely remembered how to speak the word. His friends were so few…

"No, sir, but… He took a blow to the head. He's alive, but none of us know how he's doing, or if he'll recover. Sir Nycolos, I'm so sorry."

"I…" He couldn't remember feeling so adrift, so helpless, since his earliest weeks here in Talocsa. *Perhaps this guard captain is an ill omen,* he wondered, though he knew the thought was borderline hysterical. "I need to go to the palace."

"Of course, Sir Nycolos." The soldiers stepped aside, allowing the travelers to pass.

Nycos kept his gaze downward. The road seemed oddly blurred, obscured by something beyond the gentle snows. It was almost as if—

"Nycos?" Silbeth, now also on foot, took his arm and pulled him to a halt. "Are you crying?"

"Am I?" He looked up at her. He'd shed tears, as a human, of exhaustion, frustration, pain… Never such as these. He reached up, felt the moisture in his eyes, a single trail threatening to freeze as it traversed his cheek. "I guess I am. It's a curious thing; I… don't think I care for it."

She studied him, lip twitching as though she would say a hundred things at once, and then she wrapped him in a brief but steadying hug.

"I've made my decision," she whispered in his ear. "I'll keep your secret."

She pulled away, and it took him a moment to realize just what she was telling him. Despite everything, a tiny smile tugged at the corner of his mouth. "Thank you."

"I mean, unless you give me a new reason to change my mind," she warned him, only half in jest.

"Of course." And then, again, "Thank you."

"You're welcome, Nycos."

———

He stood alone in the council chamber, staring idly at the table where maps and other documents of war so frequently lay. The guards had directed him to wait here when he'd requested an audience with the king, but they'd given no indication of how long he was to wait, or why here rather than the throne room.

During his trek through Talocsa, and then Oztyerva, Nycos had picked up on much that had happened in recent weeks. Quindacra had, indeed, not only dispatched the messages he'd instructed but reopened ambassadorial channels as well—all good signs, though he thought it unfortunate they'd sent a new envoy in place of Ambassador Guldoell.

The treaty remained intact. The attacks on communities in and around Gronch had ceased, for reasons Nycos understood better than anyone. Ktho Delian forces had concluded their supposed exercises and drawn back from the border, albeit not far. The threat of imminent invasion, it seemed, had passed.

Yet while Kirresc might not be at war, neither was the nation on a peacetime footing. Nycos had spotted far more soldiers on the street on his way to the palace, far more knights in residence once inside, and had overheard enough conversation to know that troop movements were underway all across the nation. If conflict had not yet been born, it clearly gestated, and he wasn't entirely certain why. Perhaps when his Majesty finally arrived…

"Welcome home, Sir Nycolos."

*That* wasn't King Hasyan's voice.

Nycos turned and dipped his head in polite greeting. "Dame Zirresca."

She started to speak, then seemed to think better of it, instead shutting the door behind her and moving to stand at the table. "Have you seen Baron Kortlaus?" she asked, not unsympathetically.

"Not yet."

"You should know, before you do... He won't recognize you. He's not really there. He hears us, lets us feed him, but that seems to be it. We still hope he'll recover, but... Well, I thought you should be prepared."

"Thank you," Nycos told her sincerely. "I'll go see him as soon as I've spoken to his Majesty."

"His Majesty won't be joining you this afternoon. He... spends a lot of time alone, these days. Mourning."

"I understand. I'm sorry."

"We all are," she said brusquely. "I've been instructed to speak to you on his behalf."

A faint suspicion flared in Nycos's mind. "Please, go ahead."

"First off, we're all going to assume that you left with Marshal Laszlan's permission, on a secret mission he chose to conceal."

"Um..."

Zirresca leaned over the table, her expression, her entire posture intent. "If we believed otherwise, Sir Nycolos, we would have to take punitive steps. And we can't afford that right now. We need you. You understand?"

"I do. That said, if Quindacra's not abandoning our pact after all, there should be no invasion. Why—?"

"Ktho Delios may not be put off so easily. Their scheme may have disintegrated, but we have to consider the possibility that they've merely been delayed, not thwarted."

"Come on, Zirresca." Again she looked as though she wanted to interrupt, to say something, but as she chose against it, he continued, "You and I both know that the military build-up and preparation happening around here is more than a precaution."

"His Majesty," she confessed, "is all but convinced the attack on Laszlan was orchestrated by Ktho Delios."

"Surely he wouldn't go to war with them over a suspicion! He—"

"No. He's grieving, not insane. Of course we're investigating, trying to determine for certain what happened, who was responsible. But make no mistake, Nycolos. Whether it was Ktho Delios, one of the other nations, or even some noble or organization within Kirresc itself? As soon as we know for certain, we *are* going to war."

Nycos desperately wished that he were within reach of one of the chamber's chairs.

"What I need to know, Sir Nycolos, is that I can count on you. That you won't be caught up in past grudges."

"I'm a loyal knight of Kirresc! Of course you..." He stopped, Zirresca's precise words catching up with him. His earlier suspicion crystallized into absolute certainty, and he knew what she'd already almost told him twice over.

Well, he could hardly pretend to be surprised, could he? Orban was dead, Kortlaus not far behind. He himself had been away. And she'd been the frontrunner anyway, hadn't she?

He'd nowhere else to go, no easy way to start yet another new life, and those people he truly cared for—however few in number—were all here.

So, no matter that everything he'd strived for over the past year and more was beyond his reach, that the only path he knew to a higher position and a better life was now closed to him, that his pride rankled and churned at the very notion, he gave the only answer he could.

"Of course you can count on me, Crown Marshal Zirresca. It's my honor to serve."

———

"It's all coming apart."

Vesmine Droste, officer of the Deliant, leaned her head up against the cool stone wall. "I put this all into motion. It was my plan. Quindacra, the ogres, all of it."

"Was it?" Behind her, an adolescent boy in a ragged cloak placed a wooden mug on the table and leaned back in his chair. "I seem to recall having a bit of a hand in it."

"You know what I mean. As far as Governor-General Achlaine and the rest of the Deliant are concerned, it's all me. The operation was supposed to leave our neighbors open and isolated, ripe for the taking. And now it's failed, utterly, after we've devoted a *lot* of resources. I'll consider myself fortunate if they *just* take my rank!"

"Calm down, Colonel."

"*Calm...!*" She spun from the wall, stormed over to slam her fists on the table. "How dare you—?"

"Yes, calm. We've suffered a setback—but it *is* a setback, nothing more. We'll have to take some new steps, rely on some of my failsafes. Your conquest will have to wait another year or three."

"Oh, is that all? And I suppose you expect me to convince the rest of the Deliant to be all right with that?"

"Dealing with them *is* a large part of your purpose in this little cabal of ours, Colonel."

"Don't overstep yourself, wizard!" she hissed. "You need me more than I need you! If necessary, I'm sure I could find some Inquisitors who could do the same—"

The table reared like a furious stallion, slamming Droste across the chamber with two legs. It charged after her, those same limbs colliding with the stone to either side of her, pinning her to the wall.

"There are no Inquisitors," he snarled, "no sorcerers for you to call on, who can do what I can!"

Her gaze flickered from him to the table legs, which had struck the stone hard enough to leave scratches. "They'll hear you!"

"Oh, relax, Colonel. Nobody can hear a thing that occurs within this room unless I wish them to. You might want to consider the various repercussions of that before you think to threaten or insult me again."

Vesmine nodded stiffly, and the table dropped away, returning to its spot in the center of the chamber.

"Anyway, none of this effort has been wasted," he explained. "We've identified an enemy, one I thought I'd dealt with when I arranged for the Kirrescis to locate Wyrmtaker. Trust me when I tell you it's better that we learned of him now than when our plans were further along. I'll figure out how best to deal with him, and you will yet have your war. It's just a matter of time."

"Hmph. As you say, Ondoniram."

"Yes." The ancient sorcerer smiled broadly with the stolen face of a child. "As I say, indeed."

# ABOUT THE AUTHOR

When Ari Marmell has free time left over between feeding cats and posting on social media, he writes a little bit. His work includes novels, short stories, role-playing games, and video games, all of which he enjoyed in lieu of school work when growing up. He's the author of the Mick Oberon gangland/urban fantasy series, the Widdershins YA fantasy series, and many others, with publishers such as Del Rey, Titan Books, Wizards of the Coast, Omnium Gatherum, and Dragon Moon Press.

Ari currently resides in Austin, Texas. He lives in a clutter that has a moderate amount of apartment in it, along with George—his wife—and the aforementioned cats, who probably want something.

CPSIA information can be obtained
at www.ICGtesting.com
Printed in the USA
LVHW031503191119
637871LV00001B/40/P

9 781774 000120